LOOKING AT YOU

With the tires barely rotating, the truck slowly moved forward, and some of the ghosts actually bowed and curtsied as the old vehicle passed them. Some blew kisses. Several took off hats that disappeared moments afterward.

Sunlight fragmented by green leaves slanted along the lane, and from the corner of his eye Vickery saw that the ghost mouths were all opening and closing in unison, and then he became aware of their frail voices, singing. He didn't recognize the melody, but it seemed to express fond reflection, wistful retreat.

He glanced at Castine, and she was blinking rapidly.

Vickery passed the last of them just below the steps to the mausoleum, and when he looked again at the mirror the lane behind him was empty except for a few dry leaves spinning across the asphalt.

"Poor forsaken shells," said Castine in a hoarse whisper. "What are we, royalty?"

"They, uh, were looking at you."

STOLEN SKIES

TIM POWERS

A Baen Books Original

Baen Publishing Enterprises
P.O. Box 1403
Riverdale, NY 10471
www.baen.com

ISBN: 978-1-9821-9244-0

Cover art by Eric Williams

First printing, January 2022
First mass market printing, February 2023

Distributed by Simon & Schuster
1230 Avenue of the Americas
New York, NY 10020

Library of Congress Control Number: 2021042635

Printed in the United States of America

10 9 8 7 6 5 4 3 2 1

To Tom and Debbie Gilchrist
for years of friendship and advice

With thanks to:
David Brin, Tony Daniel, Preston Dennett, J.R. Dunn,
Ken Estes, Russell Galen, Tom Gilchrist,
Brian McCaleb, Elizabeth O'Brien, Elena Pagter,
Serena Powers, Tina Princethal, Joe Stefko,
Toni Weisskopf, and Bill and Peggy Wu

STOLEN SKIES

SUNDAY

CHAPTER ONE:
Hands Like Steam Shovels

--- --- --- --- --- --- --- --- --- --- --- --- --- --- --- ---

After making good time through Reston on Highway 267, the government Chevy Suburban slowed as brake lights flashed on in the dark highway lanes ahead of it.

Slouched in the passenger seat, Ingrid Castine watched the black silhouettes of the trees alongside the highway bending in the wind against the the paler night sky. She was glad to stretch her legs several inches farther than she'd been able to during the last eight hours, in the coach seat of the American Airlines flight from London's Heathrow Airport to Dulles International.

Even with the heavier traffic, the drive would probably be less than an hour. It was a familiar ride, down past the Beltway Loop through Falls Church toward the Potomac, but she wouldn't be going to the Office of Naval Research building, as she usually did—tonight she was summoned to an office in the Pentagon.

Probably she was to be transferred again. She had been recruited into the Transportation Utility Agency right out

5

of college eight years ago, and five years later the TUA had been terminated, and she'd been shuffled to the Office of Naval Intelligence; and then last year she had been transferred to what was—as of yesterday, at least— her present job, as a field investigator with the Office of Naval Research.

The jobs had all proved to be disquietingly weird. What could be next? she wondered sourly. Was there a Sub-Department of Tactical Astrology? An Auxiliary Office of Dowsing?

She shifted in her seat and glanced at the driver. Short haircut, dark suit—apparently in his early thirties like herself. He had been professionally cheerful when he had met her at the disembarking gate and opened his wallet to show her an Office of Naval Intelligence identification card, and had obligingly wheeled her suitcase to the waiting Suburban and stashed it in the back, but when she had asked why it was ONI that was picking her up, and why she was being taken to the Pentagon, he had simply shaken his head in evident distaste. She had got the impresssion that his answer would have been, *Some damn fool thing*.

As usual, she thought now, and she shivered. And with my peculiar ability, or handicap, I seem to make things worse.

Castine had never told her employers that ever since a traumatic crisis in May of 2017 she had not been securely fixed in sequential time, as just about everyone else was; if she deliberately caused her vision to blur, and then made herself focus *past* the shapes she saw, she was generally able to see her surroundings as they had been in the recent past—from a couple of minutes earlier to a bit more than an hour. The retro-views seldom lasted longer than a minute, but during them she was blind and deaf to whatever might be going on in real time, so she only sought them deliberately when she was alone, and she had found that drinking lots of coffee could reliably keep them from happening spontaneously.

A man in California had been with her in the crisis three years ago, and shared her peculiar ability, but she hadn't spoken to him in more than a year. At that time the echo-vision, as he had called the phenomenon, had for a period of about a month shown them only sequential views of an old house where terrible things had happened fifty years earlier; but those views had been projected into the psychic ether by a man who died in 2018, and the echo-vision had worked reliably since then, in the few instances when she had ventured to use it.

Worked reliably, she amended, until last night. The Office of Naval Research travel order had come just after her supervisor in Wiltshire made his report on that night's operation.

To her right, the full moon was intermittently visible through the waving black tree limbs. Somewhere beyond them lay Fort Myers and Arlington Cemetery. There had been trees bending in a night wind in Wiltshire too, twenty-some hours ago, with this same full moon above them; and she was too tired now to push back the memory of what she had seen, or hallucinated, in that English field off the A360, just south of Tilshead.

She quickly turned away, toward the driver. "How do I get in?" she asked, just to hear her own voice here.

He rolled his wrist on the steering wheel to glance at his watch. "You've got your phone on you?"

Castine tapped the front of her coat. "Of course."

He nodded. "When you scan your ONR badge at the entrance security checkpoint, you'll get a text code to enter on a keypad there."

She hadn't run into that on her several previous visits to the Pentagon. "Okay," she said, and added, "Sorry to wreck your evening."

He just shrugged and went on squinting at the cars ahead. Evidently he didn't want to talk. She sighed and looked back out the window at the trees.

That field in Wiltshire was nearly four thousand miles behind her, but over the new-upholstery smell of the car's interior she could almost catch the remembered reek of crushed and scorched English wheat stalks.

For the last four months she had been assigned to a Naval Research field office in Southampton. One of her main duties had been to drive out into the country in the middle of the night with a team of four other special agents, and make convincing crop circles in one or another of the many fields of wheat and barley that were accessible from the main roads.

It hadn't been easy. Plant stalks in genuine crop circles showed expulsion cavities and elongated nodes, so Castine's ONR team had had to bring along a generator to power a couple of portable microwave guns that they'd jury-rigged from disassembled microwave ovens, and sweep their beams across the bases of as many of the plants as time permitted; one night they had accidentally radiated a cell phone one of the team had dropped, and the phone had exploded. And, again to match the characteristics of the real thing, they had had to heat a lot of magnetized iron pellets and toss them around. The final part of the task had been to simply drag boards on ropes across the fields to flatten the grain, using Leica laser surveying meters to make their patterns symmetrical.

And then after a few days, during which their elaborate crop circles would have been noticed and have drawn the excited attention of the public, Castine and her team would revisit the sites in their official Office of Naval Research capacity, and prove that they had been hoaxes. The exploded cell phone had proved to be so effective as a debunking detail that they had used the trick again a couple of times.

And the ONR field office maintained a fleet of drones, equipped with directional microphones and infrared scopes, that flew low over the Wiltshire fields at night to spot new, *genuine* crop circles—and the remote pilots were careful not to fly a drone directly over one because the little aircraft always lost power then, and sometimes blew up. When a genuine circle was located, Castine and her team raced to the spot and trampled conspicuous pathways from the nearest road to the new pattern of mysteriously flattened grain, and dropped cigarette butts and empty beer cans and crumpled petrol station receipts among the whorls of horizontal stalks. They generally hadn't even needed to revisit those—the curious public was quick to find the deposited litter and dismiss the sites as hoaxes without any help.

Last night—which was further in the past for her than for most people, since she had flown from east to west at

500 miles an hour for eight hours—Castine and her ONR team had got a positive signal from one of the drones, and piled into their van and sped along the A360 to the indicated wheat field a mile south of Tilshead.

There were ONR-mandated precautions to be observed when entering a genuine crop circle. Bursts of alpha and beta radiation had been detected at a couple of sites, and the research agents carried hand-held radiation meters; and lately among the cultists and cranks who flocked to every newly reported site there were wild and unsubstantiated stories of people being lifted from their feet and thrown impossible distances, and patches of cold so intense that monitoring cameras spontaneously shattered and couldn't be touched for hours. That was all obvious nonsense, but in the last month the ONR team *had* found that the sites became very cold shortly after the phenomena had occurred.

The ONR agents approached each site carefully, and they maintained continuous, if sometimes inexplicably sporadic, radio contact with the field office in Southampton. Castine always dutifully followed the procedures, but until last night in the field beside the A360 she had never encountered anything but the silent, mystifying symbols imprinted in the landscapes of grain.

And until last night Castine had not experienced any of the physical ill-effects that had sometimes afflicted her fellow agents and the tourists who visited the spots later—tingling of the skin, dizziness, spontaneous weeping, even hallucinations—but that had changed when she tried to question a woman they found in that field.

The flattened pattern in the wheat had been wide in the moonlight, stretching a hundred yards in a set of variously sized spirals and a couple of torn-up areas closer to hand. Even from ground-level, by moonlight, Castine could see that it was one of the more complex patterns that had been showing up just in the last couple of weeks, with, in ONR terms, "extensions and double-dumbbells and curling entourages of diminishing grapeshot prints." And, as often lately, she could dimly make out a whirlwind-like column of dust standing above the center of the pattern.

Castine had found the woman, cowering and unable to speak, crouched in a sort of nest she had made for herself off one of the smaller curls of the pattern.

The woman was about twenty years old, dressed in jeans and a flannel shirt, and Castine had had to pull her hand out of her mouth to stop her chewing her already bloody fingers; and Castine had spun around in alarm when the woman suddenly gasped and pointed past her; but there was nothing to be seen besides the rows of standing wheat that bordered the flattened and interwoven stalks.

Whatever had happened there, it was over—the pattern was finished and the characteristic intense chill was beginning to set in. But this woman had seen something that had frightened her out of her senses. Castine and her team had arrived within ten minutes of the drone's signal, though, so the event had been recent.

While the other agents lifted the still-speechless woman to her feet and half-carried her back toward the van, Castine looked out across the field in the direction the woman had pointed, and—quickly before she could change her mind—let her eyes unfocus.

The field and the sky were now abstract variously gray shapes in her vision, and she made herself look past their now-meaningless streaks, past the insignificantly immediate moment.

Her view of the field brightened slightly, though the light was a color comparable to copper, and she recalled that the man in California who shared the echo-vision ability had speculated that it might be infrared light, received directly in the primary visual cortex and not through the narrow-band retinas.

Tiny spots of brightness, invisible to normal sight, would be the characteristic hot iron pellets, but Castine's attention wasn't on them.

Thirty feet ahead of her in the round clearing was— had recently been, rather—what appeared to be three naked and malformed figures, hunched close together and facing away. Castine shuddered, for though the expanses of bare striated flesh were shifting and flexing, they were as dark as the standing wheat behind them, and in the echo-visions living flesh glowed.

Then, still viewing the events of the recent past, Castine saw the woman in jeans and a flannel shirt step from behind her and walk hesitantly toward the three cold, pulsing figures. In the dimness of echo-vision, the woman's resolute profile was luminous.

At that point the triple shape straightened and pivoted heavily, and Castine saw that it was actually just one thing—what she had supposed were two outer figures were now visibly two enormous hands, fists, compacting the mat of flattened wheat. Between the hands, dwarfed by them, stood a spindly humanoid figure with bulging eyes in a grotesquely long and oversized head; a long tongue protruded from its wide-lipped mouth.

The fingers of one of its hands unfolded outward, tearing up the matted wheat stalks, and then its shovel-sized fingernails dug in and pulled the narrow body forward. Its eyes rolled in different directions in its misshapen head.

The woman turned and rushed right through Castine's immaterial viewpoint, her mouth open in a muffled scream; and though there was no physical contact, Castine recoiled backward and fell onto the interwoven carpet of wheat stalks, shivering with fright and revulsion; and even as she rolled over and scrambled to her feet, the night dimmed back to normal vision and real time, and when she turned breathlessly to look behind her, the clearing was empty in the moonlight.

Certainly no such monster as she had seen could be hidden anywhere nearby. She was still shivering, as much from the shockingly intrusive overlap with the woman's past image as from the sight of the awful creature dragging itself across the stalks.

Her fall and panicky recovery, and her fast breathing, had alarmed the other agents, and the one in charge, a burly old lieutenant, had hurried up to her and pulled her aside.

"What," he'd said flatly.

"The thing that woman saw," Castine had gasped, "it—" She shook her head and looked longingly toward the van.

He had glanced quickly around at the evidently empty field. "What am I missing?"

"Not now, maybe ten minutes ago. It—"

"Oh?" He had stepped back and squinted at her. "*O*-kay. What, then—skinny, with a big head and big eyes?"

"And—hands!—like steam shovels—!"

He had slowly shaken his head. Finally he had told her, "Shut up about it for now."

The team had driven the catatonic woman to the Salisbury District Hospital, and had then returned to the field office in Southampton. As dawn filtered through the Venetian blinds of the cluttered squad room, Castine had composed a report on the night's operation—omitting, after only a moment's consideration, any mention of her brief vision or hallucination—and had then driven to her nearby flat. After she'd got five hours of restless sleep her supervisor had phoned to tell her that she was to report to the Pentagon in Washington D.C. by the earliest possible transport, which had proven to be the American Airlines flight out of Heathrow Airport.

Castine had never seen the Pentagon at night, and when her driver sped past the heliports of the Remote Delivery Facility and stopped at the foot of the stairs leading up to the River Entrance, she stared out the window at the building. The tall pillars, lit white from below, and the row of closed wooden doors behind the bases of them, looked forbidding.

The driver had got out and walked around to open her door, letting in a cold breeze that smelled of the Potomac River. "You've got a room at the DoubleTree on Army

Navy Drive," he said as she stepped out. "Your luggage will be there."

"Thanks." She gave him a nod, and walked across the pavement to the stairs, shivering in her wool coat.

Her appointment was for 11 PM, at an office on the fifth floor of the C Ring, and when she had got past security and made her way up the stairs, she walked for what she thought must have been some respectable fraction of a mile along the uniformly wainscoted corridors, past two angles of the five-sided building. A couple of men in gray business suits hurried past her at one point, their shoes tapping on the gleaming floor, but they didn't glance at her. When she arrived at last at the indicated office, she was a bit more than half an hour early.

The tall, polished oak door was closed, and she pushed a button beside it, very aware that the clothes she was wearing were ones she had put on more than twelve hours ago in England. She ran her fingers ineffectually through her auburn hair, wishing she'd found an opportunity to brush it, but at least patted it into place over the bullet scar above her right ear.

The door was pulled open by a stocky young man in blue service dress uniform with silver lieutenant bars on his lapels; he had some ribbons too, but Castine didn't know what they signified. He gave only a cursory glance to the VISITOR badge she had been wearing on a lanyard around her neck ever since passing through security, and she guessed that the guards had called to announce her arrival.

He nodded and waved her into what was clearly a waiting room—track lights on the ceiling cast a reflected glow on two brown leather couches, a low wooden table with nothing on it, and framed pictures of 1950s-futuristic jet airplanes hung on the cream-colored walls. There was a door in the far wall, and a small chrome refrigerator humming in the corner between the couches, and Castine caught a whiff of clove-scented smoke on the chilled air.

"Special Agent Castine," the young lieutenant said. "Commander Lubitz wasn't expecting you till eleven—at the earliest, what with a trans-Atlantic flight and all." He looked around at the room as if it were his job to keep it tidy. Apparently satisfied, he glanced at his watch and went on, "He'll be back in forty minutes. There are drinks in the refrigerator—sandwiches too, if the airline didn't feed you. Do make yourself comfortable." He opened his mouth as if to say more, then just bowed and left the room through the hallway door, closing it firmly behind him.

Castine stared at the closed door for a few moments, then crossed to the refrigerator and crouched to pull it open. She took out a cellophane-wrapped turkey sandwich and, after a brief hesitation, reached past a little bottle of Merlot and took a can of Coca-Cola. She carried them to the table and sat down on the nearest couch. The sandwich wrapping proved to contain also a packet of mustard and a tiny napkin. She fell to, hungrily.

Five minutes later she balled up the cellophane and, not seeing a waste basket, tucked it into her coat pocket, then wiped her mouth and pushed the napkin in after the cellophane.

She still had about twenty minutes and she wondered if the lieutenant would have left, if she hadn't arrived.

Sub-Department of Tactical Astrology, she thought

wryly. Twenty minutes—why not take a look around, in a non-chronological way? If anybody should come in, they'll imagine I've just fallen asleep—natural enough, after my noted *trans-Atlantic flight*. The echo-vision interludes seldom last longer than a minute, and if anybody should shake my shoulder, I can fill whatever remains of that time with stretching and yawning and apologizing for having dozed off.

She looked at her watch, then sat back and stared across the table toward the other couch; and within a few seconds her field of vision had lost all apparent depth, and was just varicolored shapes jostled together as if on a flat surface. She exhaled and made her eyes focus past the now-meaningless jumble.

The light was suddenly dimmer, lit only by the familiar non-color of echo-vision.

She jumped and shifted back, for there were three men visible in the room now—then, rather, however long ago this scene had taken place. Two were in business suits, one of them with close-cropped hair that appeared pale and was probably white, the other dark-haired and shorter. The third man, in a black turtleneck sweater, had a dark, theatrically pointed goatee—definitely not military. That one gestured as he spoke, and she saw that he was holding a cigarette; the tip glowed brightly. Now the older man was speaking, but Castine could catch only a faint murmur, and wished she could read lips.

She looked down at the table. Beside a glass ashtray was a stack of papers, and she leaned forward and peered at them. By the dim echo-light she was only able to read the title, which was in bigger type and bold-faced: PLEIADES.

Still in the echo-vision, the hallway door swung open and an Asian woman of about Castine's age stepped into the room. She wore a pale jacket and slacks, and her dark hair was cut short. She didn't smile as she nodded toward the two men.

The woman had just taken a step forward when Castine's vision abruptly regained light and color, and she was looking at the point in the empty room where the woman had been—had been some time ago, possibly as long ago as two hours.

Castine glanced around and verified that she was still alone, and she looked at her watch again; she had only been seeing by echo-vision, oblivious to events in real time, for a minute or less.

She stood up, careful of her balance, and was peering at the pictures of odd old airplanes when the hallway door behind her opened. She turned around, feeling a bit guilty now for having spied on the people who had been in this room some while ago, and saw the older man from the echo-vision walk in and close the door.

He crossed to where Castine stood and looked at her badge. His short hair was indeed white by the normal illumination of the track lights, and his well-cut suit was brown wool. "Special Agent Castine," he said, raising his eyes to meet hers. "I hope you're not too jet-lagged." After several seconds he turned away and opened the door in the far wall.

"I'm sure I'll be fine, sir," said Castine. The man didn't move or speak, so she repressed a shrug and stepped past him into a wide but windowless office that was harshly lit by bare fluorescent tubes recessed in the ceiling. "I, uh, only landed a couple of hours ago," she added, just to fill the silence. I wonder if I'm in actual trouble, she thought. And I must look like a corpse in this light! Shouldn't there be a plexiglass panel over those fluorescents?

Maps and graphs and shelves packed with black binders covered the walls, and more binders were stacked on the carpet. The man followed her in and waved toward two office chairs near the desk, and Castine sat down in the one whose view was not blocked by the back of a computer monitor. Again she caught a whiff of clove-scented smoke.

"I'm Commander Jack Lubitz," the man said as he made his way around the stacks and lowered himself into a chair on the other side of the desk, "and I'm borrowing you from ONR for a specific assignment." He sat back then, steepling his fingers and squinting at her over the tips of them.

At least I'm not fired, thought Castine. When several seconds had gone by in silence, she stirred and said, "Am I back in Naval Intelligence?"

"Ostensibly." Lubitz looked down at his desk. "Your supervisor in England," he said, "claims you saw something in a crop circle field last night." He looked up at her. "'Hands like steam shovels'?"

"That's what the witness told me," said Castine, reflexively lying to conceal, as always, her limited ability to see recent past events. "A hallucination, obviously."

"Obviously," echoed Lubitz, nodding.

When he said nothing further, she asked, cautiously, "What is the assignment?"

Lubitz pursed his lips, sighed, and said, "There's a man

who has . . . become aware of certain highly classified aberrant information. It's vitally important that he be located and questioned."

Castine's heart sank. Rushing her here from England by ambiguous authority—for an obviously ad-hoc 11 PM meeting with an officer in civvies—and, most telling, the word *aberrant*, which had been used by the ONR office in England to describe the genuine, mysteriously occurring crop circles: she guessed, reluctantly, who the man in question might be.

She had to ask, but tried to sound merely tired and impatient. "Who is he?"

"We believe his name is Herbert Woods," Lubitz said, "sometimes known as Sebastian Vickery."

CHAPTER TWO:
Foo Fighters

Since she had half-anticipated the answer, Castine simply cocked her head as if mildly surprised.

"The one-time Secret Service agent?" she said, then added only, "I remember him," since Naval Intelligence might not know about her history with Vickery . . . who was the only person she knew of who shared her echo-vision ability.

Lubitz asked, "When did you last see him?"

It's vitally important that he be located and questioned. That didn't sound good.

Castine whistled soundlessly and frowned past Lubitz at a map of California on the wall. The Transportation Utility Agency's records had been purged in the summer of '17 . . . but probably not completely; she must after all assume that Naval Intelligence knew about her association with Vickery earlier in that year—though there was no way they could know that the two of them had fallen right out of the world into a nightmare afterlife, and then managed to get back again, alive and incidentally able to see behind the moment of now.

And the ONI could hardly be aware of her having met him again a year later, when the visions of the abandoned house had eclipsed their echo-visions and they had got caught up in the bloody history of that old house, and several people had been killed. Vickery himself had killed two of them, and saved Castine's life. Again.

"May, it would have been," she said after only a reasonable pause, "yes, of 2017. Nearly three years ago. The west-coast TUA chief had gone badly rogue, if you recall, and decided that Woods, AKA Sebastian Vickery, and I were working against him, and that we had to be killed. Vickery and I were thrown together for a couple of days."

"As I recall, that agency was trying to summon actual *ghosts,* to supplement motorcade security."

Unable to think of a helpful reply, Castine just nodded. *And we did make progress at it,* she thought, *till the chief decided to summon some kind of godawful Cthulhu thing instead, and opened a conduit to a Heironymus Bosch other-world hell . . . which Vickery and I fell into.*

She covered a shudder by putting her hand over her mouth and yawning.

"Woods was charged with the murders of two TUA agents in 2013," Lubitz went on, "while he was still a Secret Service agent, but the charges were dismissed."

"That's right," said Castine; and *it was self-defense,* she added mentally. She wished she dared to peek at her watch. She'd had only about five hours of sleep in the last thirty-six, and she wanted to get out of this office, out of the Pentagon. A hot bath, she thought, a stiff drink, and ten hours in a hotel bed. Ponder all this unwelcome stuff tomorrow.

Lubitz rubbed his forehead, and it occurred to Castine that he too was very tired. "Excuse me," he said, "but were you . . . intimate with Woods, during those days you were together in 2017?"

Castine frowned. "We were on the run from the bent TUA. We didn't dare use credit cards, so we slept in a tomb at the Hollywood Cemetery one night, and in a taco truck the next—at that time Vickery worked for a woman who ran a fleet of them. But no, there was never any kind of romantic, sexual element in our relationship." That was true, she reflected. "I was engaged to be married," she went on, "so I wasn't open to any such business. As for him, his wife committed suicide years before I met him. That may have . . . inhibited *him*, in that area." That may be true too, she thought—reinforced by our traumatic meeting with his wife's ghost, in that terrible afterlife world.

Lubitz slid a yellow file folder from under the keyboard. Castine could see the word printed on the front of it: PLEIADES, again.

Records of the Office of Naval Research disinformation operations in Wiltshire had been kept in orange files, which signified Top Secret; and she had sometimes dealt with red files, which meant Secret, and blue ones for Confidential. She had never seen a yellow file.

Lubitz laid his hand on it. "Your security clearance," he said, "is upgraded to TS/SCI, as of now."

Castine knew that the Top Secret/Sensitive

Compartmented Information clearance was the highest of the Top Secret levels, equivalent to the Department of Energy's Q Clearance.

"That would require—" she began, then stopped. Of course, she thought.

Lubitz nodded. "A Single Scope Background Investigation, and yes, it's been done already. In fact this assignment is largely a result of that investigation."

A *result* of that investigation? thought Castine. She knew that such investigations were exhaustively thorough, and she wondered uneasily what they might have discovered.

Lubitz slid a photograph out of the file and held it out to her. "Do you recognize either of these men?"

Castine took it with a consciously steady hand, and squinted at it in the harsh light. The picture was not in perfect focus, but she could recognize the man she knew as Sebastian Vickery, wearing a denim jacket over a black T-shirt, standing with another man in a sunlit parking lot. They were looking at something on a cell phone the other man was holding. Vickery's hair was still more dark than gray, and he had shaved off the beard he'd had when she'd last seen him. He'd be ... thirty-nine or forty, now. The man beside him was older, bald and deeply tanned, and wore a scuffed brown leather jacket.

"Can you identify either of them?" Lubitz asked.

Castine nodded. "The one on the left is Vickery. Woods."

"Ah. We weren't reliably certain. The other fellow is a UAP fanatic named Pierce Plowman." Castine recalled that UAP stood for Unidentified Aerial Phenomena, a term adopted by the Navy to replace the embarrassing old Unidentified Flying Objects acronym.

Lubitz went on, "Naval Intelligence has been monitoring Plowman for years, but in this last week we've moved him, and any close associates of his, from the problematic eccentric category to, uh, high-priority acquire. We retrieved this photo and ran facial recognition software on his companion, and at first we got nothing. Too blurry. Then we ran it through the new FR system at the Air Weapons Station at China Lake— and even with their system we only got possibles, no positive. One of the possibles was in the old Secret Service personnel files, of all places—Herbert Woods— but the file photograph was eight years old, and the FR algorithm gets very dicey after six."

Castine handed the photo back. ONI evidently didn't know that Vickery had adopted a new identity sometime after their trip to hell in 2017, and taken the name . . . what was it? . . . Bill Ardmore. And, as Ardmore, Vickery had adopted the pose of a "UFOlogist" to explain his frequent solo trips out into the Mojave Desert. Actually, Castine recalled, he had set up a sort of nest under a desert freeway bridge, to consult ghosts. She tried to imagine explaining that to Lubitz.

"Was Woods interested in UAPs?" Lubitz asked.

Castine shrugged. "Not as of 2017, as far as I know." True enough, she told herself defensively; he didn't adopt the UFOlogist role until early 2018. And here's damned Sebastian Vickery back in my life again, making me deceive the U.S. government! What do I owe him? Well, besides my life.

She took a deep breath. "My assignment has to do with him?"

"We want you to definitively identify him. We think we know where he's going to be, and we'll provide you with a cover story for being there too."

"A cover story? Is he to be arrested?"

Lubitz sat back and stared at her speculatively. "Did you know him well?"

Hard to say, Castine thought. "Reasonably. We were only together a couple of days."

"He'll be detained." Lubitz spread the fingers of one hand, then made a fist. "If he is present, we'd like you to engage him in casual conversation, after you've identified him. Ask him about his current activities, and so forth. When you've learned as much as you can, you make an excuse to step away—say you've left something in your vehicle, or, I don't know, need to visit the ladies' room, or Porta Potty, or whatever might be there."

At which point you arrest him and interrogate him, Castine thought. What on earth has Sebastian blundered into now? And what sort of place is it that's got Porta Potties?

"Does his ... 'highly sensitive aberrant information' concern UAPs?" she asked.

"That's not an immediate concern of yours, at this time. Secure *compartmented* information," Lubitz reminded her.

Castine made herself concentrate. If I do find Vickery, she thought, I'm afraid I'll have to warn him off somehow, God help me. After what the two of us have been through together, I can't genuinely participate in getting him ... arrested, interrogated, very likely incarcerated!

Lubitz had a cell phone in his hand now, and he swiped

the screen and then tapped it. "I'm assigning you a partner," he said, laying it down on the desk. "She knows the procedures for reporting in and receiving any further instructions. A car will pick you up at the DoubleTree at 3 AM. At 4 AM the two of you will board a flight out of Andrews on a C-37A that will be waiting for you—that's a Gulfstream jet—and you'll arrive at the Yucca Valley Airport in California at about 6:30, California time."

Now Castine couldn't help throwing a dismayed glance at her watch. It was already well past eleven. "Three this morning," she said, just to be sure.

"You can sleep on the plane, it's a five-hour flight." Castine thought he sounded envious of her getting an opportunity to sleep.

The door behind Castine clicked and the air shifted perceptibly.

She swiveled her chair around and stood up. The Asian woman she had seen a few minutes ago by echo-vision had stepped into the room; she nodded past Castine at Lubitz, then looked at Castine and held out her hand. "I'm Rayette Yoneda," she said.

No specified rank or job description? thought Castine. This whole enterprise reeks of off-paper.

Able now to see the woman in color, not just by the muted coppery light of echo-vision, Castine saw that her jacket and slacks were light green cotton, and the hair framing her narrow pale face was raven black. Castine clasped the extended hand.

"And you are Special Agent Castine," Yoneda said, releasing Castine's hand after one shake. She turned to Lubitz and raised her eyebrows.

"It's definitely Woods," Lubitz told her.

Yoneda rocked her head impatiently, and it was clear that Lubitz would not have called her in if Castine had not made the identification. "So we go," she said. She took a step forward and turned the computer monitor sideways, then sat down in the other chair. Castine resumed her own seat, kicking aside a stray golf ball on the carpet.

Lubitz pressed his fingertips together again, and Castine thought it looked as if he were praying. "Your only concern in this," he said to Castine, "is to recognize Herbert Woods, let Agent Yoneda know who he is, and chat with him, if possible, for as long as may be informative. She will convey his identity to a team of Sensitive Assignment Specialists we'll have standing by. At that point the two of you make your exit."

Yoneda spoke up. "And if Plowman is there too?"

Lubitz waved dismissively. "The specialists will be watching for him. Your assignment is Woods."

"Where in California is it we're going?" asked Castine.

"It's a site we've prepared," said Lubitz. "It involves a sort of work you're familiar with, as it happens. Disinformation." He paused, frowning, as if trying to remember what he had been saying.

"Disinformation?" Castine prompted.

Lubitz blinked at her, and nodded irritably. "You know it's an ongoing policy to discredit all claims of aberrant events." He waved at the shelves behind him. "Planting fraudulent artifacts at reported crop circle sites, disseminating convincing videos that can later be exposed as trick photography—alien autopsies, plausible accounts of abductions, cattle mutilations. Over the last several years we've contracted with private labs to synthesize fragments of unlikely alloys, which we've planted near military bases—uh, but for this operation—"

"To deceive whom?" asked Castine. "The *military?*"

Lubitz blinked and cleared his throat. "For this operation," he went on more strongly, "we had DARPA construct a dummy *vehicle,* I suppose you'd have to call it, that conformed to the most authoritative reports of UAPs—it was a translucent sphere four meters in diameter with an aluminum cube fixed inside it. Our sphere was made of AION, aluminum oxynitride, which should be exotic enough to intrigue the amateur UAP hunters." He shrugged. "At least until we examine it and find indications that it's a Russian fake."

Castine knew that DARPA was the Defense Advanced Research Projects Agency, and she thought she saw where Lubitz was going with this, but she was too tired to be sure of her own extrapolations. She gestured for him to go on.

"Last night," said Lubitz, "we logged a flight report from the pilot of an F/A-18 Super Hornet, describing the sphere flying erratically—of course there was no such flight, really—and at the same time we had a Gremlin drone drop the sphere in the vicinity of a big boulder known as Giant Rock, near Landers in the Mojave Desert."

Castine nodded. "It's a fake flying saucer. Sorry, UAP. Like our crop circles in Wiltshire."

"Yes. And we've put notices of the flight report and crash on a couple of private online chat groups. It'll draw the UAP amateurs—the very well informed ones first."

Castine thought of the genuine crop circles that her Office of Naval Research team had salted with discrediting litter. "Should we expect any aberrant phenomena?"

"No no, this is entirely mundane."

Yoneda laughed softly. "Aberrant phenomena!" And when Castine turned toward her she rolled her eyes and added, "Foo fighters!"

Castine believed that was the name of a Seattle rock group. Before she could ask Yoneda what she meant, Lubitz pushed his chair back and stood up; the briefing seemed to be coming to a startlingly quick end.

"This should be very simple," Lubitz said, "especially if Woods doesn't even appear. But it *must not* go off the rails. It *will* not. That being so, you don't even need to think about the consequences if it *were* to."

He stood back and raised his eyebrows, inviting questions.

And Castine's mind was whirling with them. "Vickery, Woods, he knows I've been working for Naval Intelligence," she began. "What will he think —"

Lubitz's eyebrows lowered. "But you weren't, in 2017."

That's right, Castine thought with a wave of alarm; why didn't I admit from the start that I met Vickery again in August of 2018, and told him about my reassignment?

"That's right," she said out loud, with a carefully casual nod of acknowledgment. "The Transportation Utility Agency hadn't been shut down yet. Sorry, I haven't had much sleep. Okay, but he knows I was working for a government agency, at least. Won't he—if *he's* there, won't he assume *I'm* there because of this dangerous classified knowledge he's picked up?"

Lubitz cocked his head, and peripherally Castine could see that Yoneda was facing her. "I told you," Lubitz said, "that we have a cover story to explain your presence at the site. You're to be a journalist. There'll probably be journalists there."

Castine exhaled and shook her head. "He *won't* believe *that*. That stinks of a trap, excuse me."

"Very well," said Lubitz impatiently, "you and he were both fugitives from that agency in '17. You could pretend you've gone rogue again. What he says to you then might be particularly relevant."

"*I* didn't go rogue," Castine reminded him, keeping her voice level; "the TUA did. I was one of the few agents in it who weren't dismissed or prosecuted."

"If you don't think you can pull it off," said Lubitz, sounding almost peevish, "then try not to let him see you. If you recognize him, just point him out to Ms. Yoneda and scurry back to your vehicle."

"Wing it," advised Yoneda drily.

The harsh light was giving Castine a headache. She closed her eyes and shook her head. "Okay, sure, I'll see how it feels when the time comes." She opened her eyes to squint at Lubitz. "So how long are we going to be in California?"

He spread his hands. "Hours only. The plane will wait at Yucca Valley Airport, and you'll be back in D.C. tomorrow night."

"We report to you for debriefing?"

"Ms. Yoneda will make the report. You'll be flying directly back to England. This is Saturday—you should be at your usual assignment in Southampton by Monday."

Lubitz was looking away as he spoke, and Castine was suddenly sure that he was lying, or at least leaving out something important.

"Right," she said, fervently hoping that Vickery would not somehow show up at this Giant Rock place, and that she would, as Lubitz claimed, be back in England in two days and could forget about this whole disquieting interlude. Just to seem unquestioningly on board, she added, "Will my new security clearance get me different work there?"

Lubitz's smile was perfunctory. "I imagine it will." He turned to Yoneda. "Questions?"

"Just one. Will either or both of us be armed?"

The woman seemed to recite the question, and Castine guessed that she already knew the answer Lubitz would give, and had been instructed to ask, for Castine's benefit. Castine decided not to mention the small can of Fox Labs pepper spray in her pocket.

"No," Lubitz said. "You two will have left the area before our team moves in, and it'll be a very quiet apprehension in any case. In addition to your usual Common Access cards, you'll both have Field Researcher IDs, which should be enough to get you cooperation from local authorities, if that should unwisely become necessary."

"It won't," said Yoneda. Her voice was firm, and she pushed her chair back and stood up.

"There's a car for you at the River Entrance," Lubitz said. "Now—" He waved wearily, "go, go."

Castine was mildly surprised at the effort it took for her to get to her feet, and she looked forward to sleeping on the flight to California. She followed Yoneda through the small waiting room out to the corridor.

Overhead fluorescents gleamed in the polished floor as the two of them walked between the wainscoted walls and closed doors. Castine had to take long steps to keep up with the other woman. When they rounded the first corner she asked quietly, "Foo fighters?"

"And crop circles," Yoneda said, "and things with hands like steam shovels, and all that *aberrant* crap. Foo fighters was what pilots called UFOs in World War Two."

"*I* didn't see any steam shovel monster," said Castine. I didn't see it in real time, at least, she thought. And when did you hear about that?

"Carl Jung, do you know the name?"

"Sure," said Castine, a bit breathlessly. "Archetypes."

"Very good. He knew all that applesauce was just hallucinations, projections. People used to see angels and gods in the sky, but in a technological age they see … extraterrestrial hubcaps and waffle irons. And steam shovel monsters! The Army finally closed down their Stargate Project twenty-some years ago—" She glanced at Castine. "That was remote viewing, a spy in a bunk at Fort Meade trying to see Soviet missile emplacements in Kiev or someplace. But now the *Navy* wants to check out *UFOs.*"

Castine stopped and leaned against a wall to catch her breath. "UAPs."

Yoneda stopped too. "You knew the guy, this Herbert Woods?" When Castine nodded, she went on, "Are you sure you're down with fingering him?"

Castine pushed a stray lock of hair back from her

forehead and gave Yoneda a tired smile. "Orders is orders."

"So you weren't all that close with him?"

"I was on the run with him for about three days, back in 2017. It didn't...turn into anything." True, she thought.

"He was some kind of hobo, right, after he went AWOL from the Secret Service?"

"Sometimes. And sometimes he worked in those taco trucks you see all over L.A."

And sometimes, she thought, he was a driver for a very useful supernatural-evasion car service. And sometimes he was a freeway-side gypsy, charting the expanded possibility fields generated by free wills moving rapidly along the freeway lanes...and sometimes he had to deal with the ghosts that were able to manifest themselves in those fields.

Yoneda nodded and resumed walking toward the next bend in the corridor. "Well," she said breezily over her shoulder, "he'll be lucky if he ever sees a taco again."

Castine pushed away from the wall and followed her. Oh, Sebastian, she thought, don't be there tomorrow.

CHAPTER THREE:
Como Siempre

The 1952 Chevy camper truck stood near the cracked cement foundation of a long-gone diner, and the truck rocked on its shock absorbers whenever a particularly strong gust of wind swept in from the east, out of the vast expanse of the Mojave Desert.

A dozen oddly assorted vehicles were parked haphazardly on the barren plain, and even the several big mobile home trailers were dwarfed to insignificance by the titanic boulder that stood up stark against the empty blue sky and blocked most of the view to the north. The boulder was seven stories tall and half again as wide, and the narrow fringe of spray-paint graffiti around its base made it look as if it had once stood in a shallow sea of colorful flotsam. The Hopi Indians had considered the boulder sacred, the heart of Mother Earth, and prophesied that a new era would begin when one day the giant rock would split; and in fact twenty years ago one side of it *had* split off, and now rested like a beached ship beside the hardly diminished natural monument.

35

Three other massive boulders, imposing in any other setting, stood on the sand around it, and a ridge of tumbled rocks bordered the area to the west. The spray-paint graffiti on these surrounding granite and quartz surfaces were all staring eyes, or R.I.P. remembrances of people noted only by their first names. Clearly the sacred aura around this immense standing stone hadn't entirely diminished with the 1882 departure of the Hopis to a reservation in Arizona.

But any mood of spirituality on this Sunday morning was dissipating fast. The broken wreckage of the supposed UFO had been found shortly after dawn, and had now been trucked back to this plain at the north end of the three-mile dirt road that led back to the little town of Landers; and already the emerging consensus among the gathered UFO enthusiasts was that the event had been a hoax, albeit an elaborate one. The argument now was mostly whether it had been perpetrated by the Russian, Chinese, or United States government.

Cars and trucks were still arriving—a dust-cloud and spots of reflected glare to the south told of at least a couple more vehicles approaching, their drivers no doubt hoping for evidence of extraterrestrials.

Sebastian Vickery stepped up onto the running board of the pickup truck and looked across the truck's dusty roof at the scattered clusters of people visible on this side of Giant Rock. Even with a wide-brimmed hat and dark sunglasses he had to squint in the waxing reflections of sunlight on sand and stone, and the creosote-smelling wind threw veils of dust across his view.

As far as Vickery was concerned, this trip was proving

to be a waste of time; he had come in the hope that Pierce Plowman might show up, since he'd had no luck getting in touch with Plowman during these past seven days, but the old man wasn't among any of the groups of people on the plain, and Plowman hadn't been in either of the trucks that had gathered up the evidently bogus UFO wreckage.

When Vickery had driven up the long desolate track from Landers and parked here, the first thing he had done, after noting the locations of all the other vehicles and satisfying himself that he would not be disturbed sitting in his truck, was to stare through the windshield until the rocks and the sky were just random patterns of color, and then focus beyond them. And when he was seeing the recent local past by echo-light—the stony landscape relatively bright even in echo-view on this unclouded desert morning—old habits had made him scrutinize the scene, and he had detected no signs of surveillance arrangements or covert organization among the sightseers.

And then, still seeing the recent past, he had stared up at the great monolith, glowing an impossible color that was both something like brown and something like silver, and thought about dragging his easel and paint-box and a canvas out of the back of the truck.

When his vision had abruptly and glaringly shifted back to the view of real time, he had relaxed and got out of the truck to look for Plowman. Uselessly, as it had turned out.

He was glad the echo-vision worked reliably these days—a year and a half ago he and Ingrid Castine had found that the ability to see behind *now* showed them only a terrible old ruined house that had once stood in

Topanga Canyon, south of Los Angeles. In 1968 the house had been the site of a hippie cult's attempt to create a thing called an *egregore,* an autonomous group mind that would forcibly draw other minds and dissolve them into itself; the 1968 attempt had failed, but in 2018 it had been tried again by a Silicon Valley entrepreneur named Simon Harlowe. Harlowe had discovered that Vickery and Castine, with their fractured connection to sequential time, would together be the ideal Interface Message Processor . . . or switchboard, or router, or thalamus . . . of his egregore. Vickery had ultimately had to kill two people, including Harlowe, to get himself and Castine free of the soul-destroying psychic whirlpool.

Castine had stayed two nights at Vickery's trailer in Barstow, sleeping in his bed while he slept on the living room couch, and when the trouble was past, they had considered the idea of Vickery moving to Gaithersburg, Maryland, where Castine had an apartment; but ultimately he had decided to stay in California.

Though they had parted amiably, there had been no contact between them in the year and a half since. He supposed she was still working in some capacity for the Office of Naval Intelligence.

Vickery hopped down from the running board. Plowman had not appeared, and he wanted to catch the 8 AM mass at Blessed Sacrament Catholic Church in Twentynine Palms, a long twenty mile drive to the southeast.

The two vehicles that had been visible advancing up the dirt road had now arrived at the broad clear area. One was a new bright blue Jeep, and the other was a gray Ford van of '60s vintage with the back windows painted over white. They apparently weren't together—the Jeep stopped near the fallen segment of the great boulder, while the van circled around and parked fifty yards behind Vickery's truck. From old training, Vickery noticed that the van's engine sounded mutedly powerful, and that there was an extended extra mirror on the driver's side. Its tires looked incongruously new.

Two women climbed out of the Jeep and gaped up at the monolith, raised hands shading their sunglasses—but Vickery's face was suddenly cold. Even at this distance, he recognized Ingrid Castine, looking thinner than he remembered, in blue jeans and a long-sleeve white blouse and hiking boots. Her auburn hair, tossing in the wind, was longer now.

His reflexive reactions were two; a smile twitched at his lips, and his right hand touched the hard, flat bulk of the 9-millimeter Glock 43 under his denim jacket.

Then, still facing toward them and away from the van that had arrived in their wake, he opened the truck's door and climbed in. The windshield was dusty, and with the hat pulled down low over the sunglasses, he could certainly drive wide around the women and disappear to the south without her recognizing him.

He knew that would be the wisest course.

But, he thought, what is she *doing* here? One week after Frankie Notchett was arrested? Notchett's just a small-time Los Angeles poet interested in UFOs, but he was Pierce Plowman's friend and confidant . . . disciple, even. Could Castine be here looking for Plowman, same as me? I came here to warn him—what would be *her* motive?

Vickery glanced at the passenger-side mirror. Nobody had emerged from the van. He dug his keys out of the jacket's side pocket. After fitting one into the ignition slot on the dashboard, he slouched back, alternately watching the two women and the van behind him.

Perhaps Naval Intelligence was checking out the reported UFO crash, and it was simply a long-odds coincidence that Castine was one of the agents assigned to the investigation.

If I drive away, he thought, I'll never know why she's here.

And I do know, he thought, as well as I know . . . well, not my own name . . . as well as I know east from west, that she would never knowingly betray me.

Castine and her companion had at first moved forward, away from him, to mingle with the sparse groups picking over the wreckage of the fake UFO; but now they were walking back this way between the randomly parked cars and trucks. If they maintained their present direction, they would arrive at the old pavement, and pass close by Vickery's truck, in no more than a minute. They appeared to be chatting, but Castine was darting glances around at the widely spaced parked vehicles, and the other woman never took her eyes off Castine's face.

Vickery touched the ignition key, and hesitated—and in that moment Castine looked squarely at the truck's windshield, and Vickery met her gaze, and even at this distance the recognition was palpably mutual, though her expression didn't change.

Then the sudden harsh boom of an explosion behind him battered his eardrums and rocked his truck, and a white BMW was racing across the plain below the towering boulder. Vickery spun in his seat and saw a churning turbulence of flames where the van had been, and pieces of debris skittering across the dirt and spinning away through the air.

He turned back to look through the windshield— Castine was now leaning against a parked and unoccupied Volkswagen, and her companion had drawn a gun and was sprinting toward the burning shell of the van; the BMW that had sped past the boulder was now just a dimishing silhouette in a cloud of dust on the road to Landers.

Castine looked across the distance between herself and Vickery's truck, and swept her hand in a wave that clearly meant *go.*

Vickery bared his teeth, squinting after the receding BMW. He couldn't hope to catch up to it in his camper truck, but he had once been a Los Angeles police officer, and he wanted to get a closer look at that car. It was obvious that no one inside the van could have survived the explosion, and no one else had been close enough to be injured—and the woman who had accompanied Castine was now talking on a cell phone, and would probably be effectively distracted for at least a minute.

A quick glance at the cars parked in the direction the fleeing vehicle had come from was enough for him to memorize their arrangement, and then he sat back and made himself relax, breathing deeply. He stared at the giant rock and the sky and the desert, and in a few seconds he was seeing the shapes as merely a two-dimensional pattern—with specks and blobs that must have been airborne pieces of the van moving rapidly across it—and when the view was just an abstract mobile collage, he flexed his focus to look past it.

His vision regained depth, though dimmed now in brassy echo-light, and the roaring of the fire was muted; he quickly peered toward the cars he had scrutinized a moment earlier, and he saw a pale BMW among them that had not been visible there a few seconds ago in real time. He could just make out the silhouettes of two heads in it. In the remaining seconds of the echo-vision, he pushed open the door of his truck—though to his atemporal view his hand was invisible and the door did not open—and he simply stepped through the appearance of the door as if it were a hologram; and he had taken several running steps toward the evident BMW, hoping to get close enough to see its license plate and trusting to luck not to collide with somebody or trip over some unseen fragment of the van, when light and sound crashed back into his senses.

The BMW, of course, was no longer visible where it had been some time earlier, and he was ten feet away from his truck. He glanced around quickly: Castine's companion was standing a good distance back from the roaring fire, facing it and still talking on her cell phone; looking in the other direction, Vickery saw Castine push herself away from the Volkswagen and then stumble and catch her balance, evidently disoriented. She looked from Vickery's truck to where he was standing a few yards away from it, and she scowled at him and began hastily scrawling letters in the dust on the Volkswagen's windshield. The letters spelled *RUN!*

Okay, he thought, and turned to hurry back to his truck ...

But the sky was glittering. He looked up—and slid to a halt, the breath stopped in his throat.

Sunlit silvery spheres were rushing back and forth across the empty blue firmament in eerie silence, their size and distance impossible to guess—they moved and changed course as rapidly as needles on a seismograph, and in the first couple of seconds he assumed his vision had gone bad, perhaps the onset of a stroke.

But when he looked down he saw that the people closer to the rock were pointing at the sky and running in every direction, presumably toward their cars.

Vickery raised his head and again stared upward. It was still hard to grasp that the silver globes darting across the sky were real, though they were gleaming in the morning sunlight—but several of them briefly circled over Giant Rock before springing away in all directions and instantly reuniting in a helical pattern directly overhead—at a height of a hundred yards, a mile?—and he realized that there was order in their ever-changing velocities; and he was suddenly certain that their motions were deliberate, and reflected some sort of sentience or sentiences.

Vickery felt tiny and terribly exposed on this flat desert plain—he remained standing, though every nerve in his body was tensed in readiness to huddle, crawl under the truck, hide his frail identity from the shining beings in the sky.

He had to look down. Castine was staring up at the celestial prodigy, but she looked away from it long enough to stare blankly at Vickery for several seconds, and then shake her head and slap the Volkswagen's windshield.

And a moment later the sky was empty, the silvery globes having vanished as instantly and soundlessly as they had manifested themselves.

Vickery glanced quickly around at the unobstructed remote horizons to the east and south, then hurriedly ran to his truck, climbed in and started the engine. The things are gone, he told himself, if they were ever really there. Sundogs, desert mirages! Castine is involved in some government work here, and you're in danger of blowing her cover. Whatever her work is, it probably has to do with the atmospheric phenomena that just appeared in the sky, and nothing to do with you.

He took a deep breath, and exhaled.

But Castine had clearly meant, *You have to get out of here*.

He rocked the gear shift lever into first gear, and he nodded to her as he sped past her and the other cars and steered around onto the dirt track that would take him to Landers and Old Woman Springs Road and south to the Twentynine Palms Highway.

In the rear view mirror he saw Castine's companion sprinting toward the Jeep and waving at Castine. In moments they had both scrambled into the Jeep, and now it was rolling along in the dust of his wake.

Recalling Castine's evident alarm at seeing him, and the gun the other woman had been openly carrying, Vickery pressed his foot down on the gas pedal, and the old truck shook as it gained speed.

The Jeep accelerated too, bobbing over the uneven

road, and it was gaining on him. Gripping the jerking wheel tightly with one hand, he tapped the gun under his jacket and then pulled out his phone, popped the back off of it, and pried out the battery.

With both hands on the wheel again, he concentrated on the bumpy road rushing under the tires.

The Jeep would certainly have better suspension than his truck, and he was thinking about what he would do if its driver cut him off, or fired a warning shot—or worse!— but when he darted a quick glance at the mirror he saw the Jeep swerve and lose speed and then pull to the side of the track. In moments it was lost to view in the dust cloud raised by his truck.

Thinking of his tires, he let up on the gas pedal, but kept a wary eye on the mirror.

Forty minutes later, Vickery had arrived at Blessed Sacrament church. He sat close to the wall in the back pew, partly so that no other communicants would give him curious looks when he remained seated and didn't walk up to the altar for Communion with the rest of the congregation, and partly so that he could see everyone who came in through the open doors at the back of the nave.

He had not seen the blue Jeep again, but old training had kept him alert and ready to make evasive moves all the way here, and he had not yet completely relaxed.

Morning sunlight extended from the church entrance almost all the way to the altar, and he was sitting well to the side, in shadow. The altar and the crucifix were set back behind a tall, wide arch, but even from the back of the church he had been able to see the priest raise the host at the Consecration, and Vickery bowed his head.

During the past seven years he had attended Sunday mass more often than not, and he had gone to Confession nearly as often, but he had not taken Communion in that time. The two Transportation Utility agents he had killed in 2013 had very nearly succeeded in killing him first—in an attempted ad hoc execution in a desert gully outside Palmdale—because he had unknowingly stumbled onto the top-secret ghost-trafficking in which the TUA was then involved. He had had to kill men since then, one in a Los Angeles street, two in a field by Topanga Beach, and a teenager in a Jewish deli in Los Angeles, but the pair of agents in the desert had cast a shadow on his soul which the subsequent killings—justified and necessary though each of them had been—had only deepened. He knew it was shame, even to some extent a self-aggrandizing sort of shame, that kept him from consuming God's body and blood at Communion, but he had so far never managed to overcome it.

When mass ended, he waited until the last of the congregants had shuffled out, taking copies of the church bulletin and shaking hands with the priest, before he stood up and made his way to the open doors. The priest was out on the cement apron in front of the church, talking to several well-dressed elderly people, and beyond them was nothing but a trailer or two on the face of the desert that extended away to distant mountains.

No cars at all were visible at the moment on the street, and Vickery even glanced warily into the sky before he walked to the right and paused at the corner of the church. He had parked around in the back, behind some auxiliary building, but past this point was a small asphalt lot with nine parking spaces, and he had noted the cars parked there when he had arrived. Despite feeling self-conscious, he slid his hand inside his jacket now as he stepped out from behind the church wall.

His hand clenched on the grip of the Glock when he saw the blue Jeep parked in the nearest parking space, but in nearly the same instant he let his hand fall empty out of his jacket; Castine was sitting in the Jeep, alone, and he knew how she must have found him. Behind her sunglasses her expression was bleak.

He gave the other cars a cursory look, then trudged up to the Jeep.

"Hey, Ingrid," he said quietly.

She nodded. "Nearest Catholic Church," she said in a strained voice. "I Googled for it, and figured you'd try for the 8 AM." She was gripping the steering wheel tightly. "You've wrecked my life again. I assaulted a government agent, my partner—I'll probably go to prison! An— accessory! Some ONI guys *died* in that explosion. Sensitive Assignment Specialists! *Damn* it, Sebastian! Why were you there? You don't even *believe* in flying saucers!"

She touched her hair over her right temple, and Vickery recalled that she had a bullet scar there, from a time when he *had* arguably wrecked her life.

He stared at her, mystified. "I was minding my own business—looking for a guy."

"Sure, Plowman. And you apparently heard something from him that you shouldn't have heard. Why do you keep *doing* that? They're g-gonna lock you up somewhere, and you'll be lucky ever to see a taco again. Me too, now." She looked around as if noting the arid landscape for the first time, and she too glanced warily at the sky. "Where's your truck? I've got to ditch this Jeep." She climbed out and stood on the asphalt, and Vickery saw the grip of a small pistol in her waistband, no bigger than .380 caliber. Her auburn hair had been disarranged by the wind, and a strand fell across her eyes when she snatched off her sunglasses.

"Sebastian," she said in a shaky whisper as she pushed it back, "what *were* those things?"

He shivered, remembering the brief spectacle. "God, Ingrid," he said quietly, "I don't know. UFOs! Almost as if they were drawn by that van blowing up." He shook his head and glanced at the sky again, then shrugged and looked at her. "What's this about Plowman?"

"I don't know. He's a UFO nut, they've got a photo of you with him. Sorry—AAP nut. Anomalous Aerial Phenomena."

"He's a nut on all kinds of subjects . . . and he's never said anything *worthwhile.*"

"I don't think it matters."

After a few seconds in which the wind was the only sound, Vickery said, "Naval Intelligence knew those things would appear?"

"No. We were there so I could identify you, and specialists in the van were going to arrest you, because of some ultra-classified knowledge you have. Why didn't you drive away right after I waved you off?"

"I was about to, but then your van blew up and a car

over by the big rock took off fast, too fast for me to get much of a look at it. So I—I went into echo-vision to try to see it while it was still parked."

"You did? Dammit, I bet that's why I got tipped into it too. I got stuck with ten seconds of silent dark downtime while everything was going on!"

Vickery recalled that she had seemed dazed when she had pushed herself away from the Volkswagen, just as he himself had been recovering from the brief echo-vision episode. And there had been times in the past when they had both inadvertently fallen into that state at the same time.

"Sorry," he said. "At least you were holding still by that Volkswagen, not walking around."

"Let's not hold still now."

"Right." Vickery took her elbow and led her toward the church's back lot. "I don't have any ultra-classified information. Round the back here, just past that dumpster. Except maybe having seen what happened there today."

"Something Plowman told you. Slow down, will you?"

"I came to warn him about people like you. I'm pretty sure a friend of his got taken by something like your crowd." He had his keys out, and he unlocked and opened the truck's pasenger-side door. "And Plowman's just a nut, an eccentric," he said as she slid into the seat. "Flying saucers, chemtrails, he even thinks the Earth is flat." He closed her door, then hurried around the front bumper, got in and started the engine. "You assaulted a government agent back there? Why?"

She sniffed and stared out the side window at a blank stucco wall. In a frail voice, she asked, "What's chemtrails?"

"Jet vapor trails. Conspiracy nuts think they're mind-control chemicals." He had parked parallel to the building, and now drove in a circle to exit onto the street and make a left turn. "So . . . why?"

"Guess," she said flatly.

He grimaced and nodded. "Uh . . . thanks."

"I owed you," she said, and inhaled deeply. "Or so it seemed at the time. She—this agent, my partner!—she saw what I wrote on the Volkswagen's window before I could wipe it off, and she saw you take off, and then she handcuffed me and we got in the Jeep to catch you. It looked like we *would* catch you, too, so I, I *pepper-sprayed* her! She ran us off the road."

"Ah." Vickery recalled the pursuing blue Jeep slowing and steering off the dirt track, and he tried to think of something better to say than *Thanks*.

"I, uh, owe you too," he said.

"You sure do."

He turned left onto the highway that would eventually lead them south to the 10 Freeway. Old Man 10, the freeway gypsies in Los Angeles called it, and, irrational though the thought was, he knew he'd feel less exposed in its coursing flow and off these shallow-seeming surface streets.

"She was blinded," Castine went on with a visible shiver, "all hissing and choking. I got this gun out of her holster and made her give me the cuff key. Then I pushed her out and drove off, searching on my phone for the nearest Catholic church. And I took the battery out of my phone, after." Her voice had trailed away in a yawn, and she shivered again. "I can't *begin* to imagine the kind of trouble I'm in." She put her sunglasses back on and looked left and right at the drug stores and offices and restaurants widely spaced between flat, barren lots. "Where are we going?"

"Be on the 10 before long. Then—L.A., I guess. Do they know about this Bill Ardmore identity? I haven't been fingerprinted since I adopted it."

"They didn't seem to. What's in L.A.?"

"My trailer, these days. And I'd like to find Plowman."

"Why not, I suppose. Still, it'll be nice to be on the old 10 again." She tugged the little pistol from her waistband and bent forward to slide it under the seat, then leaned back and stretched. "I'm dead for sleep," she muttered, "sorry. Wake me up if we get anywhere."

Within moments her head was resting against the door window and she was snoring softly.

He looked away from the straight line of the rushing highway to glance at her sleeping profile, noting a few faint new wrinkles beside her eye and down her cheek; and he was wryly surprised at how natural it seemed, even after a year and a half, for her to be sitting beside him in a car, both of them running from big weird trouble. What had she been doing since that August?

He sighed deeply. Taking her under his wing again would certainly disrupt, perhaps destroy, the life he had lately managed to make for himself. But in an odd way he felt as if he had been expecting it, even counting on it. Marking time.

Su apuro es mi apuro, he thought, *como siempre*. Your trouble is mine, as always.

CHAPTER FOUR:
UFO, Not NLO

Two San Bernardino County fire engines and three Sheriff's cars had pulled up near the remains of the van, which was now just a steaming, blackened frame. Clouds of sand were streaming away in the wash from the rotors of a low-flying helicopter. Firemen in yellow turnout coats and pants and helmets appeared to be poking through the ruin, and sheriff's deputies in sunglasses and khaki were questioning bystanders.

Sitting in his rented Honda fifty yards away from the aftermath activity, the man currently called Tacitus Banach was furious at everyone, especially himself. He had arrived early, picked a strategic parking spot, mingled with the gathering crowd and surreptitiously photographed the license plates of all the vehicles—but in the crucial moments when things had started to happen, he had been . . . *incapacitated*. Blind, for ten seconds!

He leaned back, closed his eyes, and shivered.

And then when he had recovered his senses, the aerial

phenomenon had been happening directly overhead! He had been informally studying them for two years—buying beers for people who claimed to have witnessed UFO appearances, visiting alleged landing sites, gleaning nuggets of consistency from badly printed pamphlets and semi-literate posts online, but until this morning he had never actually *seen* the things.

The gleaming silver spheres—their sizes impossible to guess—clustering, separating, rebounding from the corners of the sky! He had been too frightened—no, too awed, humbled—to do more than gape at them, probably with his mouth hanging open like a fool.

But he had already been disoriented at that point. When the van exploded and the BMW had precipitately fled the scene, he had seen a black-haired woman in cargo pants and a khaki bush jacket draw a gun and run toward the burning van—

—and then, infuriatingly, he had fallen out of *now*. For a good ten seconds he had only dared to stand still in the muted brassy dimness, helplessly looking at the scene as it had been at some time in the recent past.

And it was when the light and noise of real time came back that the whole firmament of the sky had been glitteringly alive with the darting mirror-bright shapes, and he had been helpless to look at anything else until the impossible things vanished.

He had managed to collect himself then, and he saw the old Chevy camper truck start up; it drove away south, and the woman in the khaki bush jacket and another woman scrambled into a blue Jeep and took off, evidently pursuing the camper truck. Banach had been standing too

far away from his own car to hope to catch up to them—
which would arguably have been unwise in any case.

Banach opened his eyes now and shifted around on the
car seat, letting his gaze ascend the massive shoulder of
the great rock; and for a few moments he was able to view
the stupidities and inadequacies of this morning as
inconsequential. Tacitus Banach was sixty years old,
nearsighted, somewhat overweight, and balding. This
towering boulder had sat here, unconsidered during the
millenia before humans even existed, then worshipped,
then more recently and briefly a focus of NLO activity,
ultimately destined to watch over this desert long after
humanity was no more than an imperceptible adulteration
of the dust in this infinity of sand.

He shook his head sharply and reminded himself to
think in English. *UFO*, not *NLO*—Unidentified Flying
Objects, not *Neopoznannyy Letat Oj'jektu*. You represent
the old guard, he told himself firmly; not like those two
hooligans who conspicuously raced away right after the
explosion! The GRU—the *Glavnoye Razvedyvatel'noye
Upravleniye*, the Soviet Military Intelligence
Directorate—survived the fall of the Soviet Union
honorably intact, unlike the more celebrated KGB, but
some of these new recruits are just crude thugs, useless
for strategic work.

But maybe I'm becoming useless myself: *nikudyshnyy*,
if I may indulge for another moment. My visions of the
recent past never happened *involuntarily* before! What
use am I, how can I even drive a car, if at any moment I
might fall out of *now*, and only be able to see what has
already happened?

Since the interludes in which he viewed the past were controllable—had until now been controllable!—Banach had kept the ability a secret from his superiors. He had only been able to "look backward" in that way during the last three years . . . after one disastrous morning in March of 2017.

Born in Kaliningrad in 1960, he had enrolled in the Zhdanov Higher Military Engineering School at eighteen, and at twenty-two he was commissioned as a second lieutenant in the Soviet Army. He would most likely have been deployed to Afghanistan with the 40th Army to fight the *mujahideen* insurgents, but a Mandate Commission spotted him as a candidate for the Staff College of the Soviet Army, known as the Military Diplomatic Academy or MDA, and after a number of interviews and background investigations he had received orders to report to the MDA campus in Moscow.

At that point he had been a GRU officer, and because he was unmarried and had achieved fluency in English and had studied British and American fiction and nonficton, he was chosen to operate under deep cover as an "illegal" agent—working abroad without diplomatic cover, under an assumed name—in the United States. He had then been specially trained in covert communications, evasion of surveillance, American speech and the operation and maintenance of American cars, and as an illegal-in-training he had been forbidden to go to Moscow restaurants frequented by foreigners, or to have his picture taken in any setting identifiable as Moscow.

And after three years he had been posted to Canada to establish a "legend," a false identity. It had been decided that he would be provided with credentials allowing him to get a job in an American college as a professor of Political Science, and he had eventually worked his way up to a position at the University of Southern California. By that time the Soviet Union had collapsed and fragmented, but the GRU had continued to function as a cornerstone Russian intelligence service.

And for twenty years there, under the name Andrius Kuprys, he had taught classes in National Ideologies and Comparative Politics and Marxist Theory, and hosted discussion groups in his Mid City apartment, always watching for the occasional student with intelligence and political ambitions and strong commitment to militant socialist philosophies. "Andrius Kuprys" functioned only as a talent-spotter, passing on likely names to his handler. Direction, persuasion and the winnowing out of all but the few really likely agent candidates were undertaken by GRU operatives of whom Kuprys knew nothing.

At first Kuprys had resented his sedentary middleman position, though his superiors insisted that well-placed talent-spotters were too valuable to be put at risk as agent-handlers too. But after a few years of it he had got tenure at the university, had published essays in *American Political Science Review* and *The Journal of Socialist Theory,* and he took satisfaction in seeing a couple of his nominated students go on to positions in the California State Legislature. The first rungs of the ladder!

But in 2017 it had all abruptly come to an end. After a mass arrest of Soviet illegal agents in New Jersey and New

58

York in 2010, the FBI had been devoting a large part of its workforce to finding and arresting more such agents, and charging them with failing to register as agents of a foreign government. The captured agents were imprisoned and, in most cases, eventually traded back to Russia—there to face an uncertain future, at best.

Andrius Kuprys had very nearly been caught in the FBI net.

One morning in March of '17 he had, as often before, stuck a flash-drive into a certain patch of grass in a shopping center parking lot for his handler to retrieve, but the FBI had evidently been monitoring him for some time. As he stepped away from the grass, the doors of two tan Ford Explorer SUVs parked beside his Toyota sprang open, and a moment later Banach had found himself facing four young men in business suits, each carrying a gun and an open badge wallet.

Banach's Toyota was parked on the far side of the two SUVs, and his hands were in the pockets of his tweed sportcoat. With his left thumb he pressed the Panic/Alarm button on his key fob and in the same moment looked past the agents with a startled expression. He had long ago replaced the Toyota's factory horn with a 150-decibel Zone Tech dual trumpet horn, and when the shocking metallic bellow shook the air, sounding like a semi-trailer truck imminently bearing down on them all, he dived to his left and tried to do a forward roll between two parked cars; but his hands slipped in an oil puddle and his head collided hard with the pavement.

He had wobbled to his feet with hot blood coursing down his face, and his head ringing along with the intermittently blaring car horn behind him. An old station wagon was trundling past in the parking lot lane, and he yanked open its driver's side door and managed to pull a horrified woman out onto the pavement; and he was in the driver's seat and steering unsteadily out of the parking lot when one of the FBI agents fired three shots.

One shot struck the left front fender, one punched through the driver's side window, stinging his cheek and his left eye with a spray of glass, and the third struck the door frame and ricocheted upward to jarringly graze the side of his head.

He had been trained in functioning while concussed, and reflexively began counting, *"Adeen, dva, tree, chityri—"* to maintain continuity in what he was seeing: a driveway onto a main street, an open lane, cars swerving, probably car horns blaring in unheard protest ...

A green freeway entrance sign registered as an opportunity for speed and distance, and his hands automatically steered the hijacked car into the curving onramp lane as his foot pressed down hard on the accelerator.

He was aware that he had got onto the 110 freeway, though staying in one lane required constant and sometimes wide correction, but the station wagon's engine was stuttering—probably the bullet through the fender had damaged something. He reminded himself to check for pursuit—and the government SUVs were probably right behind him—but the rear-view mirror showed him only wind-blown dust. And through the windshield, too, he could see nothing but whipping curtains of sand. In panic he swung the steering wheel to the right, aiming the station wagon at an off-ramp barely visible through the sudden sandstorm.

Later he had learned that the Los Angeles freeways generated a field that could only be defined as supernatural, and that the field had been particularly strong on that day— to his benefit, ultimately, in a way. Probably.

No longer using the name Andrius Kuprys, Tacitus Banach now sighed and looked around at the barren plain in the now-harsh sunlight. Nearly all of the other cars had left the wide area around the giant boulder, and only one Sheriff's car and one fire engine still sat near the wreckage of the van. He couldn't see or hear the helicopter.

He started his engine, but paused before touching the gear shift lever. Having remembered his escape from the FBI three years ago, he couldn't now evade the memory of what had happened to him when he drove down that unnatural freeway offramp—nor his subsequent doubts, never to this day entirely dismissed, of his own sanity.

The freeway sandstorm had abruptly cleared, but not in time for him to avoid crashing the hijacked station wagon into what had appeared to be a big greenhouse— though when he had opened the door and stumbled out onto loose sand, the flying pieces of glass had become clumsy butterflies that didn't get far before falling to the sand and being eaten by tiny lizards. The sky was a churning cauldron of earth colors that made the horizon difficult to distinguish, though in his concussed state he hadn't been able to focus on anything for more than a second or two anyway.

The chilly air was astringent, stinging his nose and lungs, and it seemed unnaturally thick, so that walking required conscious effort; and the perspective was scrambled—a step toward the station wagon left him facing away from it. Clinging to the scrap of order that had been playing in his mind, he had kept on counting, and soon the chain of spoken numbers became remembered metrical verses of a Pushkin poem.

And somehow the verses, recited in the same metronomic tone in which he had been reciting numbers, had eventually, step by labored step, led him out of the delirium. He had found himself at last in a brightly sunlit patch of weedy dirt encircled by an offramp of the Pasadena Freeway, many miles from where he had steered into that offramp to insanity.

The station wagon was lost beyond comprehension. Banach's face was streaked with blood and his shirt was blotted with it, and a group of freeway-side gypsies encamped there had sat him down and given him a restorative cigarette and a beer. They had helped him clean up, and sold him a fairly fresh shirt, and he had walked to a train station.

He told his handler only that he had been unmasked and nearly arrested by the FBI. As expected, he had been taken to a safe house and given an interim false-name passport in order to return to Moscow by a circuitous route. Then for a month he had nominally been a "guest lecturer," one who in fact did no lecturing, at a GRU school in Bykovo, forty kilometers east of Moscow. He had expected to be charged eventually with some deriliction of duty—but, to his surprise, he had again been sent to

Canada to establish a *new* legend, a new and very different cover identity, as Tacitus Banach.

As Andrius Kuprys, he had been clean-shaven and physically fit and had spoken with a neutral trans-Atlantic accent; as Tacitus Banach he had a full gray beard and was encouraged to put on weight and affect a faint Oklahoma drawl. To secure his financial stability now that he was no longer receiving a university paycheck, an unknown person in Montana regularly mailed him packages of items like rare Barbie dolls and Lego sets and Montblanc fountain pens and Dunhill tobacco pipes, which Banach repackaged and sold on the eBay website.

His new assignment was to adopt the role of an eccentric conspiracy theorist and insinuate himself into the loose communities of flying saucer cultists in Los Angeles, and he had been pursuing that for the last couple of years ... and had learned more, perhaps, than his masters had intended.

While still languishing as a non-lecturing lecturer in Bykovo, he had one morning lost his glasses—and discovered to his astonishment that, by focusing past his blurred view of *now,* he could briefly see his surroundings as they had been an hour earlier. The light had been dim and inconsistent, but he had not needed his glasses to see clearly by it.

And he discovered that he could do it again, at will.

In those backward-looking moments he was blind and deaf to what was actually going on around him in real time, but in these past three years there had been occasions when it had been helpful to be able to see what cars had been parked at certain locations at some earlier time, or what papers had recently been on a desk, or even what number had recently been called by someone in a now-vacated restaurant booth.

It was clear that he was no longer firmly set in the moment of now, and he believed he knew when the fracture had occurred—on that day when he had exited reality and then found his way back again.

He shifted into drive and steered toward the dirt road that would lead him away from Giant Rock and back to civilization. Now he'd have to report to his handler that the opportunity to slipstream in behind the Navy's fake flying saucer gambit had been wasted: whatever chance there might have been to find Pierce Plowman among the cleverly lured crowd had been wrecked when those two idiot GRU agents had simply put a bomb under the Naval Intelligence van and then driven off immediately after the explosion, like bank robbers making a getaway! Banach would demand that those two clowns be sent back to Moscow.

The unpaved road was distinguishable in the vast flat desert only because of tire tracks and the absence of yucca and creosote bushes right in its path. Squinting ahead through his sunglasses, Banach saw the woman while she was still a hundred yards ahead of him.

She was trudging north, back toward Giant Rock, and he recognized her cargo pants and bush jacket—she had been the driver of the blue Jeep.

He was keeping his speed to less than fifteen miles per hour, so he had several seconds to think before he would reach her.

She had drawn a gun and gone running toward the van immediately after it blew up. That indicated alertness, readiness, training; the van had been covert Naval Intelligence, and she was probably an ONI field agent, assisting in whatever ONI had meant to accomplish by drawing all the dedicated UFOlogists out here this morning.

But she probably hadn't meant to be walking along this desert road now. Had the other woman forced her out of the Jeep?

As he began applying the brake, he glanced around in the car to be sure there was nothing she shouldn't see. But his own gun was under the seat, and the paper cups and old issues of FATE magazine on the floor were no harm. All that was on the seat were his glasses case and a pack of Marlboros.

She watched as he approached, and her gaze flicked past his car, then back. As he rolled closer, he saw that she was holding a cell phone in one hand and a handkerchief in the other.

When he had slowed to a stop, he lowered his window. She was Asian, very pale behind wide sunglasses, and she kept swiping her nose with the handkerchief. Perhaps she was allergic to some desert weed.

"You don't want to be out in the sun," he told her.

"No," she agreed hoarsely, trudging across the dirt to his window. "You're about the last to leave there, right?" She looked back toward Giant Rock. "Can you give me a ride? Back south? I don't want to ask the cops or the firemen."

He peered past her and mimed surprise. "You *walked* here? You missed—good God, girl, you missed—"

"I was there. I saw the things in the sky. And the explosion. A girlfriend and I drove up, but we got in a fight on the way back, and she pushed me out of the car." She brushed a sweaty strand of black hair off of her forehead. "A ride?"

"Oh, sure, hop in. Pushed you out? That's attempted homicide out here, though the cops would have found you. Nobody else would give you a ride?"

"I waved them all off." She walked around the back of the car and got in on the passenger side. "I thought my friend would come back for me," she said as she closed the door and fastened the seatbelt, "and she'd worry if I was gone, but it looks like she blew me off."

Banach lifted his foot from the brake and let the car idle forward, then touched the gas pedal enough to get back up to his moderate speed. "What do you think those things were?" he asked, with an unfeigned shiver. "I about had a heart attack. I'm Tacitus, by the way."

"Like the Roman historian," she said. "I'm Rayette. Can I bum one of your Marlboros?"

"Very good. And sure, help yourself." He squinted at her, trying to guess where she might be carrying her gun. "I think it was stuff out of Area 51 over in Nevada— experimental aircraft. Or maybe Russian stuff, spying." I wish, he thought.

"I don't know what it was," she said. She shook out a cigarette, and when he tapped the console she lifted the lid and found a Bic lighter. She lit the cigarette with an admirably steady hand, then just stared straight ahead through the windshield. "A mirage. People died in that van."

If she were indeed an ONI agent, she must regard this morning's events as a disastrous failure; and since his masters monitored most of the ONI's communications, it was a loss for them as well. Those two young GRU fools!

"Oh!" he said. "I didn't see it, I just heard the boom and saw the smoke." I didn't see you with your gun, you understand, he thought. "I was hoping it was empty, like unattended propane or something. Jeez, that's rough." He decided to press on, "Did you know them?"

"No," she said flatly.

"Well that's a mercy." Was that something Americans would say? He shook his head, and neither of them spoke for a full minute. "So," he said finally, "are you a UFOlogist, Rayette?"

She inhaled deeply on the cigarette, visibly considering the question. "Not really," she said, exhaling. "A couple of my friends are. Do you know a lot of them?" When he rocked his head and pursed his lips she went on, "Sebastian Vickery? Pierce Plowman?"

Very calmly he took one hand from the wheel to pick up the pack of cigarettes. "Pierce Plowman," he said, shaking one onto his lip, "yeah, nutty old guy. Can I have the lighter? Is he still living in that house in Chatsworth?"

"Last I heard. Right off the 27."

Banach covered his disappointment by lighting the cigarette and sighing a plume of smoke at the windshield. So neither of them knew how to find Plowman. He had picked the city name at random, and *all* of Chatsworth was right off the 27. But at least she had firmed up his suspicion that she was an ONI agent—the GRU was aware that the United States Office of Naval Intelligence was trying to locate Plowman, and here she was saying that *she* was seeking Plowman, and lying about her knowledge of the man.

"I'd like to get in touch with him," she said.

Banach felt distinctly out of his depth. I've got an apparently well-informed ONI field agent right here in my car, he thought, the result of a perfectly happenstance meeting, and she has—spontaneously and unprompted!—raised the very subject that brought me here this morning. I should play her the way a case officer would. I can't neglect the possibility that she could be made an unwitting asset of the GRU.

And she thinks I know where Plowman lives.

"I don't know his address," he said, "but I've got his cell number back home, and I'm sure I've got some emails from him in my old email file." That might or might not have been a good bluff, he thought, in this blindfold poker game, but I'm committed now.

"That'd be helpful," said Rayette, staring now at the ash on her cigarette. She started to speak, hesitated, then said, "How can I get in touch with you?"

CHAPTER FIVE:
Underpainting

Downstairs from the Sixth Street sidewalk, in the bar of Cole's, Castine tipped up her glass of beer and, after three big swallows, set it down on the table and blinked around at the dark paneled walls and the white globe lamps hanging from the ceiling.

"That's better," she said hoarsely. "Cole's, you said; where is that? How long was I asleep in your truck?"

"A couple of hours," said Vickery, setting down his own glass half-empty. "We're in downtown L.A., about a hundred miles west of where you left your Jeep."

"Wasn't my Jeep." She yawned. "I'm in big trouble, aren't I? At large at the moment, though. Are there menus?" Vickery tapped the laminated sheet on the table in front of her, and she nodded and peered at it. "Something smells good—pastrami, corned beef?"

"The French Dip sandwiches are great," he said. "They were invented right here."

She shook her head. "I had a French Dip sandwich with you a year and a half ago, and look what happened."

Vickery recalled that the two of them had been shot at, later that night. "Best not to risk it," he allowed. "I'm going to have the knockwurst and sauerkraut."

"Me too, if it's a lot. I haven't eaten anything since a late lunch in England yesterday, and they're eight hours ahead of here. No, that's right, I had a sandwich at the Pentagon last night. Oh, Sebastian, what am I going to do? Felonies—treason! People *died!*" She lifted her glass and had another swallow. "All your fault," she said, exhaling as she clanked it down. "Again."

Vickery repressed a frown, and didn't argue. "I need to know," he said levelly, "exactly what sort—sorts—of trouble we're in. You said—"

A young waiter ambled up to their table then, and Vickery rapidly gave him their lunch order and added two more Budweisers.

When the waiter had walked away, Vickery went on, "You said Naval Intelligence wants to arrest me, because of something I heard from Plowman. Do you know what *sort* of thing that might have been?"

Castine rocked from side to side, clearly marshaling her thoughts. "Probably something to do with UAPs, Unidentified Aerial Phenomena—flying saucers. They set up that fake crash out in the desert by that big rock, and posted reports about it on some UFO chat groups, as a disinformation project. They like to do that sort of thing, get conspiracy-theory types all worked up about some weird-looking event and then discredit it. But they were also, or mainly, hoping you'd hear about it and show up there. And you did, God help us."

Vickery shook his head ruefully. "I remembered the

chat sites from when I was pretending to be interested in that nonsense..." His voice trailed away. "Well," he amended, "until this morning I *thought* it was nonsense." For a moment he stared into his beer glass, remembering the impossibly fast zig-zag courses of the silver globes in the desert sky. He looked up at Castine and said, "Anyway, I only drove out there because I saw posts about the crash and I figured Plowman probably did too, and he'd show up. And I didn't see him."

"But *you* were there, like they hoped."

For several seconds neither of them spoke.

"And you were in *England* yesterday?" said Vickery. "I wonder why they needed you out by Giant Rock this morning."

"I told you, to identify you for sure. I imagine you're hard to find, especially since they don't know about your new Bill Ardmore identity. And they wanted Plowman too. Maybe they think aliens gave you guys the secret of antigravity or something."

"To identify me." Vickery leaned back and saw the waiter approaching their table, carrying a tray on which stood two full glasses and two steaming plates. Vickery glanced at Castine and said, "That too, I'm sure. But why did they *really* want you there?"

The waiter unloaded the plates and glasses, and Castine began eating hungrily. She didn't speak until she had washed down a mouthful of sausage and sauerkraut with a gulp of beer.

"You're terrible," she said, wiping her mouth with a paper napkin. "There doesn't have to be any other reason."

Vickery pulled his phone and battery out of his jacket

pocket, and when he had replaced the battery in the phone he pressed the power-on button and set it down on the table.

"Just long enough to check messages," he said.

Castine raised an eyebrow. "It made sense for me to disable my phone. But they could hardly know about yours."

"I think it's best that we work in total-precautions mode. How much do they know about us?" He pointed from her to himself.

"Just that—" She paused and scowled at him. "I *think* just that we were on the run together for three days, when Terracotta wanted to kill us."

Vickery recalled that Emilio Terracotta had been the west coast chief of operations with the Transportation Utility Agency in early 2017, and had tried to have him and Castine killed because they were obstacles in his attempt to divert the agency's national security resources to a dangerous occult enterprise of his own.

"They don't know you and I drove a taco truck into the Labyrinth," Vickery asked, "and came out . . . changed?"

The Labyrinth had been the hellish afterlife state— opened by Terracotta's attempt to summon the entity remembered in Greek mythology as the Minotaur—that Vickery and Castine had fallen into. They had managed to come back from it, alive but no longer securely moored in sequential time.

She paused with a forkful of sauerkraut halfway to her mouth. "No, I—but they wouldn't believe any of that, even if—and anyway the TUA records for May of '17 were purged—" She put down her fork. "They might."

Vickery, his mouth full, raised his eyebrows.

"Lubitz," said Castine, "the ONI Commander in charge of this, this covert and probably very *deniable* operation!—he asked me about something I saw in an echo-vision two nights ago." Quickly she described the crop circle work she'd been doing in Wiltshire, and the giant-handed monster she had glimpsed when she'd used echo-vision to view the immediate past at a genuine crop circle site.

Vickery listened to it all with an occasional raised eyebrow or muted "Huh!" but no skepticism.

"I denied seeing the thing," she added, "I told him it was what a witness had described to me, but—he did ask me about it."

"And they picked you for that crazy crop circle work in the first place."

"Oh," she said in a small voice. "Yeah. *Aberrant* work, they call it." She busied herself with cutting up her knockwurst.

"Do you think," Vickery said, "that . . . such a thing could actually have *been* there, in that crop circle?"

"Of course not," said Castine quietly. "But yes, I think it was."

Vickery nodded, understanding her. "How is Naval Intelligence going to try to find you now?"

"I don't think they can." She gave him a crooked smile. "Unless they have a sample of my blood."

Vickery was alarmed. "They don't, do they? Or at least they wouldn't know how to use it?"

"No, and no."

Vickery relaxed. A year and a half ago Simon Harlowe,

the Silicon Valley entrepreneur who had tried to generate the predatory and voracious group mind he called an egregore, had discovered that the blood of Vickery and Castine to some extent shared the temporal wobble they had acquired in their trip to the Labyrinth afterworld— samples of their blood would be pulled perceptibly toward their living bodies. Harlowe had blotted two cloths with their blood in order to be able to track them.

Those cloths had probably been thrown away long ago, and in any case the Office of Naval Intelligence would have been in no position, nor had any reason, to acquire them.

Vickery picked up his phone and turned it on, and there was a tiny red *1* on the phone icon. "A message," he said, tapping it. "I'll listen to it and then take the battery out again."

The message was from Pierce Plowman, and had been recorded just after 10 AM.

"*Ardmore,*" came the old man's scornful voice from the tiny speaker. "*I got your message, but I already knew about Frankie. If you were fool enough to go out to that site where shit happened today, and if they didn't arrest you, you're probably heading back from there. I'll be where I used to work, at three today. I'll see you, if you show up. Delete this, dipshit.*"

Vickery tapped 7 to delete the message, then laid the phone on the table and flipped open the battery cover. He was almost annoyed with himself for being relieved that Plowman was apparently all right.

"*That,*" he said as he pried out the battery, "was Pierce Plowman himself." He looked up at Castine and briefly widened his eyes. "He wants to meet me at the Hollywood Forever cemetery at three o'clock." Vickery glanced at his watch and then snagged a forkful of knockwurst and sauerkraut. "Plenty of time."

"We spent the night there once," Castine said. "In a tomb."

"That we did," said Vickery, "that we did."

"So didn't you have his number today? Or does he just never answer his phone?"

"He doesn't have one. This call would have been from a pay phone—he must know all the pay phones still standing in L.A. The phone number I have for him is his daughter's, and I left a message for him on her voicemail a week ago. When he didn't call back for six days and his daughter never answered her phone or called back, I assumed she hadn't given him the message. They don't get along—well, he doesn't get along with anybody. And he was never at his place, so I drove out to Giant Rock this morning to see if he'd show up there."

"Long drive."

"I figured I could do some painting while I was out there anyway. The desert—the rocks and bushes that stay in one place." He gave her a tired smile. "I rent a studio— well, a room—in Long Beach, and I've got paintings in galleries these days. I sign them '*Janus.*'"

"The two-faced god," said Castine. "One face looking into the past. What's—" She cocked her head, and after a moment said, slowly, "How do you paint in echo-vision?"

"Well, I can't. Obviously. But I can look at a landscape in recent-past time, and then when I'm in real time again I try to catch that echo-light on canvas. I can even sometimes," he added with a vague wave of his fork, "do a . . . a trick I think of as underpainting. Or I imagine I can."

Castine seemed glad to be talking about something less immediate. She gave him a faint smile. "Do your pictures sell?"

"In a couple of the L.A. galleries, sometimes. And at swap-meets. It's handy when they do."

"So what's underpainting?"

Vickery too was glad to digress for a few moments. "I probably just imagine it. Ordinarily it's when you lay down a color, like the shape of a figure, and then paint over it so the underlayer still shows, here and there. What I try to do is . . . get *halfway* into echo-vision, so I can sort of see things by that past light, but still see my hand in real time. It feels like peripheral vision, but straight ahead."

"I—" Castine took a gulp of her second beer and suppressed a burp. "I wouldn't drive that way." She leaned back and stretched. "Okay, tell me about Plowman."

"Well, I met him a year or so ago, when I was going to Mass at the Cathedral of Our Lady of the Angels, on Temple Street downtown. He's—"

"That's the big brown box you see off the 101? Very modern twenty years ago?"

"Right. I don't think *he's* Catholic—he was working a pair of copper wire dowsing rods in the parking garage, said he was looking for some underground pattern or symbol. Anyway, he remembered me from the Roswell UFO Festival in 2018, and we got talking, and I wound up missing Mass and going out for beers with him instead. *Mea culpa!* I've been to his place a few times, and he's been to my trailer. He must be going on eighty, and he claims he worked at Area 51 in Nevada in the '60s and '70s, though he was a groundskeeper at the cemetery when I met him. He got fired from there for being drunk and talking about ghosts." He gave her a sour smile. "You and I met a ghost there, remember? It was trying to pick up on you."

"We saw a lot of ghosts there," said Castine softly. "Sitting on their tombstones in the middle of the night, singing."

"Well, talk like that won't get you a job there. Plowman lives in a garage in Inglewood now, pays rent in cash and handyman work, and I told you he doesn't have a phone. And he's big on every conspiracy theory—there's a secret subterranean city under Denver Airport, and the eye in the pyramid on a dollar bill is proof that the country was founded by the Illuminati. Even the camel picture on a pack of cigarettes is full of clues."

"And the Earth is flat, you said. And he's a drunk? What do you hang around with him for?"

"Well—" Vickery smiled ruefully. "Most often *because* he's a drunk. Every few months his daughter calls me and tells me he's been drunk in bed for a week or so, not eating, so I bring him groceries and a carton of cigarettes and he's okay for another couple of months."

"Damn, Sebastian. It's a wonder you don't adopt feral cats."

Vickery waved vaguely. "He's actually a very intelligent guy. If you were to listen to his stories late at night, he'd half convince you."

"That the Earth is flat." Castine sounded angry.

"Half convince. Late at night. He does have answers for every point you'd raise to contradict him. And he gets insulting."

"Shit," snapped Castine, and she seemed to be blinking back tears. "Excuse me. For this I'm going to spend twenty years in Miramar? Because an old drunk told you the Illuminati smoke Camels, or whatever? Lubitz must have lost his mind."

Vickery recalled that the Naval Consolidated Brig at Miramar, near San Diego, was where all female military prisoners were housed.

He replied sharply, "Considering the sort of people you always wind up working for, you're more likely to just quietly get killed. Me too, now, thanks very much." He drained his second glass in three gulps. "And in fact if Plowman did know anything at all," he added, clanking the glass down, "he didn't tell me about it. I saw him last week, the day before I tried to call him, and he said a guy we both know had made some discoveries that he wanted to show me. Plowman insisted I'd be better off not knowing about them, but he was drunk, and I got him to give me the guy's address."

Castine opened her mouth, but Vickery waved her to silence. "It's a fellow named Frankie Notchett. He's another one who doesn't trust phones, so I went to his place next day. It's an apartment by the water in Seal Beach, I gathered he's got a boat moored nearby and goes out a lot at night. So as I was walking up to his door, a couple of guys in black nylon jackets were carrying out computers and notebooks and what I think was a Geiger counter, all in plastic bags sealed up with red evidence tape. I just kept on walking, and I drove to Plowman's garage to warn him, but he wasn't there. I left the message on his daughter's voicemail, and when I've driven past his place these last few nights, there haven't been any lights on. It didn't seem smart to park and walk up to the door."

Castine didn't seem to be listening. Her eyes darted back and forth for a moment, and then her gaze fixed on a point slightly to Vickery's left and beyond him.

He quickly spun his chair and stepped widely away from it as he turned around—but he saw nothing across the floor but framed black-and-white photographs on red velvet-patterned wallpaper.

"Sebastian?" Castine had not moved. Her voice was tense, and when he resumed his chair he saw that she was still staring past him. She dropped her fork and extended her trembling hand, and when he took it her fingers curled tightly around his.

"I don't think you're in it," she whispered, "since I guess you saw my hand." She was staring to the side now, at the empty expanse of the booth, and abruptly recoiled across the padded bench seat. "Damn—*why now?*"

Vickery knew she must be experiencing an involuntary episode of echo-vision, and that she wouldn't be able to hear him if he spoke. He patted her knuckles with his free hand.

"Good," she said hoarsely. "Just keep everybody away."

And a moment later she focused her eyes on him and freed her hand. She sat back, panting. "Why me—and not you? Why at all?"

Vickery shook his head in wary sympathy. "You drew back there for a second—what did you see?"

"Just a woman who must have been sitting here," she said, touching the bench seat to her right, "some time ago. But she *leaned close* to me!" Castine blinked at him. "Our heads would have overlapped, been in the same space!"

Vickery raised a hand, his fingers spread.

Castine picked up her glass and drank what was left, then exhaled and said, "Maybe you've never had that happen, where your head is *in the same space* as the head of one of the people you see in echo-vision! Okay, it's not the same time, but it's the same *volume*. It happened to me in Wiltshire, in England, two nights ago—that woman who was running away from that thing in the crop circle. She ran right through the space I was in, I mean the space I was in later, after her—"

"I get it."

"Well, her overlapping me—that was as horrifying as the monster!" Castine put down her glass and gripped her elbows. "It's a—a violation, a rupture of your identity. I don't want to be *mixed* with somebody!"

"Huh. Do you think *they're* aware of it?"

"I don't know. The woman at the crop circle was practically catatonic afterward . . . but she *had* just seen that monster." She shivered and looked up. "I did sense something just now, right at the beginning, when I zoned out—for a second I had the sensation of being on a boat, at night. The sky was dark, but I got the impression that there was light from below, as if the ocean were glowing."

"Not just a stray memory?"

"No, nothing I've seen before."

Vickery looked at his watch again. "We should start for the cemetery, God knows what traffic will be like on the

101." He pushed his chair back and got to his feet, reaching into his pocket for some cash to leave on the table. "Are you—I guess you might not want to fly back to D.C. today."

"On the whole, no." She slid out of the booth and stood up. "Between us we've managed to screw up that side of my life. Which is the only side there is, actually." She gave him a mirthless smile. "I'm adrift, again."

"You're welcome to stay in my trailer," he said gruffly, "of course. There's still that couch I can sleep on."

"While the guest gets the bed. I remember." Together they walked to the door, and she added, "Thanks. My familiar port in a storm."

"Especially when the ocean's glowing," he said.

"Ohh—shut up about that."

In a Super 8 motel room in Yucca Valley, only a few arid blocks southwest of the airport she and Ingrid Castine had flown in to this morning, Rayette Yoneda sat on the bed and stared at two cell phones that lay in a patch of sunlight on a pillow. One of them was an old T-Mobile flip-phone which hadn't worked since being dropped in a hotel bathtub years ago.

She had told Tacitus that she was staying here, and he had dropped her off outside the lobby doors. Yoneda suspected that the elderly Tacitus found her attractive— certainly he had kept glancing at her peripherally as he drove, and had seemed nervous and self-conscious when he had spoken. Well, good. It would ensure that he would look up Pierce Plowman's numbers for her.

When she had checked into this room and bolted the

door, Yoneda had pulled off the bush jacket and dropped it on the floor, and then simply sprawled on the bed and closed her eyes and let herself remember the things she had seen in the sky a couple of hours earlier.

They had been real! UAPs, Unidentified Aerial Phenomena! For several seconds there by Giant Rock she had forgotten the burning van and the Sensitive Assignment Specialists who were dying in it, and just stared into the sky. The things had darted back and forth hundreds of feet overhead, like mirror-bright pool balls, moving with such speed that she'd had to whip her head from side to side to keep any one of them in sight, but executing acute changes of direction with no deceleration at all.

It wasn't possible!—for anything, let alone any sort of living creatures!—but everyone there had obviously seen the same phenomenon. The shadows had flickered in crazy zig-zags across the whole visible expanse of desert. Then the things had vanished all at once, silently, as though a projector had been switched off—but they had not been any kind of projection. They had *been there*.

Foo fighters! Maybe it was all true. Maybe some of those British crop circles *weren't* hoaxes. Maybe the TUA really *had* summoned ghosts to supplement motorcade security. Maybe Vilko Cendravenir, for all his pretentious pointed goatee and clove-scented cigarettes, really *did* break the plexiglass light panel over Lubitz's desk with some golf balls he had caused to move without touching them.

Yoneda prided herself on her sensible comprehension of reality, and this line of thinking nauseated her.

At last she had got up from the bed and tapped out an email on her working phone, a costly black Kryptall. The email was addressed to Commander Lubitz via encrypted ProtonMail, and it was a detailed follow-up to her hurried phone call at the scene.

In the email she had been completely straightforward. She had given a fuller account of the explosion of the Sensitive Assignments van, and a plain, literal description of the UAPs; and, reluctantly, she had explained that Castine had warned off a man who must have been Sebastian Vickery, and that Castine had then pepper-sprayed her and taken her gun and the Jeep when she had tried to go in pursuit of him. In a concluding paragraph, hoping it somewhat lightened the email's tone of failure, she had recounted her meeting with a man who might know the whereabouts of Pierce Plowman. Finally she had tapped in the address of her present location, and, with an anxious grimace, had hit Send.

After waiting half an hour for a reply, she had cursed impatiently under her breath, pocketed her phone and walked out of the motel. When Tacitus had driven her here she had noticed a Sizzler and an IHOP a few hundred feet down the street, and the desert breeze had not yet been hot, so she had walked to the IHOP and eaten a leisurely breakfast of poached eggs and bacon and pancakes. The wind had heated up by the time she had paid and walked out of the place, and when she had got back to the motel room she had cranked up the air conditioner.

Now she sat staring at the two cell phones on the pillow.

This must not *go off the rails,* Lubitz had said. *It will not. That being so, you don't even need to think about the consequences if it were to.*

It went off all sorts of rails, Yoneda thought now. In all sorts of directions. I was ready for that sappy fool Castine to try to warn Vickery off, if he showed up, but I never expected her to physically *attack* me. I should have allowed for it. Instead I screwed up.

Yoneda's father had instilled in her a fastidious aversion to failure. She had graduated from Stanford University in 2012, at the age of twenty-one, with a B.S. degree in Geological and Environmental Sciences, and her work using data from Polar Orbiting Environmental Satellites to map areas of malaria risk in sub-Saharan Africa had drawn the attention of the Office of Naval Research. She interned with the ONR at a General Schedule rating of GS-5, but within months had advanced to GS-12, had a top secret security clearance, and was using satellite geospatial imagery to identify nuclear weapons facilities in China and Russia. She had been baffled and annoyed with this temporary transfer to the Office of Naval Intelligence.

She lifted the two phones and looked from one to the other. She dreaded the one that worked, and looked forward to spending time with the old ruined flip-phone.

As if prompted by her picking it up, the working phone clicked in her hand, and she almost dropped it. Dropping the non-working phone instead, she swiped the screen of the one she still held and—after taking a deep breath—touched the green dot on the screen.

She held it to her ear. "Yoneda here," she said, exhaling.

"I've sent out the two men you met in my office last night," came Lubitz's voice, "Finehouse and Cendravenir. They're en route now. I'm in contact with Finehouse, and they'll meet you where you are, at about 5 PM your local time. Finehouse will be taking over the operation, and you're to tell him everything that happened today. The plane will wait at the airport, and directly after you talk to him you will fly back here."

"Yes, sir. Uh—what about the guy I met who knows where Plowman lives?"

"All calls to your phone will be documented. He'll be contacted. Give me all of that back."

Yoneda's voice was level as she repeated what Lubitz had said, and she didn't protest or make excuses for her failure this morning.

"I'll debrief you when you arrive," Lubitz said, and the call ended.

She laid down the phone with exaggerated care, and looked at her watch. It was about one-thirty. She could certainly afford to get a couple of hours' sleep.

But first—she picked up the broken phone and flipped it open.

It was her personal *kaze no denwa*, her wind phone.

The idea of a wind phone had apparently started after the tsunami of 2011 destroyed the town of Otsuchi in northern Japan; on a local hilltop, a garden designer set up a phone booth containing a disconnected rotary telephone, and people in the area, and then people from all over Japan, would come there and use the inert phone as a prop to let them express their feelings to dead friends and family. There was no flavor of divination to it—no claim that the pilgrims were actually heard by departed souls—it was simply a way to focus and articulate thoughts, serving the same purpose as statues or stained glass windows in a church.

Yoneda had been ten years old when her father died of a heart attack in their New York apartment, and for some years after that she had written letters to him and burned them outdoors, where the smoke could disperse into the sky. When she heard of the wind phone custom, though, she had switched to using the old flip phone for casting her thoughts. Speaking was easier, more spontaneous, than writing.

"It went badly today, father," she said softly. "But I'll make up for it." She closed the phone and looked out the window at the desert and remote mountains. "I'll make up for it," she whispered.

It occurred to her that she had three and a half hours before her replacement would arrive. To hell with sleep.

In his walk-up apartment between Figueroa and the 110 Freeway, Tacitus Banach was alternately riffling through the yellowed pages of a 1952 paperback Merriam Webster dictionary and glancing at his computer monitor, which today was flanked by two Pink Splendor Barbie dolls. One of the dolls was already listed on eBay, and the bidding was up to five hundred dollars.

He had got home an hour and a half ago, and had composed a report to his handler in which he had described the events of the morning, including the license number of the fleeing camper truck and his meeting with a likely ONI agent. Following protocol, he had used the old dictionary to encipher the report, giving the page number, column number and line number of every plaintext word; his handler had a duplicate copy of the dictionary, and had presumably deciphered Banach's report fairly quickly, but had only now replied.

Banach was surprised at his handler's delay in responding. In the last two years his regular reports must have seemed trivial, though he had learned to take their subjects seriously himself—rotating patterns of light in the ocean seen by boats off San Diego and San Pedro in the middle of the night, sightings of impossibly fast gleaming objects over military bases, high radiation readings and intense cold in neolithic stone circles in the Mojave Desert—but his report today must call for serious attention. The fact that he had not found Pierce Plowman—a rude old person he had briefly met a couple of times at midnight UFO vigils along the Mulholland Drive ridge—paled beside his eyewitness account of the objects that had appeared in the sky over Giant Rock, and the needless killing of ONI personnel by the hot-headed young GRU agents, and Banach's fortuituous contact with Rayette.

Banach copied the last of the three-number groups from the email text on his computer monitor, then closed and deleted the email, and deleted it from the Recently Deleted file, then sat back and looked at the words the numbers had directed him to in the old dictionary: *LICENSE NUMBER BELONGS TO WILLIAM DRUNKARD-MINUS-DRUNK-MORE*, he read. A five-digit number which obviously wasn't a page number came next, after which the code resumed, *ROSECRANS*

AVENUE PERIOD DO NOT APPROACH PERIOD AGENTS IN AUTHORIZED ACTION DO NOT INTERFERE PERIOD REPORT ANY FURTHER CONTACT WITH RAY-VIGNETTE-MINUS-VIGN PERIOD AGENTS WILL ADMINISTER PERIOD END MESSAGE

Banach pushed his chair back from the desk and picked up his cigarette from the ashtray.

"Agents will administer?" he said to one of the Barbie dolls. "Administer what?"

He was afraid he knew what. He had given his handler the address of the Motel 8 where he had dropped off Miss Ray-Vignette-Minus-Vign. And probably Mr. Drunkard-Minus-Drunk-More will get the same—and Plowman too, if they discover his location. To hell with intelligence gathering, the new policy seemed to be simply the eradication of all competition, along with any information that might have been gleaned from them.

He thought of calling the Motel 8 in Yucca Valley, and telling Rayette to get out of there—but it would be treasonous to interfere, and anyway he didn't even know her last name. *I want to speak to an Asian woman named Rayette who checked in there four hours ago* . . . if indeed her name was even actually Rayette. No.

His cigarette had gone out while he'd been decoding his handler's message. He lit the half-length and grimaced at the whiff of scorched moustache hair. And *I've established unforced contact with an ONI agent!* Not a very strong contact, to be sure, but it seems likely that I could have got some worthwhile information from Rayette by spinning out my imaginary acquaintance with

Plowman. But those two GRU hooligans will surely just kill her, as they killed the ONI agents in that van this morning.

Banach remembered Pyotr Ivashutin, who had been the director of the GRU during Banach's time as a student at the Military Diplomatic Academy in 1985 and '86. Ivashutin had devoted the service to ferreting out the secrets of foreign powers, and had run the GRU, the Military Intelligence Directorate, so effectively that, while most intelligence chiefs were replaced when a new political leader came into power, he had been director of the GRU under Khrushchev, Brezhnev, Andropov, Chernenko, and Gorbachev. *Razvedka*, the gathering of information, had always been the main objective.

Under Ivashutin's leadership, the policy would have been to play today's windfall sources, learn what they knew—not simply waste the opportunities by killing them.

Banach knew nearly nothing about the new director of the GRU, Igor Kostyukov. He could only judge the man by his evident policies, and even in the newspapers there had been reports of several assassinations on his watch in recent years—a Chechen leader in Qatar in 2004, another in Turkey in 2015—as well as a number of bungled attempts, like the near-fatal poisoning of the defector Sergei Skirpal in Wiltshire, England, in 2018. In that last incident, the assassins had carried the deadly nerve agent Novichok in a perfume bottle, and after poisoning Skirpal they had thrown the bottle into a litter bin, and a random British citizen who found it had died, along with the girlfriend he had given it to.

Was this what his old service had become? Trained monkeys would have better tradecraft.

Banach recalled that one defector had stated, *I didn't abandon the USSR, the USSR abandoned me.*

And he recalled the oath he had taken, with perfect sincerity, at the age of eighteen: *I will always be ready to come to the defense of my homeland, the Union of Soviet Socialist Republics . . .*

The what? he thought now. What was that you said? The Roman Empire, was it? The Persian Empire, the Hittites?

Hoisting himself out of the wooden chair that sat in front of the desk, he looked around at his apartment, and he wondered if he had subsided too far, too complacently and even negligently, into this current cover identity. As a professor at USC, with the constant group discussions of socialism versus capitalism, and frequent re-readings of Marx, Engels, Lukacs and Ilyenkov, the abstract Communist ideal had been a constantly reinforced dogma; but among the strange vagabonds and eccentrics who had been his companions for the last two years, that ideal had become so abstract that it seemed to have no more relevance to the actual world than classical Greek grammar or Ptolemaic astronomy.

Banach walked away from the desk, past the bookshelves—crowded with clumsily printed books on flying saucers and alien abductions and unorthodox geography, as well as several boxed sets of old Topps baseball cards—to his narrow bedroom, and looked out the window.

From up here on the second floor he could see past

the soundwall at the end of the street, and the tops of cars and trucks were visible sweeping past on the 110 Freeway.

Trees were clustered below the freeway embankment, and he thought of the freeway-side gypsy nest concealed there. He had spent hours in that foliage-hidden clearing, and in ones like it alongside the 605, the 101, and Old Man 10, often bringing beer and sandwiches for the oddballs who gathered in those places. He was respectful of their stories about magical metronomes and supernatural currents and phantom cars, for hadn't he himself driven down an imposible offramp into a different and perverse world, three years ago? And they often relayed rumors, varying in value, of strange things seen in the sky.

It's a good thing, he thought bitterly now, that none of my reports impressed my masters as having any validity— or they'd probably have tried to kill all the freeway-side gypsies.

The buzzing of his phone brought him hurrying back to his desk. It was very unlikely that his handler would call him, but he hoped, forlornly, to be able to urge a more restrained program in dealing with the sources he had identified.

"Hello," said a woman's voice when he picked up the phone and swiped the screen, "is this, uh, Tacitus?" When he confirmed it, she went on, "This is Rayette, the woman you drove to a motel in Yucca Valley this morning. I hate to press you, but did you have any luck finding a phone number or email address for Pierce Plowman? I'd like to get in touch with him today."

Banach's heart was suddenly thudding in his chest. Protocol dictated that he should get her to stay where she was, perhaps by telling her he'd call her back with the information as soon as he could...

"I couldn't locate those," he found himself saying, "but I know where he lives. What do you say I pick you up and take you there?" *I could drive her to any vacant-looking house*, he thought, *and then just say, Look, he's not home, and there'd be at least the chance to obliquely quiz her during the drive.*

There was a pause during which he bared his teeth, imagining the two GRU assassins even now getting out of their car in the motel parking lot. *She probably thinks I'm sexually interested in her*, he thought, *and just trying to arrange another meeting.*

"Where are you?" she asked at last, cautiously.

"I'm in Los Angeles, but—" *But what?* "— but I've got time to swing past your motel."

He was sweating. This was hopeless. It just wasn't plausible that a stranger would offer to drive from L.A. to Yucca Valley and back, just to do her a favor. He was trying to frame an alternate direction for the dialogue when she spoke again.

"Okay. That's very kind of you, Tacitus. You remember where this place is? What time do you think you'll get here?"

Banach frowned. *She should exhibit some doubtful reluctance*, he thought, *some suspicion, if she wants me to believe her interest in Plowman is something less than officially urgent. We really are both letting our covers slip.*

He shrugged nervously. "Oh, say four o'clock?"

Again there was a pause, and he wondered what sort of schedule she might have.

"Oh hell, let's do it," she said finally. "Be a bit early if you can."

What he was going to say next would definitely wreck his pose as a harmless old UFO hobbyist, but he could see no way around it.

"I saw an IHOP restaurant down the street from your motel," he said. "Meet me there, okay? And—go there right now. And, uh—I do mean *right now*."

"I see." She ended the call.

CHAPTER SIX:
Epitaphs Over Lazaruses

Vickery parked his camper truck at the curb of one of the central lanes of the Hollywood Forever Cemetery, and when he climbed out onto the asphalt pavement he squinted around in the freshening afternoon breeze. The lane was lined with tall palm trees, but the green grass on either side was streaked with the shadows of randomly placed pine and juniper and oak trees, with variously sized headstones of black or white marble receding to apparent infinity under the mingled canopies of foliage. Plowman could be watching from anywhere, and Vickery slowly turned in a circle, making his face visible in every direction.

Castine had stepped out onto the grass, and because of anxiety about traffic cameras and facial recognition software she was wearing newly purchased sunglasses and a knitted cap. She had also bought a long black trenchcoat, and altogether looked nothing like the woman who had been at Giant Rock eight hours earlier.

"Where's the tomb we slept in three years ago?" she asked.

Vickery waved behind them. "In the southwest corner. Probably it's not vacant anymore."

"I wonder if the sleeping bags are still in it." She turned to peer down a cypress-lined walkway. "Anything your man Plowman tells us is going to be upsetting, isn't it?" She nodded, as if glumly agreeing with herself. "But at least he's crazy, right?"

"We can only hope."

She sighed. "I'd like to find out something that could somehow *vindicate* me." She gave him a frail smile. "Us."

Vickery nodded ahead, toward where a pyramidal tomb blocked the view of the mausoleum, and Castine looked in that direction. A tall, burly old man was trudging across the grass, his eyes hidden behind mirrored aviator sunglasses and his hands in the pockets of a worn and scuffed brown leather jacket. He was bald and clean shaven, and as he came closer, deep lines in his tanned face became evident. A cigarette was tucked in one corner of his mouth, trailing smoke on the breeze.

He stopped walking when he was several yards away from Vickery and Castine, and rocked on his heels, twisting his head one way and the other as if to let each of his eyes get a look at them.

"So were you out at Giant Rock this morning?" he asked Vickery. His voice was a cavernous rumble, with a hint of New Jersey in the vowels. When Vickery nodded, the old man went on, "Forget it all and hope nobody got your license number. You think you know something about this stuff, but trust me, you're a kid who's used to sandboxes trying to comprehend the Great Basin Desert. And there's Gila monsters. Go home and watch UFO videos on YouTube."

Vickery thought about the ominous interest Naval Intelligence had taken in him, and about Castine's predicament . . . and about the thing she had seen in a crop circle two nights ago.

"We're involved," he said. "And, uh," he added with a self-conscious shrug, "this isn't our first rodeo."

Castine rolled her eyes.

Plowman squinted from one of them to the other. To Vickery, he said, "Frankie told me you wouldn't listen to good advice. *I* thought you'd have a bit of sense. Especially," he added, nodding toward Castine, "if you got a girl along."

"I can take care of myself," said Castine.

"I bet." The old man looked back the way he'd come, then shook his head and exhaled. "Okay. You're both adults and apparently sober. So who was there, this morning? Military, with radar?"

"No," Vickery said. "There was a van that probably had government agents in it—Sensitive Assignment Specialists?" He glanced at Castine, who nodded. "But it exploded and they all must have been killed. Probably a bomb—"

"And UFOs!" said Castine. "In the sky!"

"I heard about the bomb," said Plowman thoughtfully. "Russians, Chinese? A more covert power?" The mirror lenses of his sunglasses turned toward Castine. "What? UFOs? Those weren't actual *objects*, sweetheart. And they don't usually show up except when they're drawn by dual-band radar, most often X-band and S-band frequencies overlapping. Military."

Castine evidently didn't relish being called *sweetheart*. "Not actual objects?" she said stiffly. "They cast shadows."

Plowman shook his head dismissively. "Sure, and they reflect everything in the electromagnetic spectrum . . . and then some. But think about it, kid. Physical objects of any appreciable mass couldn't change direction instantly at hypersonic speeds. They *are* real, though—as real as the splash when you throw a pair of shoes into a swimming pool. But what did you mean by throwing them in, eh? *That's* the question." To Vickery, he said, "Something crashed near there, last night. What was that?"

"It was a faked UFO. Some guys went out in trucks and brought it back—it looked like it was originally a translucent glass or ceramic sphere with an aluminum cube in it, about ten feet in diameter, but it was all busted up."

Plowman was frowning. "Wings? An engine?"

Vickery shrugged. "These guys said they got all there was. And it was just this broken glassy stuff and bent metal."

Castine was visibly getting impatient. "We need to ask you—" she began.

"Hold your horses, girl. Ardmore, that makes no sense. Why would they—"

All three of them jumped then, for a young man in a sweatshirt and jeans had just stepped out from behind a narrow marble tomb a few yards away across the grass. His brown hair was in tangled disarray but didn't shift in the breeze.

"Frankie my boy!" exclaimed Plowman, starting toward him.

Vickery had recognized Frankie Notchett, but his chest felt suddenly hollow and cold, and he caught Plowman's arm. "Wait a sec, Pierce."

Behind him he heard Castine's sudden gasp.

Notchett's mouth was opening and closing, and then he said, *"The stranger hundred-handed ones, who every season hope to steal the threads—"*

"What?" said Plowman to Vickery; then, to Notchett, "What?"

Castine was close behind Vickery. "Don't look at it—"

"—And weave them into wings—Listen to me! They'll take . . . and . . . glue on . . ." Notchett paused, shaking, then opened his mouth very wide.

Castine threw herself at Plowman's knees while Vickery yanked him to the side; the big man toppled, and all three of them wound up rolling on the grass as something hissed through the air above them.

"Get," said Castine through clenched teeth, *"away* from it!"

She and Vickery managed to drag Plowman back to the asphalt and around the front bumper of Vickery's truck.

Plowman sat up on the pavement, glancing quickly around. "Frankie!" he yelled, "get down!" He squinted at Vickery. "Snipers?"

"It's not Frankie," said Castine, panting, "it's his ghost."

"Bull*shit,* girl," said Plowman, getting to his feet.

Vickery had stood up, and was peering across the truck's hood at the figure that still swayed in front of the tomb. Its long tongue had retracted back into its face.

"*Wherewith to fly,*" it called, "*even beyond the reach of Chaos—*"

"Two and two is four," said Vickery clearly, "and four squared is sixteen. Take off your shoes to count it if you don't believe me."

The Frankie Notchett apparition looked down at its shoes, which were now flickering—black dress shoes at one moment, white sneakers in the next. "That's your opinion," it muttered.

"And minus sixteen it's nothing!" said Castine, standing now beside Vickery. "*Think* about it—it's cold math, etched in stone—*nothing!*"

"You think you're so smart—" The figure in jeans and sweatshirt spun to face away from them, then was facing them again, and a second later it was spinning so rapidly that its face was a blur. Then with a soft thump that shivered the air it was simply gone.

Plowman stared open-mouthed at the spot where the ghost had stood; then he snatched off his sunglasses and turned to Castine.

She spread her hands. "A ghost. I'm sorry. Frankie is dead."

"Dead?" Plowman's mouth worked. "What was the math for?"

"Ghosts . . . hate it."

"I'm not crazy about it myself, dammit, but I'm still here."

Castine rolled her eyes. "Ghosts happen because of a field the freeways throw, interaction between moving and stationary free wills. It's a violation of determinism, okay? But math is pure determinism, no wiggle-room, and if you can get a ghost to look squarely at it, the ghost's virtual wave form—its *possibility*—collapses."

After a few seconds Plowman said, "Uh huh." He turned to Vickery. "Who's your girl?"

"An old friend. I trust her."

"We need to know—" Castine began, then just looked at Vickery and widened her eyes.

Vickery nodded and said to Plowman, "What was it Frankie wanted to show me, a week ago?"

"His *ghost*," whispered Plowman, squinting again at the empty patch of grass in front of the tomb. "I'll be damned. I saw 'em when I worked here, but they just sat on their tombstones in the middle of the night, and sang. Not like this." He slowly put his sunglasses back on.

Vickery repeated his question, and Plowman squinted irritably at him. "Maybe this isn't your . . . what did you say? First rodeo? Huh. Cute. But believe me, this isn't stuff you'll be happier for knowing." He glared at Castine, who had glanced at her watch. "You got somewhere to be, math girl? You're better off there, believe me."

Castine dropped her hand and shook her head.

"Frankie wanted me to know it," said Vickery.

The old man sighed, looked back at where Frankie Notchett's ghost had stood, then patted his jacket pocket. "He sent me three copies of some of his data, and said I should pass one on to you. I brought one along, in case you had no more sense than he has. Had. You get the copy I spilled coffee on."

He pulled a sheaf of papers out of an inner pocket and passed it across the truck's hood to Vickery. "It'll scare you away, if you can understand it." He looked over his shoulder. "Shit! You're sure that was Frankie's *ghost?* Not some kind of astral projection?"

"No," said Castine. "The extended tongue—and you're lucky it didn't hit you—and the changing shoes, and the terminal Y-axis spin. That's a ghost, beyond—"

Plowman interrupted, speaking to Vickery. "So they *killed* him? Why the hell? I'm just glad some of their *Sensitive Assignment Specialists* got blown up! What were they *doing* out there this morning?" Before Vickery could answer, he went on, "Why would they drop a *fake* UFO?"

"It was disinformation," said Castine, "to discredit any saucer nuts who'd be fooled and say it was real. But it was mainly a decoy to draw *you,* and Sebastian here." She spread her hands. "They didn't know *real* UFOs would show up."

"Sebastian?"

Castine clicked her tongue. "William Sebastian Ardmore, to his friends."

Plowman tilted his head back, facing Castine, and for several seconds he didn't speak. Finally he said, "Who are we talking about? NSA, CIA? The Russians?"

She glanced uncertainly at Vickery.

"I think you can tell him," said Vickery. "I think he's an ally."

"Emeritus, at most," growled Plowman. "For remote consultation."

Castine exhaled and then took a deep breath. "Well, it's the Office of Naval Intelligence," she said, "but I think it's an off-the-record sort of operation. I can't imagine who'd blow up the van they had there . . ."

"And you know all this how, darlin'?"

Castine looked again at Vickery, who nodded.

"Until last night," she said, pushing out every word against evident reluctance, "I was a civilian employee of the Office of Naval Research. I was doing . . . crop circle work in England, in Wiltshire, but last night I was reassigned to ONI, and they sent me to Giant Rock this morning to identify Bill Ardmore."

"She warned me off before they could grab me," put in Vickery, "and then she went AWOL."

"And they want you too," said Castine to Plowman. "Because of something you know, and might have told Bill." She pointed at the papers in Vickery's hand. "Maybe what's in there."

"Something I know." Plowman took a long look around at the trees and the headstones. "I know a lot of weird things, and I don't like the way the government is likely to use 'em. What's crop circle work?"

"I, uh—well, it's classified. Hah! And anyway, it's got nothing to do with this business today."

"Frankie didn't agree," Plowman said. "Along with air-shows like what you saw, there've been sand-angels around Giant Rock for as long as anybody's been going out there. Hm? That's patterns that showed up in the desert—crop circles without the crops, you might say. Have you figured out what your crop circles are?" He laughed shortly and waved around at the headstones studding the grass. "Epitaphs. Over Lazaruses. Lazari?"

"They're graves?" said Castine. "Of what?"

"Of the ones who throw shoes into the pool. They mistake overlapping radar waves for the splash of shoes that somebody else threw in, see? So they do a counter-step—uselessly, but they keep doing it. They don't think, exactly. And when they fall into the pool themselves, as it were, then they can't help but show up as physical objects, with actual mass. But they're ghosts, then."

Castine burst out excitedly, "Do they look like creatures with huge hands?"

Plowman's sunglasses reflected her wide-eyed face. Slowly he said, "Sometimes, yeah. Sometimes they've got a hundred hands." To Vickery, he added, "And Frankie said there's a grave too deep, under downtown L.A. When you first met me, at the cathedral, I was trying to track its lines." He took a breath as if about to say more, then looked toward Castine and just exhaled. "There's notes on the photocopies you've got there."

He shoved his hands in his pockets and stepped back. "You're on your own. Good luck." He turned and began walking away.

"How can we get in touch with you?" Vickery asked.

"You can't," the old man called back over his shoulder, "and don't waste your time trying to follow me. Your girl's too much of a hot potato for me to be any kind of ally, sorry." Walking backward for a few paces, he added, "AWOL or not, they'll find her, and you, and most likely do you like they did Frankie. Not me."

Then Vickery saw only Plowman's receding back.

A full minute later, after the old man had disappeared around the mausoleum, Vickery said, thoughtfully, "He must have had sex with somebody who died near a freeway sometime."

"Yuck, thank you," said Castine, walking back to the

truck and opening the passenger side door. "I'd rather picture him having killed somebody by a freeway."

Vickery nodded and dug the keys out of his pocket. Each of them had learned that ghosts could be seen only by people who had an intimate connection with someone whose life had ended in the weird freeway-generated field, and a now-dead ghostmonger had told them, *Ending someone's earthly life for him is about as intimate as you can get.*

Vickery and Castine had both been intimate, in one way or the other, with people who had died within the freeway field.

He got in and laid Notchett's notes on the seat.

"This was a bad idea, meeting him," Castine said as she slid in on the passenger side and closed the door. "If Lubitz's people do get hold of him, he can tell them that Bill Ardmore has the information, now. And they evidently killed that Frankie guy."

Vickery nodded ruefully. "True. But they're not likely to catch Plowman in the next hour or so." He touched the papers on the seat. "Let's go to my place and at least see what we've got."

He pushed the gear shift into first and drove ahead; but immediately had to put on the brakes.

Peering ahead through the dusty windshield, Castine said, "Are they all drunk? Some funeral."

At least a dozen well-dressed men and woman were milling around on the grass and in the lane. Several had fallen down and, despite energetic aid from their companions, were having difficulty getting back up again.

One corpulent old man's tuxedo became a pair of

striped pajamas for a moment, and then was a tuxedo again.

"Don't look at them," Vickery said sharply.

"Oh. Yeah." Castine's face was taut. "Back out of here."

But the figures were moving aside, waving Vickery on. "I think they mean to let us pass."

"They'll break your windows with their tongues. Back out." A year and a half ago they had seen an SUV's window shattered by the intense cold of a ghost's tongue.

Vickery glanced at the side mirror. "They're behind us too. Solid. We go ahead."

Castine looked at the mirror on her door, then just nodded, tight-lipped.

With the tires barely rotating, the truck slowly moved forward, and some of the ghosts actually bowed and curtsied as the old vehicle passed them. Some blew kisses. Several took off hats that disappeared moments afterward.

Sunlight fragmented by green leaves slanted along the lane, and from the corner of his eye Vickery saw that the ghost mouths were all opening and closing in unison, and then he became aware of their frail voices, singing. He didn't recognize the melody, but it seemed to express fond reflection, wistful retreat.

For several moments they all held one sustained note, and for those moments their appearances didn't change; then the melody shifted and they were again a confusion of flickering clothing.

He glanced at Castine, and she was blinking rapidly.

Vickery passed the last of them just below the steps to the mausoleum, and when he looked again at the mirror the lane behind him was empty except for a few dry leaves spinning across the asphalt. He looked for some trace of fading silhouettes among the shrubbery on either side, but there was nothing.

He turned left and accelerated to ten miles an hour; and he rolled down his window, glad of the cool, jasmine-scented breeze on his damp face.

"Poor forsaken shells," said Castine in a hoarse whisper. "What are we, royalty?"

"They, uh, were looking at you."

"Well I'm not coming back here, ever." She raised her arm to press the cuff of her trenchcoat to her eyes. "Dammit, Sebastian, when did this sort of thing become our *lives?*"

Vickery didn't anwer; he just sped up, recalling the tracery of lanes that would lead them back to the entrance and Santa Monica Boulevard.

"Explain," said Rayette Yoneda.

She was standing six feet away from Tacitus's rented white Honda in the back parking lot of the IHOP, grateful for the shade of the restaurant's blank back wall, for she was wearing her jacket. Beyond the wide parking lot, one-story houses sat quietly amid palm and Joshua trees. She could feel the hot desert wind fluffing her short hair, and the only sound was the faint mutter of the idling Honda's exhaust.

The gray-bearded old man lifted his hands from the steering wheel. "I'm afraid I got you into trouble," he said. "I didn't mean to."

Yoneda made a beckoning hurry-up gesture.

"There's a group," Tacitus went on quickly, "what you might call militant UFO sympathizers, the, uh—the Zeta

Reticuli Chess Club. Zeta Reticuli is a star you can only see in the southern hemisphere, and they believe the UFO aliens come from a planet orbiting it. The chess club folks think you people have live aliens in captivity at Area 51, and they believe you want to capture more, to do experiments on, and the chess club will do anything, break the law, to stop you."

Yoneda mentally cursed herself for having waited two and a half hours for this evident madman to show up, and for having spent that time sitting in a back booth in the IHOP, to the decreasingly concealed impatience of the waitresses, when she could have got a few hours' sleep. But she wanted to know why Tacitus thought she was a government agent.

"What is 'my people'?"

"I saw you draw a gun and get on your phone when the van full of agents blew up. You've got to be Air Force Intelligence." He waved impatiently. "But the thing is, I called the chess club people and told then that, and I told them where you're staying. And from what they said then, I got the idea that they were going to send some people to that motel to *get* you."

Yoneda supposed it was possible. Sourly she wondered if the people sent to get her would have been as elderly and out of shape as this specimen.

Could there be any credit in reporting on this chess club group, if in fact this crazy old guy wasn't just fantasizing? It *would* be nice to salvage something from this disastrous day.

"You don't actually know where Plowman lives, do you?" she said.

Tacitus narrowed his eyes for a moment, then shook his head. "That was a bluff. But I do know the address of the guy who drove off in the camper truck. I got his license plate number, and one of the, uh . . . chess club members is a cop, and he got me the name and address. The guy lives in Long Beach, I can take you there. I'd like to talk to him myself, as it happens. I got the idea you were following him before your . . . girlfriend? . . . pushed you out of your Jeep."

Vickery! thought Yoneda. Finding him would go a long way toward redeeming this failure. But ONI surely checked with LAPD and the DMV for the address of any Sebastian Vickery. This Tacitus fellow might not be bluffing now—I never told him it was a Jeep that I was driving, so he must at least have *seen* Vickery's truck.

"What was the name?"

"Ah." Tacitus found a cigarette from somewhere on the passenger seat and flipped it into his mouth. "Of course." He paused to light it. "You people have access to the DMV too," he went on, speaking through smoke, "and if you knew the guy's name, your lot could just go there and get him." He gunned the engine. "Get in."

"That's all bullshit, about the chess club, isn't it?"

"We can talk on the way."

Yoneda looked around at the empty parking lot, snapping her fingers in uncomfortable indecision. Short of beating up this old man, it seemed unlikely that she could get him to tell her the name Vickery was using; and in fact the old man was seeming to be tougher than he had a few hours ago. He seemed more alert now, and he'd even lost the trace of a southern accent. Going with him would mean standing up the two agents Lubitz was sending out, when they arrived at the motel at five . . . but she had her phone.

"Nobody's likely to look in that box," said Tacitus, nodding toward the corner of the building, where a box that had once contained bottles of ketchup sat on the asphalt. "Your people will find your phone there, I imagine."

Yoneda laughed and stepped back. "On your way, saucer boy."

Tacitus shrugged and smiled, and clicked the Honda's engine into gear.

But I don't want to report that I got this far and then let it go, Yoneda thought dizzily. I can't let the screw-up stand. *It went badly today*, she had said into the wind phone, thinking of her father, *but I'll make up for it*.

She stepped in front of the Honda, holding up her phone; and when Tacitus rocked the car to a halt, she walked to the ketchup box, held the phone six inches over it, and let it drop.

Tacitus reached across the console to open the passenger-side door.

CHAPTER SEVEN:
Spiritual Danger Pay

These days Vickery's trailer was at the far southwest corner of an immense trailer park off Rosecrans Avenue. On the south side, the trailer was shaded by tall eucalyptus trees that stood at the edge of a park, and on the west by a six-foot wall, beyond which lay a narrow stretch of dirt and a service lane and then the shallowly sloping cement bank of the Los Angeles River. The flat riverbed was a hundred yards across, but water flowed only in a thirty-yard wide channel down the middle of the expanse.

"You're pretty well hidden back here," said Castine after Vickery had driven down several lanes, past dozens of trailers.

"And if villains corner me," he agreed as he braked to a halt in front of his trailer and switched off the engine, "my back door opens onto that fence or that wall." He opened the door and stepped out. "Though until today there haven't been any villains interested in me."

Castine was already walking toward the trailer's

wooden steps. "I said I was sorry," she said. "Didn't I? Anyway, I didn't send you out there."

Vickery followed her up the steps to the narrow porch, and unlocked the trailer's door and tugged it open. A puff of hot stale air ruffled Castine's hair.

"I remember the way to the refrigerator," she said, stepping past him into the narrow kitchen. He moved to the right, into the living room, and switched on the air conditioner.

Castine got out of her trench coat, hung it and her knitted cap on one of the kitchen chairs, and dropped her sunglasses on the table. A few moments later she carried two opened bottles of Budweiser into the living room and set them on an issue of the *New Oxford Review* on the coffee table.

She sat down in one of the two easy chairs and looked around at the standing lamps and the crowded bookshelves, then sighed and leaned down to pull off her hiking boots. "It's nice to be back here, somehow," she said, flexing her stockinged feet on the nearest rug, "in your little moving castle." She lifted one of the bottles and took a long sip, watching wide-eyed as Vickery pulled from his pocket the sheaf of papers Plowman had given him and tossed them onto the table. "Fan mail from some flounder?" she asked breathlessly as she put the bottle down.

Vickery could see the tension in her hands, and he grinned in spite of himself at the bravely silly reference to the old Rocky and Bullwinkle cartoons.

"Maps and lists, it looks like."

He spread them out on the table. One was a circular

map of the Earth with the north pole at the center and a white band indicating Antarctica around the circumference—clearly a map of the "flat Earth." Another was a stapled booklet, half a dozen pages of typed latitude and longitude notations, with handwritten notes at the bottom of the last page. Paper-clipped to the list were two photocopied pages of a book. The edges of the papers were stained, and Vickery recalled Plowman saying that he had spilled coffee on them.

Vickery freed the copied book pages. The first sheet was a title page: *Theogony*, by Hesiod, translated from the Ionian Greek by Francis Notchett, published in 2018 by "Notchett Press, Los Angeles." The second sheet was a copy of an inner page of the book—many lines of verse, in iambic pentameter, ten of them heavily underlined in the original book.

"Does this ring any bells?" he asked, passing the sheet to Castine.

She read the lines out loud:

"218.A - 218.J: And Night, chaste by necessity for this,
Birthed the Moirai who hold existence firm:
Clotho, who generates the thread that binds,
Lachesis, who spins out its tiny length,
And Atropos, who ties it in a knot
And clips it off. Ouranos, Gaia's son,
Restrains the stranger hundred-handed ones
Who every season hope to steal the threads
And weave them into wings wherewith to fly
Even beyond the reach of Chaos . . ."

Below it, handwritten on the orginal, was the further line, *But at what gelid, endothermic cost?*

"Those last printed lines," said Castine, holding the paper toward Vickery, "are what Notchett's ghost recited, in the cemetery."

"I guess that wasn't just ghost gibberish," Vickery said, "since Notchett underlined it and copied it while he was still alive."

"And he added that line about jellied endosperms." Castine tilted her bottle up again. "Your man Plowman," she said as she lowered it, "what did he say again?"

"He said that UFOs are like splashes when somebody throws shoes into a pool, and when the somebody *falls into* the pool, he becomes a physical object, but he's a ghost then."

"And when I asked if the ghosts have huge hands, he said sometimes, and sometimes they've got a hundred hands." She tapped the page. "So did Mr. Hesiod know about this stuff?"

Vickery shook his head. "Hundred-handed sounds like standard mythological stuff. That dog Cerberus had three heads, and Hydra the serpent had lots of heads."

But he stood up and crossed to one of the bookshelves.

"Is that one of yours?" said Castine behind him. When he turned, he saw that she was pointing at an unframed painting leaning against another bookcase below the window.

The trailer was shaded against the late afternoon sun by the trees bordering the park, and Vickery switched on one of the standing lamps and looked at the painting.

It was a view of a desert, done in sepia tones with silvery highlights. The sky was black, with a rusty full moon hanging over distant mountains, but the sand and Joshua trees appeared luminous.

Vickery pulled out two volumes of an old encyclopedia and carried them back to his chair.

"Yes," he said, setting the books on the table and sitting down. "Out by Amboy, off the 40."

"It's echo-vision," she said. She got to her feet and crossed to the painting to crouch beside it. "You've almost got the color. At least it reminds me of the color."

"Hesiod," said Vickery, peering at a page in the encyclopedia, "was a Greek poet in 800 BC, and his long poem the *Theogony* is the first known history of the Greek gods." He closed that volume and opened the other. "And *Moirai* is Greek for the Fates—well, that's Clotho and Lachesis and Atropos, like the poem said. One of them spins the thread of your life, the next measures it out, and the third cuts it off."

"In the bit of the poem you've got there, it says Clotho *generates* the thread. And the thread binds—'holds existence firm.' Does this glow in the dark?"

Vickery looked up; Castine was still peering at the painting. "No," he said, a bit nettled. "The desert did, that night, by that weird light." He picked up the lists of latitudes and longitudes and flipped to the last page, then got up and went to a different bookshelf and pulled down a big atlas.

"According to the notes at the end of this lot," he said, resuming his seat and flipping open the book's cover, "crop circles have clustered most around three parallel lines—what he calls 'the trinity of crash lines.'" He opened the atlas to a two-page map of the world, then pulled open a drawer in the table to fetch out a pencil.

"One of them," he said, using the folded edge of the *New Oxford Review* as a ruler, "stretches from 116 degrees east longitude by 50 degrees north latitude—about here, in northern China— to 110 degrees longitude by 1 degree south latitude, down here, by Borneo." He penciled a line between those points. "And he notes that it crosses Qinghe County in China. Okay."

"A long crash," commented Castine.

The next line led from a point 150 degrees west longitude by 50 degrees north latitude to a point 122 degrees west longitude by 19 degrees north longitude. Vickery penciled it in—it ran from a point in the north Pacific about 800 miles west of Vancouver to a point in the ocean about the same distance west of Mexico City.

"They're not parallel," said Castine, leaning over his shoulder now. "The first line was straight up and down, but the one by California is slanted."

"Not only that," said Vickery, "he says here that it passes just six hundred miles west of San Diego." He added a bowed section to the line. "It curves."

"And this is supposed to be patterns of *crop circles?* That line is entirely in the ocean." She stood up straight and stretched. "I bet the ghost made these notes. Ghosts are idiots."

"A ghost couldn't handle all these numbers." Vickery peered at the map. "And I think the third line is going to be even more slanted—he says it goes from England through Turkey and the Caspian Sea and the Arabian Sea to near Sri Lanka."

He marked the end-points of the third line. The first pencil dot was at 51 degrees north latitude by 1 degree east longitude, on the south coast of England, and the second dot was at 7 degrees north latitude by 80 degrees east longitude, roughly the southern tip of India. It was sharply diagonal, and Vickery noted that it would have to bend quite a bit to cross any part of the Caspian Sea. He erased part of the line and re-drew it as a curve.

"Huh," said Castine, returning to her chair. "They're not even straight, never mind parallel." A moment later she blinked and stood up again to lean over the map. "That third line crosses Salisbury, doesn't it? In Wiltshire?"

Vickery glanced at the map, then looked up and spread his hands. "You tell me."

"It does—and the upper tail of it slants northwest from there, and there *are* a lot of crop circle formations along that line, genuine ones." She touched the map and traced the line southeast. "Germany, Romania, Poland, yes, lots—and more or less along this line, too. And here," she said with an excited nod, "it's not crop circles, but they've found a lot of stone circles in the deserts in Turkey, right around the line. We were told about them in the general overview of the Wiltshire assignment. They're real old, but nobody even noticed them till the '20s, when planes flew over them." She looked up. "And I bet the name of that county in China was Qinghe," She pronounced it *kinjee,* while Vickery had rendered it as *Quinhee*.

"Okay . . ."

"Well, they've found a lot of ancient stone circles there, too. So maybe ancient peoples preserved crop circles—or dirt circles, sand angels, crop circles without the crops—by outlining them with stones. Memorialized them, if they're graves like Plowman said. And look, the China line extends across the South China Sea, down past Borneo to Java, and there've been a lot of crop circles around Yogyakarta. Which is there," she added when Vickery gave her a blank look.

"Okay." Vickery sat back and took a sip of his beer. "Even though they're not parallel, they *are* in lines. Somewhat curved lines."

"*If* he was honest in scatter-plotting location points to derive his lines . . . and *if* he didn't just cherry-pick the locations." She frowned and touched the line that ran through the blue area to the left of the American west coast. "But how could there be crop circles in the ocean? What would they *look* like?"

"They just about always happen at night, don't they? Maybe the ocean glows."

Castine shuddered and returned to her chair. She took several swallows from her beer bottle, then said, "Maybe the lines *are* parallel, on a globe. Have you got a globe?"

"Oh—yeah, I guess so." Embarrassed, Vickery got up and went into the kitchen, and when he came back he was blowing into the valve of a slack plastic bag mottled in blue and tan, and there was a black felt-tip marker in his shirt pocket.

Castine smiled. "You keep the world in a kitchen drawer?"

"Easier to store, deflated."

When Vickery had got the thing fully inflated, it was a

respectable-enough globe, twelve inches across. He sat down and uncapped the marker.

Glancing from the atlas to the convex surface of the globe, he carefully copied the lines he had drawn on the map. It was soon obvious that the lines wouldn't be in any sense parallel on the globe either, and when he was finished he held it up for Castine to see.

Castine shrugged. "You marked up your globe for nothing. What else have we got?"

Vickery shuffled through the papers again. "That's it. The poem and the crop circle notes and the flat Earth map."

"Wait a sec," said Castine, "wait a sec." She picked up Vickery's pencil and slid the flat Earth map to her side of the table. Carefully, switching her attention from the map in the atlas to the circular one on the paper and back, she drew lines on the flat Earth map. When she was done she lifted the pencil and stared wide-eyed at Vickery.

The three lines were parallel, the China and America lines on one side of the central north pole, the Middle East one on the other.

"They *are* parallel," Castine said softly, "on a flat Earth."

"Well he cherry-picked his locations then," said Vickery, "obviously, to make lines on his idiot map. These guys are—"

"Those spots I recognized *were* cluster spots. The lines *are* fairly implicit."

"Okay, the Earth is actually flat. You and Plowman would have got along." He leaned back and stretched. "Are you going to be hungry? There's a couple of good Mexican places down Rosecrans."

"I could use a shower, mainly. Though I hate to get back into these sweaty clothes. Do you have anything to eat here?"

"I've always got makings for a big omelette. And actually I still have some of your clothes from last time— jeans, a white blouse, a suede coat?"

"My La Brea Tar Pits wading outfit! I hope you didn't just put them away the way they were? They'd have fermented."

"I had them cleaned, though the coat is kind of funny-looking now."

"An omelette sounds fine, but I'd like to take a shower and get into my old clothes first." She gave him a critical look. "I won't use up all the hot water."

"Point taken."

Joel Finehouse walked back across the shadow-streaked IHOP parking lot to the new Ford SUV, where Vilko Cendravenir waited in the passenger seat. When Agent Yoneda had not been in her motel room nor answered her phone, Finehouse had traced her phone and found it in a cardboard box behind this IHOP restaurant. The IHOP security camera had shown Rayette Yoneda dropping her phone in the box and getting into a white Honda, with every appearance of willingness. A quick phone call to Washington had revealed that the license plate on the Honda had been stolen from a twenty-year-old Ford registered to a dentist in Oxhard, and the image of the Honda's bearded driver had been too oblique and obscured by reflection to be of any use in facial recognition analysis.

Finehouse was forty, of medium height and compactly muscled, with brown hair going to gray. He wore a dark blue business suit with his tie now loosened and the top two buttons of his white shirt undone. Cendravenir, peering at him through the SUV windshield, was casually dressed in jeans and a black turtleneck, and his pointed black goatee made him look like the magician he claimed to be.

Finehouse found the claim distasteful, but he had been in Commander Lubitz's Pentagon office last night when Lubitz had persuaded Cendravenir to demonstrate his peculiar ability. Lubitz had taken six golf balls from a desk drawer and laid three of them on the desk near where Cendravenir had been sitting; the other three Lubitz had commenced to juggle. After Cendravenir had stared for a few seconds at the three balls that remained on the desk, they had sprung into the air without his having touched them, circling one another above the desk in mimicry of the ones the Commander was juggling. The fact that they had shortly spun out of Cendravenir's telekinetic control, one of them shattering the plexiglass panel over the ceiling fluorescent lights, had really only made the whole show more impressive. Lubitz's secret Operation Pleiades had seemed actually remotely feasible, assuming that Sebastian Vickery and Ingrid Castine really did suffer from what Lubitz called *distempor*.

But someone had bombed Lubitz's backup van, Agent Castine had gone AWOL, and now Agent Yoneda seemed to have done the same. The players, like the golf balls last night, were spinning out of control.

Before getting back into the SUV, Finehouse pulled his phone from his jacket pocket and tapped in Lubitz's number, and when the Commander answered, he explained the current situation.

Then for nearly a minute he just listened; and when he pocketed his phone and got into the SUV, he told Cendravenir, "We're going to L.A. It seems Commander Lubitz isn't willing to write this off as a failure yet."

"'Tis ill-advised to seek a newer world'," said Cendravenir, refastening his seat-belt as Finehouse started the engine, "I want danger pay. Your Sensitive Assignment Specialists are broiled lizard snacks now, *n'est-ce pas?* I'm a fairly sensitive fellow myself, as it happens." He pulled a pack of Djarum clove-flavored cigarettes from his leather satchel, but sighed and put it back when Finehouse scowled at him.

"I'll note your request in my report," said Finehouse, starting the engine and steering out of the parking lot. "But this next step looks like a cold trail." When Cendravenir raised his eyebrows, Finehouse explained, "There's a woman Sebastian Vickery used to work for, off-and-on, before he went dark in February of '18. She runs an unlicensed *santeria* car service, and Lubitz thinks Vickery might try to contact her."

"Very well, then I want *spiritual* danger pay."

Finehouse considered what freeways to take in order to get to Eighth Street in the Koreatown area of Los Angeles. A *santeria* car service, he thought; and Castine and Yoneda have disappeared, and I'm traveling with a guy who can juggle golf balls without touching them, and the implausible goal of it all is to establish communication with a lot of silver balls that appear and disappear in the sky. We should all be getting insanity danger pay.

"I'll note your request in my report," he said stolidly.

Finehouse had joined the Office of Naval Research in 2005, right after graduating from MIT with an engineering degree, and at the Naval Research Laboratory in Washington D.C he had been developing one-piece aluminum-alloy armor for the undersides of military vehicles operating in foreign city streets, where improvised explosive devices often detonated under vehicles. A simplistic but high-priority interruption of his work had been to assist DARPA in designing the fake UFO that was dropped near Giant Rock last night, and he had shortly found himself reassigned to the Office of Naval Intelligence, working under Commander Jack Lubitz on Operation Pleiades.

Finehouse had grown up in a tiny east Tennessee town called Cosby, raised by his grandparents in a small clapboard house off U.S. Route 321, and his goal since childhood had been to find his way to the bright expansive world he saw on television—and that way was immersing himself in the crystalline logics of physics and mathematics. Over the years he had shed his accent and the naïve beliefs of his grandparents, and prided himself on his coldly rational world view—and he was annoyed with himself when the old Appalachian superstitions occasionally intruded, and he found himself momentarily worrying that an accidentally swallowed watermelon seed would grow inside him, or that closing a pocket knife that someone else had opened would bring bad luck.

Operation Pleiades was in many ways uncomfortably reminiscent of those superstitions, and he longed to get back to developing alloys for vehicle armor.

He drove out of the IHOP parking lot and turned onto Twentynine Palms Highway, and after a few moments he realized that he was driving too fast, as if to get sooner to the end of this crazy operation, this distasteful interruption of his life.

Vickery, now in faded black jeans and a Death Records T-shirt, had checked the coolant and oil levels in the truck, and crouched by all four tires to measure the air pressure, and finally stood up and stretched. The sun had gone down beyond the L.A. River, and the sky was dimming. He walked up the trailer steps and opened the door.

Castine had turned on two of the standing lamps in the living room, and she looked up from the old science fiction paperback she had found on one of his bookshelves. Her hair was dry now and haphazardly brushed, and she wore the fresh jeans and the white cotton blouse.

"Do we go to a Mexican restaurant or eat here?" Vickery asked, closing the door.

"You said big omelette."

"Coming up."

He washed his hands at the kitchen sink, then hauled out a cutting board and cut an onion and a red bell pepper into narrow strips. He tipped a splash of olive oil into a cast-iron pan and turned the heat on under it, and after a moment rocked the pan back and forth to coat the bottom. He scraped the onion and bell pepper strips off the cutting board into the pan and stirred them around with the knife blade.

There was a fresh carton of eggs in the refrigerator, and

when he had pulled it out, he called, "Are you very hungry, or just somewhat?"

"Well," came her voice from the living room, "the onions smell wonderful, and it's been a long time since lunch at Cole's."

"Ages," Vickery agreed. He broke eight eggs into a glass bowl, assessed the floating yolks, then broke the last four in as well and began stirring them all with a fork.

He had just begun pouring the beaten eggs from the bowl into the pan when a flare of white light from the window dazzled him, and he lost his balance; he caught the refrigerator handle with one hand, and then pressed strongly upward on it, for his feet were lifting from the linoleum. He tossed the bowl into the sink, where it shattered, throwing long strings of beaten egg toward the ceiling, and he gripped the handle tightly with both hands. His face was hot, and though he wasn't able to take a deep breath, his nose stung with the smell of burning plastic.

Castine half-fell into the kitchen, bracing herself in the doorway; her face appeared to be stretched back toward the living room, as if she had moved too fast for her right cheek and eye to fully catch up. Then gravity came back on, hard, tugging her slack face downward.

Her mouth twisted open, and over a sudden trilling sound like mechanical birds she choked, "Crop circle. Run."

Then she had warped around and pulled open the front door and disappeared down the steps, with Vickery stumbling along right behind her. Down on the pavement, he found it easier to run if he took a look at the rippling lane between the undulating trailers and then just closed his eyes.

After a dozen pounding steps the tightness in his chest loosened, and he opened his eyes.

Castine was two yards away, crouching with her palms flat on the asphalt, gasping for air in the chilly fresh breeze. She looked up at him and panted, "We're out of it, or it's over." She straightened, and Vickery was glad to see that the visual distortions had stopped.

Dust and scraps of paper were being blown up the lane; some of the papers were scorched and smoldering. Trailer doors were banging open and people were hurrying outside.

"You said crop circle?" said Vickery hoarsely, and when Castine nodded he said, "In a trailer park?"

Castine had stood up and was pointing over the roof of the trailer. Vickery looked around and saw a narrow, perfectly regular column of dust against the darkening sky; it appeared to be a few hundred yards away.

"What's past that wall behind your trailer?" Castine asked, stepping in that direction.

Vickery caught her elbow. "Whoa, don't go back into that!" he said, but she shook him off and sprinted toward the wall. He followed, calling, "The L.A. River!"

Tacitus had consulted Google Maps on a laptop in his car, and he had insisted that he and Yoneda approach the trailer from the riverbed side. He had parked in a cul-de-sac south of the trailer park, and the two of them had trudged through the brush along the riverside chain-link fence until they had found and stepped through a gap where a car had apparently once driven through it.

They had crossed a service road and then hopped and

slid down the cement slope to the broad, flat pavement of the riverbed, and walked north. The evening breeze was at their backs. To their left was the narrow band of rushing water in the middle of the gray expanse, and then more pavement and the western slope with trees along its crest, and far ahead of them were the pillars of a freeway overpass; the only other figures visible on the geometric landscape were a couple of skateboarders flitting like gnats around the distant pillars.

During the long drive west Tacitus had stuck to his obviously improvised story about a Zeta Reticuli Chess Club. Whatever might be the truth about this Tacitus fellow, Yoneda was sure that the object denting the back of his jacket as he walked was a handgun in a waistband holster.

For several minutes Yoneda had been mentally rehearsing how she would disable old Tacitus if he should draw the gun or in any way exhibit insanity; she had made him stop at a 7-Eleven for cigarettes during the long drive, but she had not insisted on finding a pay phone and calling Lubitz, since this pilgrimage had every likelihood of being a misidentification or an outright fantasy.

And there *was* still the chance that she might be able to find Vickery and report his license plate number and street address to Lubitz, which would salvage a big part of the day's assignment. She would have to make some mention of Tacitus in her report, too—after ditching him.

She had been watching the trees visible at the top of the near embankment, and stopped. "It should be right up here."

Tacitus had stopped too, and blotted his sweaty forehead with the sleeve of his jacket. He had stared up the cement slope, his glasses misty with exertion, and it was clear that he wasn't at all sure of what he intended to do if they should find Vickery. When Yoneda began walking up the incline, he shrugged and followed her.

"Well," he said, breathlessly, "let us go see Mr. Ardmore."

Yoneda halted and looked back. "That's the name he's using? *Ardmore*?"

Tacitus had taken two stretching steps past her, but now abruptly hunched forward to brace his hands on the rough cement surface of the slope. He opened his mouth, but produced only a grating whine.

The sun had gone down, and a moment ago the riverbed had been in dimming twilight, but now a sudden bright light from above cast the man's shadow starkly on the cement under him.

Yoneda crouched and spun, squinting up, then dove to the side and rolled diagonally back down the incline to the flat surface.

A brightly incandescent sphere, perhaps several yards in diameter, hung a hundred feet over the upper slope of the embankment, and it was either growing larger or descending.

Tacitus had roused himself and now came tumbling after her. In the moment when he crawled past her toward the channel of water she saw that his clothes and beard were dotted with red sparks.

Yoneda scrambled to her feet and ran away from the light, but after only a few steps her shoes were barely brushing the pavement; her course was diverging upward from the riverbed surface. Reflexively she began making swimming motions with her arms, and she expelled her breath as if she were in water and wanted to sink. The erratic wind was full of leaves like schools of fish.

Her momentum carried her farther away from the descending bright sphere, and her shoes and then her knees collided with the cement surface; she slid on her hands and one hip, and then she was up and limping, trying desperately to move in a straight line southward in spite of the apparent warping of the brightly lit riverbed and her own shadow twisting fantastically in a hail of leaves in front of her. The broad watercourse echoed with shrill staccato noise like a rapidly spinning wheel with a bad bearing.

A few seconds later she was panting in a steady cold wind and sudden darkness, batting at embers now visible on her pants. She looked back—the sphere was gone, and for a few seconds the shrill metallic twittering was accompanied by choppy back-and-forth gusts and then the air was still and silent. Her nostrils twitched at the oily smell of ozone. When she tried to take a deep breath, and could do it only in hitching gasps, she realized that she was crying.

She heard splashing and then wetly slapping footsteps to her left, and saw the bulky silhouette of Tacitus, his arms held out to the side for balance, plodding in her direction from the water channel. Yoneda forced her breathing to be steady.

When Tacitus had come to within a few feet of her he stopped, and for several seconds they simply stood silently, staring at the dark, empty riverbed. Tacitus inhaled and audibly opened his mouth, then shut it.

Yoneda could hear scuffling now from the service road up the slope to their right, and a woman's voice that she believed she recognized called, "Are you two all right?" It was Agent Castine at the crest of the bank, looking away from Yoneda and Tacitus now to scan the broad riverbed.

Yoneda followed Castine's gaze, and saw that dust and water formed patterns across the stretches of cement; the streaks of water were evaporating and the dust was dispersing, but she could see an intricate curved line of connected circles and coils of dots.

Castine and a companion—Vickery? Someone named Ardmore?—were making their way down the slanted surface in a semi-skating gait, and when they reached the level expanse Castine's eyes widened at the sight of Yoneda.

Before either of them could speak, Tacitus spoke hoarsely to the man. "Excuse me—do you own a 1952 Chevrolet pickup truck?"

CHAPTER EIGHT:
Free Will's a Bitch

Because Castine had been looking for it, Vickery had noticed the fleeting patterns of dust and dampness spread out on the face of the riverbed, and he remembered Plowman saying, *crop circles without the crops*.

Down on the flat surface now, he looked at the two strangers and remembered what the bearded man had asked.

"It's not for sale," Vickery replied shortly. He noticed that the man who had spoken was soaking wet. "What in hell happened here?"

"It was a UAP," said the man's companion in a shaky voice. Peering more closely at her, Vickery tensed. Cargo pants, khaki bush jacket—this was the Asian woman who had been the driver of the blue Jeep this morning.

"And it's a crop circle now," said Castine, "with what looks like double-dumbbell patterns and Fibonacci entourages extending God knows how far."

As if he could no longer hold it back, the bearded man burst out, "Are you William Ardmore?"

Vickery answered, "Ardmore *won't* sell the truck, trust me."

The Asian woman stepped back and asked, in a tone of almost light-hearted exhaustion, "Are you Sebastian Vickery? You're here with Agent Castine."

"Try Rumpelstiltskin—" Vickery began, then stared past her and roughly pulled Castine backward by the elbow. Castine looked over her shoulder, gasped, and then began scrambling back up the cement slope. The two newcomers were already sprinting away south. Halfway up the slope, Vickery paused and looked back, his eyes wide and his scalp tightening.

Two enormous dark hands, each as big as a couch, were uncurling their fingers out across the wide pavement. Between them stood a skeletal figure with an oversized head, its lips and tongue and ears protruding grotesquely; its eyes were just oversized bumps in the rippling texture of its face. Pieces of the tripartite thing were falling away, and Vickery saw that they consisted of leaves and water spray.

It lifted the huge hands and turned its distorted and apparently blind head from side to side, and the tinny trilling sound sprang into audibility again but went silent a moment later; and then the thing broke up into clusters of soggy leaves rolling away in the wind.

Crouched a couple of feet above Vickery, Castine said, "Radiation, and I've got no meter—back to your place, quick."

Vickery nodded and followed her up to the crest,

where they crossed the narrow access road to the six foot wall of the trailer park.

Vickery had just crouched to make a stirrup of his hands to give Castine a boost when the woman and the bearded man came puffing up to the road.

"Check this out," said the woman.

Vickery looked up from where he was crouched by the wall, and saw that the woman was holding a revolver; and that the bearded man, standing back from her, looked angry and chagrined.

Castine spread her hands. "What do you want, Yoneda?"

"I see you're not carrying my gun now," Yoneda said. "Where is it?"

"In the truck. Under the passenger seat."

Vickery recalled that his own gun was in his jacket pocket, on the bed in the trailer.

"It better be nowhere else," said Yoneda. Stepping to the side and addressing Tacitus too, Yoneda said, "I'm going to sit up on the wall, attentively, while the three of you climb over. Then we'll go to Rumpelstiltskin's place and talk of many things."

"Whoever goes in first," said Vickery, "turn off the fire under the pan on the stove."

Yoneda tucked the revolver into her waistband and sprang, caught the top of the wall and swung one leg up, and a moment later was straddling it and holding the gun again.

She was panting, but her voice was steady as she told Vickery, "You can go in first. Your hands will be visible and I'll have this gun aimed at the center of Castine's back."

"I gather you live in a trailer?" the bearded man said. "If you have a flashlight, and Miss Rayette here doesn't object, could you look around under the trailer for a bomb, before we all go in? It would be what they call C-4, and it would look . . ."

"I know what it would look like," Vickery said. "I've got alarms, but I'll check."

Yoneda nodded. "We'll all wait on the pavement while you do."

Ten minutes later the four of them were in Vickery's narrow living room. Vickery and Castine sat stiffly in the easy chairs, and the portly bearded old fellow was huddled on the couch. Yoneda was standing in the kitchen doorway rapidly tapping the old man's revolver on her thigh; she had not stepped out to get to Vickery's truck and retrieve her own gun, but she had leaned into the kitchen and turned off the fire on the stove.

The bearded man, who Yoneda addressed as Tacitus, was now wearing an old bathrobe of Vickery's, for his wet clothes had proved to be dotted with tiny *worms* from the river and had been thoroughly rinsed off in the shower, and were now hung on a towel rack in the kitchen. Vickery's jacket was dusty from his having crawled around with a flashlight under the trailer, making sure that no assassins had got past his alarms and planted a bomb; and none had. A layer of smoke under the ceiling glowed in the lamplight, for Yoneda and Tacitus had lit cigarettes; the air reeked of tobacco smoke and charred onions. There was no more beer, and a bottle of Maker's Mark bourbon and four already-replenished glasses sat on the coffee table.

Yoneda had several times opened her mouth as if to say something, then snapped it shut; finally she just shook her head and looked across the room at Tacitus. "Okay," she said, "to *start* with, would people who might plant a bomb under this trailer be the same people who blew up that van this morning?"

Tacitus had combed his beard and scanty hair while Vickery had been rinsing off his clothes, but he was still nervously fingering his moustache. He paused and pursed his lips, clearly regretting having mentioned the possibilty of a bomb since there hadn't been one.

"I don't know," he said finally. "I suppose so. It just seems like a day to be cautious."

"You specified C-4."

Tacitus let his hands drop to his lap. "Well, I gather that's what people use these days. I didn't want Mr. . . . our host to be looking for black bowling balls with burning fuses sticking out of them."

Vickery wondered sourly if his crawl under the trailer had simply been humoring a deluded old man.

"We'll get back to that," said Yoneda. She swept a glance over all three of them, and took a deep breath. "Right," she said. "So. What—*happened!*—down in the river?"

"I told you," said Castine, "it was a crop circle, without the crops. The chirping noises, the distorted vision, the heat—that was probably the microwave radiation that cooks nodes in wheat stalks, in ordinary crop circle appearances. There'll be a lot of magnetized iron pellets scattered around too. And there was probably some alpha and beta radiation—and—" She paused, glancing around defensively, then went on, "—what seemed to be changes in gravity."

Vickery nodded. "There were."

"Shit," said Yoneda with evident resentment. "Yes, there were. And for a few moments there was—that—" She raised her free hand and spread her fingers.

Castine picked up her glass and drank half its contents. "That thing with the big hands," she said, exhaling. "I saw one of them in a crop circle in England two nights ago." Nodding to Yoneda, she added, "I know I told you it was a witness who claimed to have seen it—I didn't want you to think I was crazy."

Yoneda waved the gun impatiently. "But what *are* they?"

Castine just shook her head.

Tacitus was bent down and tugging uncomfortably at the hem of Vickery's bathrobe. Vickery had offered to loan the man a shirt and a pair of pants, but Tacitus had declined, and they wouldn't have been wide enough for him to button or zip up in any case.

"Your clothes should be dry before too long," Vickery told him. "And I did rinse all the worms off."

Tacitus sighed and straightened up. "They are cortical homunculi."

"I'm sure you're right," said Vickery. "I hope you didn't swallow any."

Tacitus pursed his lips irritably. "Damn your worms! I mean the things with the big hands and distended faces. When the extra-dimensonal intelligences fall into occupation of physical mass, they often helplessly assume what they comprehend as our physical appearance.

According to reports, they can only sustain the form for a few moments. As was the case tonight."

"Hah!" said Yoneda. "Our physical appearance? Some of your chess club pals must be very weird-looking dudes."

"Okay," said Castine, "that went right by me."

"Do explain," said Vickery.

Looking distinctly uncomfortable, Tacitus said, "The chess club is a group of militant space alien sympathizers, and they resent—"

"A *chess* club?" interrupted Castine.

"Oh. Well, that's sort of their *cover*, you see." Ignoring a derisive snort from Yoneda, Banach went on doggedly, "They resent your, what they believe are your intentions toward the aliens. You being, I gather, Air Force Intelligence."

Vickery was sure the old man's story was a lie, a clumsy one, and he could see that Castine and Yoneda thought the same but were willing to let it stand for the moment; and he wondered what sort of group, if any, old Tacitus might actually be a member of.

Yoneda flicked ash off her cigarette and stepped forward to pick up her glass from the table. "So that *thing* in the riverbed is what aliens think humans look like?"

"Yes," said Tacitus, "and in fact it's a more accurate likeness, from one perspective, than the way they used to appear. Their forms are made of whatever mass is at hand—dust, clay, leaves—and until a few months ago the forms were a crude mimicry of our *external* appearance: oval heads on slender four-limbed bodies. But lately—"

"The grays," said Castine. "The typical image of aliens, like in *Close Encounters*."

"Exactly," said Tacitus. "And not a bad sketch of the human figure, really, from the outside, considering that they're not accustomed to comprehending physical shapes at all."

Vickery looked up from refilling his glass and nodded. "I always thought those aliens you see in pictures were too human-like to be how real aliens would look."

Castine was frowning at Tacitus in amused puzzlement. "You said that thing in the riverbed was a more accurate likeness of us."

"Yes, in an essential way. What we saw down there is the human form as comprehended from the *inside*, in the somatosensory cortex of the brain. The areas of the body that are allotted more sensory nerves there—hands, lips, tongue—are understandably taken to be bigger."

Yoneda stepped into the kitchen and dragged a chair into the living room and sat down. "Comprehended from the inside," she said. "What does that mean?"

Tacitus spread his hands. "They have begun to perceive human brains."

"It didn't," said Yoneda hesitantly, "have, uh . . . gender."

"Thank God," muttered Vickery, trying not to imagine how the thing would have manifested that.

Castine rolled her eyes and nodded.

"Male and female characteristics appear to cancel out," said Tacitus, "in their view. It may be that they don't have any referent for sexuality."

"Do they ever," asked Castine hesitantly, "have a hundred hands, rather than just two big ones?"

"It would be an effect of the same cause," Tacitus began.

But Yoneda gave Castine a sudden sharp glance. "In Wiltshire, you arrived at that crop circle with a . . . team, right? It must have been a good ten or fifteen minutes after the circle was formed. The big-handed thing hung around that long? And none of your team even *saw* it?"

Vickery could think of nothing he could say that would help Castine out; and spilling his drink or faking a coughing fit would be transparent attempts at distraction.

"It was a broad pattern," said Castine, with at least no haste or change of expression, "and the middle of the night. I walked a good distance into it—"

"They don't last ten minutes," said Tacitus flatly, leaning forward. "They don't last one."

Castine raised her eyebrows. "This one did," she insisted.

"This morning!" said Tacitus with imperfectly suppressed excitement, "a certain state was . . . forcibly *imposed* on me, though before that it had always occurred only when voluntarily sought. And immediately after that the things appeared in the sky."

He stood up quickly from the couch, and Yoneda raised the gun, but the old man simply crossed to the window and picked up the canvas leaning against the bookcase below it.

He stepped close to the nearest standing lamp and peered at the umber and tan and silver brush-strokes in the desert landscape. After a few seconds he put it down and stared at Vickery.

"You too!" he said. "Was it simply because the three of us were there, or," he added with a glance toward Castine, "did one of you enter the retro view deliberately, triggering me, and probably the other as well?"

Vickery cocked his head. "Sorry? What?"

"Did you once," Tacitus asked, almost in a pleading tone, "drive down a freeway offramp into a region of insanity?"

Castine's gasp was faint, but Tacitus spun toward her, nearly losing Vickery's bathrobe. "You did! And now you can see the infrared past, as you surely did in England two nights ago." He laughed harshly. "The three of us in that state this morning—a triangle of retro points puncturing the fabric of now, a localized radiating discord like conflicting radar waves—we called them into the sky!"

Yoneda was staring blankly at Tacitus.

Castine cast a desperate glance at Vickery, who didn't move for a moment and then sat back and smiled wryly.

"Yes, we did," Vickery said, "three years ago. You?"

"Also three years ago." Tacitus returned to the couch and sat down. "And now we are not secure in our slots in sequential time, eh? We . . . rattle from side to side, a bit."

"Yes," said Vickery. "Only toward the past, though—there seems to be some kind of temporal headwind."

"I think," said Tacitus, "there must not be many of us."

"There was another," said Castine softly, "who drove down an offramp like that in 1960, but he was killed a couple of years ago. Yes, it's probably just the three of us now."

"We few," said Tacitus, "we unsteady few."

Yoneda waved Tacitus's gun. "Okay, you're all going to—"

A low buzzing noise interrupted her, and in the next moment Vickery had vaulted up from his chair and snatched the revolver from Yoneda's hand. He glanced at the bookshelf over the door, on which stood three glass figurines shaped like monkeys; the one on the left, with its hands over its eyes, was glowing red.

"Under the trailer for real this time," Vickery said, and took hold of the doorknob.

Before he could turn it, though, Tacitus caught his elbow. "I'm afraid I must deal with this."

Vickery looked past Tacitus to Castine, who shrugged and nodded.

"I can't let you have the gun," said Vickery.

"I don't need it." Tacitus stepped past Vickery, took a deep breath and pushed the door open.

Vickery was now standing beside the doorframe with the gun raised. The evening breeze, cool on his damp face, smelled of car exhaust and the river, and there was no one visible now on the lane between the trailers. Tacitus shuffled forward onto the landing, and called in a loud voice, "Stoy! Vlast'yu direktsya! Voz'mi svoye ustroystvo idi—Eto pod kontrolem."

Looking past Tacitus's shoulder, a few seconds later Vickery saw a young man in a dust-streaked black windbreaker staighten up as he hurried away from the base of the trailer, and then another, who was carrying a box. Both had fair hair cut short. The first man turned around and called, "Kto ti?"

Tacitus stepped forward so that his face was clearly illuminated by the porch light. "Anatoly Kazakov. Kto-to bol'shim avtoritetom. Prover'te, chto ya govoryu, prezhde chem pytat'sya snova."

One of the men barked a question in the same

language; Tacitus replied curtly with what might have been a series of numbers.

After a moment's hesitation and a brief exhange of whispers, the two men hurried away into the shadows of the narrow lane; their backs were briefly lit by a streetlight, and then Vickery heard a car start, and wondered if it was the BMW that had raced away from Giant Rock after the explosion this morning.

Tacitus stepped back inside and closed the door, and when he turned to the room his face was bleak. *"U menya ne bylo drudgogo vybora,"* he whispered; then, focusing on the others, he said, "I had no choice."

Vickery reached up to the glass monkeys with his free hand and re-set the motion detector, then walked back to his chair and sat down, holding the gun in his lap. "That was Russian."

Tacitus nodded and spread his arms. "You see before you an orphan."

"What did you tell them?" asked Castine.

"I told them to stop—by the authority of the Directorate—and take their device and leave, that the situation had changed and was under control. I gave them my name, my real name, and told them to verify what I said before they took further action." He shook his head. "Idiots. They'll be reprimanded for leaving."

"Which Directorate?" asked Vickery.

Tacitus walked around the table and sat down on the couch. Raising his glass of bourbon in his trembling right hand, he said softly, as if to himself, *"Mais ou est l'Union d'Soviet Socialiste Republiques d'antan?"*

It was a paraphrase of a line from the French of

Francois Villon, and Vickery mentally translated it: *But where is the USSR of yesterday?*

Tacitus looked up. "The Soviet Military Intelligence Directorate, *Glavnoye Razvedyvatel'noye Upravleniye.*"

"The GRU," said Yoneda. "Not a—a *militant chess club.*"

"No," said Tacitus, "that was a hasty improvisation... there is such a chess club, but I've never had any contact with them." He yawned, and Vickery knew it was from tension, not weariness. "It is said," Tacitus went on, "that in the GRU complex on the Khoroshevskoye Highway in Moscow there is an incinerator—a crematorium—for traitors. Ivashutin said it was just for burning documents, but I wonder if it is my destination now."

Vickery recalled the van that had been blown up this morning by Giant Rock. What this potbellied old man was saying now might be true.

Vickery gestured toward the floor of the trailer. "Why would the GRU want to kill *me?*" he asked. "How would they even be aware of me?"

Tacitus's head swung from side to side as if, thought Vickery, he were looking for some way forward. "I didn't abandon it," he muttered at last. "It left me abandoned."

Tacitus leaned back now and stared at the low ceiling. "There was to be an operation at Giant Rock this morning. We—they!—knew that the U. S. Office of Naval Intelligence was sending two agents and a backup van." He gave Yoneda a wan smile. "I knew from the start that you were ONI, not Air Force Intelligence." He shook his head and went on, "I'm not operational, I was told to go and observe, and to identify Pierce Plowman if I saw him—I've met him a couple of times." He looked at Vickery. "I photographed the license plates of all the vehicles there, and when you fled, pursued by what I took to be an ONI vehicle, I relayed both numbers to my handler. And the policy of the Directorate, it seems, is to eliminate every ONI agent involved in, ah, UFO investigations; as well as anyone who seems to be of value to those investigations."

"Good God," said Yoneda with a visible shiver, "you guys are barbaric!"

"Regrettably inclined toward a blind clean sweep these days," admitted Tacitus.

Vickery turned to look at Yoneda. "Why did *your* lot kill Frankie Notchett?"

"Frankie is dead?" exclaimed Tacitus. "When?"

"I don't know anything about that—" Yoneda began.

"Sometime during this last week," said Vickery.

Yoneda finished her sentence, "—I only knew someone by that name was apprehended."

Tacitus was staring at Vickery. "I spoke to him no more than a month ago! Are you certain?"

Castine nodded. "*Oh* yeah."

Tacitus swiveled his head toward her. "You saw the body?"

"Uh," said Castine, "no. We—we saw his ghost, actually, this afternoon."

"Oh for God's sake," breathed Yoneda.

Tacitus switched his attention from Castine to Yoneda. "Rayette," he said, "you don't believe in ghosts?" When she just cocked her head mockingly, he said, "You should. You saw one half an hour ago."

"What, the thing with the hands? Made of leaves and dirt? Whatever that was, it came down in that glowing ball."

"It came down *as* that glowing ball," Tacitus corrected her, "dying. I believe the three of us here," he added with a wave toward Vickery and Castine, "poisoned it when we ... *impinged* on its identity this morning. And when we three came into mutual proximity again this evening we provided the place for it to die. They are purely deterministic, they have no metaconsciousness, and overlapping with free wills awakens them, so that they die."

"Free will's a bitch," Castine observed, then looked sheepishly at the floor.

"I was going to try cooking something again," said Vickery, standing up, "but since Mr. Tacitus's comrades might come back at any time, I'm afraid we're all leaving."

"Not my comrades any longer," said Tacitus mournfully.

Castine too had stood up, and Vickery handed Tacitus's gun to her. "Watch them while I pack. Tacitus, you can get dressed. Your clothes are wet, but at least they've got no worms on ,em."

"Small mercies," whispered Tacitus, standing up.

CHAPTER NINE:
Some Kind of *Brujos?*

"Agent Castine," said Yoneda with quiet urgency when Vickery had hurried away toward the bedroom and Tacitus was pulling his pants on in the kitchen, "listen to me carefully, and *think*. We have Vickery—that *is* him, right?—and *a GRU defector!* You and I both screwed up today, but we can come up with a story to explain it all, and come out ahead." She nodded toward the bedroom. "Just point the gun the other way."

Castine gave her a tired smile and didn't move.

"Right now," Yoneda went on, "you can still have a life. I can way downplay your attack on me this morning. Are you going to throw yourself away, and what?—live off the grid or something?"

Castine considered the course of her life since it had collided with Sebastian Vickery's. In 2013 she had been a twenty-eight-year-old agent of the Transportation Utility Agency and Vickery had been a thirty-two-year-old Secret Service agent named Herbert Woods. She had had him arrested for breaking protocol during a

Presidential motorcade—he had entered a restricted Countermeasures vehicle and inadvertently heard highly classified ghost chatter on a radio—and he had very nearly been summarily executed for it, escaping only by killing two TUA agents. Four years later she had found him among the freeway-side gypsies in L.A., living under the name Sebastian Vickery, and this time she had *saved* him from arrest by the TUA. It had led to . . . well, it had led to the TUA murdering Eliot Shaw, her fiancé, for one thing. And it had led to Vickery and herself driving a taco truck into the nightmare afterlife known as the Labyrinth; and when they had made their tortuous way back to reality, they had discovered that they no longer fitted securely into sequential time, and could see the recent past in what Vickery called echo-vision. The following year she had flown back to Los Angeles to find him again, for echo-vision had begun intrusively showing both of them the terrible old house in Topanga Canyon that had been torn down in 1969 but was eventually to reappear in a supernatural maelstrom on the tumultuous night of Halloween in 2018.

In the course of all of this, she and Vickery had saved each other's lives many times. It didn't even occur to her now to point the gun the other way.

"I've done it before," she told Yoneda. And I've somehow managed to come back afterward, she thought. I wonder if I can possibly come back from this without going to prison, or worse.

Vickery reappeared from the bedroom wearing his denim jacket and carrying a black briefcase in his left hand and a .45 semi-automatic in his right.

He eyed the revolver Castine was holding, which had been Tacitus's. "You okay with that?"

Castine nodded.

To Yoneda and Tacitus, who was standing in the kitchen doorway tucking his wet shirt into his dripping pants, Vickery said, "I think it'd be a good idea for you to finish your drinks and go. I'm going to turn the lights out and leave the door open, so if our Bolsheviks come back they might decide the place is abandoned now."

Tacitus stepped forward and picked up his glass. "Not Bolsheviks anymore," he said. He drained the glass and set it down. "Hooligans now. Will you come with me, Rayette?"

Yoneda gave Castine a last, disappointed glance, and looked away. "Yes. Please. I think we should walk the long way around to your car, by the street, not back through the riverbed." She turned to Castine. "Can I get my gun?"

"Not tonight."

"Can we take the bottle?" asked Tacitus, nodding toward the fifth of Maker's Mark, still half-full.

"Not tonight," said Vickery.

Tacitus nodded sadly, then waved at Vickery's painting leaning against the bookcase. "If we get an afterward," he said, "I would like to buy that painting. I don't know how you managed so nearly to get that strange light."

"Underpainting," said Castine.

"If we get an afterward," said Vickery, "I'll let you have it. We few, we unsteady few."

Vickery and Castine backed into the kitchen then, as Yoneda and Tacitus shuffled to the door and descended the steps. Over Vickery's shoulder Castine watched them recede up the lane, into the pool of streetlight radiance and then out past it into darkness.

Vickery closed the door. He stepped back into the living room and laid the .45 on the coffee table and unzipped his briefcase.

"A motel?" said Castine.

Vickery tightened the cap on the bottle of bourbon and tucked it into the briefcase, beside several .45 and 9-millimeter magazines and three thick rubber-banded bundles of twenty-dollar bills; and she recalled that a few years ago he had cashed out his old Secret Service 401k and a settlement from the Transportation Utility Agency.

"I don't mean to be paranoid," he said as he folded the papers Plowman had given him and slid them in alongside the bottle, "but Tacitus said the GRU wants to kill both of us, and they've got my name and license plate number—they might have my credit card number too."

"A tomb?" said Castine. "A taco truck, that condemned house up on Mulholland?" she added, thinking of the places in which they had found overnight shelter in previous times.

Vickery straightened and slung the briefcase strap over his shoulder. "My studio," he said. "I pay cash for it, and the owner is an old guy on Social Security who doesn't declare the money. It's got a cot and reclining beach chairs."

"Best yet."

Vickery tucked the .45 into his jacket pocket. He crossed to the front door and opened it, and crouched to peer around the jamb in both directions.

"Okay," he said, standing up, "We're out of here."

Castine followed him down the steps. "Are you going to turn off the lights?"

"Gas and electric both," he said, moving toward a meter and a metal box at the side of the trailer—but the trailer's lights went out before he got there, and Castine's streetlight shadow disappeared in sudden darkness.

And above the trailer and beyond it she saw again the column standing vertically against the now-dark sky. It was dimly luminous, and wider than it had been an hour and a half ago; in twilight it had been made of dust, but now it seemed to be whirling snow.

Sebastian walked up beside her and said, "Power failure all over, but I switched it off anyway," and then he looked where she was pointing.

For several long seconds neither of them spoke, staring at the silent, swirling, alien column.

"We should look," whispered Castine.

"I . . . suppose."

They both hurried around the trailer. Vickery pulled himself up to straddle the wall, and reached down to catch Castine's wrist, and in moments they had crossed the service road and stood again, panting, at the crest of the cement slope overlooking the riverbed.

And they stepped back, for an impossibly icy wind was whirling up the slope at them. The base of the milky white column was nearly as wide as the riverbed, and the narrow band of water that ran down the center shone white in the dim glow of the urban sky.

Castine was shivering. "It's frozen!" Her breath was a cloud of steam.

Then Vickery had grabbed her arm and pulled her

back. A line of tall weeds ran alongside the road, and he pushed her down at them. She felt his hands clutch the back of her coat.

Castine gripped the weed stalks, and she had to tug on them to pull herself down to the roadside dirt. Vickery reached past her and caught two handfuls of weeds, and he just held on. He was lying above her back, but she felt no weight.

Then she did; he was sprawled heavily across her, and she was pressed against the dirt. He rolled off of her and lay on his back on the pavement.

"Gravity's back on," she gasped.

Vickery got to his feet with evident caution, and Castine stood up carefully and stepped with him to the crest, shivering and hugging herself against the frigid air.

The pale column was breaking up into clouds of snow, and in moments it was gone. All that was left of the phenomenon was the frozen river.

"That snow," said Vickery. "I don't think it melted."

Castine shrugged, clenching her teeth to keep them from chattering. "It's gone."

"I think it sublimated. I don't think it was water."

She gave him a blank look.

"I don't know," he said, taking her elbow and turning back toward the wall. "Nitrogen, probably. I hope the power's back on—the truck has to start."

Castine thought of reminding him that the truck's electical system had nothing to do with the city's power grid, then wondered if that mattered. Either way it was electricity, after all.

But lights glowed in the windows of the other trailers

along the lane, and the truck's engine started after stuttering for a few moments while the battery reasserted itself. Vickery backed the truck around and shifted to drive, and in moments the trailer, looking forlorn with its windows dark and its door open, had disappeared behind rows of other trailers.

"Sebastian Vickery," said the woman, stepping around a gleaming single-post car lift, on top of which sat a new Ford 150 pickup truck with no wheels. She was hardly more than five feet tall, but stocky, and the piercing eyes in her wide brown face twinkled with unpredictable merriment. Her black hair was cropped short and she was wearing stained jeans and a khaki jacket. She might have been in her forties.

"Yeah, I sure do remember him," she said.

Behind her, several men in overalls squatted on the cement floor, carefully gluing pennies and playing cards to the inside surfaces of new tires. On the street side of the maintenance bay, behind Joel Finehouse and Vilko Cendravenir, the sectional maintence bay door was fully raised; the sky outside was dark, but the bay was brightly lit by fluorescent tubes in the high, corrugated steel ceiling. Finehouse noticed that Vilko Cendravenir was ostentatiously wrinkling his nose at the mixed smells of motor oil, solvent and Mexican food, and kicked his foot.

"Ms. Galvan," Finehouse said, "We're trying—"

"If he's in trouble I won't help you," Anita Galvan interrupted. "He's making payments to me, regular, for having ruined the upholstery of my best car, a year and a half ago." She cocked her head. "Not that he doesn't deserve trouble."

"How does he pay you?" asked Finehouse.

"Five twenties, most months, in an envelope with a joke return address. He doesn't want me to know where he lives, 'cause he knows I'd have *mis amigos* go beat the shit out of him." She laughed. "He punched me in the stomach and stole the car, and when he returned it the next day there was *tar* all over the seats!" She looked over her shoulder at one of the men rolling a tire across the floor. "Bend it," she called, "lean on it! Make sure the pennies stick!"

Finehouse went on, "If his debt were paid off—"

"Twice over," put in Cendravenir, his teeth gleaming between his moustache and his silly pointed goatee.

Finehouse forced his suddenly clenched jaw to relax. "—do you think you could find him?" he finished, keeping his voice level.

Galvan rocked back and forth on her heels. "Who are you?"

The tire got away from the man who had been rolling it, and in his lunge to catch it he only managed to slap the tread, giving it more speed. It came careening straight toward Cendravenir, who gave a startled cry and jumped aside to let it pass him and roll out onto the lot.

One of the men back in the bay exclaimed hoarsely, and Finehouse looked past Galvan. The man was staring up at the raised pickup truck, and after a moment Finehouse noticed that the truck's exposed hubs and brake rotors were spinning.

Galvan had turned away and taken several steps toward

the steel lift post. Finehouse glanced at Cendravenir, who was trembling and sweating; clearly he had been badly startled by the tire rushing at him. Finehouse nudged him and whispered, "Stop it!"

"That thing got all-wheel drive?" yelled Galvan. "Bring it down far enough to turn it off!"

"It *is* off," called one of her employees, "and it *don't* have A-dubya-D."

Beside Finehouse, Cendravenir closed his eyes and held his breath, and the car's wheels stopped spinning.

Galvan stared at the lifted truck for several more seconds, then turned to face Finehouse and Cendravenir. "Who are you guys? I want more than twice what the upholstery cost—I'd probably have to pay somebody to find out where Vickery is, *and* he's an old friend. He used to be one of my drivers, and I think he saved my family from being wiped out by devils. Twice."

"But you'd like to have him beaten up," Finehouse pointed out.

"Sure. To the hospital. Not the morgue. So are you some kind of *brujos?*"

Finehouse believed the word meant sorcerors; and he wondered if it would help to have Cendravenir give this woman a demonstration more impressive than just making a car's wheels spin.

But he remembered the golf balls breaking the light panel over Lubitz' desk; depending loosely on the stimulus, Cendravenir might helplessly throw that car into the street, or set somebody's intestines twisting into knots. Finehouse knew it could happen, and shuddered at the irrationality of it.

He patted his sport coat to show that it was flat, then reached behind the lapel and pulled out his badge wallet.

"Naval Intelligence," he said, flipping it open.

Galvan glanced at it, then stared at Finehouse. "I couldn't live with myself if I sold him out for less than ten grand."

"We could subpoena you," Finehouse said, though he knew Lubitz wouldn't even consider such a grossly conspicuous move.

"Do it, Navy boy. I'll tell the truth under oath—I don't know where he is."

Finehouse glanced past her at the car on the lift, then turned to look at the cars out in the lot. "We might ask you about other things. Licenses, permits, taxes."

"Fifteen," said Galvan cheerfully.

Finehouse didn't move for five seconds, then said, "Ten," and drew a card from the wallet and gave it to her. It was one of the ones with nothing on it but a phone number. "Give me a call when you know where he is," he said, putting the wallet away, "and when we've verified it, I'll bring you the money."

"It'll be accurate," Galvan said, "since you know where to find me. I'll give you his location when I'm holding the money. Fifteen. And leave *him* at home," she added, nodding toward Cendravenir. "I don't need my cars rolling around."

Finehouse stared coldly into her steady brown eyes, but after a few seconds had to look away. "Right," he said. "Call me."

He turned and stalked away across the dark yard, hearing Cendravenir hurrying to catch up.

Finehouse got into the SUV and started the engine; Cendravenir climbed in a moment later, panting. Craning his neck to see out the rear window as he backed out onto Eighth Street, Finehouse said, "You had to do your mimicry trick?"

"Yes," said Cendravenir flatly. "I'm tired, I'm nervous—where the hell are we?" He fastened his seat belt and sat back. "If moving stuff scares me, well—other stuff's gonna move too."

Finehouse supposed the man was right, and hadn't been able to help setting the pickup truck's hubs spinning. Cendravenir suffered from telekinetic latah—ordinarily the ailment known as latah was a "startle disorder" in which a sudden surprise caused its victims to mimic the actions of people nearby. But Cendravenir was telekinetic, and so when he was startled he caused physical objects to mimic the behavior of other physical objects.

It was a psychological disorder, and Lubitz had told Finehouse that it was related to the malady of the 19th century Jumping Frenchmen of Maine, who, when startled, would—after jumping—follow any orders they were given. Disorder or not, Cendravenir's ability was the hinge-pin of Operation Pleiades.

Finehouse turned right onto the next street and sped between rows of parked cars in front of old brick apartment buildings with fire escapes criss-crossing their facades, turned right and quickly turned right again, and drove nearly all the way back to Eighth Street. He swung in to park at a yellow curb and switched off the engine.

"You forgot something?" asked Cendravenir, for they were now just around the corner from Galvan's lot.

"If anybody has a problem with the way we're parked," Finehouse said, "stall them." He climbed between the front seats to the back of the SUV. "I think she'll make a call right away." He opened a laptop computer that was connected to a Stingray 2 cell-site simulator and booted both of them up, then swiveled one of a pair of pole-mounted antennas to point it directly toward the back of Galvan's building.

Cendravenir had twisted around in his seat. "What's all that?"

"We're going to be a fake cell tower," said Finehouse as he crouched over the computer monitor and clicked on the controller icon while the Stingray box scanned the local cell-signals environment and insinuated itself into the network. "We've got a power amplifier and we're only a hundred feet away, so Galvan's phone is going to think we're the nearest cell tower—five bars!" He looked up and saw Cendravenir's blank look. "We're the man in the middle. The data stream from her phone goes through this," he said, patting the Stingray box, "and instantly on to the nearest cell tower, and vice versa."

He tapped through several screens on the laptop. "I show six subscribers within our narrow bubble, and IP connectivity to only one of them at the moment." He clicked on it and a black window appeared on the screen with all of the target cell phone's data listed in tiny white letters, and he turned off the target phone's encryption.

He put on headphones and clicked on the phone code.

"—want him for?" said a young man's voice from the headphones.

"There's some secret agent types looking for him,"

came Galvan's remembered voice, "and I want to warn him."

"If I can find him, I can warn him myself," said the young man. "Why should you pay me?"

"There's *details*," said Galvan.

"You're going to sell him out again."

Finehouse clicked on the bar that opened a window displaying Galvan's phone number and the number she was connected with, and he highlighted them and copied them to a file on the laptop.

Galvan said, "No, they didn't offer me any money. But Vickery might pay to know about them. I got their license number."

Finehouse heard a sigh in the headphone speakers. "If I can find him, I'll tell him what you've told me. For old times' sake."

The call ended. From the front seat, Cendravenir said, loudly, "We're waiting for some guys to bring out a refrigerator!" and when Finehouse pulled off the headphones and climbed back into the front seat he saw that Cendravenir had lowered the passenger-side window. An old man was standing on the sidewalk, apparently objecting to the SUV being parked at a yellow curb.

"You can have the refrigerator," Finehouse called to the old man, and put the vehicle in reverse. He backed up the street until he was able to swerve into a driveway, then shifted to drive and turned left, heading north.

After a few blocks he made his way back down to Eighth Street, and he turned in at the brightly lit parking lot of a Korean barbecue restaurant. Without switching off the engine, he pulled out his cell phone, leaned back to keep Cendravenir from seeing the screen, and texted to Lubitz an account of their interaction with Galvan, not omitting Cendravenir's inadvertent telekinetic slip.

While Finehouse waited for a reply, Cendravenir lit one of his clove-flavored cigarettes. Finehouse just sighed and turned up the air conditioning.

Lubitz's reply arrived only a few seconds later: *Find and secure Vickery at all absolutely NECESSARY cost. Find and secure Castine; find Yoneda: commit or omit. Keep Cendravenir ready and tranquil.*

Finehouse turned off his phone and put it away. "We've got reservations at the Holiday Inn Express downtown. I think we'd better get room service."

"I won't have any problem in a restaurant, assuming nobody throws anything at me." Cendravenir drew on the cigarette, and sparks fell in his lap. "I was nervous with that Galvan woman— jumpy, ill at ease!—right from the start. She seems *volatile.*"

Finehouse put the SUV in gear and steered back out onto Eighth Street. "True. Okay, we can try a restaurant. Take a Xanax."

"Yes. And I'll stay at the hotel tomorrow if you go to talk to that woman again. You think she can find your Vickery man?"

"She seems to be trying. And we may be able to step right over her."

He glanced at his watch; it was 8:30. He made a right turn on Western Avenue.

"Who *is* Vickery?" asked Cendravenir.

"He's a guy who has information he shouldn't have."

"Sure, I know that, but—what *else* is he?"

Cendravenir was staring straight ahead, sucking on his spicy cigarette. Vickery, Finehouse thought, along with Castine, will ideally comprise your opener of the way, set the stage for your biggest performance. This morning they proved, unexpectedly but pretty dramatically, that they can do it.

Finehouse let the question go unanswered. He looked to the side at Cendravenir—then glanced ahead and instantly shoved his foot down hard on the brake. A car had abruptly swerved from a left-turn lane into the lane in front of him and then stopped short for a yellow traffic light.

Finehouse's arms were braced on the steering wheel as the front end of the SUV dipped, and he could feel the vehicle's momentum being forcibly strangled by the brakes. After two long seconds the SUV rocked to a halt, its bumper only inches from the bumper of the car ahead.

Cendravenir had pitched forward against the restraint of the seatbelt, and he had dropped his cigarette. Finehouse looked at him quickly, but the man just unfastened the seatbelt and groped around between his feet, and when Cendravenir straightened up, holding the cigarette, Finehouse was relieved to see that he was not sweating and trembling.

"Don't scare me like that," Cendravenir muttered, and inhaled on the cigarette. More sparks fell in his lap.

The traffic light ahead switched to green, and Finehouse lifted his foot from the brake pedal and let his hands relax on the steering wheel.

"Take a Xanax right now. Take three."

✧ ✧ ✧

Tacitus Banach stared moodily across bowls of tortilla chips and salsa at Rayette. They had found a table in a far corner of El Parian on Pico Boulevard, under a row of blue pennants that spelled out CORONA, and the warm air smelled wonderfully of grilling beef and enchilada sauce. There was no risk of being overheard, but Banach wished their order would arrive so that he could delay answering her questions by chewing something more substantial than the chips.

"I may simply get a job," he said finally. "Here, or—anywhere, San Diego, San Jose, Barstow. Be a genuine American. Just because I'm a, a deserter doesn't mean I must be a defector."

"I've got to report you," said Rayette. "If you don't claim defector status, the FBI *will* find you, and arrest you for failing to register as an agent of a foreign government. As a defector, though, you'll be given immunity and a new identity, and some income."

Banach smiled. "And you'll reinstate yourself with your superiors, after falling out of communication today."

Rayette shrugged. "That too."

A waiter walked up with the two bottles of Corona beer that they'd ordered and set them on the table. Banach picked one up and stared at the label until the waiter moved away.

"Some defectors from the GRU haven't lived long as such, in spite of new identities," Banach said, thinking of the crematorium at the GRU complex in Moscow. "The GRU does not forget or forgive. And how can you report me?" He scooped up some of the salsa on a chip. "You don't even know the surname I've been living under, and the license plate on my car—oh, I saw you note it!—is, it saddens me to say, stolen. I will leave no fingerprints on this bottle. And of course you have no phone, or gun, and you may be assured that you can't overpower me."

Rayette slumped in her chair and pulled a flip-phone from her pocket. Banach pushed his chair back—regretfully, for he had been looking forward to the tacos he had ordered—but Yoneda showed him the open back of the phone. There was no battery, and the inside surfaces were rusted.

"It doesn't work," she said. "It's my—sort of good luck charm." She laid it on the table.

Banach relaxed. Certainly if it had been functional, as a phone or GPS tracker, there would have been consequences by now. But he was intrigued—she seemed to lean toward it as if listening.

"Old ghosts?" he asked gently.

"No—not real ones, anyway. Reminders." She nodded and pushed the old phone aside. "'Get a job somewhere,' you said. Sure. How do you make a living now? Does the GRU send you money?"

Banach took a sip of beer. "Actually," he said with a smile, "they send me collectible items which I sell on eBay."

"What, like old comic books?"

"That sort of thing, yes."

"And that's been funding your investigations into these UAPs, UFOs—"

"NLOs," Banach agreed. *"Neopoznannyy Letat Oj'jektu."*

"Right." Yoneda sat back and gave him a quizzical look.

"Am I the only one at this table who can see how...
involved you are in all of that? You know about monsters
like that crop circle thing we saw in the L.A. River an hour
ago, and—what was it? Seeing the infrared past? Hah! Oh,
and the three of you forming a triangle that made those
flying saucers show up this morning, and—and all the rest
of that crazy shit."

The waiter returned, this time carrying plates that he
slid onto the table. He warned that they were hot, agreed
to bring more salsa, and strode away.

Yoneda gave Banach a skeptical grin as she dug a fork
into an enchilada. "And you're going to go get a job at a
Jiffy Lube somewhere? A Burger King? Investigate crop
circles and UFOs on your days off? You *could* work full-
time with Naval Intelligence, the way Wernher von Braun
worked for NASA—you could be a consultant, a
researcher, working for the officer who's heading up this
current project."

Banach was sure Yoneda didn't entirely know what she
was talking about, but... if he officially defected, it made
sense that he'd be able to pool his tormentingly
incomplete knowledge of these things with the knowledge
Naval Intelligence had amassed. The GRU had covertly
gleaned some of what ONI knew, but certainly not all.

And what could be more important, more fascinating?
Truly alien entities, almost entirely outside our four-
dimensional comprehension, impinging on our world like
a man dipping his fingers into a pond, interrupting the
pond's two-dimensional surface.

Banach knew that Yoneda was watching him closely as
she chewed and swallowed and took a sip of beer. He

poured some salsa on one of his tacos and picked it up, then paused.

"But you killed Frankie Notchett," he said. "Did you find out everything he knew about these phenomena first? Everything? I wonder if you're much better than the GRU."

"Oh, who says we killed him? I know, Castine and Vickery saw a ghost. If it said it was Notchett, it was probably lying. Who takes a ghost's word for anything? Shit."

"I think he is dead. But can you find out how he died? Would your superiors tell you the truth?"

"Yes, once I've explained why I fell out of the loop today. I can say I'd like to question Notchett. They'll tell me his status—they want me to be equipped with the facts."

"Would you tell *me* the truth, once you find out?"

Rayette cocked her head. "I don't know. I do think it's unlikely that they—" She gave him a bleak smile. "I don't know."

Banach took a bite of his taco. Eventually he wiped his mouth with a paper napkin and said, "That is satisfactory. Tomorrow you will be at a time and location I'll specify, alone, and I'll watch you from a distance. If Naval Intelligence killed him, you will be holding a newspaper. If they did not, if he is not dead or died from some other cause, your hands will be empty. Right? And I will make up my mind whether to trust you, join you, or to—disappear."

"Disappear to a Jiffy Lube in Barstow. Okay." It seemed to Banach that she spoke to the ruined phone on the table when she added, "it's all I can do."

CHAPTER TEN:
Little Frisbees

Vickery's studio was a flat-roofed room added onto the back of a small one-story stuccoed house on 16th Street in Long Beach. He had attached a ladder to the outside wall, and laid boards across the roof and put up railings, making an elevated deck of the rooftop. Poles at the four corners supported a retractable tarpaulin for shade. Down in the studio were cabinets and a refrigerator and a long table crowded with spray cans and coffee cups bristling with paintbrushes. Below a window that by day looked out on an overgrown backyard was a stack of variously sized blank canvases, while finished paintings leaned beside the door and a half-finished view of a mountain stood on an easel by the other window. The studio had no air-conditioning and smelled of spray-sealer, so Vickery had opened all the windows and then he and Castine had climbed up to the roof. They now sat in a couple of nylon-web beach chairs beneath the fluttering half-retracted tarpaulin. Vickery had brought along the bottle of Maker's Mark and two hastily rinsed coffee cups.

For several minutes neither of them spoke, then Castine asked, "What does *gelid* actually mean?"

"Really really cold."

"Huh." She took another sip of bourbon and stretched her feet out across the boards. "What are you going to do?"

"Well, speaking of cold, I've got some Stouffer's frozen dinners in the studio refrigerator, and I was thinking of putting them in the microwave. Would you like lasagna or Beef Stroganoff?"

"I meant what are you going to do about . . . all this trouble today?"

"Oh—I think I'll hide out here for a while. Then, if things still seem agitated in a week or so, figure a way to sell the trailer to a fictitious name and relocate it— at least to a different county, maybe out of state." He glanced at her. "How about you?"

"Beef stroganoff, please. And I *am* sorry! Again! For wrecking—unwittingly helping to wreck—your life. Again." She shook her head. "Actually I think I might be okay. With a good lawyer, I bet I could just get fired. I'm a civilian. The thing is, nobody saw me pepper spray Yoneda. The Jeep— well, I was authorized personnel, so I don't think running off in it was theft, exactly." She smiled crookedly. "And at least I left it at a church, right? I'll have to get another job pretty quick, though. Huh. I wonder how much lawyers charge." She scratched her scalp over her old bullet scar. "What was the other word? Not endosperm."

"Endothermic. A reaction that absorbs heat. As opposed to exothermic, which is a reaction that releases heat." He stared up at the overcast sky and recited, "'*But at what gelid, endothermic cost?*' What was the bit before that?"

"Something about the three Fates. And hundred-handed guys that wanted to steal their threads."

Vickery frowned thoughtfully. "Whatever it was that happened in the riverbed was endothermic."

"And how. In Wiltshire we measured some sudden drops in temperature at crop circle sites, but never near as cold as that." Castine clasped her elbows and shivered. "Stroganoff?"

"Right." Vickery stood up. "I'll fetch Notchett's papers too. Give me ten minutes, and don't finish the bourbon."

"I promise," she said, "nothing."

Fifteen minutes later they were eating out of plastic trays with plastic forks. Vickery had brought up a battery-powered work light and hung it on a rope that supported the tarpaulin. Scents of garlic and onions and sour cream contended with the reek of diesel exhaust on the chilly night air.

At last Vickery set his tray aside and picked up the papers Plowman had given him.

"What have we got," he said. He pulled the loose pages free of the paperclip on the stapled booklet. "Let's see. *'The Moriai who hold existence firm...'* Well that's unorthodox, the Moriai are the Fates, and they measure out the length of a person's life, they don't hold existence firm. And it says Clotho 'generates the thread that binds.' Again, that's not how the myth goes, the threads are lifetimes, they don't *bind* anything. *'Lachesis, who spins out its tiny length'*—okay, though it's discouraging to call lifetimes 'tiny.' Then *'Atropos, who ties it in a knot and clips it off.'* Well that's right."

Castine had finished her dinner and set her tray on the

floor planks. "I don't think he's talking about lifetimes," she said. "I think he's using—this is a translation Frankie Notchett made, right?—I think he's using that myth as cover to talk about something else." She leaned over and tapped the paper. "See, it gives line numbers, 218 A through 218 J—I bet in the actual Greek *Thingummy*, line 218 is just followed by line 219, without these . . . ten extra lines."

"Theogony."

"That's what I said. And Ourang-Outang—" She peered at the paper. "'*restrains the stranger hundred-handed ones/ Who every season hope to steal the threads,/ And weave them into wings wherewith to fly/ Even beyond the reach of Chaos . . .*'"

Vickery squinted out past the edge of the roofs at the lights of Long Beach. "Ouranos," he said absently, "not Ourang-Outang. It's a different spelling of Uranus."

Castine said nothing to that.

"So let's suppose," Vickery went on slowly, "that in this poem Frankie was writing about our hundred-handed, or big-handed, creatures—our cortical homunculi, as Tacitus said—wanting to steal these threads that hold existence firm."

"But the threads are tiny, it says here. How are they going to hold anything firm?"

"Tiny threads," said Vickery, "knotted and cut off, passed around among the three Fates. And they hold existence firm." He looked across the paper at Castine. "At Cole's you told me that there's electromagnetic screw-ups at your crop circles?"

"Right, phones and radios don't work half the time, and

if you fly a drone directly over one, it totally loses power. Sometimes they've just exploded."

"And gravity lost power back there—when we were in the trailer, and again when we went to look at the riverbed after it was all over, and everything was frozen and there was that column of snow. Which I don't think was frozen water."

"Nitrogen, you said."

"Or methane, maybe; that doesn't have to be quite as cold to freeze." He lifted the bourbon bottle and refilled his coffee cup. "Gravity, electromagnetism, and—and the tiny threads that hold existence firm."

Castine didn't say anything.

"But where would they *go?*" said Vickery, half to himself. "I can see reactions to their sudden absence, new equilibriums, but—they can't just *disappear.*"

"Who," said Castine, "the homuncular guys?"

"No. Forces." He stood up and paced to the railing overlooking the backyard. "Plowman said the UFOs we saw weren't physical objects—he said they're real, though—as real as the splash when you throw a pair of shoes into a swimming pool. Disrupting the surface, see? The actual *things* aren't at the surface, but the surface experiences their interaction. And the surface is all we know, our whole universe."

"Of course," said Castine. "That explains everything. But shoes? Did that homunculus we saw even have feet? I don't recall. Now *gloves*—if it had *gloves,* you could throw one in a pool and float six people on it." She nodded firmly.

Vickery gave her a sour grin. "You ever hear of a book

called *Flatland?* It describes two-dimensional creatures that live in a plane, a two-dimensional surface, like . . . like animate oil smears on the surface of a pond, say, who can't comprehend the air above, or the water below, because their whole world is the surface of the pond. Everything they see is straight ahead, visible only as either a dot or a horizontal line, because horizontal is all they've got." He held his palm out flat and moved his hand back and forth. "The only way they'd could know that something was circular would be if they moved all the way around something they saw as a straight line and it didn't get wider or narrower as they went around it."

"Like parameciums on a microscope slide."

"Okay, assuming there was no room for them to go over or under each other. Now what if one of them threw a, a frisbee at another of them, but, before it reached its target, *we* leaned in from above and poked one of your microscope slides into the surface, at a slant, so the frisbee went scooting up the slide?"

"The parameciums would figure it just vanished."

"Right, but it still had its momentum, it was still moving just as fast as when the little guy threw it—just in a direction the parameciums can't comprehend."

"Up. Out of the pond surface. Out of their universe." She took a sip of bourbon and breathed, "Oh, this is nice after Beef Stroganoff."

Vickery returned to his chair. "Maybe I'm crazy. But the forces of gravity and electromagnetism are conveyed by force-carrying particles—gravitons and virtual photons."

"Little frisbees."

"Well, they don't exactly have mass. But yeah. And it seemed like they were getting deflected away, back there by the riverbed. The forces were still working, probably ... just somewhere besides where we were."

"You think we're the equivalent of flat parameciums, to whatever sort of aliens are dipping into our ... reality?"

Vickery drained his cup and shrugged. "Right now I think it."

"Okay," Castine went on, "so the peculiar-handed creatures are stealing our gravity and electromagnetism, at crop circles. I get the frisbees—where do the threads come in?"

"There's another force. Two more, actually, but the strongest of all is the one that holds quarks together in protons and neutrons. There's three quarks in each of those, and this force extends from one quark to another and no further; extremely powerful, but very short range."

"Ah. A tiny length, and Atropos ties it in a knot and clips it off. Does this force have frisbees too?"

"Sure. They're called gluons, and they—"

"Sebastian! Frankie's ghost said that! He quoted the 'weave them into wings' line, and then he said something about 'glue on.'"

Vickery tried to remember what the ghost had said, but didn't recall that. "Are you sure?"

"Yes. Frankie's way ahead of you. Was. So why would it get real cold—real gelid!—if the homuncular guys steal the gluon frisbees?"

"Well, I think the universe has no choice but to instantly reconnect the quarks. Restore the stolen force, replace the hijacked frisbees. And to do that it has to suck energy, a whole lot of it, from the surroundings. Endothermic as all get-out."

Castine frowned. "They do it more, lately. It wears off pretty quick, but—just in the last month or so, sometimes it's got cold enough in crop circles to make metal break like glass. And there's stories about funny gravity lately too. It used to be just the electrical stuff getting messed up."

Vickery shifted uneasily in his chair. "Well, I guess if they only do it at crop circles . . ."

"But there's more crop circles all the time. All over the world. And there's gravity screwups now, too, and *extreme* drops in temperature."

Like leaks in our gas tank, Vickery thought. He pulled his phone and battery out of his pocket and opened the back of the phone. But surely, he thought as he fitted the battery into the slot, it's a really enormous gas tank! He held the phone's power button down for several seconds, then laid it on the planks beside his chair.

He poured more bourbon into both cups, then raised his and inhaled across the aromatic surface of the liquor. Far out among the night-time streets of Long Beach a siren wailed into audibility and faded. The stars were lost behind dim, low-hanging clouds. He took a sip and set the cup aside.

"Your phone's awake," said Castine.

Vickery glanced down and saw that its screen was glowing. He sighed and picked it up and ran a finger across the screen. There was a tiny red *1* over the phone icon.

"I've got a message." He touched it, then tapped in his password and held the phone to his ear, and after the automated voice noted that the call had occurred at 8:32

PM, an hour and a half earlier, he leaned sideways in his chair so Castine could listen in.

"Mr. Ardmore," came a woman's angry voice from the little speaker, "this is Trudy Plowman, Mr. Shithead's daughter in Yucaipa. FedEx delivered some damn radar machine here today, and he was here just now and took it. He ordered it, paid for it with my Visa numbers, in my name! You tell him if he doesn't return that thing tomorrow I'm calling Visa and telling them it's fraud, identity theft—nine-hundred dollars! Shit!"

The call ended. Vickery tapped the top number listed under Recent.

"Radar?" he said to Castine as the phone made the connection. "He said there must have been radar at Giant Rock, I wonder if he wants to . . ."

The call went to voicemail, but Trudy Plowman broke in as soon as Vickery identified himself.

"I'll tell him to return it immediately," Vickery said, interrupting her repetition of the complaint she'd made in her recorded message, "but to know where he is, I need to know exactly what the radar machine was."

"What? Why? Nine hundred—!"

"If I know what it is," said Vickery patiently, "I'll know where he plans to use it."

"Oh. Let me get the receipt." Trudy Plowman was back on the phone almost immediately. "Wide Range Underground Detection Locator. Ground Penetrating Radar. Does he think he's going to find gold? That damned old—"

"I'll deliver your message if I find him," said Vickery, "and I'll let you know." He tapped the red dot while Trudy

Plowman was still talking, and immediately turned his phone over and pried out the battery.

"I know where he's going to be tomorrow," he told Castine, "the Cathedral of Our Lady of the Angels, where I first met him. He was in the parking structure off Hill Street that day, working a pair of copper wire dowsing rods. I guess he figures he needs more sophisticated technology."

"Are you going to tell him to return his radar gadget? It's rough he charged it to his daughter's Visa."

"It's a family dispute, and he wouldn't listen to me anyway."

"She'll probably call you back."

"I may never put the battery back in." He looked at his watch, then folded Notchett's papers and slid them into his pocket. "It's after ten," he said, "and it's been a . . . an eventful day. I've got a folding cot in the studio, and these chairs recline." He raised his hand to prevent any protests. "And the guest gets the cot."

"Okay." Castine got to her feet. "Is there a bathroom?"

Vickery dug his keys out of his pocket and held one up as he handed them to her. "The door by the ladder leads you into the hall, and it's on your left. The old guy who owns the house is asleep by now, but lock the door just in case."

She nodded, holding the key. "Plowman said the crop circles are epitaphs over graves."

Vickery stood up and folded his chair. "I remember," he said, and tossed the chair down onto the shadowed grass.

"And he also said they're Lazaruses. I wonder if all of them are going to rise from their graves at once. Take *all* the frisbees."

"Could be." Vickery picked up the plastic trays and dropped them into a bucket at the corner of the roof.

"If the aliens—the living ones that we can't perceive, not their deformed, mass-bound ghosts—if they see the Earth like Notchett's map, then—"

"Then what Notchett called their crash lines are parallel, I remember." He unhooked the work light from the tarpaulin rope and held it up.

"Yeah," said Castine, walking carefully toward the ladder at the edge of the roof, "and all the force-disrupting columns standing up over the crop circles are parallel too, vertically. All over the world, all pointing straight up in the same direction, from that perspective."

Castine had said, *I wonder if all of them are going to rise from their graves at once,* and it fleetingly reminded him of an old Steppenwolf song lyric. And he recalled the lines from Notchett's translation of the *Theogony*: "*every season hope to steal the threads,/ And weave them into wings wherewith to fly/ Even beyond the reach of Chaos . . .*" and Notchett's afterthought line, "*But at what gelid, endothermic cost?*"

Vickery spoke reluctantly. "Plowman said there's a— that is, he said Notchett told him there's a 'grave too deep' under downtown L.A., and when I saw him at the cathedral messing around with dowsing rods—I bet he was trying to locate it. Maybe he meant it's too deep for them to rise out of."

Castine was already a couple of rungs down the ladder, but looked up, the house key gleaming in her hand. "You think he means to push the things into it?"

"No. He's—I guess he's always been—a sort of oracle.

He learns how things work, and once in a while he'll tell somebody something. Like giving us these papers."

"Do you think *anybody* is going to push the things into the grave?"

"Notchett might have meant to. Probably there's other people."

Castine nodded. "Plowman seemed to know a lot more than just what's in those papers."

"He doesn't want to see you again. Me either, by association."

She stepped down another rung, and now only her face was visible above the edge of the roof. She opened her mouth as if to say something, then just stared at him.

Vickery sighed. "We can talk about it tomorrow. There's more frozen dinners for breakfast."

Nobody had noticed that the Hispanic teenager who mowed the front and back lawns of the old house appeared in the afternoons on his puttering 125-cc Honda motorcycle and left the place in the mornings; unsurprisingly, since the house was at the far end of a cul-de-sac, between a radiator repair shop and a City of Bellflower Vehicle Maintenance Station. The 1950s ranch-style house had been vacant since 2004, to judge by the newspapers the boy had found scattered on the floor when he first took up covert residence.

His phone was now charging at an electric socket that he could reach through the folding security gate of the radiator repair shop's garage. Back in the house, he had parked his motorcycle in the dark kitchen, and blankets were hung over the bedroom window so that the light from his battery-powered lantern wouldn't show outside.

He was sitting on the cement floor, surrounded by shoe boxes, and as he sorted through their oddly assorted contents he mentally replayed Galvan's phone call: *Santiago, I think Sebastian Vickery's back in town. You've found him for me in the past—you think you can do it again? I could put the word out among the freeway-side gypsies, but I just want to know where he is, so I can get in touch with him myself. I'll pay you a hundred dollars and a month's free food at any of my taco trucks.*

Among the contents of the boxes were a couple of handguns with dubious histories, a set of lockpicks, several forged driver's licenses, a small New Testament and a half-pint bottle of peppermint schnapps with an inch of clear liquor still in it . . .

The only things he always kept on his person were the handgun he had taken from an unconscious and possibly-dead government agent three years ago, and the leather bands around his wrists, into which were subsumed the ghosts of his mother and father, killed by a hit-and-run driver on the 5 Freeway while sneaking into the country with their then-twelve-year-old son.

Santiago pushed an emptied shoe box aside and opened a fresh one; and it was evidently from the right time, for on top of the litter inside was a medallion that had belonged to an old man called Isaac Laquedem, who had taken Santiago in and taught him how to stay alive in the cold streets of Los Angeles after the deaths of his parents. Santiago lifted it aside and set it down carefully;

then pulled from the box a four-inch wire framework with a tangle of brown fabric stiffened around it.

He carefully pried at the fabric until he had separated it into two handkerchief-sized squares of hard, wrinkled linen; and he wiped his fingers on his shirt, for the brown color and the stiffness were dried blood.

A year and a half ago, after killing Isaac Laquedem, Simon Harlowe had decided that Sebastian Vickery and Ingrid Castine were essential parts of the group mind he wanted to start up, because after they drove one of Galvan's taco trucks into some kind of hell, and came back again, they were supernaturally *loosened* in a way that fitted Harlowe's plans. Even their blood was weird—a blot of it anywhere would be detectably pulled toward the living body it came from. And to be sure of not losing track of Vickery and Castine, Harlowe had got blood from Vickery on one of these cloths and blood from Castine on the other.

Got it pretty liberally, Santiago thought now, eyeing the twisted brown shapes.

On the night of Halloween in 2018, in a clearing at the bottom of Topanga canyon, Vickery and Santiago had both shot Simon Harlowe, and Santiago clung to the conviction that it had been his bullet that had killed the man.

Earlier on that day Santiago had learned that Harlowe had been tracking Vickery by using one of these cloths as a directional pendulum, and before fleeing the scene of the shooting Santiago had quickly peered through the windshields of the cars parked on Topanga Canyon Boulevard, and spotted this wire framework with its attached dark cloths on the dashboard of a Chevy Tahoe.

Always alert for something that might prove to be of value to someone, the boy had broken the car's window and snatched the frame and the cloths, and then fled.

He had thought of selling the cloths to Vickery, but the man had disappeared immediately after that violent night.

But now Vickery was apparently in L.A. again. Santiago would not sell him out to Galvan and her "secret agent types"—Vickery was a friend, or something close to that— but he might give Vickery a chance to outbid Galvan.

Santiago gingerly picked up one of the stiff cloths, and didn't detect any lateral pull. He lifted the other, and again saw no tilt in the way it hung from his thumb and forefinger.

Santiago untied one of his shoes and pulled the shoestring out through all the grommets, and he tied it around a corner of one of the cloths and held it up.

The cloth was dangling at an angle that diverged visibly from the vertical. One of them is back, he thought. He untied the shoestring and tied it onto the other cloth, and held it up. It too hung at an unnatural slant, and in the same direction.

Vickery and Castine are both in to win, thought Santiago, and certainly together. He let go of the shoestring and sat back.

Twice in the last three years Vickery and Castine had been in L.A. together, and both times it had been connected with a big disaster about to happen, which in their clumsy ways they helped to cancel. And only a couple of hours ago something very weird had happened in the L.A. River down by Rosecrans; and Santiago had heard that a bunch of flying saucers had zipped around over the Mojave Desert this morning.

Santiago made his irregular living by keeping track of what was going on in the paranormal or supernatural subcultures of Los Angeles—following people, watching the tides of the indeterminacy fields the freeways generated, acting as courier for people who didn't trust conventional means of communication.

Whatever Vickery and Castine were involved in was probably something he should take into his considerations.

He lifted the medallion, its string still stiff in places with old Laquedem's blood—once magical in the same way that Vickery's and Castine's blood was, but with no living body anymore for it to point toward—and he draped it around his neck and tucked it inside his shirt.

Santiago began putting the rest of the mementos and guns and tools back in the shoe boxes, but he kept the bloody cloths to one side, and when he stood up he glanced around uncertainly, then carried them into the kitchen and put them in the refrigerator. The house had no electricity and the refrigerator wasn't cold, but he doubted that he'd be able to sleep if he imagined the cloths slowly moving across the floor in the dark.

✧✧✧
MONDAY
✧✧✧

CHAPTER ELEVEN:
A Different Method Now

The radiator repair shop didn't open until 10:00, and Santiago retrieved his phone and charger at 8:00 the next morning. The air was chilly and he heard thunder in the distance, and he buttoned up his gray hoodie and tapped the heavy angular bulk in his right pocket.

Back in the kitchen, he hung one of the bloodstained cloths from the motorcycle's clutch lever housing and tucked the other into his left jacket pocket, wheeled the bike outside, and fastened the padlock on the door. He tromped on the kick-starter, and when the engine started he rode quietly out to the street.

The bloodstained cloth hanging from the clutch swung steadily south, and he stopped only occasionally to verify the direction as he rode south on Woodruff Avenue through the suburbs of Lakewood, but when he stopped just past Heartwell Park the pendulum was pulling to the southwest, and he took Los Coyotes Diagonal toward

Long Beach. When he came to the big traffic circle he turned west on Pacific Coast Highway—and then after riding several miles he had to reverse course and follow a residential street to the south, past jacaranda trees and apartment buildings and old Spanish-style houses.

He was riding slowly, and when an old green camper truck swept past him going the other way, the pendulum swung back.

The truck's windshield had been dusty, and Santiago hadn't been able to make out the driver, but it had to be either Vickery or Castine. He leaned the bike around in a tight half-circle and sped after the truck.

The truck drove up to Pacific Coast Highway and made a fast left turn, but Santiago had to wait for a couple of cars to pass before he could follow, and just when he had caught up and was about to pull alongside and wave, the truck steered away onto an onramp to the 710 freeway.

Santiago rode up the onramp too—nervously, for 125-cc bikes weren't powerful enough to be legal on freeways. He was able to keep the high camper shell in sight, but the truck was doing about seventy miles per hour in the middle lane, and Santiago, roaring along in fifth gear and watching his rear-view mirrors for light-bars on Highway Patrol cars, wasn't able to gain on it.

Santiago was at least able to see the truck, most of the time, as it sped for fifteen miles through Bell Gardens and Commerce, but it increased its speed to get onto the northbound 5, and Santiago gave up the chase and rode down the nearest exit lane back onto surface streets.

Now he had to stop every few blocks to hunch over the bloody cloth, and his course was a frustrating series of right and left turns; but the cloth consistently pointed northwest, toward downtown.

As Santiago rode at a more comfortable speed past liquor stores and shacky outdoor restaurants, and rows of little markets and dental offices and off-brand churches painted in different bright colors to distinguish one from another, he noticed a new sort of tent in the homeless encampments along the sidewalks—these were simply made of strings and yellow police tape and scavenged used car lot pennants, useless for blocking sun and wind, much less any eventual rain. When a man came crouching out of one of the frail constructions and began spinning rapidly and then disappeared, Santiago realized that many of the figures slouched on mattresses or shambling aimlessly were in fact ghosts. He kept his bike close to the centers of the streets, and only stopped to check his morbid pendulum in empty parking lots.

Whittier Boulevard was a straight course northwest, and he sped along it without stopping. He crossed the Sixth Street bridge and rode quickly past more crowded and malodorous tent clusters on the sidewalks—noting several of the new ghost tents—and took a northbound street, toward downtown and safer curbside spots to check the pendulum.

A few minutes later he rode up onto the sidewalk by the entrance to a four-story tan parking structure, switched off the engine and flipped down the kickstand.

He got off the bike and walked along the sidewalk, carrying the dangling brown cloth, and after a dozen steps it swung toward the parking garage's entrance. Santiago had noticed three rows of big bells in a wide opening in the wall next to the parking structure, and he recognized the place as the Cathedral of Our Lady of the Angels. The lopsided bell tower wasn't visible beyond the high wall.

Vickery or Castine—probably both of them—were obviously in the parking garage. Santiago walked back to where he had parked his bike and flipped up the kickstand, but didn't start the engine; instead he began walking it back toward the garage entrance.

There was nobody in the ticket booth between the garage's entry and exit lanes, and Santiago pushed his bike up the driveway, past the horizontal bar and into the shadowed parking structure. He quickly wheeled it to the right and stopped beside a van tall enough to conceal the motorcycle. He tucked both of the blood-stiff cloths into the gap between the tachometer and speedometer dials.

Square blue and white pillars stood at every third parking space, blocking some lines of sight, but there were not many cars parked in here on this Monday morning. Peering over the sloped hood of the van, Santiago could clearly see Vickery and Castine standing by a walled pedestrian ramp fifty feet away, near a bald old man who appeared to be holding a handgun pointed at them. A moment later Santiago realized that it must be some sort of tool, for though the old man held it steadily, the cylindrical gold barrel swiveled from side to side, and when it was pointing away the boy could see a red light on the back of it.

When the old man turned and took two measured steps in Santiago's direction, the boy recognized him by his bald head and scuffed leather jacket—it was Pierce Plowman, a flying-saucer nut he had met a few times in the freeway-side gypsy nests.

The parking garage ceiling, low and ribbed with a network of suspended pipes, provided good acoustics. "Obviously it works," said Plowman irritably, "L.A. is silty clay soil from the 134 south to the 10, with a dielectric resistance of about eight. This thing," waving the device in his hand, "sends ultrawide radar waves, very low pulse power in the C band, and these antennas are partly iron fulgurites from a sand angel out by Giant Rock. It can detect stuff thirty meters down."

The gold barrel of Plowman's hand-held device began spinning. With an air of proving a point, he crouched and made a mark on the cement floor with a piece of blue chalk. Santiago saw now that there was a curved line of such marks across the cement floor behind the old man.

"That's the last of it." Plowman stood back and pulled an old Kodak One Step camera from his jacket pocket. "I've been here since 6:00," he said, speaking around the camera as he took a picture of the chalk marks, "and I've got all the missing sections now. You two can take off, you're not part of this."

Castine burst out, "Not *part* of this? Who was it that a UAP just about *sat on* last night? A UFO, that is. And who—"

"And you're AWOL from Naval Intelligence," Plowman interrupted, "and they're probably hot on your trail right now. Go get caught somewhere besides where I am!" The camera ejected a picture, and he held it up to his face and blew furiously on it.

Santiago's pocket was warm, and when he pulled out

his phone he saw that its battery was already down to 74 percent. Somebody was apparently using it remotely, almost certainly tracking it; possibly Galvan, but from what Plowman had just said, Santiago guessed that it was the men Galvan had described as "secret agent types"— Naval Intelligence, pursuing Vickery. Big government guys like that could surely have eavesdropped on Galvan's call to Santiago, and got his phone number.

And his phone had been in one place all night, charging; and if they had followed it this morning, they would not have had to stay close enough for him to notice the tail.

They could be right outside.

Santiago dropped his phone and sprinted across the empty parking spaces and the exit lane; the three people by the ramp heard his tennis shoes squeaking on the cement floor, and were staring at him by the time he reached them.

"Up the ramp!" he gasped, "crouched low behind the wall!"

The sunlight at the garage entrance dimmed as a vehicle pulled into the driveway and paused at the ticket dispenser.

Castine, Vickery and Plowman had all instantly obeyed Santiago, and a moment later they were following the boy up the ramp, staying below the wall-mounted hand-rail, and then hurrying across a lobby past ticket payment kiosks. Once through the glass doors on the far side, they were out in a gray paved couryard, squinting up at the tall brown angularity of the cathedral towering stark against the blue sky. Again Santiago heard remote thunder.

"What are we running from?" whispered Castine. Her hand was inside her coat, and Santiago was sure she was gripping a gun.

He just waved and led them forward.

The four of them ran up a set of gray cement steps to a broad tan plaza. Castine glanced toward a garden area on the north side of it, but Santiago ignored that and ran past a row of palm trees toward a black marble doorway at the base of the sheer cathedral wall a hundred feet away. To the left of it, a decorative steel gate was open onto Temple Street and a groundskeeper truck had backed through it onto the plaza.

Santiago could hear the other three pounding along behind him. A uniformed security guard by the doorway had stepped forward, shading his eyes, but Santiago veered left, toward the open gate. When he reached it he quickly unzipped his hoodie and pulled it off, shivering in just a white T-shirt. The jacket swung heavily in his hand.

Castine, Vickery and Plowman crowded up, panting, and the four of them stepped through the gate and began walking rapidly west on the Temple Street sidewalk, in and out of the shadows of curbside pepper trees. Vickery was visibly shortening his stride so that the other three could keep up.

Santiago noticed that Plowman was still carrying the gold-barreled radar device, which he now saw had six short, crooked stone rods attached to the bottom of it, and told him sharply to put it away. Plowman nodded and hastily pulled the rods out of the device and tucked it all into his jacket, which was already bulky with the camera in his pocket.

"I've seen you in the nests sometimes," the old man said to Santiago.

Santiago nodded and made sure to hold his balled-up hoodie in front of him, out of sight to anyone back at the parking garage.

Three stout middle-aged women in sun-hats and bright, flowery dresses were strolling along ahead of them, and Castine said quietly, "Let's hide on the far side of these nice ladies."

Vickery nodded, and one by one they sidled around the women, who were soon several yards behind them.

For several seconds none of them spoke, and the only sound was the scuff of various shoes on the sidewalk.

"I'll look back," said Santiago finally. He turned all the way around as he kept walking, briefly peering between the hats of the three women, and when he was facing forward again he said, "Some guys standing by the driveway. Keep walking, slow."

"Looking toward us?" asked Vickery.

"Looking all around, it seemed like."

Castine was facing straight ahead as she strode along, but she took a moment to glance down at him. "You're Santiago. I remember you."

"I remember you guys too."

"Who," she asked him, "are we running from?"

"Probably what Mr. Plowman said," answered Santiago, "Naval Intelligence? I, uh—I think I led them to you. Well, it's Galvan's fault."

"We're parked under the Music Center up here on Grand," said Vickery. "Let's cross at the light. *Galvan?* How?"

"Some guys went to see her yesterday," Santiago said, "wanting to know how to find you. She told me they didn't offer her money, but I think they did."

"She wouldn't have acted on it otherwise," said Vickery sourly.

"Well," said Santiago, "she called me to see could I find you, and I think the *Naval Intelligence* guys got my number and tracked my phone. The battery was way down just now, and the phone was hot. I left it in the garage—along with my bike." He thought of telling Vickery about the blood cloths, but decided that *that* news could wait at least a few minutes.

"And my car's in there!" said Plowman. He scowled at Vickery. "I told you yesterday to keep away from me, and now you've got Frankie's murderers right where I left my car!"

Santiago looked at Vickery. "Your turn to see if they're coming."

"Okay." Vickery turned as if to speak to Castine, and took the opportunity to glance quickly behind them. Several men were indeed standing in front of the parking garage, one of them out in the street. They appeared to be looking in all directions.

"They're there," he said, "but they're not coming this way."

Santiago nodded, but watched traffic and sidewalks, ready to sprint away from the others if black cars should suddenly drive up onto the sidewalk to block their way. He glanced up at Vickery, then at Castine, and wondered what sort of trouble they had got themselves into now. Vickery was tanned, and his hair had more gray in it than it had a year ago; Castine was maybe thinner than she had been when he'd last seen her, and she looked tired.

We've worked together in the past, Santiago thought, but whatever their troubles are now, they're not mine.

At the Grand Street intersection the crosswalk light had just turned green, but Santiago glanced to the east and said, tensely, "Wait! Cross two at a time, slow, and break up Vickery and Castine. Be tourists."

Plowman grudgingly offered Castine his arm, and the two of them stepped forward into the crosswalk; four seconds later Santiago nodded to Vickery, and they sauntered along several yards behind the others.

They regrouped at the corner, and crossed Grand Street paired again. On the far sidewalk, finally out of sight of the parking garage, they all began walking rapidly south.

Castine glanced from Santiago to Plowman. "We can all drive around for a while, and drop the two of you back there after they've gone."

"After we get a few questions answered," added Vickery. "For instance," he went on, looking to the side at Santiago, "I get it that some guys who might be Naval Intelligence apparently followed you here by tracking your phone—but how did *you* find *us?*"

"Ahh," said Santiago on a long exhalation. "I came to warn you about Galvan and those men. And I told you to duck and hurry up that ramp, right?—so they wouldn't get you?"

"Right. And thanks for that. How?"

Santiago looked back toward the cathedral corner, but the men he had seen come out of the parking garage entrance had not followed them to the intersection.

"A year and a half ago," the boy said slowly as he strode along, "I shot that Harlowe man, down by the beach. Well, you did too. A couple more people got shot that night, and everybody ran away. Not me. I went to the parked cars—"

On the other side of Vickery, Castine stopped, then hurried to catch up. "Oh my God," she said softly, "I bet Harlowe had them in his car! Did you break into his car?"

"It didn't seem like a big thing," said Santiago defensively, "after killing him."

"Had what in his car?" said Vickery; then, "Oh! Yeah."

"Where's *your* goddamn car?" growled Plowman. "I've got to get out of this whole area."

"The cloths with our blood on them," said Castine, ignoring Plowman. "Where are they?"

Santiago shrugged miserably. "On my bike. Shoved into the top of the fork. But those guys won't know what they are."

Vickery looked across Santiago at Castine. "Would they know what they are?"

"I told you yesterday at Cole's," said Castine crossly, "No, they—they haven't—"

She paused, and Vickery raised a hand, prompting.

Castine shook her head. "Let's hope those guys don't find them."

They had reached the entrance to the Music Center's underground parking garage. "In here," said Vickery. "I think we'd better start driving in big fast circles."

Joel Finehouse led Vilko Cendravenir and the three Sensitive Assignment Specialists back into dimness of the parking garage.

There had been no difficulty in following the target phone, which had clearly been carried by the young man on the little blue Honda, until the bike had exited the 710 freeway. Down in the surface streets, the young man had ridden such an erratic course through the city, pausing frequently to get off the bike and hunch over something, that they had followed a block or so back, trusting the phone's signal to keep them from losing him. They had not seen him ride into this parking garage, and had driven past and had to find a way back to it—and when they had turned in and parked, the phone had been lying on the cement floor near the motorcycle, but there had been no one in the garage.

Finehouse had immediately sent two specialists up to the cathedral's plaza level, and one of them had radioed to report that a security guard had seen four people run out of the plaza by a gate onto Temple. Finehouse, Cendravenir and three of the specialists had rushed out onto the sidewalk, but there had been pedestrians visible in both directions, none hurrying, no group of four, and no visible boy in a gray hoodie. It seemed likely that the four runners had got into a car.

Finehouse tucked the radio back into the pocket of the casual green windbreaker he wore today, and looked around the extent of the dim garage.

The little motorcycle was the only vehicle in the garage whose engine was hot, and another specialist, a man Finehouse believed was named Atkins, was just finishing the job of attaching a GPS tracker inside the bike's left side cover and snapping the cover back in place.

Cendravenir lit one of his clove cigarettes. "I suppose

one of the four people running out of the gate was your man Vickery."

"Probably." Finehouse waved the smoke away and walked to the center of the exit lane. He looked down at the blue chalk marks that made a curve across the cement floor, then at the sunlit garage entrance.

"The kid's phone was motionless all night," he said, mostly to himself, "down around Bellflower, and at eight he rode down to Pacific Coast Highway, then he rode up the 710 for fifteen miles and got off in East L.A. At that point he started the stop-and-go zig-zag pace till he got here. He must have been tracking Vickery, by sight and then by remote, same as we were tracking *him*." To his annoyance, he heard a trace of east Tennessee in his voice, and cleared his throat. "We need to talk to the kid."

Cendravenir dropped his cigarette and brushed sparks off his turtleneck sweater. "Are we going to wait for him to come back for his bike? I haven't had breakfast."

"We can't wait around here," said Finehouse. "We'll catch up with the boy later, when he's in some less populated area."

"Chief," called Atkins, "this is weird."

Finehouse walked over to where Atkins was standing by the bike; two stiff brown rags lay on the seat now, and Atkins was wiping his hands on his shirt.

"They were shoved between the tach and the odometer dials," Atkins said.

Finehouse saw that each rag had a wire tied around it, and he gingerly took hold of a wire and lifted one of them.

"That's dried blood," said Cendravenir. "You remember how he kept stopping the bike to mess with something? I bet he was using these as pendulums to point toward Vickery."

"You think that's Vickery's blood?" asked Finehouse.

"It's not fresh, obviously," said Cendravenir, "but it was Vickery he was supposed to be trying to find, right?"

Finehouse wrinkled his nose in distaste. This assignment was already outside the bounds of sensible science, but now it was beginning to sound like witchcraft.

"And these chalk marks on the floor mean something," Cendravenir added. "Magic symbols, maybe."

"One of you guys photograph the marks," said Finehouse tiredly. To Cendravenir he said, "Can that happen? That pendulum business?"

"I never heard of doing it with blood," said Cendravenir, "but people dowse with pendulums all the time, and anybody's vulnerable to all sorts of stuff if they leave samples of their blood lying around." He lifted one of the rags by its attached wire and held it out in front of him. His hand was steady, and the brown rag stopped swinging after only a couple of seconds; and it was hanging a few degrees away from vertical, toward the southwest.

With his free hand, Cendravenir pointed in the same direction. "I think Vickery is that way."

He might be, thought Finehouse—assuming startling new extensions of science can be discerned in vulgar litter in the hands of society's detritus.

"I wonder why he needed two," said Cendravenir. He lifted the other rag, and after a few seconds it hung with a visible inclination in the same direction as the other. "They both seem to point to Vickery."

"One's pointing to Agent Castine," said Finehouse with weary certainty. "They have a history together...and apparently at some point somebody took some of their blood, to keep track of them."

"That's a history, all right," allowed Cendravenir, putting the things back down on the motorcycle seat. "Breakfast?"

Finehouse, staring at the two blood-stiffened rags, didn't answer.

Commander Lubitz had briefed Finehouse on Vickery and Castine. He had mentioned that the Transportation Utility Agency, where Castine had been employed until 2017, had tried, with some evidence of success, to summon and use ghosts in aid of motorcade security. Lubitz believed something traumatic happened to both Vickery and Castine at around that time, something that left them with what he called distempor—imperfect mooring in discrete sequential time.

When the TUA had been closed down in a flurry of nondisclosure mandates, most of its personnel had simply been fired or pensioned off—but Ingrid Castine had been transferred to the Office of Naval Intelligence, and then to the Office of Naval Research, because of certain anomalies in her record and behavior.

What these branches of the government had begun doing was covertly testing her for possibly useful extrasensory skills. In briefing Finehouse, Lubitz had described arranged situations in which, for example, an important Top Secret file in Castine's custody was taken from her desk while she was in the rest-room; when she had returned to her desk, a hidden video camera in her office had shown her several times freeze, staring into space, after which she had gone unerringly to the person who had taken the file. And one time when they'd known that she'd be eating alone in the cafeteria at noon, they had told one of her co-workers to occupy Castine's usual table half an hour earlier and leave a red-banded ONI flash-drive on Castine's usual seat, as if by accident; and when Castine had arrived at the vacated table, she had stood and stared at the seat for nearly a minute, and then returned the flash-drive to the co-worker.

Telepathy, clairvoyance? Lubitz had come up with the distempor theory instead: that in these instances she had looked into the recent past.

Lubitz had told Finehouse that he had immediately thought of Sebastian Vickery. Vickery and Castine had both been subjected to the same ordeal, whatever it had been, in 2017, and so Vickery might have acquired the same ability that Castine had.

But tracing Vickery had been difficult.

Under his real name, Herbert Woods, Vickery had been a Secret Service agent, but after he killed two TUA agents in 2013 he had effectively disappeared until briefly resurfacing four years later to participate with Castine in the TUA debacle. It was known that he had previously worked for Anita Galvan's "supernatural evasion" car service, and Lubitz had found evidence that he had on at least a couple of occasions been quietly employed by an LAPD detective to *describe the recent past* of fresh crime scenes. Good enough evidence of distempor.

And so Lubitz had conceived Operation Pleiades, on

the then-dubious supposition that—since UAPs moved in ways that seemed impossible within the limitations of normally measured sequential time—two minds simultaneously violating the boundaries of the moment of now, in a location noted for UAP activity, might attract and focus the attention of the theoretically atemporal UAPs.

Operation Pleiades was a private hobbyhorse project of Lubitz's, and he had planned to try it later in the year, after definitively locating Vickery and conducting further tests of Castine's ability. But everything had come to a head very quickly—Lubitz had learned that he was soon to be transferred to a European embassy, and three nights ago Castine had fortuitously confirmed her ability by looking a few minutes into the past in a crop circle in England.

Lubitz had arranged Castine's immediate reassignment to ONI and forced the re-scheduling of the fake-UAP drop, and had planned to capture Vickery and Castine together, and then fly Finehouse and Cendravenir to California to do the actual operation some days later. Vickery and Castine would then have been induced to look into the past, thus ideally summoning a cluster of UAPs, at which point Cendravenir was to have done his mimicry trick with a bunch of chrome-plated aluminum spheres. Lubitz believed the UAPs would have perceived the mimicry and responded, establishing the beginning of communication.

Hah! thought Finehouse now.

Given Vickery's documented involvement in the flying saucer subculture, it had been a natural but costly mistake to draw him out of hiding by faking a UAP crash at Giant Rock and having Castine be there to identify him. But Lubitz should have considered the possibility that the two of them might—as had evidently happened— simultaneously do their distempor trick there and then.

"What?" said Finehouse now. "Oh—we can stop at a McDonald's and get some stuff to eat in the car. Atkins, fetch those . . . those *pendulums*. I believe we're tracking Vickery and Castine both, now."

And he would have to report this new development to Lubitz. It would be good to capture both Vickery and Castine, but Finehouse wasn't looking forward to phrasing the report: *Using rags soaked in the blood of the subjects as directional pendulums* . . . Lubitz would probably take it in stride, and anybody hacking their communications would surely assume it was code, but Finehouse resented the circumstances that made it necessary.

He walked to the SUV and opened the passenger side door. "Let's move on. Atkins, are they still together?"

"Both in the same direction, anyway. Pretty directly south now."

"Okay," said Finehouse, "everybody get in the vehicle." He reminded himself that this was science, arguably—but he felt as if he'd swallowed a watermelon seed, or closed a pocket knife that somebody else had opened.

His phone buzzed in his pocket, and he pulled it out and touched the screen. "Finehouse."

"I've just now had a report from Agent Yoneda," came Lubitz's voice. "She's unwisely chosen to go solo, but she's still functioning, and she's given me an address for Sebastian Vickery, though he's likely to have abandoned it."

"We're tracking him now. He's moving."

"By that phone number you got last night?"

"That, at first," said Finehouse. He took a deep breath. "We're using a different method now . . ."

CHAPTER TWELVE:
Parasitoid Wasps

- -

Vickery had driven south on Grand and turned right on First Street, and now he was speeding southeast between parking lots and low, government-looking buildings. Plowman was crowded against the passenger-side door, with Castine between him and Vickery, and Santiago was peering in through the open back window of the cab. The side windows were rolled down, but the sun was in their faces and Vickery wished he'd taken off his denim jacket before getting in. The radio was tuned to a talk station, nearly inaudible.

"Okay," said Plowman finally, "What did you mean, a UFO nearly sat on you?"

Castine quickly described what had happened at Vickery's trailer the night before, and what the Russian had said. From the corner of his eye, Vickery could see that Santiago was listening wide-eyed.

"And," Castine concluded, "it happened because that GRU agent and I were tipped into echo-vision when

Vickery here stepped into it deliberately, out at Giant Rock. That agent said we made a triangle of ... punctures in *now*. He said it was a—" She turned to Vickery.

"Localized radiating discord," Vickery said, "like out-of-phase radar waves." He turned north on Spring Street. "We'll go west on Sunset then south on the 110, loop around. If they've figured out the blood rags, this should keep 'em running in circles."

"Radar waves," muttered Plowman.

"And so," Castine went on, "the thing that threw the shoes into the pool yesterday morning fell into the pool last night, in the L. A. River bed, and ... became a ghost, the thing with the big hands." She nodded. "And it was gelid as all hell."

"Gooey?" put in Santiago, clearly mystified. "The pool?"

"Cold," Castine told him, "and *the pool,* the surface of it, means our—universe, reality." To Plowman she added, "And lately crop circles have been very damn cold, and there's more of them all the time, these last few months. It's—Sebastian, tell him about the gluons."

"Sebastian," said Plowman. "Vickery." He squinted sideways at Vickery. "There's stories about you." He turned to Castine. "And I bet you're the woman in the stories. Hah!" He slapped his thigh. "You flew a hot-air balloon out of Hell, is how it goes."

"It was a hang-glider," said Vickery. "But in Frankie Notchett's poem ..." He explained their interpretation of Notchett's added lines in the *Theogony*. "So some kind of higher-dimensional entities are deflecting the electromagnetic, gravitational and Strong Nuclear force-carrying particles out of our four-dimensional reality by way of crop circles, which you said are their graves."

"Yes," said Plowman, "and I said they're Lazaruses. And I guess they're a lot damn closer to their mass resurrection than I thought. It's like when cicadas all come out of the ground on the same day, after being buried for some prime number of years." He tapped his distended jacket. "And I've got the complete negation symbol now. I'll give it to you."

"Negation . . . is that the 'deeper grave' you told me about once?" Vickery caught a green light and sped across the 101 freeway overpass, glancing to the side at the tight ranks of cars in the lanes below.

"Yeah," said Plowman. He took a deep breath and turned to Vickery. "You're bullshitting me—a hang-glider?"

"You had to be there," said Castine soberly.

"If," said Vickery, "each crop circle—and there are even the equivalent of crop circles in the ocean, according to Notchett's charts, and in deserts; and," he added with a mirthless bark of laughter, "add one in the L.A. River bed!—if each of them hijacks our forces at once to fly beyond the reach of chaos . . . where does that leave us?"

"I imagine our forces would regenerate themselves instantly," said Plowman. "But at the cost of a winter like maybe they get on Pluto."

"This is *soon?*" asked Santiago.

"I don't know," said Plowman. "What's 'soon' in these kinds of terms?"

"I wish I had the latest reports from England," said Castine, "but I think it's soon."

Plowman jumped when Santiago tapped him on the shoulder. "This deeper grave," the boy said, "it's the *lineas de muerta* under the freeway? Lines of death?"

"Eh? I guess so—it's where one of 'em withdrew, thousands of years ago—dug a hole and pulled it in after itself, no way out, end of story. Its pattern isn't symmetrical like most crop circles—it's like a big knot, and it spells *finito* to others of that tribe."

Santiago narrowed his eyes and nodded. "People been putting sugar and honey on the streets, up Broadway and on Sunset, around the big robot. Trying to make the devils come to the lines. *Negation,*" he said carefully. "But people don't know where all the lines are."

"Robot?" said Castine. "A robot now?"

"It's that Arts High School on the other side of the 101 from the cathedral," said Vickery. "It looks like a giant robot pointing a ray-gun at the cathedral."

"And a lot of lines of the symbol are under it," said Plowman. He leaned to the side to twist his head and look at Santiago. "People know about this? Sugar and honey—like a trap?"

"Sure," said Santiago, "but they don't know where all the lines are, and the lines are mostly under buildings anyway." He looked at Vickery. "And you got Russians trying to blow you up, and Navy guys that want to put you in jail?" When Vickery rocked his head and nodded, the boy went on, "You all can't just drive this truck in big circles forever to keep away from everybody."

"Oh," said Vickery, catching the boy's meaning; and he added softly, "Good Lord."

Castine gave a short exhalation that might have been a cut-off nervous laugh. "*If* they're using the blood cloths. Maybe they're not."

"We could just stop somewhere," said Vickery, "and see if they show up and arrest us, or kill us. Then we'd know." His chest felt hollow, and the dew of sweat on his forehead wasn't entirely caused by the cramped seating and Santiago breathing on his neck.

"But *can* we go see *her?*" asked Castine. "What will she . . . *do?*"

"Last time you saw her you punched her in the stomach," Santiago reminded Vickery. "And took her car."

"I saw her again after that," said Vickery defensively. "Ingrid and I returned her car the next day." He shifted his hands on the steering wheel and added, reluctantly, "After I stole it, yeah."

"We returned it with the seats soaked in stagnant water and smeared with tar," Castine recalled mournfully, "after our dip in the La Brea Tar Pits. Just for you and I to get away alive, you had to convince her that you'd saved her family from the egregore group mind."

"At least she let us go," said Vickery. "After I swore to pay her a hundred a month for eternity."

"Sounds like my daughter," grumbled Plowman. "My Goneril. My Regan."

Vickery recalled that Goneril and Regan were the two heartless daughters of Shakespeare's King Lear; and he wondered if Plowman might have another daughter, corresponding to Cordelia, Lear's forsaken loyal one.

"Is there a Cordelia?" Vickery asked.

Plowman frowned and waved the question away.

"You should return that radar gun," said Castine. "Get the refund on her Visa card."

"You talked to her—!" Plowman began, but Santiago interrupted him.

"See?" said the boy, nodding to the right. "Lines of sugar."

Blue tarpaulin tents and shopping carts and folding chairs were crowded on the sidewalk, and the people slouched or walking among them didn't seem particularly aware of the blurred white streak that extended between a couple of tents and into the street. A few yards ahead another streak, at a slant, also stretched from the sidewalk fence and partway across the street. Passing car tires had erased segments of it.

"The lines are behind the fence too," said Santiago, "and in the dirt on the other side of the street. There's more lines, all the way up to Cesar Chavez, and west. People can't afford that much sugar, but they buy it anyway, to try to trap the devils. And they don't even know where all the lines are."

Castine and Plowman didn't say anything.

After several seconds Vickery spoke up. "I think I should approach her alone. Galvan, not Plowman's daughter."

"She'll just sell you to the ONI agents," said Castine hopelessly.

"Maybe, maybe not. But you and I need a vehicle that conceals us from our pursuing blood." To Plowman and Santiago, he said, "If I can get one of her shielded cars, we can drop you two off back at the cathedral parking lot. The ONI agents will probably be gone by then. And if Galvan won't cooperate—well, you're on your own, and better off away from us."

Plowman had been silent while the truck had rolled over the costly, useless lines of sugar on the street, but now he shifted against the door and cleared his throat.

"No," he said. "Damn it."

Vickery waited a moment, then said, "No?"

"I—have to!—take you someplace first. If I can remember how to get there. It's been many years." His head jerked slightly, with a shudder or a suppressed laugh. "They're a secretive lot, but they'll let you in if you're with me. Or throw us all out. Sort of like approaching your Galvan woman. You need to be careful, though—these people do *not* want the aliens to be exposed to the negation symbol. But they do know stuff you need to know."

Vickery waited, and Castine finally asked, "Who are they?"

"They call themselves the Zeta Reticuli Chess Club," said Plowman. "They've got a place up in the hills."

"Huh!" said Castine. "The Russian was pretending he was one of them, for a while. What are they, besides a chess club?"

"Oh—they're like a monastic order, playing anti-king chess in shifts, twenty-four hours a day for the last fifty years or so. Several generations."

Vickery didn't even ask what anti-king chess might be. "I'll leave you all in a parking lot," he said, "and talk to Galvan alone."

He felt Santiago's breath on his neck as the boy whistled silently, and peripherally he saw Castine shake her head; but nobody objected.

The breaking surf two hundred feet to her right was a steady muted crash and retreating hiss, punctuated by the cries of seagulls circling in the cloud-streaked sky. She had heard distant thunder intermittently, but the sky was quiet now. The only other people visible along the broad bone-white beach were a couple of surfers in black wetsuits a hundred yards away, carrying boards down toward the water. Rayette Yoneda kept an eye on them, but only from habit.

Tacitus had told her to be at the Hermosa Beach pier at 10:30 AM and to walk south through the loose sand to the second lifeguard tower, and after ten minutes she had plodded her way to the first one, which was just an empty blue-painted shack on a raised platform of criss-crossed beams. She had been making her way along a track in the sand that had been flattened for vehicles, but walking in the yielding sand was still tiring, and she wished Tacitus had told her to follow the paved road that ran in front of the houses and apartments a hundred feet to her left, on the far side of the volleyball nets. She supposed he had deliberately told her to take a route that would make progress slow, and running difficult. The cold wind from the sea made her turn up her jacket collar and clench her fists in her pockets, and the second lifeguard tower looked half a mile away.

She was not carrying a newspaper—Naval Intelligence had not killed Frankie Notchett.

Last night she had got Tacitus to drop her off at a Hertz car rental at the Long Beach airport, and had then driven a newly rented Toyota Camry down here and got a room at a place called the Sea Sprite Motel. This morning she had found a cell phone repair shop and bought two thirty-dollar Consumer Cellular phones, and had finally called Lubitz on one of them.

It had been a difficult call. She had started by telling him plainly everything that had happened since she had dropped her official phone into the ketchup box behind the IHOP in Yucca Valley yesterday, including all the extraordinary details of the UAP's descent in the riverbed and the subsequent manifestation of the cortical homunculus, and what Tacitus and Vickery and Castine had said afterward, and the intrusion of the pair of alleged GRU assassins.

At the end of it Lubitz told her, with some perceptible reluctance, that she would at least for a while continue to be an active agent in the field—and she had known that he would soon ask her for her current location and the license plate of her rental car. She had hoped to evade that, for she didn't want Finehouse and a fresh team of Sensitive Assignment Specialists intruding on her efforts to persuade Tacitus to formally defect.

Quickly, to keep her promise to old Tacitus, she had asked how Francis Notchett had died.

Lubitz had told her curtly that any information about Notchett was compartmented; and she had insisted that she needed access to that particular compartment in order to function in this situation.

Lubitz had audibly shifted in his chair. "The various

possible directions of your . . . *whole future,* you realize,"
he had said in a reflective tone, "will very much depend
on your actions in these next few hours. I'll give you this:
he hanged himself with his belt, on a doorknob."

"Why?" When Lubitz had let several seconds go by
without answering, she had pressed, "Dammit,
Commander, I'm in the field, I'm in the animal *soup* with
these people!"

Lubitz had sighed, and she had thought she could hear
him drumming his fingers on his desk. "Notchett didn't
approve," he'd said finally, "of our plan to establish
communication with the UAP intelligences. He said
they're like *parasitoid wasps,* was his phrase, which lay
eggs in other insects, and that they'd . . . *destroy the world*
when they made their exit from our plane, as he believed
they meant to do soon. He said we have to kill them
somehow. The man turned out to be just a lunatic, you
see. He killed himself because he imagined we would use
coercive methods, force him to tell us what he knew about
the alien intelligences."

He imagined that, did he, thought Yoneda.

And then, scarcely believing it, she had watched her
hand extend to the side and drop the phone into a glass
of water on the bedside table.

I am not an orphan, she had told herself. Tacitus
abandoned his service, or was abandoned by it, but I'm
just exercising initiative in the field.

She had quickly picked up her old broken phone and
flipped it open.

"Pray for me, father," she had whispered.

❖ ❖ ❖

An overweight man in a blue sweatsuit was now trudging through the sand from the street by the apartments. His scanty, wind-blown hair was dark and he was now clean-shaven, but Yoneda recognized Tacitus. They both kept walking on their intersecting courses, and when they were only a few yards apart, Tacitus stopped.

"No need to walk all the way to the second tower," he said, speaking just loudly enough for her to hear him over the boom and hiss of the surf. "I've been walking along the next street over, parallel to you, and there's been nobody keeping up with you." He cocked his head. "You are not holding a newspaper."

"Notchett killed himself," said Yoneda, "while in captivity." She told him what Lubitz had said about Notchett's reason for suicide, parasitoid wasps and all, and when she had finished, Tacitus just stared past her at the sea, squinting in the wind.

"I believe it," he said. "And—excuse me, but I have nobody else with whom to be frank—I wonder if taking defector status, and working with your people, might not lead me to wear a stout belt and note the locations of doorknobs."

It occurred to Yoneda that she too had no one else with whom to be frank, aside from the absent father she imagined in her inert wind phone.

"We can set ground rules in place," she said. "Assurances, guarantees." She ran her fingers through her short black hair.

"Ground rules, guarantees—consisting of what?"

"I don't know. Think of something. Wouldn't you *like* to establish some sort of communication with those beings?" She looked around in all directions, at the houses and the beach and the sea and the distant long centipede of the Hermosa Beach pier. She assured herself that Tacitus would have been careful in coming here, and that it was very unlikely that a sniper was lying prone on one of the rooftops. "And isn't the GRU out to kill you now?—along with all the rest of us? You don't *have* to be an orphan."

Tacitus's face was pale where his beard had been, and the dark brown dye in his hair was sharply at odds with the wrinkles around his eyes and the newly visible lines in his cheeks.

"I need to talk to Frankie," he said, and held up his hand to forestall her obvious objection.

"Okay . . ." Yoneda said cautiously.

"After I dropped you off at the airport, I went to my apartment—fast, because I had been ordered *not* to interfere with things like bombs under trailers, and of course my handler knows my address. I packed some things and fled, never to return." He too looked around the beach, and was clearly reassured by its windy emptiness. "Would you like to get breakfast somewhere?"

The shave and dye-job don't make you look any younger, Yoneda thought; then frowned in self-reproach, for it was obvious that Tacitus was not interested in her sexually.

"May as well," she said. "Where are you parked? I'm in a lot back by the pier."

Tacitus started walking across the sand in that direction. "I abandoned my car last night, and engaged several taxis to get here."

"Old fashioned."

"Uber requires that you use a phone."

"Fair enough." Yoneda took his arm and turned him toward the lane that ran in front of the houses. "Not through all the sand again. So how are you going to . . . talk to Frankie?" She wondered if Tacitus had something like her wind phone, and meant a hypothetical sort of talk; then she remembered Castine saying that she and Vickery had allegedly seen Notchett's ghost yesterday.

Tacitus nodded and walked beside her, away from the surf. "I took two books from my apartment," he said, "a copy of Hemingway's *The Sun Also Rises*, the true first edition with the word *stopped* misspelled on page 181— that should get us some cash at a good rare book store—and a tattered paperback copy of *New UFO Breakthrough,* which Frankie loaned me a year or so ago."

"Useful reference?"

"No, it's misguided and naïve. But it belonged to him, you see—he read it, even made some pencil notes in it. It should constitute what the freeway-side gypsies call a handhold, a way for Frankie's ghost to manifest, if I summon it."

Yoneda forced herself not to ask if Notchett's ghost might join them for breakfast; and then she had to restrain a smile, for there were several Mexican seafood restaurants locally—the ghost would probably want the seafood cocktail called *vuelve a la vida,* return to life.

Instead she asked, with a straight face, "Did Vickery and Castine have a handhold for it when they saw it yesterday at that cemetery?"

Tacitus gave her a wry look. "They said Plowman had

some papers Frankie had given him. That was evidently a close enough reach."

"Touché." She was certain that it was a waste of time, but to humor the old man, she said, "I have a motel room—do you want to call him there after breakfast?"

"No, the ocean has no current—well, not the kind of current I need. It doesn't cast an indeterminacy field. I've got to be very close to a generating freeway, in one of the gypsy nests."

My hard-won career, Yoneda thought wonderingly, *now seems to depend on getting this old fool to defect. If he goes bumbling along on his own, getting some low-level job and consulting ghosts in freeway-side gypsy nests on weekends, the FBI will surely track him down. Maybe I should let Finehouse and a Sensitive Assignment Team just take him.*

But, "Okay," she said.

As they plodded toward the lane at the inland edge of the sand, she let herself wonder, gingerly, what a ghost might actually look and behave like, and if it might be susceptible to argument, or misdirection, or even charm. *Frankie*, she thought, *if you fuck this up for me, I swear I'll get a priest to exorcise you—hard.*

CHAPTER THIRTEEN:
Lineas de Muerta

Vickery walked quickly east on 8th Street, past *carnicerias* and narrow check-cashing and eyebrow-threading businesses, and shops whose Asian signs and tinted windows gave him no clue about what goods or services might be dispensed in them. He had left Plowman, Santiago and Castine in the truck, with the ignition key, in a nearby parking lot with two exits and no gates. Castine had wanted to come along with him, but he had reminded her that Galvan didn't like her, and—to her objection that Galvan didn't like him either—pointed out that at least he was paying the woman a hundred dollars a month in recompense for the various damages and destructions the two of them had inflicted on her vehicles over the years.

Galvan's yard was only half a block ahead of him; the chain-link fence, masked with green netting, was obliquely visible, and the gate was of course pulled open at this hour. Vickery hurried to it and stepped up the broad driveway.

He made himself walk at a more leisurely pace between the two rows of cars, toward the long maintenance bay and the silver Airstream trailer that sat off to the left. On the other side of the lot was the two-story building, its windows painted over white, in which Galvan had her office.

As he neared the open bay doors, squinting into the dimness and wondering if any of the several mechanics visible had worked here long enough to remember him, a voice from his left called, "You get right the fuck out of here."

Vickery looked toward the trailer. A bald man in a T-shirt now stood in the doorway, squinting in the sunlight and glowering at him.

"Hi, Tom," Vickery said. "She'll see me." He waved toward the office building. "Is she in there?"

"I'll call her. Wait where you are till she tells the guys to beat the shit out of you."

Vickery nodded, and decided not to compound his imminent offense by presuming to pour himself a cup of coffee at the cart by the maintenance bays; he had left his .45 with Castine for the same reason. He took a deep breath of the chilly morning air, spicy with the smells of solvents and chorizo, and tried to relax his shoulder muscles as he exhaled.

He remembered being one of Galvan's drivers, back in 2016 and 2017, taking fares to airports and churches and consulates in Galvan's supernaturally shielded cars, and he reflected that it had not been all that different from when he had been a Secret Service agent standing post along one secured boulevard or another, in one city or country or another, as motorcades drove past. Assuring secure transportation.

And he had worked in Galvan's fleet of taco trucks too, parking alongside malls and high schools and construction sites to sell tacos and enchiladas to the faces that crowded up to the little service window.

It seemed there had never been a particular *place* where he worked; or even, considering his plan to move his trailer again, where he lived.

"Vickery," came the woman's well-remembered voice from behind him. He turned toward the building and saw Anita Galvan striding toward him, her face creased in a wide smile. "A guy's going to give me fifteen thousand dollars for telling him where you are. *Contrata.*"

Having expected this development, Vickery held his arms out to the sides so that the mechanics she had just summoned would have no trouble frisking him.

He believed the word *contrata* was Spanish for *hire*, and he had never understood why she used it as a signal to her employees that whoever she was facing was to be immediately and forcibly detained. He knew without looking around that at least one of the mechanics would now be standing off to the side and holding a gun pointed at him, and he didn't jump when hands from behind began patting him down thoroughly.

"You don't need to call the guy," Vickery said. "He'll be here before long anyway. He's tracking me by my blood, the bloody cloth that guy Harlowe had, in 2018— remember?" At any rate he may very well be, Vickery thought. He went on before she could speak, "That's why I need to borrow one of your supernatural evasion cars."

He turned his head to look toward the street, past one of her men who, sure enough, was holding a semi-automatic pistol aimed at his middle. "Very quickly, if you don't mind. The, uh...world?...hangs in the balance." He ventured a smile. "Again."

He held the smile, but he could feel sweat at his hairline in spite of the cold breeze. A rumble of thunder rolled across the cloud-streaked sky.

Galvan was staring at him with no expression. After several seconds in which, uncharacteristically, there was no chugging of an air-compressor or clang of a dropped wrench from the open bays, she looked past him and clearly got a shake of the head from one of the mechanics, indicating that Vickery wasn't armed. Then she held open her khaki jacket to show the black rubber grip of a revolver tucked behind her wide leather belt.

"You—" she said to Vickery, and seemed unable to think of anything further to say. She started to turn away, then spun and drove her fist with surprising force into Vickery's abdomen.

Vickery bent double and fell heavily onto his shoulder on the asphalt, unable to breathe. His throat spasmed, trying to draw air, but his diaphragm was paralyzed. His cheek rolled on the gritty asphalt and his hands clenched and unclenched as if trying to encourage his lungs to work.

At last he was able to suck air in, in noisy whoops, though he immediately lost it all each time in painful involuntary coughing—but eventually he was able to breathe in and out steadily. He sat up, wiping drool and sweat from his cold face and wondering if the ONI agents had arrived yet.

"I," he gasped, squinting up at Galvan, "think you ruptured—everything."

She squatted and grinned at him face to face. "The guy can take you to a hospital when he shows up. I owed you that since August before last, when *you* punched *me* in the stomach. And I did you a favor here, you know—you insulted me in front of my men, and really I should have killed you for it. They'll probably think I'm getting soft, and I'll have to crack a few heads."

Vickery started to get up, then thought better of it and just looked around. The mechanics had all gone back into the bay and seemed to be deliberately occupying themselves with work at benches along the far wall. One, before turning away, gave Vickery a mildly sympathetic glance, and Vickery believed he remembered the man from his days as a driver here.

"I didn't—" Vickery began; then reconsidered and said, "How did I insult you?"

She laughed and slapped his face hard. She began counting on her fingers. "Three years ago you stole my Ford Taurus and left it in Hell, then you stole one of my taco trucks and left *it* in Hell too, and I . . . *forgave* you for those!—because you saved my nephew—"

"And your whole family. And everybody else in L.A."

"Do you know what that car and truck *cost?* And then! After that! A year and a half ago you punched me and stole my best car! That one you returned, but even after I changed out the wrecked seats it never stopped smelling like a swamp."

Her eyes had narrowed as she spoke, and Vickery thought she might be about to hit him again.

"And," he said hastily, "that time when I took your best car I saved your nephews and nieces who had looked at that brainwashing coloring book. They'd have—"

"I know, their minds would have been eaten by that egregore thing. But today you come in here and say give me another of your cars, Galvan! Quick! Kiss off all that money the Navy man will give you! You say it in front of my men!"

"I'm sorry, that was—abrupt, but—"

"And some kind of 'nother damn save the world? What now, zombies, dinosaurs?"

Vickery took a deep breath and let it out, and decided that he might not, after all, have suffered some internal injury. "Up around the cathedral on Temple Street, and north to Cesar Chavez, have you seen the lines people are making on the streets? With sugar, and honey?"

Galvan rocked her head back and gave him a quizzical look. "Sure. It's to catch spacemen. I have family around there, they say there's lines under the streets, and if the spacemen can see enough of the lines they'll be stopped, like a chicken if you draw a line in the dirt and lay him down with his beak on it." She must have caught Vickery's incomprehension, for she added impatiently, "The chicken can't stop staring at the line, can't move. He's hypnotized. When I was a kid there was sometimes six or eight chickens in the yard, laying down like that."

"Okay, yes, it's like that." Vickery restrained himself from looking again toward the driveway. What if the ONI agents had followed the course indicated by *Castine's* blood cloth? They might be arresting her right now. "There's a guy who has figured out all the lines," he went on quickly, "and wants us to make the, uh, spacemen look at them, and that will—yeah, like the chickens, it'll make 'em . . . stop." He was still sweating.

"My nephew Carlos borrowed money from me, to buy sugar to make lines in the streets. He's plenty scared about the spacemen." She shrugged. "But you remember Carlos is crazy."

"Dammit, boss—" He paused; it had been a long time since he had called Galvan boss. "Trust me, the *spacemen* aim to fly away, but for fuel they're going to take all the Earth's heat." Close enough, but he sounded insane even to himself. "The Earth will freeze. No joke. And the spacemen have been very active lately—it's probably going to happpen soon. Those people around Cesar Chavez, your family, they sense it."

"Hah!" Galvan smiled and squinted at him. "You *believe* it!"

"Yes, I—dammit, yes, I believe it."

She looked at her right hand, and flexed it gingerly. "You've been right about some things before, I think."

"You *think?* Do you remember the—"

"Shut up."

Galvan straightened up smoothly and extended a hand to Vickery, who took it and got to his feet like an infirm old man.

"You see that 1970 Cadillac DeVille?" Galvan said, pointing at a gleamingly white 20-foot long sedan in the bay. "That's my best car, not a single microprocessor in it, and a big damn EMP generator in the trunk. And it's insulated against every kind of attention—ghosts, angels, devils, electromagnetics, baptism-signature scanning . . . it's hard to even focus your eyes on it for very long. The fare's a thousand an hour, and I got a waiting list for rides in it. Rich old folks hiding from God, mainly." She grinned and punched him in the arm. "I wouldn't let the *Pope* borrow it, if he was to come here and beg me."

Vickery nodded, trying to conceal his mounting anxiety. He forced himself not to look at his watch.

It was Galvan now who cast an uneasy glance toward the street. "Why does the Naval Intelligence man want you so bad?"

Vickery burst out, "They don't want us to draw the line in front of the chicken! They want to *talk* to the chicken!"

Galvan bit her lip. She gripped Vickery's arm and said fiercely, "Okay, *pendejo*. I got a busy schedule today, lots of urgent rides, but over there's a 1998 Dodge Intrepid, and it's plenty shielded enough to at least hide your blood like you don't even exist."

Vickery squinted at the dusty car, noting that a stick of bamboo stood where an antenna should be. No radio reception, probably.

Galvan went on, "Is Betty Boop with you?"

Betty Boop was the name Castine had given when first introduced to Galvan. "Yes, around the corner, along with that kid Santiago. The Navy guy is following her blood too."

She looked past him and called, "Tonio! The keys to the old Dodge, *rapidamente!*" To Vickery, she said, "Save my family again and I'll cut your debt in half. And that Dodge isn't much, but if you leave *it* in Hell, I really couldn't go on doing business unless I have you killed. You're way past due already, if I wasn't so sentimental."

"I understand," said Vickery, and when Tonio tossed

the keyring he caught it and limped toward the Dodge. Thunder boomed across the northern hills.

Vickery pulled the Dodge in behind his camper truck and got out without turning off the engine. He hurried to the passenger side of the truck, and when the door proved to be locked he banged on the window. Behind the glass, Plowman frowned at him.

"Out!" Vickery called. "Everybody into the Dodge!" He hit the window again as Castine opened the driver's side door and Santiago opened the camper hatch and hopped to the pavement.

"Castine," Vickery said to her over the truck roof, "grab the briefcase—and the first aid kit from under the seat. And Yoneda's gun! Quick, quick, everybody!"

When Plowman and Santiago had climbed into the back seat of the Dodge, Castine got in on the passenger side and Vickery folded himself painfully into the driver's seat.

Castine had tossed the briefcase and Yoneda's gun on the floor and was holding the old metal first aid box. "Did she hit you, or did she get one of her guys to do it?" she asked, rocking in her seat as he started the car and reversed away from the camper truck.

"She did. A debt of honor." He looked at the street and snapped, "Get down out of sight!—you too, Pierce!"

He stopped the car at the parking lot entrance while a black SUV drove past slowly; and when it had caught a green light and driven on north past Eighth Street, Vickery swerved out of the lot and caught the end of the light to make a left turn on Eighth. He remembered to look at the gas gauge, and was reassured to see that the tank was half full.

"Can I get up?" said Castine at the same time that Plowman said, "Dammit, Bill, what did you see?" His camera and ground-penetrating radar device had fallen onto the floor.

"An SUV that might have been them. Ingrid, get a couple of gauze pads out of the kit—and the razor." He was driving fast, peering ahead. "What," he muttered, speaking to himself, "a bus, a delivery truck . . ."

Castine had torn open a cardboard package and was holding two squares of loose-knit white cotton. "You're right-handed?" he said. "Cut a left-hand finger and get blood on one of them."

She didn't protest or ask why, and when she had done it he took his left hand from the steering wheel and held it toward her; he winced when she cut the knuckle of his little finger and blotted the blood with the other pad.

"You better stick them on some vehicle quick," she said, wiping the razor on one of the pads. "If Harlowe's old blood cloths go inert for too long back there, the ONI guy is going to think about how close it is to Galvan's lot." She put the razor back in the box and closed it.

They were driving past markets and offices and restaurants that all had Korean letters over the doors, and when he was approaching Western Avenue he swerved into a strip-mall parking lot, grabbed the bloodied gauze pads from Castine, and opened the door. He took a deep breath, got out and straightened up in spite of the ache in his abdominal muscles, and walked as fast as he could to the intersection.

To his relief, an orange L.A. Metro bus was idling at the curb, the entire side of it covered with a wrap-decal advertising *Star Trek: Picard,* and the LED lights in the destination sign on the back read *207.* He recalled that the 207 line ran up Western to Franklin Avenue in Hollywood.

He hurried across the sidewalk and stood by the back of the bus. Below the three stacked right-side tail-lights was a broad black composite bumper, and when the air brakes released with a hiss and the bus began to move, he reached out and tucked the two spotted gauze pads behind the upper edge of it.

He walked quickly back to the Dodge and got in. The engine was still running, and he waited for a gap in traffic and then accelerated to make a left turn on Western, heading south.

"If they *are* using our blood to track us," he said, "they'll chase that bus up past Hollywood Boulevard. I'll just get out of the area and then we can get lunch—there's a good Korean barbecue place on Olympic—though we'd better eat in the car. Castine and me, anyway." Seeing Plowman's irritated puzzlement in the rear view mirror, he added, "This car is insulated against supernatural attentions."

The explanation sounded crazy, but Plowman's eyebrows lifted and he nodded.

"And if they are following the blood," said Castine, nodding toward a four-inch metronome mounted on the dashboard, "the insulation's working."

The metronome's pendulum was intermittently swaying back and forth, no more than would be caused by the motion of the car.

All of Galvan's stealth cars were equipped with metronomes like it, each one capped with a lump of something organic—bone, wood, leather—into which a ghost had been subsumed. The ghosts were inert, but they made the pendulums knock back and forth quickly when they were in a strong supernatural field. Rapid clicking could indicate a particularly powerful field being generated by the motion of free wills on a nearby freeway—which was cause for caution—or it could be in response to a reciprocating hunting signal, in which case the car's location had been supernaturally detected—which would be cause for immediate alarm.

Plowman demanded to know what Castine was talking about, and Vickery explained the metronomes. "It's like piezo quartz crystals that contract when an electric current runs through them," he said in conclusion.

"Huh!" said Plowman, sitting back. "Does that Galvan woman sell those things? I'd like have one in my car, one in my house . . ."

"And one on a hat," agreed Castine. "This negation symbol you found under the cathedral parking lot—this 'deeper grave'—what is it, exactly?"

"I'll show you when we're parked."

"Can you front me the price of lunch?" asked Santiago from the back seat.

"Sure," said Vickery. "You saved us from getting caught by the ONI team. Naval Intelligence," he added, seeing the boy's blank look.

"After leading them to us," whispered Castine just loud enough for Vickery to hear.

Vickery made a right turn onto Olympic and drove for

half a mile past obscure medical and chiropractic offices, then steered into a parking lot on the south side of the street, in front of a two-story building with a blue-tile roof and a couple of restaurants occupying the bottom floor. The one on the right, Bak Kung, was fronted with false stonework between the windows, and it was to this one that Vickery directed Plowman and Santiago, after giving them five twenty-dollar bills.

Thunder rumbled in the distance, and Castine remarked that none of them were dressed for rain. Vickery replied that it wouldn't matter unless the car's roof leaked.

When Santiago and Plowman had got back to the car ten minutes later, carrying several bags, paper plates were passed back and forth and over the front seats, and soon the air inside the car was stuffy with the smells of marinated beef and spicy chicken and seafood pancakes. Plowman took a deep sip of his iced tea and then topped up the cup from a flask.

When everyone had finished and Santiago had carried the plates and empty cartons to a trash can and hurried back, Castine turned around in the front seat to stare disapprovingly at Plowman.

"So what exactly is this 'deeper grave'?" she asked him.

Plowman took a long sip of his fortified iced tea. "You saw Frankie's map? The three crash lines? That's where the things happened to intersect with our sort of spacetime, and a lot of them got simplified down to mass—*died* is the closest word for it. And the patterns they leave when they die, your crop circles, induce *more* of them to die, so the lines are always getting more emphasized, more compelling. You said yourself the numbers of them are increasing."

Plowman drained the cup and set it on the floor. "I told you yesterday that they don't exactly think—they're deterministic, and it was the . . . cloud of supernatural *in*determinism on Earth that tripped them up, confounded them, caught them in a sort of accretion disk. Free will all over the place down here, violation of strict cause-and-effect everywhere you look. So they're stuck here, and more and more of them are what-you-might-call dying."

"Lazaruses," prompted Castine.

"Yeah. All the crashed ones, the ones in the crop circles, have found themselves occupying our stuff, our atoms, which are like a lot of stretched rubber bands—they're gonna release 'em all at once and slingshot themselves right out of their entanglement with our irrational local spacetime. It's like they got stuck in Alice in Wonderland, and they're gonna bounce back out to where they came from.

"But, see," Plowman went on, "*a few* of the ones who crashed kind of committed suicide. I mean, they died, but they also turned all the way inward, negated their potential to rise again." He stopped talking and looked out the window, and the lines around his mouth and eyes seemed deeper now.

After a few seconds of silence, Santiago asked, "You gonna take me back to my bike?"

"Oh, right," said Vickery. He started the truck's engine and backed around to face the street.

"Go on," said Castine to Plowman.

"Those suicide ones," said Plowman, "they left patterns, too, symbols, but not on the surface. This ... species? ... mostly comprehends surfaces—topology. The patterns the suicide ones leave are *off* the surface—underground." He cocked his head. "Maybe they do 'em up in the air, too—but those wouldn't show up, or last. Anyway, I know of four sites where these underground patterns are. One's in the mountains in Nepal, one's in Peru, one's in Africa—and one's under L.A., between Sunset and Temple."

"The *lineas de muerta*," said Santiago softly, watching the traffic as Vickery made a right turn on Olympic. "Where the people are making lines with sugar and honey."

"Yeah," said Plowman, "I admire the effort they're making, but you need the whole symbol, and anyway these *entities* have got no reason to look at lines of sugar, they're not houseflies. But if they could be *forced* to see a full negation symbol, they'd *comprehend* it—helplessly—"

"Like laying a chicken down in front of a line in the dirt," said Vickery. He was driving east on Olympic, and sped past the Western intersection in case the SUV he had seen might have doubled back.

He noticed that Castine was staring at him blankly. "A chicken?" she said.

But Plowman nodded. "Exactly. They'd all crystallize, fossilize, die for real."

Castine shifted around to face him. "You've got the whole symbol now?"

Plowman reached into the pocket of his leather jacket. "I only had to fill in the corner the *L.A. Times* left out.

Yeah, I've got the whole thing now, as of this morning."
He pulled out a dozen Polaroid photographs and some
folded sheets of paper.

He handed the papers over the top of the seat to
Castine. "You gotta line 'em up, they're photocopies of
newspaper pages, which were too big to fit whole on a
photocopier."

Vickery glanced at the sheets as Castine held them up.
"What are they?"

"It's copies of a couple of pages of the *L.A. Times,*"
Castine said, "from January 29, 1934." She raised one and
read, "*C. W. A. Will End Abuses . . . The Four Horsemen of
the Apocalypse,* that looks dire . . ."

"That's the top of the page, about an art exhibit," grated
Plowman. "Look at the copy of the bottom of the page."

Castine looked at the next sheet. "Oh—'*LIZARD
PEOPLE'S CATACOMB CITY HUNTED*'—is that it?"
When Plowman nodded, she read, "'*Engineer Sinks Shaft
Under Fort Moore Hill to Find Maze of Tunnels and
Priceless Treasures of Legendary Inhabitants.*' Uh . . . '*the
secrets of the Lizard People of legendary fame . . . Warren
Shufelt, a geophysical mining engineer . . . a radio x-ray
perfected by him for detecting the presence of minerals and
tunnels below the ground, an apparatus with which he says
he has traced a pattern of catacombs and vaults . . .
continued on page 5.*'"

She gave Vickery a tired, skeptical look, which
Plowman caught.

"So look on page five," the old man said, "you've got it
there."

Castine looked at the next page. Vickery saw her visibly

restrain a laugh, but her voice was level as she read, "'*Did Strange People Live Under Site of Los Angeles 5,000 Years Ago?*' And it says there's gold down there."

When Vickery glanced at the page he saw what appeared to be a map of very crooked interconnected roads. Castine held up another page, which was evidently the bottom half of the map.

"The spacemen are lizard people?" asked Santiago.

Castine gave Plowman a brightly inquiring look.

"No, that was just what a clan of the Hopi Indians was called. There was also the Snake People, the Sand People, the Cactus People, I don't know what all, and none of 'em had anything to do with this besides living in the area. But white folks heard 'Lizard People' and pictured something you'd need Spider-Man to deal with."

"I saw that movie," said Santiago.

"Well, they weren't that. And what Warren Shufelt's radio x-ray machine detected weren't catacombs, they were the lines of the alien's suicide pattern."

Vickery looked at Plowman in the rear view mirror. "No gold?"

"No gold. That was all a misunderstood Hopi myth. But the suicide inversion compacted sand and stone down there, dense enough to register on a detector." He leaned across the seat and pointed at the two papers Castine was now holding. "Put them edge to edge," he told her. "Shufelt did track the lines—see?—back when you could walk everywhere, when they hadn't yet built a big robot on Fort Moore Hill—and the lines are all right there, except for that area in the bottom corner where the *Times* overlaid a picture of Shufelt and his machine." He leaned forward to wave the photographs in front of Castine. "Those were under the cathedral parking garage," he said. "Here, take the pictures. Now you've got that missing section too."

Castine hesitated, then put down the papers and took the photographs. "*We've* got it? So what do we do with it? Make a poster and wave it in the air?"

Vickery saw tension behind her reflexive sarcasm, and touched her arm. She nodded and slumped in her seat, squinting at the tall glass front of the Koreatown Galleria as it swept past.

Plowman's face was bleak. "I don't know. Figure something out." He leaned back and exhaled. "Shit. I really wish all this had come up about ten years ago—or ten years from now."

When he didn't go on, Vickery started to speak, but Plowman was talking again. "I was a contracted security guard at Groom Lake in '67 and '68. That's Area 51, at the Nevada Test Site."

The old man's voice was low, and Vickery had to lean back to hear him. Castine had turned half around in her seat, and her face had lost its derisive squint.

"I was mainly assigned to the North Gate," the old man said, "what we called Second Base, right off Highway 375, and if any unauthorized people—hunters, campers— happened to drive up the road, I told 'em they had to turn back because of unexploded ordnance in the desert. Actually the Air Force was testing weird new airplanes out there, like what they called the Oxcart, which I saw a couple of times. Looked sort of like a modern Stealth bomber, but longer and flatter."

Vickery caught Castine's eye and shook his head slightly. Let him work through whatever it is, he thought.

"But in '68," Plowman went on, "the Air Force wasn't doing much of anything there. They'd got hold of a lot of Soviet radar systems from Arabia or somewhere, and set 'em up in the hills around Groom Lake to see how they worked, and the Russians were mad about that. And then the Air Force got an actual working MiG to play with—that was the Russians' supersonic fighter jet, very secret design—and the Russians got so mad they sent up orbital satellites that passed over the test site every forty-five minutes! So the Air Force guys couldn't even bring the Oxcart out of the hangar because the commie satellites would photograph it from space. Every day was what we called Nightshot Condition, meaning don't do anything satellites might see, and the Air Force guys got so bored that they started to paint silhouettes of impossible airplanes on the runway, and heating 'em with portable heaters, so the Russian satellites would photograph 'em and pick up the heat signatures and Moscow would think the Air Force had jets shaped like octopuses and eggbeaters."

Vickery switched lanes to pass a Metro bus, and wondered if the ONI agents had already caught up with the Route 207 bus and discovered that the blood-spotted gauze pads—if the agents were indeed following those—had led them astray; and he wondered fretfully what other means ONI might have for finding himself and Castine.

Olympic slanted southeast at Alvarado by a car wash whose arches and tile roof made it look like a drive-through Spanish mission. Ten more minutes would get

Vickery's mismatched company up to Temple Street, where they could drop Santiago off. And then—a chess club?

The skyscrapers of downtown were visible ahead now. Castine was slurping through a straw at the last bits of ice in her cup.

"But one day in '68," Plowman continued slowly, "they were using X-band and C-band radar frequencies at the same time that they had the very low-frequency L-band Soviet radar systems turned on, and somebody had painted a thing like a, a goddamn Moebius cat's cradle on the runway—and then—" He cleared his throat and went on, "And then the sky was full of silver globes darting from horizon to horizon. Impossible changes in velocity, like . . . like laser dots if a bunch of people in a dark room were whipping laser pointers around. Too fast to be actual *things*, see."

Vickery heard him pick up his cup from the floor and shake it, then grunt as he put it down again. "Well," Plowman said, "you saw 'em. And that night all the field sensors went off at once and we had a Category Five alarm, '*Bogey*,' which meant airborne intruder, which . . . was an understatement. A glaring white light, and this incandescent thing came down out of the sky and landed out by Pahute Mesa at the northwest end of the range. And when we drove out there with weapons and spotlights, there was nothing but an acre-wide sand angel." He sighed. "At first."

Plowman didn't go on, and Vickery glanced at him in the rear-view mirror. The old man's tanned, seamed face was like weathered mahogany.

"What after at first?" asked Santiago.

"There was . . . a *thing*, there. Not like your thing with huge hands," he said, apparently speaking to Castine, "those didn't start showing up till much later. This was . . . as if you took a child and stretched him till he was six feet tall; big eyes, spidery white fingers. It—moved, quickly."

Vickery could almost feel the old man's shudder.

Plowman was silent for several seconds; then, "After that," he went on more easily, "it apparently fell apart, just blew away as a cloud of sand. By daylight we could see that the sand angel was a bunch of interconnected rings, like the Audi logo." He looked up. "Triple-band radar and a cat's cradle snagged the thing's attention, and it died. I suppose there'll be a column standing up on that spot too, soon, drawing all the heat for miles around, when all the things rise from their graves."

"At the cemetery," said Castine, "you said they don't think, as we understand it. Uh . . ."

"I said what I said."

None of them spoke for several moments; then Vickery cleared his throat and nodded toward the papers Castine was holding. "Well," he said, "even if your *negation* symbol there is accurate, we can't get radar to summon the things." He turned to look briefly at Santiago. "We'll be at the cathedral in a couple of minutes. I'll—" I probably owe it to him, he thought, "— I'll park around the corner and wait, and if guys are monitoring the parking garage you run back to the car and we'll scram."

Plowman rolled his eyes. "You've got your localized radiating discord, when you and Irene switch to viewing the infrared past in tandem, right? That might—"

"Ingrid," said Castine.

"My bike will probably be safe there for a while longer," said Santiago. "It's a Catholic cathedral. I can ride along with you guys for a while."

"Sure," said Vickery tiredly, "Catholics don't steal stuff. Pierce, how do I get to this chess club?"

CHAPTER FOURTEEN:
Visiting Old Friends

"It says no trespassing." Yoneda looked back at Tacitus, who was still getting out of her rental Toyota parked at the cul-de-sac curb. She was standing in front of a solid-looking wooden door in a long six-foot-high cinder-block wall, and she nodded at the two signs bolted to the door. "It says it twice." Over the top of the wall she could see tall eucalyptus trees bending in the wind, and hear the fast-pulse rush of cars on the freeway beyond.

Tacitus closed the car door and came puffing up to her. "Certain people have had keys made," he said, reaching into his pocket. "If anybody asks, you can pretend to be a city worker, can't you?"

Yoneda looked around nervously as the old man fitted a key into the door's lock, but nobody was stepping out of the Craftsman-style houses along the street or peering from the windows of the one visible apartment building.

She was carrying a six-pack of Budweiser beer in a plastic 7-Eleven bag, and it probably wasn't very cold anymore. This would be the third "freeway-side gypsy nest" the two of them had visited; the first one, off an exit of the 101 Freeway north of Hollywood, proved to have been colonized by belligerent homeless folk since Tacitus's last visit, and the second one had been physically occupied by a car that had crashed through a shoulder rail, and had been surrounded by ambulances and police cars.

Tacitus got the wooden door open, and the two of them shuffled through onto a narrow dirt path shaded by overhanging boughs and bordered on the freeway side by thick oleander bushes. From the left Yoneda heard a rapid knocking, and she quickly looked in both directions along the path as Tacitus closed the door behind them, but nobody else was immediately visible; she peered through the bushes and saw a dirt and ivy slope that led down to the busy lanes of the 10 freeway. The breeze, sifting through the shrubbery, smelled of car exhaust and rosemary.

"This way," said Tacitus, picking his way along the path toward the knocking sound. Castine jumped when thunder cracked overhead, followed by a diminishing rumble.

"There's hardly a cloud in the sky!" she said, and was annoyed to hear the petulance in her own voice.

Tacitus looked back. "That's not thunder."

Yoneda pursed her lips and resolved not to ask the indicated question. "What's that knocking sound?" she asked instead.

Tacitus stepped into a clearing that was littered with beer cans and cigarette butts, and he nodded toward what appeared to be an upright broomstick rocking rapidly back and forth on a hinged iron housing set firmly in the dirt, striking the raised edges of the housing at each stroke. Yoneda saw that the swinging wooden pole was capped by the skull of a small animal.

"I'm glad traffic is moving down in the lanes," said Tacitus, "we need a good current." He pulled from his jacket pocket the battered paperback copy of *New UFO Breakthrough* and began riffling the pages. Sunlight filtering through the surrounding greenery gleamed on his damp forehead.

He paused and lookd up. "I won't ask you personal questions," he told Yoneda, "but it's entirely possible that you won't be able to see Frankie's ghost. If I succeed in summoning it, you may simply see me apparently talking to myself. But if you *can* see the ghost—don't look it in the eye."

Yoneda was bleakly amused to realize that she was disappointed. It seemed there would be no actual ghost after all, just this old fool pretending, perhaps believing, that he was talking to someone who wasn't there.

"Okay," she said.

She put down the bag with the six-pack in it and stretched her fingers. After getting five-hundred dollars for the Hemingway book at a rare book store on Santa Monica Boulevard, and topping up the Toyota's gas tank, Tacitus had insisted that she buy the beer to mollify any vagabonds who might be loitering in whatever nest they found. She swore to herself that she wasn't going to carry the bag one step further.

Tacitus held the book open and touched a page. "Frankie," he called softly in the direction of the slope. "Frankie, it's Tacitus. You're free of those men now. Tell me what they mustn't know."

The breeze sighed through the leaves, and the traffic down the slope whined past, and after a few seconds Yoneda shifted her feet in the dirt. She would really have to call Lubitz again soon.

"Frankie," Tacitus went on, "we've seen your notes, but we don't know what to do. Help us."

For another half a minute the two of them stood still; and Yoneda had just opened her mouth to finally protest at how ridiculous this whole enterprise was when suddenly there was another person in the clearing.

She jumped backward, caught her balance, and stared down at the dirt, breathing deeply. Her heart was pounding—she could see the newcomer's white sneakers, and they were floating an inch or so above the dirt. From long, disciplined practice, she forced herself to stand steady and ready, and to be acutely aware of everything around her.

The leaves on all sides thrashed, and for a moment Yoneda thought a whole phalanx of ghosts was manifesting itself, and she was about to allow herself to run; but the leaves subsided and no other figures appeared. Her gaze crept up the wavering figure of what was evidently *actually* Frankie Notchett's ghost—black dress shoes now, and jeans, a tan sweater—but didn't focus on the vaguely youthful face under a thatch of brown hair.

"It's the rings," quavered the ghost in a high, piping voice that made Tacitus wince, "the shining rings in the sea at night . . . that's how you can approach them."

"Okay, Frankie," Tacitus said gently, "tell me about the rings in the sea."

"Out past the jetties, in the open ocean—you can't

know where they'll be, you just watch . . . hope, or fear, that they'll appear . . ."

"Buncha *boo*shit," came a hoarse voice from the bushes.

Yoneda spun in that direction; a burly, deeply tanned old fellow with white hair tumbling over the shoulders of a threadbare woolen coat was pushing aside a branch to step into the clearing.

"Got no rings in my seat," the intruder added belligerently.

Yoneda noted that the man's ruptured old shoes pushed aside twigs and dragged tracks in the dirt; clearly *he* was not a ghost. She crouched and opened the 7-Eleven bag, and when she straightened up she was holding one of the beers.

"Here." She held it out to the ragged intruder, who snatched it. "Shut up."

She looked back at the ghost. It was rippling now, as if it were painted on a clear sheet of plastic. "But when it *was there*," it said in evident windy lament, "at last, on the deck in the cockpit, I—ran!—to the controls!—and gunned away, out of the ring!" The figure broke up into segments, then re-formed. "Ach—don't look at me!"

The old hobo had opened the beer and chugged three big swallows, then wiped his mouth on his sleeve and looked around at the clearing with no particular interest. Clearly he couldn't see the ghost.

A phone buzzed in the pocket of Yoneda's jacket, and her hand automatically pulled it out; but it wasn't the second Consumer Cellular phone she'd bought this morning. It was her old ruined flip phone—her wind-phone, her *kaze no denwa*.

Her vision narrowed until the old phone in her hand was all she could see. Her arm twitched with the impulse to throw it away—this impossibly vibrating phone, along with the tormented apparition hovering in the clearing, was a stark contradiction of her certainties in the world—but instead she gripped it so tightly that she felt its buzzing in the bones of her hand.

The ghost broke through her shock with a shrill whine: "You think *you'd* have had the guts to stay, Tacit Ass? You think you're *better* than me?" Even without looking at its face, Yoneda saw the hole of its mouth expand widely.

Recalling what Vickery and Castine had said last night, she grabbed Tacitus's arm with her free hand and yanked him aside as the ghost's tongue suddenly extended six feet, slapping against the cinder-block wall. Tacitus fell heavily to the dirt, face down, and the tongue began to retract and then evaporated.

Yoneda was watching the ghost, ready to jump to one side or the other, and she became aware that she had opened her old flip-phone. "Daddy," she whispered into it, "make this thing go away!"

From the phone came a clearly audible voice: "Rayette!"

All at once the ghost rotated ninety degrees to horizontal, and was now obviously suspended in mid-air.

The hobo stepped right through it, still casually holding his beer can. "I can see that phone got no battery," he mumbled. "Lemme look at it."

The ghost rotated further, and was now upside down; and then kept rotating, faster, until within seconds it was spinning like a propeller behind the hobo.

Tacitus had scrambled to his feet, and was staring

wide-eyed at the spectacle. Abruptly the ghost disappeared, and the surrounding shrubbery shook once again.

"C'mon," said the hobo, "lemme see your phone." He grabbed at it, and when Yoneda pushed him away he swung a fist at her face.

She ducked it, but had to halt her instinctive counterstrike when Tacitus's foot pistoned horizontally into the man's midsection. The beer can flew to the side and the man grunted explosively and sat down hard.

Tacitus recovered his stance and strode past Yoneda. "Come on," he panted, "we've got to get to Frankie's boat."

Yoneda paused to hold the old flip phone to her ear. She mouthed the word *Daddy?* but the phone was once again just an inert construction of metal and plastic.

The breeze was chilly on her face, and she impatiently cuffed away tears and hurried along after Banach. "His boat?" she said. "Why?"

"Logs, notes—the state of his compass—"

"You need to let me take you to—ONI, safety, damn it!"

"After, maybe."

Yoneda rolled her eyes. "You can have the godddamn beers!" she called back toward the clearing.

Following Plowman's directions, Vickery got off the 101 Freeway at Gower and turned straight up Beachwood. As the street mounted toward the Hollywood sign visible on the green hills in the distance, Santiago was peering out the side window at the neat apartment buildings behind geometrically trimmed hedges . . . and the turreted and balconied houses that were as big as the apartment buildings and set well back from the street ... and the grass strips, bright green in the mid-day January sunlight, that extended from the curbs to the sidewalks.

"I never get this far north," he muttered.

"This place we're going is further up," said Plowman. "It was some kind of Theosophical temple in the '20s, but after the Battle of Los Angeles in 1942—"

"The what?" said Castine, turning around.

"One night in February of '42," said Plowman impatiently, "some silvery things showed up in the sky, and everybody thought it was Japanese bombers because an actual Jap sub had shelled an oil field near Santa Barbara the day before, and a lot of Navy radar systems along the coast were activated. So the Coast Artillery Brigade fired a million machine guns and a ton of anti-aircraft shells at the things in the sky. They wrecked a couple of buildings and cars in Long Beach, but of course they didn't hit any flying saucers, and eventually the Air Force said it had just been meteorological balloons. *Any*way, right after that night, a psychic and/or schizophrenic woman called Mimsy Borogrove—"

Castine was chewing a fingernail. "'Twas brillig, I'm sure," she said quietly.

"Mimsy Borogrove bought this temple," Plowman went on, overriding her, "and started up a cult to try to contact the space people. At first she ran it as a square-dance club, with apparently some very weird calls and steps, but after a while she decided that anti-king chess was the best way to connect with the flying saucers." He sat back and crossed his arms. "Last time I was there it still looked like some kind of temple. I should know it when I see it."

After less than a mile, Vickery drove between the two

stone gates that once marked the entrance to the 1920s Hollywoodland development, and then he was steering Galvan's old Dodge up the curling, narrower extent of Beachwood Drive. Here walls or garages or thick hedges crowded right up to the curb, with just roofs or chimneys or upper stories visible on the slopes beyond them, while towers and the top edges of long white walls indented the blue sky at the hill crests on either side.

At a gesture from Plowman, Vickery turned left up a narrower lane, and Castine said, "That sign said road closed—local traffic only."

"Pierce is visiting old friends," Vickery told her.

"I hope," said Plowman faintly.

"You used to be a member?" Castine asked him.

For several seconds the old man just looked out at the close shrubbery the car was passing. "Not really," he said finally. "Borogrove's grand-daughter and I were . . . an *item,* you could say, in the late '70s, early '80s. She'd have been about thirty." He sighed shakily. "I don't know that I was entirely a gentleman, in those days."

As of course you are now, thought Vickery, and he knew Castine must be thinking something similar.

"What are we hoping to learn there?" he asked.

"What?" said Plowman, clearly called back from other thoughts. "Oh, I told you. They've made some connection with the UFOs, and kept it up. First with square dancing, then chess. They're—" He paused, then went on carefully, "It's like they're a seismograph with delusions that it can solicit earthquakes, okay? But they *are* a seismograph, as it were. If anybody knows the resurrection timetable, it's them."

"Why do we say we've come to visit?" asked Castine.

"I'm going to tell them that Bill here," Plowman said, nodding toward Vickery, "is a friend of mine, and today he told me about taking you out to Giant Rock yesterday to see the crashed flying saucer, and you both saw all those things in the sky. Go ahead and describe that, but don't mention your thing in the L.A. River last night, it's too coincidental that you were both there for that too. And don't mention any of that crap about infrared retro-vision. And girl, don't say you're with ONI, or anything about crop circles. You're just Bill Ardmore's Pasadena girlfriend, okay?—probably a waitress somewhere."

"Sister," said Castine.

Plowman squinted from her to Vickery. "I'll want to hear the story about that hang-glider one day. But the thing is, these chess-folk do effectively monitor the UFOs. If we can get 'em to open up, they can give you a pretty accurate picture of what the things are doing, and when."

"I wish they were still square dancers," said Castine. "I like the way they dress up."

"This crowd dresses like hippies," said Plowman, "or they did in the '80s. And for God's sake—listen!—no mention of the negation lines, right? Put the papers and photos under the seat now." He looked sideways at Santiago. "Not about the sugar and honey lines either."

Santiago nodded. "The *lineas* are no good anyway. The giant robot is sitting on most of them."

"Stupid robot," muttered Castine.

"Guns under the seat too," added Plowman. "They might frisk us. Hell, they might even have metal detectors by now."

Vickery thought about it for a moment, then reluctantly pulled the .45 from his jacket pocket and leaned down to tuck it under the seat. Castine was doing the same with the revolver that had belonged to old Tacitus until last night; Vickery heard it clink against Yoneda's .380 semi-automatic. Vickery wasn't altogether surprised to see Santiago lean forward to reach behind himself and then push something under the driver's seat.

The road wound up between overhanging pine trees now, and between the houses were ivied slopes held back by retaining walls made of horizontally laid railway ties. Some of the retaining walls looked ready to collapse, with the vertical anchor ties leaning toward the road. Vickery recalled that such anchors were called "dead men," and they reminded him of the wooden metronomes the freeway-side gypsies set up in their nests. He glanced uneasily at the little metronome on the dashboard, but it was still just rocking with the motion of the car.

After a few more ascending turns they had left the trees behind, and the bunker-like houses they passed on the right seemed to be single-story because their other floors extended down the side of a ravine not visible from the road. Yuccas and sparse bushes dotted the brown slopes on their left.

"Around the next curve," said Plowman, leaning forward. "There's a driveway paved with pennies instead of gravel, must be a million dollars worth. Drive slow and everybody keep your hands visible—last time I was here they were all hippies, like I said, but *armed* hippies."

Vickery steered around the sharp turn, and the white building that swung into view did indeed look like some kind of temple. A turret with narrow vertical windows flanked a tall arched façade, and as he drove cautiously along the road in front of the place he saw stairs in the shadow of the arch leading up to a second floor, with the top of a dome visible further back. Several pickup trucks were visible beyond the turret, and two men in white robes stood in the shadow of the arch.

"Driveway on your right," said Plowman. "Hands visible, everybody!"

Vickery turned into the driveway, which appeared to be paved with broken glass, glittering in the sunlight, not pennies.

Plowman waved through the windshield at the pair in the shadows. "Park here and walk up."

Vickery switched off the engine and pulled up the emergency brake lever, then opened the door, letting a chilly breeze smelling of clay and creosote sweep into the car. He looked down before he stepped out, and saw that the driveway was paved with what must have been thousands of broken pairs of eyeglasses; and under the fragments of glass and wire and black earpieces he could, here and there, make out the brown disks of an infinity of pennies.

The two men walked out from under the arch, their white robes flapping in the breeze as they trudged across the dirt yard. As he stepped out of the car and straightened, Vickery saw that their heads were shaven and their faces were at once both pale and weathered-looking—squint-wrinkles around the eyes, lines down the cheeks.

Plowman had got out too, and called, "Afternoon,

gents! I'd be much obliged if you could tell Linda Loma that Pierce Plowman is here with two eyewitnesses to the business out by Giant Rock yesterday."

He had to repeat his name, but then the two robed men told Plowman's party to wait where they were, and went back through the arch and up the stairs into the building. Vickery peered up at the glaringly white façade, and noticed that the stepped top edge bristled with tiny black and white and red spikes. To keep away birds? he wondered.

"Linda Loma was your old girlfriend?" he asked Plowman quietly as Castine and Santiago got out of the car, stepping carefully on the broken glasses.

Plowman pursed his lips, perhaps at the term *girlfriend,* then nodded. "She was born in Loma Linda, see. They had a theory in the '60s about linking people's names with the land—there's a woman named Laurel Canyon, even a guy named Forrest Lawn."

Both of the robed men came back down the stairs and walked out onto the broken glasses and pennies. "Who's the kid then?" one asked.

"My nephew," piped up Castine. "I'm watching him for the day."

"Well, purification is for everybody," said the other man, stepping forward while his companion stepped back. "Arms out to the side, please," he said to Vickery, and when Vickery complied, the man patted him down efficiently.

Second time today, Vickery thought sourly.

The man did the same with Santiago and Plowman, and then just had Castine open her jacket and turn around while he poked her ribs and stomach and the small of her back with one finger.

The man nodded and turned away, and Vickery and his three companions glanced at one another—variously baffled, irritated and uneasy—and followed the man across the yard, under the high arch and up the stairs.

A woman was standing in the open doorway at the top of the stairs, also wearing a white robe, and their guide sidled past her into the building. Stepping out of the sunlight into the sudden shade and peering up, Vickery was at first only able to see that the woman was tall, with short gray hair and a round face.

Her voice was a startling falsetto: "You waited until the last, Pierce. But you're here, bless your recalcitrant soul. Becky will be pleased, I know. But who are your friends?"

"These two," Plowman said, nodding toward Vickery and Castine, "witnessed the apparition at Giant Rock yesterday morning." He visibly thought of saying more, but made do with just nodding again.

"They're welcome," said Linda Loma. She raised her hands, and her teeth showed in a smile. "In the end you came back, Pierce! To atone."

She stood aside, and after a moment's hesitation they all cautiously filed up the stairs and into a wide, high-ceilinged lateral hallway with framed abstract paintings on the walls. The floor was black-veined marble, and the hallway smelled of air-conditioning and, faintly, marijuana.

Vickery glanced at Plowman, wondering how the old man was taking the word *atone*. Plowman's eyes were narrowed, and he briefly held up crossed fingers.

Five wooden chairs were arranged around a mosaic-topped table to the left, below a narrow window, and Linda Loma waved toward them. Everybody took a seat, and Vickery wondered if the robed bald man who now stood several yards back had made sure there were enough chairs for the group.

Plowman introduced Vickery and Castine as he had said he would; and between the two of them they gave a vivid and complete description of the events of the previous morning, including the exploding van.

"Those things you saw," said Linda Loma when they had faltered to a stop, "aren't actually things. They are angels coming to Earth to guide us all to Paradise. One of the ones you saw alighted in the Los Angeles River last night and established a shrine there. They descend from the astral to the material, for us."

By the daylight through the window, Vickery saw that the woman's face was hatched with so many fine wrinkles that he thought it must in its time have expressed every emotion there was. Repeatedly. At the moment her face seemed to radiate suppressed excitement, and her hands were clasped as if to keep them from trembling.

"They are our saviors," she said. "When all the thrones and dominions, cherubim and seraphim have finally descended to Earth, they will rise again, all together, carrying us—and we'll be like them, acting without decision, aware of ourselves only in our reflection in others, as they perceive themselves only in their mutual reflections . . . forever in mutual check . . ." She raised her eyes to the high ceiling, then looked toward a pair of polished wooden doors in the inner wall. "Soon."

Santiago gave her a sharp look, then glanced back toward the front door.

"I—I think I sensed that," said Castine. "I think I sensed their *hands,* ready to lift us up."

Vickery kept an earnest look on his face, but he wished he could signal Castine to take it easy; and Plowman shifted on the chair beside him.

"Hands!" exclaimed Linda Loma. "Yes, their huge hands are ready to gather us, soon. You are blessed, daughter!"

Vickery decided to jump in. "I could see that they weren't physical apparitions—astral, like you said." He looked out the window at the blue sky, then met Linda Loma's gaze. "Soon?"

"I think you can understand," the woman said, "and Pierce did bring you here." She looked at Plowman. "I wish Frankie Notchett had come back too. Did you know he's dead?" When Plowman nodded, she went on, "We spoke sometimes, but he never repented his apostasy. Out on his boat at night, trying to *capture* angels!" She shook her head; then stood up, and the others followed suit. "Let me show you our spirit radar." She crossed to the wooden doors and pulled them open.

Vickery stepped up beside Castine and peered over her shoulder. The octagonal room beyond had probably been big enough for dozens of square dancers, and the high white walls with wide Corinthian crown molding under the ceiling simply dwarfed the five tables set up across the worn parquet floor.

Three robed men sat around each table, and as Linda Loma led Vickery's party into the room he saw that the tables were inset with wide triangular patterns of black and white squares; and then he saw six-inch-tall black and white and red chessmen standing in various positions on the squares. What Vickery at first thought were shot glasses beside every player's right wrist proved to be tiny hourglasses.

"We communicate with the angels this way," said Linda Loma, waving at the tables. "It's anti-king chess. When one game ends, another will be in mid game and another is opening up. Day and night, the games have never stopped since my grandmother initiated this form of contact in 1949."

As Vickery watched, a player at one table and then another moved a chesspiece and inverted his hourglass. At the far side of the room a player called, quietly, "Incarnation," and all three players at that table leaned forward and began rearranging the chess pieces. Another man hurried to the table and replaced one of the red pieces with a duplicate.

"Anti-king?" Vickery said.

"There are three players in each game, as you see." Linda Loma's eyes were bright as her gaze darted around the tables. "Three sides. Each of the three kings must continually be in check—that is, be the focus of attention of a piece from one of the other colors. If a king must move to a square where it is not in check—becomes isolated, falls out—it's considered incarnated, and that king is enshrined."

The man who had switched chess pieces at the far table hurried out of the room.

Vickery was suddenly sure he knew what the spikes

along the façade top were. Did these people imagine that
the enshrined kings functioned as antennas? "What," he
asked carefully, "is the . . . *goal,* of each player?"

"Simply to prolong the game, maintain steady contact.
The angels can be read within the strict logic of the
chessboard, moves governed by geometry, mathematical
logic—and allow the kings to fall into incarnation only
when the board logic dictates it."

"Incarnation," called a player at a closer table, echoed
by another at a table beyond it. Another of the robed men
stepped past Vickery to hurry to the first table and replace
the isolated king.

"They come in waves," said Linda Loma, "contractions,
and they're getting more frequent. I believe they're
building toward a crest now—in ten minutes or so they'll
all be calling, and we'll probably replace a dozen kings."

Vickery suppressed a shiver as he realized that if
Plowman was right about these people, each replaced
king commemorated a new crop circle, or sand angel, or
oceanic equivalent, somewhere on the globe.

Santiago licked his lips and spoke up: "When does it
end?"

Linda Loma gave him a startled look, as if she'd
forgotten he was there. "End? Say *begin!* It *begins* when
the incarnated angels gather to themselves enough grace
to . . . fly away! With us!"

Fly even beyond the reach of Chaos, thought Vickery.
And they won't be taking us with them, any more than
track runners take their starting blocks with them.

"Soon," Linda Loma said. She spread her arms toward
the tables. "We've watched the pattern grow ever tighter,

and the frequency peaks will soon merge into one culminant event. You've heard that sound like thunder today? You'll hear it more. The pattern has begun to grow exponentially, and we calculate that the ascension will occur sometime tomorrow night." Her voice had deepened as she spoke. "The critical High Mass will occur, the incarnate shrines will unite. And all of us will be raised up, transformed."

Vickery's face was cold, and he could feel his heart beating in his suddenly hollow chest. *Tomorrow night?* he thought. If these crazy people know what they're talking about—and Plowman said they're a seismograph for this stuff—and if our interpretation of Notchett's poem is correct, which this woman seems to be obliquely confirming—then tomorrow night we'll all be transformed, sure enough. Blocks of ice, we'll be.

He knew that if he were in his trailer, in his truck, in a bar, even just out in the sunlight, he would easily, and quite sensibly, dismiss this woman's wild statements. But in this weird hilltop temple, watching these people intently pursuing their occult purpose, he couldn't help being alarmed.

Sneakers squeaked on the marble floor, and when Vickery looked around he saw Santiago racing to the front door; the boy yanked it open, and disappeared, and his footsteps could be heard tapping rapidly down the stairs outside.

Linda Loma was blinking in surprise at the open door.

"My nephew, uh, gets restless around grown-up talk," said Castine, stepping back into the hall. "I'm afraid we'll have to get him home."

"His home," said Linda Loma, "is in Heaven. Fetch him back. And you," she said to Vickery, "please give your car keys to the facilitator." She looked past Vickery with a smile, and when he turned he saw that the robed man was now standing behind him, also smiling.

"No," said Plowman firmly. "You have some claim on me because of Becky, but these people are . . . civilians." He looked up and down the hall. "Is Becky here?"

Linda Loma's eyes widened and her voice was strained. "Pierce?"

"What?"

"You don't even know that our daughter is dead, Pierce? That she died by her own hand eleven years ago?"

Plowman stared at her, expressionless. "You're lying," he said hoarsely, but Vickery could see that he believed her.

Linda Loma closed her eyes for a moment, then opened them, staring back at him. "You must make atonement before your apotheosis," she said gently, "surely you can see that." She turned to Vickery and Castine. "You'll be made comfortable, children. Don't give a thought to—"

Plowman took Castine's arm and turned toward the door, followed by Vickery, but the robed man blocked their way.

"I will show you fear in a handful of dust," the man said.

"You show *me?*" blustered Plowman. "I show *you.* I got your handful of dust right here." He raised his free hand in a fist.

The man stepped back, still blocking the way to the door, and his hand had darted under his robe and emerged holding a stainless steel revolver.

The gun barrel moved left and right, covering Vickery and Castine as well as Plowman. Vickery was resentfully gauging the distance between himself and the armed man, and slightly twisting his left foot to estimate how much traction he could have, when Santiago's voice broke the tension:

"Drop the gun, mister, or I'll shoot the old lady."

All heads swung toward the boy, and Vickery wasn't surprised to see that Santiago was holding in both hands a Sig Sauer P229 semi-automatic pistol, probably .40 caliber. Santiago had stolen it from an unconscious Transportation Utility agent three years ago. The barrel was tilted up, pointing above the heads of the five people in front of him, but not far above.

"And kick it over here," Vickery said.

The robed man hesitated, then crouched slowly and laid the revolver on the marble floor; and after an appraising glance at Santiago, he kicked the gun across the marble floor toward Vickery, who quickly picked it up. Vickery opened the revolver's cylinder—it held six rounds of half-jacketed hollow points.

He snapped it shut, and with his free hand he dug the keys out of his pocket and tossed them to Castine, and rocked his head toward the front door.

She nodded and followed Plowman and Santiago out the door and down the steps.

Vickery backed to the open door. "I'll leave the gun," he called, "in the driveway." And how the hell, he thought bitterly, did I end up having to hold a gun on these strangers?

Linda Loma was shaking her head sadly. The robed

man had straightened up and now stood with his hands open at his sides. Another was now standing in the hall behind the woman, hesitant and peering.

Vickery stepped over the threshold and then hurried down the stairs, looking back and keeping the gun pointed toward the doorway. Out from under the arch and down on the level dirt, he ran to the driveway, his shoes crunching on old eyeglasses; the Dodge's passenger-side door was open, and as he hiked himself in, Castine accelerated back to the road in reverse, spun the car and shifted to drive, and sped around the curve. Vickery had hung onto the door frame with one hand during the maneuver, and now pulled his legs in and shut the door. He simply pitched the revolver out the window.

"I said I would," he told Castine breathlessly.

Castine slowed down as the road curved. To their left now were the tops of trees rooted further down the slope, and beyond them a view of rooftops among wooded ridges and the gray towers of downtown L.A. on the horizon. Vickery kept glancing back to make sure no pickup truck was pursuing them.

No one was looking directly at Plowman, and Vickery thought he was aware of it. "Atone," the old man said finally. "How do you make amends to someone who's dead?"

Vickery thought again of Cordelia, King Lear's loyal but forsaken daughter.

Without looking away from the road rushing under the tires, Castine said, "You've got another daughter."

Plowman just slumped back in the rear seat, his eyes closed.

Santiago glanced at him uncertainly, then asked, "How was the Notchett guy trying to catch angels?"

Plowman rubbed his face with both hands, then dropped them in his lap. He sighed and looked at Santiago. "I owe you, kid. We all do. If you hadn't come back in with that gun ..." He leaned forward to peer out the window. "Frankie? I didn't know that's what he was trying to do. He did go out on the *Ouranos* a lot at night."

Vickery looked at him sharply. "That was the name of his boat? *Ouranos?* Like in his poem?" When Plowman raised one hand in vague question, Vickery turned to Castine. "Where did we put Notchett's papers?"

"In your briefcase," she said without taking her eyes off the curving road, "You've got your feet on it."

Vickery bent down and unzipped the briefcase. The papers Plowman had given them yesterday were at the bottom, under the .45 and 9-millimeter magazines and the bundles of twenty-dollar bills, and he pulled them free.

He flipped to the photocopy of Notchett's amplified translation of Hesiod. *"Ouranos,"* he read, *"Gaia's son, restrains the stranger hundred handed ones—"* He looked back at Plowman. "Did he hope to restrain them with something on his boat? Your Linda Loma said he went out at night on it to try to capture angels. Never mind," he added when the old man just shrugged.

"Do you know where his boat is?" asked Castine.

"It's at Howard's Landing in Huntington Beach, maybe a mile from his apartment."

"Would you be able to find it, recognize it?"

"Sure, I've done a lot of maintenance on it for

him—even hoisted one of the engines out last year, to replace the flywheel. I've never been out on it with him at night, though."

"ONI might be watching it," said Vickery.

"They probably don't know about it," said Plowman. "Frankie bought everything with cash, and he got a bill of sale for the boat but never sent in the transfer-of-ownership papers. On paper, some Canadian still owns it."

Vickery noticed that Castine's knuckles were white on the steering wheel. "I'm afraid we should look at it," she said. Then added, firmly, "While the sun's still up."

CHAPTER FIFTEEN:
A Couple of This Old Lady's Fingerbones

- -

Oak trees, wide grassy meadows, widely scattered cement picnic tables—Joel Finehouse wouldn't have guessed he was still in Los Angeles, though in fact he was only two miles north of Hollywood Boulevard.

He had left Agent Atkins staked out down the street from Anita Galvan's garage, and just after three o'clock the agent had reported that Galvan had driven out of the lot and was moving west on 8th Street. Finehouse and Cendravenir and two other agents had been searching an unoccupied trailer in Long Beach, by the L.A. River— Agent Yoneda had given Commander Lubitz the address yesterday, and claimed that it was the home of Sebastian Vickery, but papers and mail in the trailer indicated that it belonged to someone named William Ardmore. Fingerprints had been taken and would soon be identified, but Finehouse had concluded that Yoneda or her allegedly GRU informant had probably made a mistake.

It was nothing, though, to the mistake Yoneda had

made at a little after 2:30 this afternoon. Finehouse had had to tell Lubitz how Yoneda had evaded a Highway Patrol traffic stop, and afterward Lubitz had simply ended the call, without comment.

In any case, Finehouse had more questions for Galvan.

He had called off the search of the trailer, got Cendravenir and the two agents into the SUV and set off to find Galvan.

After twenty minutes Atkins had reported that she was on Los Feliz Drive, northeast of Hollywood, and Finehouse had taken the 710 Freeway up through Bell Gardens and Commerce, and by the time he had switched to the 5 and was passing Dodger Stadium, Atkins had radioed that Galvan had entered Griffith Park and stopped by the ruins of the old Los Angeles zoo, and got out of her car and begun to walk. Finehouse had told Atkins to wait for him near her car.

Fifteen minutes later Finehouse had parked beside Atkins' car, and when he opened the SUV door and stepped down to the weathered cement pavement, he just looked around at the wide green meadows and the oak trees and the hills beyond, and filled his lungs with the woodland air. There was not a building in sight, and for a moment he was reminded of his boyhood in Cosby, Tennessee.

Agent Atkins got out of the SAS car and hurried over to him, breaking the nostalgic spell.

"That old Cadillac is Galvan's," Atkins said, nodding toward a long white sedan parked a few spaces away. "She's alone. She walked down that path between the trees to the south."

"Cendravenir," said Finehouse, "you and Atkins come with me." To the pair of agents still in the SUV he called, "I've left the keys. If she comes back and leaves before we show up, follow her."

Finehouse walked around to the rear of the SUV and lifted the back gate, and from a black plastic case he took a narrow ten-inch shotgun microphone and a pair of Bluetooth earbuds. He slid the microphone up the left sleeve of his windbreaker; with the end of it flush with the edge of his cuff he couldn't bend his elbow, but he could shuck the thing out in a hurry. From another case he took a pair of binoculars and slung the strap around his neck.

He led Atkins and Cendravenir across a strip of grass between two lanes, then up a narrow paved path beneath overhanging boughs. Birds twittered among the leaves, and Finehouse realized that this was the first time since he had arrived in Los Angeles that he could not hear at least the remote swish of traffic. The shotgun microphone should work perfectly, if they located Galvan and she talked to anyone.

Cendravenir was already sweating in his black turtleneck sweater. "Did the Highway Patrol know Yoneda's an ONI agent?"

Atkins stepped ahead, his hands in his pockets and his eyes on the pavement.

"We just told them 'Persons of Interest,'" said Finehouse shortly.

Commander Lubitz had learned last night that Yoneda had rented a car at the Long Beach airport, and he passed the license number on to Finehouse; Finehouse, in turn, had given the license number to the LAPD and asked that they put out an Attempt to Locate bulletin for the car, describing Yoneda and her companion as persons of interest to Naval Intelligence. And an hour ago a Highway Patrol officer had spotted Yoneda's Toyota Camry on the southbound 110 freeway, and pulled her over; but while the officer was still in his vehicle, reporting the fact that he had located the subject car, a crash-priority report of multiple shots fired and officers down on a nearby street had come over the radio, and the officer had sped off to assist—and of course the call had been a ruse, and Yoneda's burner phone had been found on the freeway shoulder.

She'll have ditched the car, Finehouse thought. They're probably on a bus now, headed God knows where, with God knows what purpose. And Vickery, if that was Vickery running away from the cathedral this morning, managed to set me off on a wild goose chase after a bus that yielded nothing but a couple of bloody bandages stuck behind the bumper.

Cendravenir was stroking his disordered goatee, clearly trying to restore its pointed shape. "I bet the Highway Patrol is pissed," he remarked.

They'll certainly demand some information, thought Finehouse, which Lubitz will have to fabricate. I should start thinking seriously about how to disassociate myself from him if—when—operation Pleiades collapses and comes under harsh review.

After a hundred feet the path emerged from the trees onto a circular area of grass about three hundred feet across, on the far side of which, abutting a wooded slope, ran a blocky tan stone wall with three irregular holes which might have been entrances.

Finehouse quickly scanned the people standing or sitting on the grass, but none of them was Galvan. Looking more closely at the stone wall, he saw that it extended to the left, with two more entrances. The wall appeared to be made of giant stone blocks haphazardly stacked, and he wondered if it could be an abandoned movie set, until he remembered that Atkins had said it was the ruins of an old zoo.

Cendravenir was ambling to the right across the grass, and Finehouse caught Atkins' eye and nodded. Cendravenir did claim to be a magician, and in this insane context his instincts might have value.

A narrow paved road ran in front of the wall, and to the right, past a cluster of trees and shrubbery, stood a line of cages. Cendravenir seemed to be walking toward them.

Finehouse caught up with the magician and, taking him by the shoulder, turned him around. "If she's in one of those cages, she mustn't see your damn Svengali beard again. Sit down. We're picnickers, see? Sit," he added to Atkins.

When the three of them were seated on the grass, Finehouse raised the binoculars and looked over Cendravenir's shoulder at the cages a hundred feet away.

The cages were of close-set horizontal and vertical black rods, with a low stone wall and bench at the rear of each. The gates to the cages were all open, probably fixed. The cages weren't big enough for an adult to stand upright inside, and Finehouse saw that only one had people in it.

He sharpened the focus, and recognized Anita Galvan's profile in the shifting dappled shade. Sitting on the stone bench near her, facing Finehouse, was a young girl with long black hair, dressed in a white skirt and a paisley shawl.

Finehouse twisted the earbuds into his ears, then shook the shotgun microphone out of his sleeve, switched it on, and slid it back in place. He extended his arm and rested his wrist on Cendravenir's shoulder.

"Hold still," he snapped when Cendravenir tried to wiggle away. "I have to aim."

He moved the microphone by fractions of an inch one way and then the other, and at one point the background whisper was suddenly voices.

"— tonight," the girl was saying. "My father took his boat out at dawn for yellowtail, way out past Catalina and San Nicolas Island, and early this morning he radioed me—he saw the spacemen in their silver helmets, flying around in the sky. And the fishermen know—*Naves espaciales por día, anillos de luz en la noche,* spaceships by day, light rings at night—there will be the wheels in the sea tonight."

"Wheels . . . in the sea," said Galvan, almost too quietly for Finehouse's microphone to pick up. "Okay. So the spacemen have shown up out at sea before? That's no use—can't lay lines of sugar and honey in the ocean."

The girl's voice said, "The spacemen many times appear where they've appeared not long before—it's like coming through a hole they already made, before it can close up again." Finehouse heard cloth shifting on stone, and the girl went on, "The symbol would maybe stop the spacemen, but even on streets the sugar and honey lines of it are . . . wooden swords and toy guns, okay? Your friend says he has the whole picture—how big? Like a poster? How can he get the spacemen to look at it?"

"Beats me," came Galvan's voice, "but he's been clever in the past." She laughed shortly. "To my cost. I loaned him a good concealment car this morning, but lately I've been putting back doors in 'em."

"The *brujas* say ghosts are up," came the girl's voice again, "metronomes going like castanets, noise in the sky like thunder that is not thunder, pigeons flying everywhere marking the edges of the freeway auras. A vision of a woman in water at night intrudes on a lot of their visions."

"A woman under water?" came Galvan's voice.

"I think—no—more like the water is enclosing her. Some think it is the Virgin Mary."

Finehouse slid the microphone out of his sleeve and turned it off, then yanked the earbuds out of his ears.

"This is just *santeria* bullshit," he said to Atkins and Cendravenir. "Let's go talk to her." He stood up, wondering uneasily what the girl had meant by *the symbol*. Could these back-alley fortune-tellers actually have some means of impeding the UAPs?—preventing Operation Pleiades? And if so, what outlandish, undignified measures might he have to take to stop them?

Finehouse and his two companions strode across the grass, and when they were still fifty feet away, both faces in the cage turned toward them, and the girl in the shawl crouched out through the gate and began running down the road to the right. Atkins glanced at Finehouse, who shook his head.

"We just want to talk to Galvan," he said, handing the tubular shotgun microphone to the agent.

Galvan had lit a cigarette, and she smiled at the three men when they walked up to the cage. Finehouse gestured for Atkins and Cendravenir to wait out on the road, and walked up the three old stone steps and bent to shuffle into the cage. He sat down on the stone bench where the girl had been sitting.

He sighed, then said, "It would be difficult to arrest you."

"More difficult than you know," Galvan agreed.

"Hah. I believe you." He stretched and looked at the old bars overhead. "I think you meant to tell me how to find Vickery, last night when you telephoned that boy. You told him I hadn't offered you any money, while of course I offered you ten thousand dollars." Galvan opened her mouth to correct him, but he raised his hand and went on, "We followed the boy to the Catholic cathedral on Temple this morning—he seems actually to have found Vickery by using old cloths soaked in blood!"

Galvan looked past him at Cendravenir, who had moved back to stare to the right, toward the eccentric old zoo architecture. "Traveling with him," she said, "you should be used to some weird developments."

"I'm getting there. Faster than I'd like. We got the bloody cloth—two of them, actually—but instead of leading us to Vickery, they led me to a bus. Vickery put fresh blood on a couple of bandages and stuck them behind the bumper. We burned those, but now the bloody cloths just hang limp. No reception." He sat back and smiled at Galvan. "I wondered why they had stopped working till I heard you say just now that you loaned him a concealment car."

Galvan gave him a mocking grin. "The cold iron cage is just to stop ghosts from butting in. You're showing off."

Finehouse laughed quietly. "I guess I am. But you also said you've been putting back doors in your concealment cars—I assume that's like backdoor code in computer software, to evade encryption and authentication. I don't want to know what kitchen sorcery you use for it, but I assume you can override your own concealments and get in touch with him."

She just stared at him.

"If you can," Finehouse said, "tell him this. We will inevitably catch him and Ingrid Castine, but if he turns himself in, surrenders to me—you still have my card? Good—Ingrid Castine will face no charges or penalties, or even demotion, for anything she's done in these last two days. If he doesn't, she'll be charged with all sorts of felonies. Theft of a government vehicle, assault on a government agent, abetting the escape of a suspected traitor, and those are just off the top of my head. She will certainly lose her current and any substantial future livelihood and spend a long time in prison. And I'll see that you get ten thousand dollars if he surrenders as a result."

He shifted as if to get up in the hunched posture the cage necessitated, then sat back and gave her a quizzical look. "A symbol in sugar and honey?"

Galvan just shrugged.

"To stop the spacemen," Finehouse went on, "if they'll look at it? Why would you *want* to stop us from getting in touch with the spacemen, as you call them? Can you imagine the benefits that contact with them might bring? A cure for—"

"Cancer," said Galvan, "sure. Or Alzheimer's or something. And anti-gravity cars." She gave him a direct look. "Or maybe they'll freeze the Earth solid."

Finehouse cocked his head, frowning. "Freeze? Why should they freeze the Earth?"

Galvan opened her mouth, then snapped it shut. Finally she said, "They're spacemen. Who knows why they'd do anything?"

This time Finehouse did get up. "I'm afraid you have a closed mind."

"And maybe you're opening yours too wide. Careful you don't fall out."

He sighed. "A risk of the trade, it looks like."

Finehouse ducked out of the cage and stood up straight. He turned back to face her through the bars and said, "Ten thousand dollars. And immunity for Castine."

"If I hear from Vickery, I'll tell him."

At Franklin, Castine pulled in to a grocery store parking lot to switch places with Vickery, and he was now driving south on the 110 Freeway, with the skyscrapers of L.A. on his left. In a couple of miles he would pass the Third Street exit.

In the seat beside him, Castine was looking around. "Isn't this . . .?"

Vickery nodded. "Just on the other side of the median, in the northbound lanes, is where we took an offramp that didn't exist."

"Three years ago?"

"Three years this April."

Plowman leaned forward from the back seat. "Is that when you drove a taco truck into Hell? And flew out on a hang-glider?"

In the rear view mirror Vickery saw that Santiago was listening wide-eyed.

"It might as well have been Hell," said Castine with a shiver. "It was the Labyrinth—Minotaur and all." She peered to the left, but the median was too high to see over. "We had to make the hang-glider, out of vellum and fishing poles."

"Which," said Plowman, leaning back, "is of course impossible."

"You should have seen these fishing poles."

"And," said Vickery, "we had to fly it into a tornado to get out. The hole back to the real world was up in the sky."

"Somewhere over the rainbow," muttered Plowman.

"It's true," said Santiago quietly. He didn't go on, but Vickery recalled that a man who had been a surrogate father to the boy had driven a car into the Labyrinth in 1960, and got out again somehow.

Vickery had his eyes on the lane ahead when the dashboard metronome began rattling furiously back and forth and a scuffling started up in the back seat. He darted a quick glance at the rear view mirror—and his face was suddenly cold.

There was a third person in the middle of the seat back there, and Plowman and Santiago were crowded against the doors.

Castine had looked back, and now popped her seatbelt loose and turned around on her seat.

Vickery corrected his involuntary swerve in the lane and then peered into the rear-view mirror again for a closer look at the intruding figure.

It was an old woman in a shapeless black dress, with a thick black veil over her face.

"Don't look her in the—" began Castine, but closed her mouth. It was clear that the veil would prevent anyone from looking the thing in the eye, if it had eyes.

Vickery could hear Plowman and Santiago breathing quickly through open mouths; and he caught a scent of mingled cocoa and mildew.

Vickery almost swerved again when the figure spoke. Its voice was a hoarse monotone against the staccato racket of the metronome: "Vickery, Betty Boop."

Vickery just gripped the steering wheel, staring straight ahead at the rushing pavement, but Castine exhaled and then said, "Uh . . . what?"

"This is Galvan," the figure said.

"They—*killed* you?" grated Vickery; for the thing in the back seat was clearly a ghost, as Castine had instantly realized.

"No no," said the ghost, "shut up, I plant tethered ghosts in my cars since you stole my Cadillac in '18. I've got a back door link, and there's a couple of this old lady's fingerbones in the car for a handhold, and a couple more in this telephone I'm talking on. I can override her ghost, and talk."

Vickery bent to grope on the floor, and found an empty paper cup; he straightened and put it over the metronome like a candle snuffer. The cup shook, but the rattle was muffled.

The ghost burst into a torrent of fast Spanish, and Santiago said quietly, "Saying the Rosary."

In spite of the disruption, Vickery found a moment to pity the ghost, which like all ghosts was a semi-aware scrap of identity cast off when the trauma of death had separated the old woman's body from her soul. The body, except for some finger bones, apparently, had doubtless gone into a grave, and the soul had gone on to whatever eternity awaited it—the good one, he guessed, unless praying was a habit this thing had picked up after its death— but the ghost must have wandered, lost, until Galvan had caught it and installed it in this twenty-year-old Dodge.

The ghost's voice sputtered and choked to a halt, and Galvan came back on. "The Navy man has the old blood cloths Santiago tracked you with—he chased a bus you put fresh bloody bandages on, that was a good trick—and he knows you've got one of my cars, so don't come back here until you've got rid of all the spacemen. A bunch of—"

The old woman's ghost took over again, babbling in Spanish, and was again choked off.

"Damn," said Galvan's distorted voice. "I gotta get better control of these things. So listen—a bunch of flying saucers were over the ocean out past Catalina this morning, and there'll be light-rings in the sea tonight. *Naves espaciales por día, anillos de luz en la noche,* spaceships by day, light rings at night. And the *brujas* have been having a vision of a woman enclosed in water who

they think is the Virgin Mary. Don't ask me. The
spacemen appear in places they've appeared not long
before, because the hole hasn't all the way closed up yet.
Don't ask, I'm just telling you all the stuff I heard from
my grand-niece, she walks around and talks to the quiet
people. And—are you—"

The steering wheel jerked in Vickery's hands in the
same moment that the ghost exclaimed, "Hah!" and the
lane divider bumps were a rapid drumming under the
right-side tires. Vickery had just steered the car back into
its lane when it happened again. He was vaguely aware
that the ghost was bobbing in the back seat, and that
Santiago was gripping the back of the driver's seat. The
paper cup had been flung off the metronome, and Castine
picked it up and shoved it back over the wiggling
pendulum.

"Don't math her out!" gasped Galvan from the ghost's
ectoplasmic throat as Vickery straightened the speeding
car once more. "I can—hold her." The car remained
steady for several seconds, and then for several seconds
more. "There," said Galvan, "I'm holding her back. She
lived in Cerritos, I think she wants to drive back there.
The Navy man gave me a message for you, Vick—turn
yourself in, and Betty Boop won't face any of the felony
charges they're ready to hit her with. Total immunity, even
keep her job, or else years in prison and work in a car wash
when she gets out. I can give you his phone number."

"He doesn't want it," said Castine.

"Well, we ought to have it in any—" Vickery began,
then had to shove the gear shift into neutral, for the gas
pedal had dropped away from his foot and now lay flat

against the floor. The engine went on roaring as the car coasted in the lane and he signaled for a lane-change to the right. He was sure the old engine would blow its head gasket, but after ten long seconds it subsided, and the temperature gauge needle stayed vertical.

He clicked the gear shift lever back into drive and kept his hand on it, but the car was behaving normally again. The speed had dropped to sixty miles per hour, but he didn't accelerate to get back into the faster lane.

"She wants to get to Cerritos in a hurry," he said breathlessly. He looked in the rear-view mirror, but Plowman and Santiago were alone back there. Castine slumped down in her seat.

"Boss?" Vickery called. "You still with us?"

There was no answer, but the muted metronome was still shaking the paper cup. The steering wheel began straining to the right, and he had to exert increasing counter-pressure to hold it steady.

Castine patted the dashboard beside the covered metronome as if soothing a restive dog. "Can you drive?" she asked Vickery. "If we ditch this car, that ONI guy will be able to track us by our blood."

"Sorry," said Santiago meekly.

"Done is done, kid," said Vickery. The ghostly tugging at the wheel abated, slowly enough so that he was able to let his muscles relax and keep the car from swerving again. He kept a firm grip on the steering wheel with his left hand and kept his right hand on the gear shift lever, ready to throw it into neutral again.

"Santiago, I can drop you and Plowman off somewhere as soon as I get this thing off the freeway." He glanced at

Castine and said, "I can drive, if I hang on tight and be ready for her tricks. But I don't dare do it on freeways."

Castine shook her head in agreement. "As long as we're getting off the freeway, I wouldn't mind finding a rest room."

"Seconded," growled Plowman.

The radio wasn't turned on, but over the rattling of the paper cup a hoarse voice shook out of the speaker: *"Los truenos son ellos."*

"The thunder is them," translated Santiago. "I'll go with you, for a while, at least. Laquedem would." Vickery recalled that Laquedem was the name of the old man who had taken care of Santiago when the boy had been a homeless fugitive.

Vickery glanced at him in the rear-view mirror. He had known of Santiago for years, probably since the boy had been about ten, and since 2017 their paths had intersected from time to time. The boy must have been about fifteen by now. Santiago had always apparently made some sort of living in the supernatural underworld of Los Angeles as a courier and watcher. Three years ago Vickery had described him to Castine as *freelance—not loyal, but honest, to an extent.*

"Thanks," said Vickery.

"For a while, at least," Santiago repeated.

"I," Plowman began; then went on more quietly, "I last saw Becky in 1993. She was ten years old. Birthday party. She—loved me."

Vickery recalled Linda Loma saying that Becky had killed herself eleven years ago, therefore at the age of . . . twenty-six. There was really nothing to say.

He steered the car off the freeway at the Seventh Street exit and drove carefully past the big Salvation Army headquarters.

"Trudy," Plowman said, and Vickery recalled that that was the name of the old man's daughter who currently lived in Yucaipa, "hates me. But maybe by saving her . . ." He shifted on the seat. "I'll go with you. God help me."

"God help us, every one," said Santiago softly.

CHAPTER SIXTEEN:
What There Is to Do

Howard's Landing was a big marina down Pacific Coast Highway from Seal Beach in Huntington Harbor, behind a very new-looking beige shopping mall, and the low sun was silhouetting the buildings and palm trees on the peninsula by the time Vickery was able to wrestle and coax the haunted car off the highway into the parking lot, and, finally and with much jerky backing and filling, into a parking space.

Vickery switched off the engine at last, evoking a faint wail from the radio speaker. He sat back and exhaled, flexing his hands.

Plowman shifted in the back seat, fumbling for the door lever. "What, did she die?"

"It's a ghost," Santiago pointed out.

"As soon as Castine and I step out," Vickery said, "we'll be trackable, though the Naval Intelligence guys are probably way north of us right now."

"Maybe they gave up," said Castine, "after a couple of hours of getting no response from the bloody rags."

"They know we're in one of Galvan's evasion cars," said Vickery, opening his door and stepping out onto the asphalt. "And they know we've got to get out of it sometime."

The others climbed out of the car. Castine stretched, then hugged herself, gripping her elbows.

The evening breeze from the west was cold, smelling of the open ocean, and he found that he wanted to get Castine back inland, away from the edge of the sea, as quickly as possible. *Light-rings in the sea tonight,* Galvan had said through the old woman's ghost; and *a woman enclosed in water.* He remembered too Castine's description of the spontaneous echo-vision she had had yesterday at Cole's—*for a second I had the sensation of being on a boat, at night. The sky was dark, but I got the impression that there was light from below, as if the ocean were glowing . . .*

And when she had driven away from the chess club temple, she had said, reluctantly, that they should look at Notchett's boat, but had specified, *While the sun is still up.* And the sun was now going down.

He slammed the door and squinted at his companions. "Search the damn boat for whatever it might have been that Notchett thought could restrain the angels, and then let's get the hell away." Turning to Plowman, he asked, "Where's this boat?"

The old man led them around the north side of the shopping mall and across an empty lot to a walkway that overlooked ranks of boats in slips along several long docks stretching out into the harbor channel. The far shore was five-hundred yards away, and lights were on in some of the windows over there.

Plowman had hopped down onto the dock and was striding along it, past gleaming white hulls and chrome bow railings. Vickery, Castine and Santiago trotted along behind him.

"Ahoy, Fishmeal!" came a call from one of the boats, and Vickery saw a tanned young man stand up to wave from a high bridge.

"Sammy," Plowman acknowledged with a nod, not slowing down. When the four of them had walked a few yards further, Plowman looked over his shoulder at Vickery. "After I did that flywheel for Frankie, some of the other boat people hired me for repairs."

"Handy."

Castine was looking back, toward where the sun had now disappeared behind the low buildings on the far side of Pacific Coast Highway.

"Here we are," said Plowman, stepping past one of the white shore-power pedestals that studded the long dock. He walked out along a narrow finger pier between two boats, running his palm along the hull on the left.

Vickery leaned back to look at the boat, glad to see no yellow police tape or official warning signs. The boat was a cabin cruiser about thirty feet long, and the bow and stern angles were short, so that the overall length was only a few feet more than the waterline length. The sheer line swept back from the cabin roof in a shallowly descending curve that became the edge of the cockpit coaming. Like most of the boats in the marina, it was moored bow-in, so a four-step ladder had been set up across the water gap and over the high cockpit gunwale.

Plowman climbed up first, then turned around and

went down another set of steps to the cockpit deck. Vickery followed, and stepped out onto a black rubber mat laid over the broad wooden deck, which was shifting slightly with the new weight. Low padded benches were installed along both long sides, with several circular life-preservers hung above them. At the cabin bulkhead, under a blue tarpaulin awning, was the dash panel and wheel of the topside helm and a door to belowdecks.

Soon Castine and Santiago were standing on the deck too, leaning on the chest-high gunwale, and Vickery took a step toward the door in the bulkhead—then halted, his hand darting to the .45 in his jacket pocket, for the door swung open.

A middle-aged man with implausibly dark hair was peering angrily out at them, and it wasn't until Vickery saw Rayette Yoneda behind him that he recognized the now clean-shaven face of the alleged GRU agent, Tacitus.

"Pierce!" said Tacitus. "Tell me you didn't step on that mat."

"Tacitus?" said Plowman. "Huh. Losing the beard was smart, but stay gray." He glanced back at the mat on the deck, then turned to Tacitus with a shrug and a nod.

"We," said Tacitus, "had the wit to jump past it."

Santiago looked quickly toward the ladder.

Castine crouched and flipped the mat over. A flat white plastic box was connected by wires to one corner. She looked up. "A transmitter?"

"It's not a box of Tic Tacs," said Yoneda, blinking as she stepped up onto the deck. "Welcome aboard, and now we've all got to get out of here."

Castine waved toward the mat. "ONI?"

"GRU," said Tacitus, "It's a standard trick. If your Office of Naval Intelligence had known about Frankie's boat they would have cordoned it off." He looked down at the mat and made a sour face. "We're fortunate that my onetime comrades weren't sure who might come aboard."

Vickery blinked at him, and Castine explained, "No bomb today."

"Your comrades?" said Plowman, stepping back to squint at Tacitus with one eye and then the other. "GRU?"

"It's all right," said Tacitus. "It seems I'm a defector."

Yoneda took his arm. "Come on, your *onetime comrades* will be back here any time now, thanks to our heavy-footed friends. We've *got* to get you to Agent Finehouse, and safety. We've wasted the whole day."

"*Was* it entirely a waste?" said Tacitus, letting her guide him across the mat toward the ladder. "I spoke to an old friend's ghost, and I believe you spoke, briefly, to— someone?"

Yoneda looked away and yanked harder on his arm. "Shut up and come along."

"Old friend's ghost," said Plowman. He hurried forward and stepped between them and the ladder. "What old friend's ghost? Hah? Was it Frankie?" When neither Yoneda nor Tacitus denied it, he demanded, "Where, what did he say?"

Yoneda took a step back, blinking and shivering in the cold wind. In a strained voice she said, "Oh, I'm in a mood to mess you up, grandpa, if you don't get out of our way."

Plowman didn't move.

After a tense moment her shoulders sagged. "Well it

was just gibberish," she said breathlessly, "nonsense about rings in the sea—now will you please—let us by!"

But Tacitus spoke up. "Yes, it was Frankie's ghost. In one of the freeway-side gypsy nests off the 10, four or five hours ago. He said—" He closed his eyes, nodded, then opened them and stared out over the ranked masts as he recited, "*It's the rings, the shining rings in the sea at night, that's how you can approach them. Out past the jetties, in the open ocean . . . you can't know where they'll be, you just watch . . . hope, or fear, that they'll appear . . .*'"

Tacitus lowered his eyes and rubbed his forehead. "At that point the ghost became agitated. More agitated! It said, '*But when it was there, at last, on the deck of the cockpit, I ran to the controls and gunned away, out of the ring. You think you'd have had the guts to stay?*'"

"That was it," agreed Yoneda. "Now come on, we've got to get out of here."

"Oh . . . shit," said Castine.

When everyone paused to look at her, she said, "We've got to get out of here, all right—but that way." She pointed past the stern toward the open harbor, then looked across the deck at Plowman. "You can get this running, can't you? Hot-wire it?"

"You go your way," said Yoneda, "and we'll go ours. Will you come *on?*" she added, tugging again at Tacitus's arm. "I've got to get Finehouse to square me with the Highway Patrol."

"Wait," he told her.

"I could hot-wire it," Plowman said to Castine. "Why would I?" He shook his head and squinted at Tacitus. "A GRU defector?"

"Ingrid," said Vickery, "we'll be safe in the car, and we can be out of here as soon as we get Frankie's charts or logs or notes—"

"All gone," interrupted Yoneda. "Tacitus and I were looking around, and there's not a scrap of paper aboard. The GRU got whatever there might have been."

"So let's get the hell back to the car," said Vickery.

"No," insisted Castine. She turned a haggard look on Vickery. "You heard what he said—the rings in the sea are how you approach the things, but it sounds like Notchett got scared when one showed up, and he ran. Dammit, Herbert, do you think I *want* to go out on the ocean, tonight? This is the last night to—*do* anything."

"Herbert?" muttered Plowman.

"Tomorrow night," Castine went on, "the aliens are going to exit our four-dimensional universe, and take away all our energy to do it. The gelid, endothermic cost. But," she said with a wave to the west, "they'll be out there tonight. There were UAPs over the ocean this morning, and—how did Galvan's aphorism go? *Spaceships by day, light rings at night*, right? Wheels in the sea, Galvan said. Crop circles in the sea." Her voice had grown fainter as she spoke, so that the last sentence was almost a whisper, and she seemed to be blinking back tears. But, "Dammit," she went on strongly, "they'll be *out there tonight*—and the three of us," she said with a wave that took in herself and Vickery and Tacitus, "we *affect* them."

"Affect," began Vickery, "but how—"

Castine spoke over him: "Notchett named this boat the *Ouranos*, and in his poem he said Ouranos restrains them!"

"How?" persisted Vickery, "with none of his charts or logs or notes?"

"With a passenger, passengers! If we could communicate—even just let them know somehow—that we're alive, sentient!—maybe they'd—"

Yoneda started to speak, but Tacitus interrupted her. "What do you mean?" he asked Castine. "Exit . . . take away all our energy . . .?"

Castine took a deep breath and let it out, then pushed her disordered hair back. "Well," she said, "if you picture our world, our universe, as a two-dimensional plane, like the surface of a pool—" She waved at Vickery. "You can take it from there, Sebastian."

"I *knew* you were Sebastian Vickery!" muttered Yoneda.

Vickery wanted very much to get Castine, and himself, too, off the boat and back into the concealment car; but he quickly explained how the lines of iambic pentameter that Notchett had added to the Hesiod translation seemed to describe an extra-dimensional diversion of the force-carrying particles that maintained the structures of protons and neutrons.

"And the force instantly re-establishes itself," he said in conclusion, "by confiscating energy from the surroundings. It's an endothermic reaction. Ingrid and I went back to the riverbed last night after you two left, and everything was frozen—there was a column of spinning snow, and I think it was frozen methane or nitrogen."

"Lately at the crop circles in England," added Castine, "after a few minutes it gets cold enough sometimes for metal to just shatter. And all along there have been variances in electromagnetism at the sites, and reports of gravity failures."

"As of last night," said Tacitus, "we can report a gravity failure ourselves!" He moved away from Yoneda. "EM and gravity are propagated by virtual photons and gravitons. Having no mass and spreading widely, they might have been easier to divert, at first, than gluons." He nodded sadly. "This is consistent with certain reports from Georgia and Azerbaijan in the 1980s. And today all day there has been something like thunder." To Castine he added, "Of course we have to go."

For a few moments none of them spoke, and sighing of the wind from the sea and the intermittent slap of water against the hull were the only sounds.

"Okay, dammit," said Plowman finally. He clenched his fists, then spread his fingers. "I gotta check over the engines first, okay? Everybody off the Russki mat." The others shuffled to the starboard gunwale and he pulled the mat to one side, exposing two flush-set deck hatches. He lifted the bigger one, and Vickery saw only darkness below the open rectangle.

Tacitus said, "No, I must go along with them," and when Vickery looked to the side he saw the man pull his arm free of Yoneda's hand. "How could I walk away from a possible meeting with. . ." He finished by waving vaguely at the sky.

"Tacitus," Plowman said, "I bet your commie pals didn't bother to take Frankie's flashlight and toolkit." He pointed to the door in the bulkhead. "In the drawer, below the main helm." To Santiago he said, "Kid, you can sit here and hand me tools."

Tacitus nodded and hurried below.

Santiago thrust his hands in his pockets and rocked around on one heel to face the ladder; then he turned back to Plowman and pulled his hands free. "Okay."

When Tacitus returned with the items, Plowman took the flashlight and lowered himself into the engine compartment, while Santiago sat down on the deck and opened the toolbox. Peering over Santiago's shoulder, Vickery could see the flashlight beam on one of the blue-painted engines down there as Plowman checked the oil dipstick.

"Crescent wrench," came the old man's muffled voice, and Santiago handed one down to him.

Vickery stepped back. Yoneda was standing at the top of the ladder, looking toward shore. Tacitus stood near her, alternately casting anxious glances at the shore and the open deck hatch. Castine was leaning on the gunwale and looking out past the stern at the harbor water. Vickery crossed the deck and stood beside her.

"There's no really good reason to do this," he said.

"It's what there is to do. We both know I'm going to be aboard."

"Why, because of that flash you had at Cole's, yesterday? That was *destiny* or something? No, there's nothing—"

Castine interrupted, "It'd be a good idea to get Santiago ashore, at least. But we're going out." She looked past him and raised her voice: "Santiago! It's time you went ashore. Wait in the car till we get back."

The boy shook his head. "I gotta see the spacemen. But you better buy me a bike if mine's stolen."

"Don't argue with me," Castine began, but Vickery caught her arm.

"He won't budge," he said. To Santiago he called, "We'll all chip in for it."

Plowman climbed laboriously up out of the engine compartment and lowered the hatch back in place. "Got oil, batteries look okay, sea strainers got no fish in 'em, engine seacocks are open." He got to his feet and limped across the deck to the helm, wiping his hands on his shirt. He crouched, grunting, opened a panel and tugged some wires down from behind the dash panel.

"Will it start?" asked Santiago, who had picked up the tool box and followed him.

"Got no excuse not to, that I can see," Plowman said, pulling a couple of wires free and twisting their ends together, "but we just want power first." He leaned back to see the dash panel, then reached up to push a button on it. "Gotta blow out all the gassy air down there first."

"Do that after we're clear!" said Yoneda, striding forward. "The GRU assassins might be arriving in the lot out front right now!—thanks to these clumsy—" She kicked the mat and didn't finish her sentence.

"They *might* be close," ventured Castine.

"If there's fuel fumes anywhere down there," said Plowman stolidly, "and I start the engine, *we'll* be arriving in the parking lot. From overhead."

At last he reached up to switch off the blower, and touched a loose wire to the ignition housing; the deck shook as the engines started up.

Plowman got to his feet, in stages. "Somebody toss that mat onto the dock and bring the ladder aboard.

Bill—Sebastian, whoever you are—get out there and cast off the lines." He looked at Yoneda. "You sure you don't want to get off?"

"Stay with the mat beacon?" She waved toward the harbor and shook her head. "Let's go, floor it."

Four miles out past the long stone jetties that enclosed Anaheim Harbor, Plowman throttled down and shifted to neutral and let the *Ouranos* rock in the low waves. The still-glowing western sky silhouetted the cliffs of San Pedro, and clouds like fragments of eroded marble shone pink in the west but ash-gray in the darkening sky over the mainland. Seal Beach and Sunset Beach were lines of bright pinpricks in the boat's wake, and the permanently moored ocean liner *Queen Mary* was a brighter spot across the water to the northwest. To the west, the black ocean extened to infinity.

The wind was from out there, and very cold; Plowman soon went below to operate the boat from the wheelhouse helm in the main cabin, and the others joined him. Now he swiveled the captain's chair around to face aft.

Vickery and Castine sat on a bench just forward of a sink on the starboard side, and across from them, separated by a formica-topped table bolted to the deck, Yoneda and Tacitus perched on swing-down seats against the port bulkhead. Santiago sat on the top step with the cabin door at his back. A single overhead light threw a chiaroscuro lemon glow onto the six faces. The heater, after some delay, was producing a draft of warm air that smelled of scorched dust.

Plowman nodded toward some wires that stuck out

from a hole in the port bulkhead just below the wooden ceiling. "They took the radio and any GPS stuff, and Frankie's compass points every which way but north. I really don't want to get out so far that I can't see the shore lights."

"But can't you steer by the stars?" said Castine. "According to Galvan, the UAPs were seen way out past Catalina."

"I'm a fair mechanic, but I'm no mariner. Anyway, in the car you said you three got 'em to make a crop circle in the L.A. River, right? Because the three of you were together, and you have an effect on 'em? Well—you're together here. Funny it didn't happen back at the marina, in fact."

Vickery thought the old man was trying to conceal relief that nothing seemed likely to happen; and realized that he was doing the same.

"It's not night yet," Castine pointed out. "Spaceships by day, light rings at night."

Yoneda shifted on the wooden bench. "What are you going to *do*," she asked, "if something shows up?"

"Well—dammit, try to communicate," said Castine, a bit defiantly. "At least make obviously deliberate gestures, two, three, five, seven, primary numbers."

"That's as far as you'll get with two hands," said Yoneda.

"So you can help take it to nineteen." Castine turned toward Tacitus. "According to you, they assume what they comprehend as our physical shape, and they take that grotesque form—big hands, lips, tongue—because they've begun to comprehend human brains, and our brains have more nerves connected to those parts." She looked around at the others. "They've begun to comprehend human brains!" she repeated. "Communication, at least recognition, might be possible."

"But they only appear for a few seconds," said Tacitus. "What can you do?"

"Speak, maybe," said Castine desperately. "I didn't notice their ears, either time I saw one, but I bet we've got a lot of nerve endings in our ears. And maybe they last longer, when they're made of sea water instead of dirt and wheat chaff."

"Sure," said Yoneda. "Surface tension and all."

"We should have stopped somewhere for sandwiches," Vickery began, getting to his feet—

—When the bow was suddenly a glaring triangle through the windshield and the porthole rings shone white, and a racket like a stuttering electric drill started up outside.

Santiago had leaped away from the cockpit deck door, and Castine got up from the bench and pulled the door open—and Vickery was right behind her when she crouched out onto the open cockpit deck, which was brightly illuminated from overhead.

Squinting upward, Vickery saw a brightly shining white sphere expanding in size against the contrastingly black sky, high above the boat. But it wasn't expanding, it was *descending*, and fast—thinking it might be about to crash into the boat, Vickery was bracing himself to throw Castine and then himself overboard, when the thing swept down and extinguished itself in the sea a hundred feet astern. The staccato noise stopped abruptly.

There was no splash, but a burst of oven-hot air swept

across the cockpit deck, and then Vickery's shoes were scuffing ineffectually at the deck and he grabbed the edge of the cabin roof as it began to sink past his right shoulder.

In the sudden darkness, Castine was a darker silhouette dotted with spots of fire; she was extending one arm toward him, and he made sure to catch her wrist firmly with his left hand, for her feet were rising away behind her.

The cabin roof was smoking under his right palm, and Vickery felt points of sharp pain in his scalp and chest. He and Castine were rotating upward on the fulcrum of his right hand, which was locked onto the edge of the scorching roof. Gritting his teeth as he clung to the smoldering wood and Castine's wrist, he was aware that the black horizon was both tilting and sinking.

Then the boat was dropped bow foremost into the sea, and Vickery and Castine tumbled forward across the cabin roof and plunged deep into churning, icy salt water. Vickery was still holding Castine's wrist, and with his free hand he clung to one of the bow railing stanchions.

After five long seconds the bow deck was pressing upward under him and the weight of sea water sluiced away to the sides. Castine was sprawled on top of him at the forward end of the short bow deck, both of them wedged against the bow railing.

Castine rolled off him and sat up, coughing and spitting; she pushed her sopping hair away from her face and blinked around wildly at the dark empty ocean. There was no light behind the windshield, but someone inside the boat pounded against the glass. Vickery waved, then pressed his hand against the wet glass and swept it back and forth in a more visible wave.

Notchett's boat didn't have even the narrowest side deck, so Vickery and Castine clambered back over the wet cabin roof and dropped down to the cockpit deck. The boat was still pitching back and forth, and they both wound up sitting and sliding down the deck to the transom, along with a lot of foaming salt water. At least, Vickery thought dazedly, the patches of fire everywhere got extinguished.

The bulkhead door banged open behind them, and Vickery heard Yoneda call, "Whoa!" He looked around and saw her leaning out of the doorway. "You two nearly had to swim home."

Vickery helped Castine up, and the two of them leaned on the transom, shivering, as Yoneda walked across the rocking deck toward them. Water was sloshing around her ankles and she held her arms out to the sides for balance.

"Plowman lost a tooth," Yoneda called, "and Tacitus has a sprained shoulder or something. That kid just rolled like a monkey." She looked up from her feet, past Vickery, and her face emptied of all expression.

Vickery quickly shifted around to look aft; and then he just stared.

Glowing white lines like the spokes of an enormous wheel stretched across the dark face of the sea, rapidly but silently rotating under the surface. Castine stood beside him, and their faces were alternately in shadow and then whitely underlit as the shining lines moved past under them.

Vickery took a quick look back. Yoneda and Santiago

were right behind them, and Tacitus was standing in the bulkhead doorway, gripping one side of it.

The sight of Tacitus reminded Vickery of last night in the riverbed. "Get back belowdecks!" he shouted, pulling Castine away from the transom. Santiago turned and slipped, and Yoneda jumped over him and fell herself, both of them sliding halfway to the forward bulkhead. Vickery and Castine separated and moved carefully around them on the rocking deck, gripping the gunwales. They had made their way to the bulkhead, Vickery bumping into the canopied helm, when Castine shouted hoarsely.

Vickery looked at her, then quickly looked in the direction she was pointing.

A figure was standing back at the transom end of the deck now, glowing internally and then dimming as the light spokes moved past in the water behind it, and it seemed to be made of smoky glass: about seven feet tall, with thin legs and torso supporing a slowly bobbing, elongated head, and spindly arms that extended to the sides over the high gunwales.

Yoneda and Santiago had glanced back and then scurried forward and knocked Tacitus aside as they crowded in through the door. Vickery waved at Castine to follow them, but now she was staring wide-eyed at something above and behind him in the vast oceanic night.

CHAPTER SEVENTEEN:
A Confederacy of Bums

Ingrid Castine almost froze—the huge glassy cylinders curling behind Vickery's head looked like the tentacles of some leviathan—but she knew they must be the fingers of the alien's enormous right hand, lifted from the sea.

Several phobically inhibiting images flashed across her mind in the instant before she moved: the terrified woman in the crop circle in Wiltshire, whose echo-viewed form had passed right through Castine; and the near-overlap with another woman seen in echo-view, at Cole's restaurant yesterday; and, somehow, the face of Eliot Shaw, the man to whom she had been engaged and who had been killed by the rogue Transportation Utility Agency in 2017.

She broke through the momentary paralysis by convulsively pushing away from the bulkhead in a fast forward somersault across the wet deck, and when she rolled to her feet her momentum made it impossible to avoid colliding with the big-headed translucent figure swaying at the aft end of the cockpit deck.

301

There was a sensation of icy envelopment, and free-fall in an unsuspected direction—and then she was *inside* it, surrounded and supported by cold sea water, and her head was up inside the elongated head of the alien whose death had made the rotating light-wheel in the sea.

It had died, and Castine experienced the devastating phase-change of its death—but in this unsought post-mortem communion she knew that it was nevertheless aware of her intrusion in its fallen material form. Castine was helplessly participating in its death, her frail identity fragmenting in the thing's dissolution, and when she desperately tried to comprehend its nature as something distinct and separate from her own, she found herself picturing triangles, trinities, the three-sided chessboards at the Zeta Reticuli Chess Club temple; it seemed that there were only three of the alien entities—no, they consisted of three sexes, or existed on three axes or polarities—and comprehension of chaotic free wills was what killed them and had killed this one: had mortally rendered this one self-aware, broken it out of the eternal three-way reciprocation of attention that sustained its kind.

For one timeless instant she nearly comprehended the existence this entity had lost—and to which it would surely be restored: something like the breathless moment of springing from a high diving board, or an orchestral chord that never faded.

Castine's body was clenched in vertigo and revulsion. A small and diminishing part of her knew that she was on a boat on an ocean on the spherical Earth, but the concept of curvature seemed to be an optical illusion, a simplification so crude that it was meaningless; substituting the idea that all surfaces were parallel was less inadequate.

She comprehended that in their unfallen state the entities had no personal memories or intentions, but this fatally individualized one knew, without thought, that its . . . companions? kin? . . . both quick and dead, were experiencing something comparable to an increasing pressure, and that when the pressure burst its constriction they would all be released from the web of indeterminist unreason that had ensnared them here; and the concept of that bursting was something her mind could encompass only by analogy from its own store of images: a firestorm rising over a city, Dracula as a bat flying away from a shrunken and drained corpse, a blistered and opaque magnesium flash bulb.

With the last strength of her will, she drew partway back from her psychic overlap with the alien entity, and she tried to muster and project a thought—a desperate solicitation of recognition; but it was clear that the thing didn't and couldn't perceive the thought. Her call for its attention existed in discrete moments of time—but, for this alien being, time was a long wavelength that stepped right over her mental gesture.

Then it recoiled away from her intrusion by bursting into spray, and she collided with the transom and collapsed, sitting down on the deck and panting as if she'd just run a grueling race.

Hands were on her, lifting her up. In the few moments it took for her personality to reclaim her mind, she cringed at the deliberate individual attention. She was aware of noises, and then recognized that some of them were speech.

"Are you okay?" said a voice that she knew: Sebastian Vickery. "You dove right through it!" he added.

I'm not dead, she thought. I'm a physical body, but somehow not dead.

She managed to say, "I'm—freezing."

She moved her head from side to side and made her eyes focus. Vickery was holding her up with an arm around her waist, and Santiago was tucking a, a *gun* back into his jacket pocket, and two others, Yoneda and Tacitus, were hurrying this way across the deck, glancing nervously at the sky and the sea.

"Some communication," said Yoneda breathlessly. "You pop him like a water balloon and then bounce on your ass."

Castine forced her mind to work. "It was—" she stammered, "it wasn't a him. Or a her, but not exactly neuter—I was *in* it for a while." She tried to wipe sea water away from her eyes, but the cuff of her suede coat was sopping wet. "Wasn't I?"

"Maybe for one second," said Vickery, leading her toward the bulkhead door.

Plowman was crouched below the topside helm, cursing.

"Let's get inside," said Vickery. "We're stalled, and it's likely to get very cold here shortly."

"Only one second?" said Castine vaguely. "It was an illuminating second."

She tried to straighten up and walk without help, but to her annoyance she wasn't able to work her legs correctly, and she let Vickery take most of her weight as they crossed the deck, and she let him lift her down the steps to the main cabin. The overhead light had gone out. Yoneda and Tacitus and Santiago followed, and Vickery led Castine to the bench where they'd been sitting two minutes earlier. The door swung in the cold wind, and Castine could hear Plowman cursing out on the deck.

At last the engines started, and the overhead light came on. A few moments later Plowman came clumping down the steps and pulled the door closed. He stepped past the others to sit down at the cabin controls, and after gunning the engines a couple of times he worked the gear lever and then steered the boat back toward the lights of the coastline.

"Go fast," said Vickery.

"Sure," said Plowman, "but I'll want some help figuring out where we came from." He seemed to catch some of Vickery's urgency—the engines were roaring under the deck and Castine could feel the vibration through the soles of her shoes.

"Just get the boat ashore anywhere," advised Yoneda. "We can ditch it." She glanced at Castine, who was shivering, and added, "Is the damn heater on?"

"Yes," said Plowman. "You can't just park a boat somewhere. I'd like to find the marina."

"And the same slip?" said Yoneda. "Good luck. Anyway, the GRU probably has assassins waiting there."

"Unlikely," spoke up Tacitus. "They'll have found the mat, and know the trap was discovered. Only crazy people would go back to the same slip after that."

"Crazy people," echoed Plowman, nodding.

"And Galvan's concealment car is parked there," said Vickery. "I don't want Ingrid and me walking far with our blood exposed."

"I watched when we came out," said Santiago. "I'll know the way back."

"Even in the dark?" asked Yoneda, and the boy nodded.

Castine had recovered enough to perceive that none of them, not even Yoneda, was ready to talk about what had happened within the last couple of minutes; and she guessed that they were surprised and embarrassed by their hesitancy.

Am I ready to? she wondered. *I feel drunk, or concussed. I can't even put words to the things I learned about the alien, just my own images of what the things remind me of. Dracula? Flash bulbs?*

She ran cold-numbed fingers through her wet hair, pressing on her scalp. *For at least a moment there,* she thought, *I had to break through my phobia about overlapping with people—people, much less aliens!—to save Sebastian from I don't know what. There was the girl in the crop circle in England who seemed to walk right through me, and the woman at Cole's yesterday who seemed about to lean* into *me—but why did I think of* Eliot?

Her mind was still too shaken for her to avoid the next thought.

Was my promised marriage to Eliot one of those things you busily and sincerely make plans for—but know, deep inside, will not actually come to pass?

No, she told herself with as much firmness as she could muster. *No, you're like the rest of them here, just using* any handy distraction to avoid addressing what happened back there on the cockpit deck.

Then she tried without success to keep from remembering a line about marriage in the gospel of Mark: *And the twain shall be one flesh; so then they are no longer twain, but one flesh*. And she shuddered.

Quickly and too loudly, she said, "I communicated with it." When all of them, even Plowman in the captain's chair, turned toward her, she went on, "Or no—at least I saw into its mind. Or something. For more than a second, subjectively."

She took a breath to say more, but her voice caught and she suppressed a sob. None of the others spoke, but she gasped, "Shut up, never mind." She inhaled again, leaned her head back against the paneled bulwark and stared at the low ceiling.

Plowman turned away from her and spoke, slowly. "I'm sorry it was you it happened to," he said, speaking loudly because the engines were roaring and he was facing the windshield. "It should have been me, again. That happened to me on that night in '68, out by Pahute Mesa at the Nevada Test Range. The thing was made of sand and dust, and it had a big head but long limbs and narrow hands . . . it was running around in the spotlights, in confusion, maybe, and it . . . it ran right *through* me. I was it, for a long, long second, and it was me, and we both . . . *hated* that."

Santiago pointed ahead, and Plowman altered their course slightly. "I never managed to get *close* to anybody," he went on, "after that. But—yeah, I saw what you saw."

"Thank you," said Castine, exhaling. When Yoneda made a beckoning gesture, she went on, "There's three of them—no, that's not right. They come in threes, or think of themselves in threes . . ."

As the bright line of Seal Beach through the windshield widened and became individual lights, and the three yellow-lit stacks of the *Queen Mary* became visibly separate on the close port horizon, Castine did her best to convey what she had learned in her moment of communion with the dead alien. She was aware of Vickery looking at her with sympathy—no doubt recalling her horror at even sharing space with another *human*—but she addressed herself mainly to Tacitus and to Plowman, who kept his eyes on the lights ahead in the darkness but nodded from time to time as she spoke.

Santiago was standing beside Plowman, occasionally pointing out particular lights, and he soon identified the lights at the ends of the two arms of the Seal Beach jetties. "Go between them and turn right when you can," the boy said, "go back under the freeway bridge and then it's just past the restaurant that looks like a water tower, I'm sure that's lit up at night." He turned away from the helm and said to Castine, "Dracula?"

"That's just what its concept made me think of," Castine told him. "It wasn't anything about drinking blood—or even about people."

"Emptying something of its vitality," said Plowman. "The way a fire-storm ascends by using up all the oxygen below."

Tacitus nodded. "And I'm surprised you remember flash bulbs!" he said to Castine. "They were for one-time use—each one was destroyed in producing light, energy, for a photograph."

"And tomorrow night's the flash," said Vickery.

Santiago had moved back to the cockpit door to peer through its window. Now he gasped, and when everyone turned toward him he just tapped the glass.

Vickery got up and looked out, then motioned the boy aside and carefully opened the door, dispelling the scarcely warmed air of the interior. Knowing what she would see, Castine got up and stood beside him.

On the rippled black plain of the sea a couple of hundred yards astern, a tall pale column was dimly visible against the night sky. Warm breath on her neck let Castine know that Yoneda had stepped up behind her and was staring out too, and she heard Tacitus, and then Plowman, shuffle across the deck to join them.

"I'm glad you got the engines started," Vickery said to Plowman. After thirty more seconds he softly closed the door. Plowman returned to the helm, and the others resumed their seats.

Castine sat back down on the bench, aware again, more forcefuly, of being cold and exhausted. "I'm afraid the good ship *Ouranos* didn't restrain the hundred-handed ones tonight," she said, with a big shaky yawn that mixed tears with the salt water on her cheeks. "The thing was aware of me, but I—I couldn't even get its attention!"

Tacitus frowned at her. "You did far more than poor Frankie dared to do. When one of the things appeared to him, on this boat, he just ran to the controls and sped away."

"I—" She paused, and mentally finished the sentence: I had to save Sebastian. "I suppose I did," she said instead. She watched the jetty lights pass on either side as

Plowman steered into the calmer waters. "I should have been carrying your negation symbol, Pierce."

"The alien wouldn't have been able to see it," said Plowman over his shoulder, "with its *now* spread out like you say."

"I don't think a drawing of the negation symbol would catch their attention anyway," said Vickery, "even if you paint it on a parking lot and leave it there for hours. You'd have to *draw* their attention to it somehow."

"Sugar and honey," said Santiago.

"Or something," said Vickery quietly.

Castine shook her head. "So what *do* we do, before tomorrow night? Just—be sure to get to Confession and an early mass?"

"I don't know what," said Plowman from the captain's chair, "but I bet I know where. That old ghost woman in the car said the spacemen show up in places they've appeared at recently—she said it's 'cause the hole of their intrusion hadn't closed up all the way yet."

Castine saw Vickery press his lips together, and she realized that he wished Plowman hadn't said that in front of Yoneda and Tacitus; and she guessed that he did have some sort of plan.

"Ah," said Yoneda, slumping in her wet clothes. "Back to Giant Rock."

"I missed the show yesterday," said Plowman.

For several seconds none of them spoke. The engines droned on, and the boat bobbed steadily over the waves.

Yoneda spoke up. "In the meantime the three of you," she said to Vickery, Castine and Tacitus, "should split up as soon as we're ashore. We don't need another monster dying on top of us tonight. But you said they don't do the crop circle death thing by daylight—so where do we meet up tomorrow morning? I can't drive all the way out to the damn desert with the Highway Patrol watching for my car—even," she added with a nod to Tacitus, "with stolen plates."

"We?" Castine frowned and looked across the table at her. "I thought you were going to take your GRU defector to Agent Finehouse. He won't let Tacitus participate in . . . trying to *mummify* all the aliens with the negation symbol. That's not Commander Lubitz's plan."

"And I think I cannot, after all, defect," said Tacitus. "I agree with Miss Castine that your masters would not sanction this effort." He stretched and ran a hand through his thinning dyed hair.

Yoneda's mouth was open as she looked at Tacitus, and then at the others, but she didn't say anything. Slowly she took a small object from her pocket, and Castine and Vickery both tensed when they saw that it was a cell phone; but it was an old flip phone, surely soaked with salt water, and when Yoneda held it up, the battery compartment was visibly empty and corroded.

She opened the phone and the cover came right off. She laid both pieces carefully on the table. "I must transfer my allegiance," she said, "from recognized authority to . . . a confederacy of bums. I must." She carefully fitted the cover back onto the phone, though it was still unattached, and put it back in her pocket; and Castine noticed that Tacitus was giving Yoneda an odd, possibly sympathetic look. Yoneda continued, "No, Lubitz and Finehouse would not sanction it. But I can't pretend I don't know what I know." She nodded toward the cabin door. "Or seen what I've seen. My career is over, and I don't even know what the penalty *is* for making a false police report to avoid arrest!" She gave Tacitus a faint, for-once-frightened smile. "I'm an orphan too."

Vickery caught Castine's eye and shrugged. I know, she thought, it would be interesting to hear the story of that false police report and the Highway Patrol. If we ever have time.

The boat purred into Anaheim Bay and under the Pacific Coast Highway bridge, and then they were in Huntington Harbor, and the water glittered with the lights of houses on the starboard side and the buildings of the Sunset Beach Harbor Patrol to port. With Santiago's help, Plowman found the four long docks of the Howard's Landing Marina, and Castine was surprised at how smoothly Plowman worked the gears and throttle to ease the boat bow-first between the finger piers of a slip—presumably the correct slip.

Castine stood up, bracing herself with a hand on a low ceiling beam. The car, she thought, the heater turned on full, solid pavement under the wheels, some store for dry clothes, a couple of big greasy tacos drenched in hot salsa, and several shots of bourbon neat.

Perhaps guessing her thoughts, Vickery nodded and said, "Another and another cup to drown/ The memory of this impertinence," which she recognized as lines from Omar Khayyam's *Rubaiyat*.

The bow of the *Ouranos* bumped gently against the fenders at the front of the slip, and Vickery stepped up to the cabin door and pulled it open. To Santiago he said, "You can help me tie her up, I'll show you how."

Castine crossed to the steps and gripped the door frame with her left hand to pull herself up to the deck level just as a softball-sized metal sphere sailed over the cabin and bounced on the deck—and even as she recognized the fuse assembly protruding from one end of it she was diving forward, catching it on the first bounce and using its momentum to flip it over the starboard gunwale.

"Fire in the hole!" she shouted as she let her dive become a roll across the wet deck to the opposite gunwale.

Vickery had seen the grenade fly past his shoulder, and he had spun to try to grab it and get it overboard before it detonated—but when Castine threw it over the gunwale he continued his spin to knock Santiago down and fall on top of him.

The explosion sounded like a sledge hammer punching a cinder-block wall, and the deck shook. A moment later Vickery was drenched in cold spray as he rolled off Santiago. Through a sudden churning mist he saw Castine getting to her feet holding Tacitus's revolver, and he realized that he had pulled his .45 out of his jacket pocket.

They'll have heard the grenade detonating under water, he thought, and not on the deck or in the cabin.

He ran to the cabin and vaulted onto the roof, and he slid prone and scanned the long dock over the pistol's barrel. He could hear shouts from the other boats.

A man in a heavy jacket and knitted cap stepped cautiously out from behind the bow of the boat in the next slip, and a moment later a similarly dressed man appeared behind him. The first man was holding a round object, certainly another grenade; Vickery sighted on him and rested his finger lightly on the trigger. The man had not drawn his arm back for a throw, and Vickery quickly calculated what shot would put the grenade into the water on the far side of the dock.

But two shots cracked from behind him, and the man simply sat down on the dock; his hand opened and the grenade rolled across the planks. His companion lunged toward him, one hand darting toward the grenade.

Vickery buried his head behind his crossed forearms, and the hard *bam* threw shrapnel whistling overhead and striking the nearby hulls. He must have fumbled it, Vickery thought.

Raising his head, he saw a ragged hole in the dock below a curling smoke cloud, and when he turned to push himself back off the cabin roof he saw Santiago on the roof behind him, holding the Sig Sauer pistol. The boy hopped down to the cockpit deck, and Vickery landed in a crouch right beside him, pocketing the .45. The air was sharp with a smell like burnt gunpowder and ammonia.

Yoneda and Tacitus were out on the tilting deck now, and Vickery waved them back toward the transom, where Castine stood holding Tacitus's revolver. A glance past the cabin showed him several people already hurrying up the dock, with a couple more standing at the bows of the other boats.

"We all swim away from this," said Vickery, hurrying to the transom. He tugged his shoes off and shoved them inside his jacket. "Fast but quiet. Try to come ashore somewhere without being seen. Plowman, Santiago, meet us at the car, we'll wait for you for a while." He swung one leg over the transom gunwale.

"And us?" called Yoneda.

"You two," Vickery said, nodding back toward her and Tacitus, "tomorrow at seven AM at—"

He hesitated, and Castine said, "Canter's, on Fairfax."

Vickery barked a quick laugh, for he and Castine had had a hectic reunion at Canter's a year and a half ago. "Canter's," he agreed.

Castine tucked the revolver under her waistband, shrugged out of her soaked coat and vaulted right over the transom. Vickery heard the quiet splash as she knifed into the water, and he swung his other leg over and jumped.

The water was breathtakingly cold, and when he surfaced he was panting. Castine was treading water six feet away, her hair streaked across her face, and she brushed it back and nodded reassuringly. Vickery looked back and saw Yoneda and Tacitus clamber over the transom and drop, and then Santiago. Tacitus and Santiago were both carrying life-preservers.

Vickery and Castine quickly swam out away from the marina docks, and when they were about halfway between the docked boats on either side of the channel they paused, treading water. At the moment no moving vessels were within two hundred yards of them. Vickery didn't see the other three swimmers, and he was glad Santiago and Tacitus had grabbed life-preservers.

Castine's head was just a bobbing silhouette against the now-distant marina lights. He listened to her breathing, and she was taking deep, unhurried breaths. "You okay?" he asked. "I can tow you if you get tired or too cold."

"Your old Secret Service training," she said. Her voice was tight but not panicky. "If the limo went off a bridge. I'm okay."

"This way," Vickery said, beginning a slow sidestroke east along the channel, and Castine adopted the same energy-conserving stroke. Vickery's right side ached, and he wondered if Galvan had cracked a rib when she punched him. "We'll find an empty dock in front of a dark house, a good distance from the explosion."

For several minutes they swam silently through the black, glittering water, each occasionally rolling to give one arm a rest. Vickery watched Castine, alert for signs of diminished coordination due to hypothermia, and he hoped this immersion in sea water wasn't rousing traumatic flashbacks of her envelopment in the alien.

"You still okay?" he asked quietly, wanting to assess her speech.

"Damn cold. Find us a dock." She spoke clearly, to his relief. She rolled to face him, her right arm now taking its turn at doing most of the swimming. "You shot the grenade guy?"

"Santiago did. Got the guy and his pal, both."

"Good God."

Vickery had been regularly craning his neck to watch the shoreline on their right, which was a long row of white two- or three-story houses with docks in front, but though he had seen a couple of empty docks, lights were on in the houses and rock music rolled faintly across the water. He didn't want Castine and himself to be seen and questioned as they came ashore, but his own muscles were beginning to ache even with the relatively easy sidestroke, and the cold water was leaching his strength, and he knew Castine must be nearing the end of her endurance.

He had spied the white lamp of a channel marker ahead, indicating side traffic, and when they had paddled their way to it—SLOW NO WAKE was stenciled on its three-foot-tall white column—he lifted his head and tried to see over the low waves that lapped at this chin.

He saw a roughly fifty-foot gap in the row of houses, and a street light a couple of hundred feet further back. The gap had to be a boat ramp—and at this hour it wasn't surprising that no pickup truck was backed onto the ramp to launch or retrieve a boat.

He caught Castine's eye and nodded in that direction. "Ashore there," he said, and the slack exhaustion in her answering nod made him wish he'd led them ashore at one of the empty docks they'd passed.

But she rocked her head back and looked in the direction of the ramp, and there was new strength in her stroke as she swam toward it; and in minutes they had crawled up the grooved concrete slope and got shakily to their feet. They left the ramp darkly streaked with water behind them.

Castine was barefoot, and Vickery pulled his shoes out from his jacket and gave them to her. When she demurred, he said quietly, "Put them on, we're carrying guns—we've got to look as normal as possible walking back to the car, and I bet I can walk barefoot better than you."

"No contest." She crouched, and soon had the shoes on and tied. "You don't mind," she said hoarsely as she pressed her hands on the pavement and then on her knees to straighten up again, "if I lean on you. A lot."

"Good idea. Look like we're a couple."

"Sure. Your Pasadena waitress girlfriend."

Vickery thought of reminding her that their blood was still exposed, but as they began shuffling forward it was clear that she was walking as fast as she could. For all their strenuous effort to get this far, the car was only a few hundred yards away.

When they got to the car and climbed in, Vickery started the engine and drove to a parking space on the other side of the lot, from which they could see anyone approaching the previous spot and, if necessary, exit directly onto Pacific Coast Highway. He switched off the headlights and shifted the engine to neutral. He had turned the heater up to the maximum, and every few seconds he had to wipe steam from the windshield.

"Santiago's got that gun, unless he lost it in the channel." He rolled down his window to be able to see the driver's side mirror, and he flexed his aching and stinging feet. The soles of his socks were almost completely worn away.

Castine nodded. Several times she opened her mouth as if to say something, then closed it. Finally she said, "I suppose the boat sunk."

"Probably the one next to it too," agreed Vickery. He looked at her leaning over the heater vents. "If you weren't so quick catching that grenade, we'd be dead. Santiago too."

"I was on the girls' softball team in high school," she

said. "Shortstop." She lowered her head to get the hot air blowing into her hair. "There was a second explosion—not underwater."

"There were two guys—probably the same ones that were under my trailer last night. One of them had a second grenade, but Santiago shot him and he dropped it. His . . . comrade tried to get it and pitch it at us or drop it in the water, but he was too slow."

"God help us, every one." She sat back and ran her fingers through her tangled hair. After a few moments she said, "Our fingerprints are—"

She stopped talking, for the dashboard metronome had begun clicking back and forth, slowly; and even though he was expecting it, Vickery jumped when he looked in the rear-view mirror and saw the figure of the old woman's ghost in the back seat again. In the shadows, the thing's opaque black veil made its lowered head seem like an extension of its hunched shoulders.

Castine looked back, and just widened her eyes.

"Are you there, boss?" said Vickery wearily. He caught again the smells of cocoa and mildew.

The ghost began speaking rapidly in Spanish.

"The Rosary again, I bet," whispered Castine. "If I'd brought mine along, I'd say it with her."

Vickery turned around to face the fortunately impenetrable black veil. "Boss?" he said. "Galvan, you there?"

The ghost just kept reciting in Spanish.

"Two hundred Hail Marys," said Castine quietly, "if she does all the Mysteries of the whole Rosary." She shivered and turned to face the windshield. "I wonder if Mary hears prayers from ghosts."

"I imagine it's like replaying prayers left on an answering machine," said Vickery. "Boss!"

The Spanish prayers were choked off, and the voice said, more slowly, "Vickery? What?"

"Did you try to call us? The, uh, speaker has started up."

"In Spanish, right? If it's me it'll be in English. How are you doing with the spacemen? Is my car all right?"

"Your car's fine," if a bit wet, he thought. "And Castine—Betty Boop—got to talk to one of the spacemen, sort of. But how do we make the old lady stop talking when it's not you speaking through her?"

"You can't," said the monotone voice, so unlike Galvan's own voice. "It's prayers, I bet. Pray along with her, you could use it."

"Naval Intelligence is probably still after us with the blood cloths," Vickery protested, "we're going to have to sleep in the car. How can we—"

"You get out of my car to eat, understand? I don't want grease all over the upholstery. And to go to the bathroom. And it had half a tank of gas when it left here, it better be the same when you bring it back."

Vickery looked at Castine and rolled his eyes. "Understood, boss."

The flat monotone managed to carry some emphasis when it added, "And don't math out my walkie-talkie ghost!"

"She tries to grab the wheel when I'm driving! And pushes the gas pedal! I can't—"

"You telling me you can't outwrestle an old lady? A *dead* old lady?" It was jarring to hear the words seeming to

emanate from the old lady in question. "So hang onto the
wheel! Put it in neutral if she plays with the gas! Jeez, Vick,
how you gonna handle spacemen if you can't even—"

"Okay, boss. I gotta go—catch you later."

"Don't fuck up."

After a moment the voice started up in Spanish again.

Castine exhaled. "Can she hear us now?"

"I don't think so. I had to call to her to get her on just
now." Vickery was looking through the damp windshield
at the bamboo antenna, which was visibly swaying; after a
few seconds it stopped.

"So," said Castine, speaking over the ghost's endless
prayers, "earplugs, to sleep?"

"Hm? Oh." Vickery shrugged. "We'll figure something
out."

Castine peered impatiently through the steamy
windshield, then said, "How long do we wait for them?"

"Another few minutes. They're both—" Vickery saw
motion in the driver's side mirror, two trudging figures;
when they passed in front of a brightly lit shop window he
recognized them. "Ah, here they are."

Castine turned around in her seat and looked out the
back window. "What do we do with them?"

The ghost droned on.

"Drop them back at the cathedral parking garage—
though I'll stay off freeways, with our stowaway trying to
take the wheel and drive to Cerritos. The *parking garage,*"
he repeated more loudly to be heard over the ghost. "If
Santiago's bike's stolen, Plowman can give him a ride.
Plowman should put him up and feed him. And buy him
a new bike."

"I think he would, though he'd put it on his daughter's VISA. What do *we* do, after?"

"Drive to my studio, quickly change into dry clothes— and get some socks and shoes!—and heat up some more Beef Stroganoff and bring it and a bottle of something out to the car." He rocked his head back toward the praying ghost. "And not spill anything."

"And sleep in the car."

"We slept in a taco truck one time."

Castine nodded. "And a tomb, one time before that. And some towels, these seats are wet. In fact the world can wait while I take a hot shower."

"Not too much to ask. A quick one."

Vickery switched the headlights on and off; and in the mirror he saw Santiago tug on Plowman's sleeve and point toward the car.

"And pillows and blankets," he said. "It's likely to be a cold night."

Castine held her hands out in front of herself and spread her fingers, as if trying to gauge the shape of something. "And a colder day."

When Plowman and Santiago walked up to the car, they opened the back doors and then stepped back. The old ghost had not stopped praying.

"Get her out," said Plowman.

"She's part of the car," said Vickery wearily, "and she can't hurt you as long as she's got the veil on. Come on, I'll take you back to your car."

The steering wheel jerked suddenly under Vickery's hand and the engine roared in neutral. After a moment it subsided to normal idling.

Plowman stepped even further back. "That was her, wasn't it, doing that? I ain't goin'."

Vickery sat back and closed his eyes. His muscles ached with fatigue from having swum three hundred yards in cold water, and from having more-or-less continuously wrestled the steering wheel on the drive down here. The soles of his feet stung, and he dreaded the effort of pressing them on the pedals.

He sighed and opened his eyes. "Santiago, can you do multiplication in Spanish? You know, two times two is four? Loud?"

Castine pursed her lips, but nodded.

"Sure," said the boy, peering into the car at the ghost. "I've met these before."

Vickery waved toward the back seat. "Two times two is four, then four times four. Make her hear it."

Santiago leaned toward the open door and began reciting in Spanish. After he had said a few short sentences, the ghost stopped speaking, and was shifting in evident discomfort on the seat.

Castine glanced at Vickery. "I hate to be interrupting her in her prayers."

"It, not her."

She nodded, her lips pressed together. "Santiago," she said with evident reluctance, "now tell her that the last number, minus itself, is nothing. And repeat that."

"Y eso, menos en sí mismo, no es nada," Santiago told the ghost. *"Nada!"*

Vickery jumped, for the ghost emitted a flat, prolonged wail and was suddenly upside-down, with her feet blocking the back window; then all he could see in the back seat was flickering patches of black and gray, like a spinning kaleidoscope filled with ashes.

Castine was bracing one hand on the dashboard. "Terminal spin," she said through clenched teeth, "in a confined space!"

The wail was cut off abruptly, and Vickery exhaled as the air shifted in the car. The ghost was gone.

"Like a damn *buzz*-saw," muttered Plowman. "Just like Frankie." He got into the back seat, slowly.

"Wow!" said Santiago breathlessly. He got in and closed his door.

The dashboard metronome was motionless now. Vickery opened the driver's side door and stepped out, wincing as his abraded soles pressed the cold asphalt, and cringing at the breeze on his wet shirt and pants. He limped around the front bumper and took hold of the bamboo antenna, and with one yank wrenched it off.

A white object the size of a cigarette butt fell out of the base of it and clicked on the pavement. He tossed the bamboo stick away and crouched to pick the thing up.

It was a bone—almost certainly a finger bone. He tossed it after the stick.

When he got back into the car, Castine gave him a questioning look. "I wondered about that antenna," he said. "One of the old lady's finger bones was in it. It was Galvan's monitor—the way *she*, at least, could keep track of her concealment car."

"So why . . .?"

"She's gonna be pissed that we mathed out her ghost—maybe pissed enough to reconsider the money the ONI guy offered her to turn me in."

"Probably would," agreed Santiago from the back seat.

"Uh," said Vickery, "good job back there."

In the rear-view mirror he saw the boy look away and nod.

Vickery shifted the engine into gear, pressed his bare sole onto the gas pedal, and steered toward the exit onto Pacific Coast Highway.

TUESDAY

CHAPTER EIGHTEEN:
Yo, Samson

Morning sunlight threw a strip of brightness along the linoleum floor at Canter's, and the warm air smelled of bacon and pickles. Vickery had stopped on the way here to buy a lot of sandwiches and beer and bottled water for later in the day, but Castine, sipping her second cup of coffee, was thinking about ordering pork chops and eggs right now, in spite of Vickery's insistence that they shouldn't stay out of the concealment car in one place for very long. Across from her in the orange vinyl booth, Vickery was ignoring his coffee and glancing repeatedly toward the street door.

"We spread a lot of chaff last night," she reassured him, then cleared her throat and had another gulp of coffee. The cut on her left forearm ached under the tight bandage, and she reminded herself that they had cleaned and disinfected their new self-inflicted cuts, and in any case had bigger concerns today.

✧✧✧

After they had dropped Plowman and Santiago off at the cathedral parking structure last night, Vickery had driven to a 24-hour Target store on Firestone in South Gate, and Castine was now wearing a black leather bomber jacket, a men's flannel shirt, a pair of bootcut blue jeans and tan hiking boots, for all of which Vickery had paid $135 in cash without complaint. Vickery had claimed that his own clothes were nearly dried out, and in any case he had more at his studio.

They had also bought a package of paper towels, and before they had driven out of the Target parking lot, Vickery had cut his arm and blotted half a dozen paper towels with his blood, and Castine had insisted on doing the same. Vickery had paired the two sets of stained paper towels like socks, and immediately tucked one pair behind the license plate of a Target delivery truck. On the way back to his studio he had stopped several times to dispose of the other five pairs—on a couple of buses, in a gas station restroom, on the roof of a taco stand, and one pair stuffed through a slot in a manhole cover.

"It's decoys—chaff," he had said as he'd got back in the car after planting the first pair, "like fighter jets throwing clouds of tinfoil scraps to confuse radar, in case your man Finehouse is still monitoring those old rags."

They were back at his studio before midnight, and Vickery brought his briefcase in. While Castine heated the Beef Stroganoffs, he taped Plowman's old newspaper pages together so that the sections of the negation symbol were lined up, tacked them to a white sheet of cardboard, then sketched in the missing corner of the symbol from Plowman's snapshots. He pulled a six-foot by eight-foot

canvas out from behind a rack of shelves and set up a
projector to throw the complete negation symbol onto the
upright canvas.

When he had traced the lines onto the canvas with
orange chalk, and then switched off the projector and
defined the pattern in black acrylic paint, he ate his
cooling dinner while Castine was in the shower. He got in
the shower after she was out, and by twelve-thirty they
were reclining in the tilted-back seats of Galvan's old
Dodge, which Vickery parked in front of an empty lot
around the corner from his studio. The nearest streetlight
cast only dim highlights on the dashboard.

Vickery had brought along a battery-powered alarm
clock, and he set it for 6 AM.

He pulled a blanket over himself and tried to shift to a
comfortable position on the still-damp seat. "I think
Galvan cracked a rib."

"Just imagine," came Castine's muffled reply from the
passenger seat, "what she'll do when she sees you busted
off her bamboo antenna."

"I'll say spacemen did it."

For a while neither of them spoke. Long after Vickery
had assumed Castine had fallen asleep, she said, "I caught
a *live grenade* tonight!" She exhaled. "Those two under
your trailer last night—that just seemed like . . . *'You kids
get out of here,'* you know? But that grenade was real."

Vickery nodded, then said, "Yes, it was."

She shifted around to face him. "And Santiago killed
them?"

"Yes."

She nodded, and after a while she said, "They figure

they owe something to dead people, don't they. Plowman and Santiago."

"Most people do."

"But they're really putting themselves out on the green felt table, at the mercy of the dice. Plowman especially— he found the negation symbol, but he's too old to *do* this. *Try* to do this. And he *knows* the things—he knows the, the free-fall loss of identity, overlapping with one of them."

"He's still got one daughter he can save. Even if it's not the one he'd have chosen."

"And guys with grenades." Castine lifted her right arm from beneath the blanket to touch the side of her head, and Vickery knew she was touching the scar from when she'd been shot three years ago, on an L.A. street about ten miles north of here.

"Always like this," she said softly. Then, "It's probably already tomorrow, isn't it?"

"Somewhat."

"I hate sequential time."

She said nothing further, and soon they both slept.

As she finished her coffee and put down the cup, Castine saw Vickery's eyes narrow, and when she looked around she saw Yoneda and Tacitus shambling past the restaurant's bakery section by the front door. Castine thought they must have found a Target too, for Yoneda was now in black jeans and a khaki jacket with a lot of pockets, and Tacitus wore an olive-green windbreaker and brown corduroy pants and a canvas hat. His right arm was in a blue cloth sling. They both looked tired.

"The desert," said Castine as the newcomers saw them

and began walking toward the booth. "We should have bought hats too."

Yoneda slid in beside Vickery, and Castine made room for Tacitus on her side of the booth.

Yoneda rubbed her eyes, then dropped her hands and gave Vickery a belligerent look. "You two can't be out of your stealth car for long, right? Would you mind going and sitting in it till Tacitus and I have breakfast? I'm literally starving." She picked up a laminated menu from the table. "You guys slept in that car? We slept in mine. I should have rented an SUV."

Castine explained about their midnight decoy distribution, and added, "I'm *going* to get pork chops and eggs."

Pierce Plowman came shambling up then, still in his jeans and leather jacket. "Who's skinniest scoot over," he said. He seemed to have a lisp, and Castine recalled that he had lost a tooth last night when gravity re-took its hold on the *Ouranos*.

Yoneda pushed Vickery against the low partition at the side of the booth. "Here you go, champ."

Castine thought Yoneda didn't yet have a persona to fit her new status—or non-status—as an uprooted fugitive, and in the cold light of morning might be reconsidering.

"You get used to working without a net," Castine said, and Yoneda laughed tightly.

"I'll just have a Coors beer," said Plowman to a waitress who had walked up to the booth.

The others ordered fairly lavish breakfasts, Tacitus ordering scrambled eggs because of his injured arm, and even Vickery asked for a Denver omelette.

Tacitus was blinking around at the already crowded and noisy restaurant, and Castine guessed that he didn't like being up this early. "Do you," he asked Vickery, "have some agenda, for us, today?"

"Last night," Vickery began; he picked up his coffee and took a long sip, frowning, then set it down and went on, "last night I made a copy of Pierce's negation symbol on a big canvas, and this morning I unstapled it from its frame and rolled it up and stuck it in the trunk. I think if I lay that out on the dirt by Giant Rock and let it sit till it extends an hour or so into the past—"

"It's gonna move into the past?" said Yoneda flatly.

"It won't *move*," said Vickery, "it'll *become* further in the past. Sheesh, everything does." When she shrugged and nodded, he went on, "Tacitus and Ingrid and I will all go into echo-vision simultaneously, which should draw *them* again—and then, before we fall back into real time, while we've still got the attention of the things—we'll be holding hands, I think—all three of us look at the symbol." He leaned away from Yoneda and yawned. "Excuse me. That should imprint the symbol on all of them."

"But they're all over the world," said Tacitus.

"They're all in line-of-sight with each other," said Plowman. "It's a good idea. It'll be like dropping a seed crystal in a supersaturate solution. *Crrk!*"

"No," persisted Tacitus, *"all over the world.* Some are probably on the other side of the globe."

"Globe!" said Plowman. "Everybody falls for that. Trust me, the columns standing up from every crop circle in the world are parallel, all aimed straight up in the same direction."

"That apparently *is* how the aliens see it," ventured Castine.

"Shit, girl, it's how it is, excuse me. If it was a damn globe, how come you can see the North Star from everywhere? And why does it take forever to 'circumnavigate' the south pole? Because you've got to go all the way around the whole rim of the world to do it! Why can you set up flags along a six-mile line and see 'em all exactly overlapped through a telescope? Why do you think—"

Yoneda clenched her fists and whispered, "I've thrown in my lot with lunatics."

"No," insisted Castine, "it's true, I mean from the aliens' pespective. Curvature is an optical illusion to them, all they see is surfaces, and the surfaces all appear to be parallel. I don't think 'the other side of the globe' would mean anything to them, if you could even convey the idea to them."

"Well, good," said Vickery, "flat it is, at least for today. And then I imagine it'd be a good idea for us to get away from that whole area quick—I don't know what it'll be like to have the whole population of them go mummified at once, but—well, like you swim well clear of a sinking ship."

Plowman leaned forward to peer past Yoneda at him. "Yo, Samson—you figure to get clear of the collapsing temple?"

The breakfast dishes arrived then, and the steamy smells of bacon and pork chops and brined salmon and fried onions stopped the conversation; as Castine forked an egg onto a slice of buttered toast and cut it open, and then waited impatiently for someone to pass salt and Tabasco, Plowman's statement was ringing in her mind.

In the Biblical *Book of Judges,* Samson was captured by the Philistines and blinded and eventually chained between two load-bearing pillars in the Temple of Dagon, and he managed to push them apart—and in the resulting collapse Samson died along with all the Philistines.

Did Plowman know enough about all this for his apparently offhand comparison to be valid? Should we, Castine wondered, find a Catholic Church and go to Confession before we set out for the desert?

Before she could frame a queston, Yoneda put down her fork and shifted around to be able to face Plowman. "So—what, they're gonna fall on us?"

Plowman was waving his emptied beer glass toward the nearest waitress. "What? Sure, darlin'. When they die they become mass. Unless we stop for lunch, this is probably our last meal. Can somebody catch that waitress' attention?"

Tacitus's eyes were wide. "You seem at peace with the notion."

"God's holding each of our markers for death," said Plowman with a shrug, "and a guy who pays it off this year is square for 2021. Could I have two more Coorses, please?" he called to a waitress passing nearby.

Castine caught Vickery's eye and mouthed, *Samson?*

He pointed at her and then himself, and raised his eyebrows, which she took to mean, *What, you and me?*— and by extension, *We've survived worse*. She gave him a tight smile.

"Why are you coming along, then?" Yoneda asked Plowman. "Why am I? *Am* I?" She pulled out her old wrecked flip phone, opened it and laid it beside her plate of lox and bagels.

"I'd turn eighty this year," said Plowman more quietly. "It seems I've been aimed at this day—this reunion—for fifty-some years. I can't walk out on the show now." He smiled. "And we don't know the ending. Maybe God will have to hold our markers a little longer."

"Huh. I may just stay here and read about you all tomorrow in the papers." Yoneda touched her inert phone.

"You should," said Castine seriously. "You can probably save your career, with a little creative reporting."

Yoneda gripped her phone, and for several seconds her face had no expression. Then she scowled across the table at Castine. "Don't patronize me! When I burn a bridge, I don't try to swim back, okay?"

Castine raised her hands. "Fine."

"If I decide to throw in my lot with bums, I damn well stick with the bums!"

"Was that young man going to be joining us?" asked Tacitus hurriedly.

"That boy's got some sense," said Plowman. "He'll be looking out for himself." He leaned forward again to peer around Yoneda at Vickery. "You got rid of that ghost that was jerking your car around yesterday, right? If there's only five of us, we can all fit in it. My old Ford's on its third trip around the odometer, and it's past due for a compression check." He looked more closely at Yoneda and added, "You got a problem with that, girl?"

"For God's sake," she breathed. "Tacitus sits between us."

Castine hoped there would be no fights in the car on the two-hour drive.

"Can I have my you-know-what back?" Yoneda asked Castine.

Castine didn't glance at Vickery. "Yes," she said. "It's in the car."

Now Castine looked at Vickery, and he gave her a wry smile and a slight shrug. Well it *is* her gun, she thought.

"I would ask for mine," said Tacitus, raising his right elbow in the sling and wincing, "but the question is moot."

It was clear that everybody had eaten as much as they intended to, and Vickery was looking at his watch. As they slid out of the booth and stood up, Plowman insisted on paying the bill.

Ten minutes later Vickery was driving south on Fairfax, with Castine in the passenger seat beside him and Plowman, Tacitus and Yoneda crowded in the back seat. The car reeked of onions and lox now, in addition to stale sea water.

The metronome on the dashboard was clicking rapidly back and forth.

Plowman reached between the front seats to point at it. "Does that mean the old ghost woman is going to come back? I'm out of here if she does."

"No," said Vickery, "I think it's indicating that we're in a big indeterminacy field, probably cast by the 10 freeway. That's a couple of miles south of us."

"A couple of miles!" said Castine. "That's a broad field."

Vickery shrugged. "Heavy weather," he said, just as another burst of thunder rolled across the blue sky.

For several blocks none of them spoke. Then Tacitus said, "My real name is Anatoly Kazakov."

Yoneda looked across Plowman at him. "Okay."

"Among comrades," Tacitus went on, "I won't die under a false name."

Castine turned around to shake his hand, but her attention was caught by lines of people standing on the sidewalks along both sides of Fairfax. They were all waving, apparently at the car.

Vickery had clearly noticed it too. "Look at their clothes," he said.

And Castine noticed that some were in sweatsuits, some in tuxedos and formal gowns, some in pajamas. One hefty old fellow was naked. Thunder cracked in the clear blue sky.

"It's like what happened at the cemetery two days ago," Castine said.

In a hushed voice, Yoneda asked, "Why are they waving at us?"

"I believe they're waving at Ingrid," Vickery said. "I think the ones at the cemetery on Sunday were too."

"What," said Castine angrily, "like I'm supposed to join them soon? I'll be sure to dress better than most of these."

"I bet it's because you dove into one of the aliens and blew him up," said Plowman solemnly.

"But I hadn't done that yet, when they were waving— to me?—at the cemetery."

"It doesn't make any sense," agreed Plowman, "if you assume that ghosts don't talk to each other." Apparently getting a blank look from Yoneda or Tacitus, he went on, "Who says next month's ghost can't talk to last month's

ghosts, hah? You think they respect the order of days on
calendars?"

"In that case," said Tacitus, "are they waving
congratulation or . . . goodbye?"

"I doubt they know." Castine raised a hand and
tentatively waved at the crowd on her side. "Poor old
things," she said.

Vilko Cendravenir had at least got a couple of hours of
sleep in his room at the Holiday Inn Express, and was now
fidgeting in the back seat of the SUV; but Joel Finehouse
had been up all night, driving down to Huntington Beach
and to the Naval Intelligence office on Wilshire and then
back to the Holiday Inn.

And now he was driving again, east on the 10, just
passing the Ontario Airport. The sun was in his eyes,
which were already smarting from the clove-scented
cigarette Cendravenir was smoking in the back seat.
Behind the SUV, four Sensitive Assignment Specialists
who had been flown to L.A. yesterday followed in a new
Ford van.

A fireball had been reported falling into the ocean
about ten miles off the Long Beach coast at a little past 8
PM last night, and at 8:37 two grenades had been
detonated at a Huntington Beach marina, thirteen miles
northeast of where the fireball had occurred. One of the
grenades had killed two men, so far unidentified, and the
other had gone off underwater and damaged two boats.
One of the boats, the *Ouranos,* was registered to a man
in Canada, but when questioned by the Harbor Patrol, the
owners of nearby boats had said that it belonged to one

Francis Notchett. That name was still flagged by Naval Intelligence, and Finehouse and his team of Sensitive Assignment Specialists had got down there by ten o'clock. After some minutes of explanation and verification, officers from the Harbor Patrol and the Huntington Beach Police Department had let Finehouse and his team approach the scene. Sheets of plywood had been laid over a hole blown in the dock.

The *Ouranos* had sunk to the gunwales, the cockpit deck awash and the cabin sumerged, but Finehouse's team had recovered a couple of oily fingerprints from the topside helm, and he was waiting for identification of them.

Back in his room at the Holiday Inn by dawn, Finehouse had got an email report on the fingerprints that Atkins had lifted from the William Ardmore trailer yesterday: they belonged to Agent Rayette Yoneda, Agent Ingrid Castine, a onetime Political Science professor named Andrius Kuprys, and the ex-Secret Service agent Herbert Woods, more recently known as Sebastian Vickery.

More information about Andrius Kuprys had quickly followed—he was suspected to be an illegal GRU agent who had worked for twenty years as a talent-spotter at the University of Southern California, and in 2017 had narrowly avoided arrest by the FBI. It was decidedly odd to find him again, or still, in the United States—usually illegal Soviet agents who were discovered but managed to escape arrest wound up back in Russia, never again to stir outside its borders.

And what had Mr. Kuprys been doing for the last three years? Agent Yoneda had apparently met him out at Giant

Rock in the desert two days ago—he must be involved in all this Anomalous Aerial Phenomena business—and she had thought he might be persuaded to defect. Yoneda had gone offline to pursue that. Was she still pursuing it, or had she gone rogue herself? Or been killed?

Finehouse glanced to the side at the tracker screen mounted on the SUV's dashboard. The beacon was still ahead of them, still moving east.

In the passenger seat, Atkins also looked at the screen. "That might not be the motorcycle," he said. "The kid might have found our tracker and stuck it on a car."

The signal from the GPS tracker that Atkins had attached to the boy's motorcycle had shown a steady location all night, in the Bellflower area. This morning at about six it had started to move—northeast on the 91, and now steadily eastward on the 10.

"I'm sure it's him," said Finehouse, squinting through the faintly glittering windshield at the cars ahead of him. "And now that we're out of the city, I bet I know where he's going."

"Where?" asked Atkins.

Finehouse didn't answer, not wanting to alarm Cendravenir, who was shifting uneasily in the back seat and no doubt dropping sparks from his foolish cigarettes onto the upholstery.

The girl in the zoo cage with Galvan yesterday had said, *The spacemen many times appear where they've appeared not long before—it's like coming through a hole they already made, before it can close up again.*

That has to be at that Giant Rock place, Finehouse thought, in the desert out past San Bernardino.

Atkins must have felt his phone vibrate, for he had it out and was swiping the screen. After a few moments he looked up and said, "They identified the prints we got off the helm of that sunk boat last night. Pierce Plowman."

"I imagine he'll be there too," said Finehouse.

Atkins asked again, impatiently, "Where?"

Finehouse stretched and yawned, bracing his hands on the steering wheel. "Where the kid on the bike is evidently going."

Finehouse was curious about Plowman. Lubitz had only told him that Plowman had worked at the Nevada Test site—Area 51—in the late '60s and early '70s, and that later he had been an eccentric bum, working odd jobs and joining the disorganized population of saucer-nuts in southern California. A harmless screwball, one would have supposed, like so many in the L.A. area, but the old weirdo had apparently got hold of some very sensitive information.

And it would have to be the sort that the Office of Naval Research called *aberrant*.

Last night Finehouse had driven to the Los Angeles Naval Intelligence office and picked up the six boxes that contained the lightweight chrome-plated aluminum spheres that Cendravenir was to telekinetically juggle, when and if an appearance of the Anomalous Aerial Phenomena could be provoked. The boxes were in the back of the SUV now, and it didn't seem out of the question that they might be needed today.

Cendravenir clearly thought the same thing. He kept leaning forward to peer over Finehouse's shoulder at the cars ahead, and his ridiculous pointed goatee stood out against his pale face.

"I opened a couple of these boxes back here," Cendravenir said now. "They're the silver balls I'm supposed to juggle, aren't they? You didn't have them yesterday—why have you got them now?" Finehouse heard a metallic knocking back there.

"It's possible we'll do Operation Pleiades today," Finehouse told him without looking away from the freeway lane.

"You're all making assumptions about what I can do," Cendravenir said. "We were supposed to have time to practice. Silver balls! What if they're—I don't know, slippery?"

You'll do it reflexively, thought Finehouse, if you're scared. And if my guess is right, if Vickery and Castine and the Russian spy are planning what I think they're planning, I imagine you'll be adequately scared.

"I don't *want* to," Cendravenir said. "I quit." He lunged forward and reached past Finehouse for the steering wheel; Finehouse batted his arm away at the same time that Atkins did, and Cendravenir fell forward, grabbing Finehouse's right leg to steady himself.

The SUV leaped forward as Finehouse's foot was briefly pressed down onto the gas pedal. He had glanced away from traffic for a moment, and when he looked up he saw that he was about to collide with the back end of a Ralph's delivery truck, and his foot instantly sprang to the brake and tromped down hard on it.

The SUV's front end dipped and the tires yipped and the whole vehicle began to slew around sideways. Finehouse's view was blocked by a basketball-sized silver sphere that came flying from the back and bounced off the dome light onto his braced arms. The SUV ground to a halt, not quite touching the truck ahead of it, but was jolted when the following Sensitive Assignment van hit the back bumper.

And cars in every lane around Finehouse were sliding on screeching tires and banging into one another.

The Ralph's truck, untouched, rolled on down the lane, and Finehouse straightened the wheel and carefully pressed the gas pedal; the SUV moved forward after only a brief tug to free itself from bumper of the van behind it, and Finehouse sped up, leaving behind a cluster of stopped cars.

Cendravenir had slumped back in his seat, and Finehouse flung the silver ball into the back. "Is the goddamn van still with us?" he asked Atkins.

Atkins lowered his head to peer at the outside mirror. "Yes. They look okay. Unlike everybody who was around us."

"Everybody stopped at once," said Finehouse. He was breathing more easily than he had a moment ago, though his heart was still pounding. Belatedly his hands tingled with tension.

Atkins was now leaning forward to look at the sky. "What the hell happened?"

"Smoky Joe back there got scared when I hit the brakes," said Finehouse. He was watching the speedometer and the truck ahead, careful not to make a mistake in the fading rush of adrenalin.

"But what—oh. Yeah." Atkins peered warily back at Cendravenir.

Cendravenir was groping on the floor, undoubtedly for

his cigarette. "If a thing does something scary suddenly," he said, and Finehouse couldn't tell if the man spoke defensively or defiantly, "other things are gonna do the same."

"I should have you blindfolded all the time," said Finehouse, "with earplugs."

"And sedated," agreed Cendravenir, straightening up and puffing on the cigarette. "Wher*ever* we're going, I'm not getting out of this car."

With four agents in the van behind us, thought Finehouse, to whose more substantial concerns you've now added damage to two government vehicles, I think you'll do as you're told.

When Anita Galvan hit the brake, the gray Cadillac CTS came to a smooth, quick stop, well short of the bumper of the car ahead, but all around her tires were screeching and cars were slamming together. The Cadillac was jolted as the car behind collided with the back bumper.

She gripped the steering wheel and blinked around angrily. All the cars she could see on the freeway lanes were stopped, many of them at odd angles. Far ahead she saw the top of a big grocery delivery truck moving away, but she was blocked in.

"That was goddamn magic!" she snarled at her nephew in the passenger seat. "Look at that new Honda, that Chevy! They've all got anti-lock brake systems same as we do. But we're the only car that didn't lock up."

Carlos blinked at the other cars, then shrugged and nodded.

"This car is *shielded*," she reminded him. "All these other cars aren't. Somebody *did* this."

Carlos as usual had nothing to say, but Arturo in the back seat said, "To stop you?"

"Nobody knew I was going to go out there today. It might be just something that *happens* now, like the thunder. A new *phenomenon*." She waved at the cars ahead. "Get out and clear me a path out of this mess."

"They're jammed together, boss!" protested Arturo. "Why do you want to go there anyway?"

"I'm sure that's where Vickery is with my '98 Dodge."

Thunder, she thought, snowstorms in the L.A. River, fireballs in the ocean, my relatives all pouring sugar and honey on the streets! Yesterday Abril told me, *The spacemen many times appear where they've appeared not long before—it's like coming through a hole they already made, before it can close up again.* And everybody says they were out at this Giant Rock on Sunday. Vickery will be there.

She added, "He mathed-out my back-door tracker ghost. I bet he's bunged up the car."

Carlos opened the door on his side and stepped out.

"How are we supposed to get the cars out of the way?" asked Arturo, who hadn't opened his door. "Why do we have to go there anyway? Vickery will bring your car back, even if it's messed up. He always does." He paused and bobbed his head. "Except when he leaves them in Hell."

"Push 'em, get one car to push another, I don't know, point a gun at the drivers! Just get 'em out of my way so we can keep going!"

Arturo exhaled wearily, but opened his door and got out.

Vickery's been right in the past, Galvan thought, in his half-ass way, but he's a fuckup. He'll need help. And if he's messed up my Dodge, one of you can drive it back and he can damn well hitch-hike out of the desert. Limping.

And, she thought as she watched Carlos and Arturo slouch toward the stopped cars ahead, I do want to see the spacemen.

CHAPTER NINETEEN:
They Go Off by Themselves Lately

When Vickery had driven out here two days ago he had been noting the bleak landscapes—the endless flat expanses of weed-studded desert, the occasional house set well back from the generally empty two-lane road, a lonely cluster of mailboxes on posts indicating houses so far back on dirt roads that their sun-faded roofs were indistinguishable among the sand and Joshua trees and tumbleweeds—but this morning he stared straight ahead, and when he passed the last paved street and bumped out onto the dirt road that stretched away to the north, he could already see the enormous boulder that lay three miles ahead.

In the back seat, Yoneda said, "When you picked me up out here on Sunday, I thought you were just being a Good Samaritan. But you already guessed I was ONI."

"True," said Tacitus.

"And *you*," Yoneda went on, "you *pepper-sprayed* me!"

"Do you wish we hadn't done what we did?" asked Castine, who was also staring ahead through the dusty windshield.

Vickery glanced at Yoneda in the rear-view mirror; she was frowning out at the endless sunlit desert to the east. "I'd still have a career," she said. She held up a hand and added, "I know—till midnight. More things in Heaven and Earth than are dreamt of in our protocols."

As if to punctuate her statement, the sound that was like thunder boomed in the empty sky.

There hadn't been lines of ghosts alongside the freeways as they had driven out here, but twice on the long stretch of the 10, Castine had pointed out cars that shifted in color and shape and then winked out of existence. The figures inside them had been blurry, but might have been waving.

"I haven't been out here in years," said Plowman quietly, squinting out at the desert. "In the early '60s I went to a couple of the flying saucer conventions they held around the rock every June. Barbecues, tents everywhere, costumes, hundreds of people. Even a year-round café and airstrip, and they said Howard Hughes would land there for a sandwich any time he was flying over. I wonder if anything's left."

"You can see a foundation or two," said Vickery.

"Huh." Plowman leaned forward to peer ahead. "The guy who started it all back in the '50s said an alien from Venus landed there, and talked to him. Gave him a tour of its spaceship. So I guess he always figured that was where they'd show up, if they ever came back again."

Castine turned around, her head bobbing as the car rocked over the uneven dirt road. "Do you think he really did meet an alien?"

Plowman sat back. "Don't be dumb, girl. You and I know what it's like to *meet* one of them."

Now the rock dominated the horizon ahead, crouched like a headless stone lion beside a smaller but still enormous boulder. As on Sunday, a number of cars and trailers were parked around the natural monuments, and after another minute of rocking progress Vickery was able to see individual people among the vehicles or out on the plain.

When the road widened out to the hundred-yard clear area, Vickery drove between the widely spaced vehicles and stopped where he had parked on Sunday, beside the cracked cement foundation of what might have been the long-gone café Plowman had mentioned. Vickery was surprised at the number of people who had made the trip out here on a Tuesday morning—looking back between the heads of Tacitus and Plowman, he could see the glint and dust-cloud of at least one more vehicle driving up the dirt road from the south.

The burned-out skeleton of the ONI van had been carted away, and Vickery couldn't now even see a scorched mark on the sand where it had stood.

He paused before switching off the engine, and none of the others opened their doors. He looked past Castine at the ninety-foot wide base of the primordial stone—he couldn't see the high shoulders of it, much less the top, from where he sat—and for the moment it seemed to be the center and summation of the barren desert that extended to the horizon in all directions except where the stone loomed massively in the way. The closed doors and roof of the car were a frail container of small, precise definitions, and he hesitated to rupture it.

"If they're still using our blood to track us," he said, "we last showed up on Fairfax in L.A. about two hours ago. We can afford a half hour of exposure here, and then Ingrid and I should get back in the car for a while. Ideally we'll be able to sneak fresh blood samples onto a vehicle that's about to leave."

Castine took a deep breath and opened her door, and the dry desert wind, scented by miles of creosote bushes and baking stone, swept in past her. Vickery switched off the engine and stepped out into the harsh daylight.

When all five of them had got out of the car and stood shading their eyes in the glare of sun on stone and sand, Plowman squinted to the north and said, "I thought that boy had sense."

Vickery turned in that direction and saw a little blue motorcycle bobbing toward them. Evidently it had circled the area first.

Vickery shook his head and walked around the car to the trunk. "Let's get this spread out," he said, opening the trunk. "Give it some duration in one spot."

At his studio at dawn he had rolled up the canvas and bent it double to fit in the trunk, and now Plowman got one end of it and helped to lift it out. The two of them shuffled to the edge of the old pavement and let the canvas roll drop, kicked it straight, then knelt and began unrolling it across the cracked cement surface.

When the canvas was completely unrolled and Yoneda and Castine were lining the flapping edges with rocks, Plowman stared at the irregular tangle of lines that Vickery had painted on it last night.

"I guess that looks right."

"It is," Vickery told him shortly. "Now we wait an hour or two and just make sure the wind doesn't flip up any corners."

Santiago came riding up on his puttering bike, and he pushed up sunglasses to peer at the lines painted on the canvas.

"It looks the same," he said, and when Vickery asked him what it looked the same as, the boy nodded toward the eastern side of the plain, past a couple of trailers a hundred yards away. "People over there laying out sugar and honey. Others over there don't like it."

Vickery squinted in that direction, then shrugged. "As long as they keep it over there."

Santiago switched off the bike's engine and flipped down the kickstand. "I brought you this," he said, digging in the left pocket of his hoodie. He held out an old corncob pipe. "You already got one thing like it, but maybe you could use 'em in stereo some way."

Vickery guessed that it was one he'd seen before, at the house of a dead ghostmonger years ago.

Yoneda stepped over to where they stood, pushing damp hair back from her forehead. "It's hot out here already," she said, and then she peered at the corncob pipe and nodded. "Only thing we were missing. Thank God you came along, kid."

"This pipe is like the knob on the metronome in the car," said Vickery. "There's a fossilized ghost subsumed in each of them."

"That's true," said Castine; then her eyes widened and she added, "That's true! Fossilized. It's like the negated alien under the robot in L.A., isn't it?"

"Kind of parallel cases," agreed Vickery. To Santiago he said, "Thanks, we might find a use for it." He slid it into his shirt pocket.

Santiago nodded and got off his bike, squinting around at all the strangers standing further off, widely separated out across the plain.

"*Robot?*" muttered Yoneda.

"Jack up the back end of the car," suggested Plowman, "and duct tape the pipe onto the wheel and the metronome pendulum onto the fender, then get the motor running, so you got a moving one rotating by a stationary one. Get a negation induction current running."

"Eye of newt and toe of frog!" Yoneda burst out angrily. "You guys know these things are *big*, right? I saw that one in the riverbed two nights ago, and we all saw the one that fell into the ocean last night. And I don't mean big in a size way." To Vickery she said, "They live in higher space-time dimensions, right?—and just interact with our lot the way we might step through a spider web?" She stamped her foot on the packed-sand ground. "And you're gonna stop them with a corncob pipe duct-taped onto a car tire?"

Vickery frowned at her, then looked past her and saw Castine biting her lip and blinking.

Yoneda went on, "Thrift-store junk against... something like gods?"

"Well," said Vickery as a nervous smile tugged at his own lips, "Ingrid and I once saved L.A. from blowing up by flying a home-made hang-glider through a hole in the sky of Hell."

Santiago nodded solemnly.

Plowman laughed. "That's the story. I heard it was a hot-air balloon, though."

"And," said Tacitus, "I drove a car into that Hell myself, three years ago. I was able to walk out, though."

Plowman pulled a metal flask from his inside jacket pocket, unscrewed the cap and took a swig of what smelled like bourbon. "Hang-glider my ass," he muttered.

Vickery thought Yoneda was near tears, and he recalled that she had probably sacrificed her career, and possibly her liberty, in order to join them in this. He was framing a way to remind her of the convincing bases of their fears and proposed action when Plowman began talking, loudly.

"It seems like a fool's errand," the old man said, nodding toward Yoneda, "hoping to negate 'em all over the world with just the stuff we got right here, but it reminds me of one time I had ants in my yard, and I took a bucket of gunpowder outside—I used to do my own reloading in those days—and I turned it upside-down on top of the biggest anthill, and two days later I took the bucket away, and nearly all the gunpowder was gone! So I struck a match and tossed it onto the anthill, and my whole yard blew up."

Yoneda looked past Vickery at the other vehicles parked out across the wide cleared area around the stone. Perhaps she was looking for another ride. Almost too quietly for Vickery to hear, she said, "And is a *robot* going to show up?"

"That's just a nickname," Vickery said quickly, "sorry, for a building in L.A." He waved at the six-by-eight canvas spread out on the old pavement. "The original of this symbol is partly under it, underground. Nobody thinks the building is a real robot, okay?"

Tacitus laid a hesitant hand on Yoneda's shoulder. "These people," he said, "*we* people—aren't actually insane."

Yoneda looked back at him. "Too late now anyway," she said. "I'm not going anywhere."

Plowman's expansive mood seemed to have collapsed. He looked around at the bleak landscape as if trying to fix it in his memory. "I don't think I am either," he said to Yoneda. He took a few steps away from the car and the weighted canvas, then walked back. He slid the flask back into his jacket, and after a moment's hesitation pulled out a tattered envelope with a rubber band around it. He handed it to Castine.

"If you make it out of here," he said, in a gruff voice that didn't invite reply, "get this to my daughter."

Vickery saw that the envelope was bulky. Castine just nodded as she tucked it into her own inside jacket pocket.

"Food and beer," Vickery said quickly, stepping around to the trunk. He popped it open and lifted away the lid of a new styrofoam cooler, revealing a brace of submarine sandwiches in cellophane and two stacked six-packs of Budweiser. Several plastic bottles of water were tucked in among it all, and another six-pack, probably not very cold, sat beside the cooler. "You too," he added to Santiago, who was hanging back.

Soon they were all sitting in a rough circle around the brightly sunlit canvas, using the edges of it between the stones as a tablecloth. Vickery and Castine had forgotten to get napkins, but Vickery reflected that napkins would have blown away in any case, and he set the example for the others by wiping his mouth on his sleeve. Plowman declined a sandwich, citing his missing tooth, and stuck to beer. The black lines of the negation symbol shone on the white canvas.

After finishing half of her own sandwich and washing down the last bite with a swig of beer, Castine looked up and asked, "About an hour, you think? It's been about a half hour already."

"An hour," said Vickery, "or a bit more. Gotta make sure the canvas is already here, at the retro moment we wind up seeing. You and I should get back in the car."

"An hour," echoed Plowman. He pulled out another envelope and passed it to Santiago. "Hold this for me, kid," he said. Santiago nodded and tucked it into the left pocket of his hoodie.

For several seconds Vickery had been aware of shouting from the eastern side of the plain, past a couple of trailers, and now Santiago stood up, looking in that direction.

"They were arguing already when I rode by there," he said. "Some are like that crazy lady at your chess club, and they don't like it that others are laying out the *lineas de muerta* in sugar and honey."

Vickery looked past Castine at the trailers. Already the sun was raising heat distortions, and the trailers seemed to ripple. "I wish they'd all just—" he began, but the pop of a gunshot interrupted him. It was followed by two more.

Vickery got to his feet, nervously touching the .45 semi-automatic in his jacket pocket. The others all stood up too, and Castine's hands were in her pockets and Yoneda's right hand was inside her khaki jacket.

The sound like thunder shook the air, and the wind from the east was stronger, raising swirls of dust, and the distant shouting became rhythmical—chanting.

"There'll be cops," Yoneda said, nodding toward the dirt road that led back south to Landers. Vickery glanced that way and saw several more vehicles approaching.

"We keep our heads down," said Vickery, "and San Bernardino County Sheriffs have got no reason to look twice at us." He turned to Santiago, who of course had one hand in the heavy pocket of his hoodie. "Over there," Vickery said, waving toward the trailers, "do you think it's just the sugar and honey that some people are objecting to? I mean—would they recognize the symbol in black paint on canvas?"

The chanting from the other side of the trailers was louder, carried on the wind.

"How close they looked at it," said Santiago, "I don't know. But," and he waved at the canvas, "the lines on the sand looked like that. Tangled."

"If anybody starts coming here from that direction," Vickery said, "Let's all stand blocking the view of the canvas. But casual!"

"All we needed," said Plowman.

The wind caught a corner of the canvas and lifted it, tossing aside several rocks that had held it down.

"How about if we all just *lie* on it?" said Castine, brushing windblown hair out of her face and crouching to replace the rocks.

"For how long?" said Vickery. "As much as a minute?

We don't want to go into echo-vision and just see *us* all lying there!"

A roaring engine caught his attention, and when he looked to the east he saw a grotesque vehicle plunging diagonally across the uneven dirt.

Vickery squinted at it. It might have been some sort of Jeep with no windshield, but the grille was hidden by an aluminum-foil-covered mask of the popular-culture "alien" image, the inverted-teardrop shape with big slanted eyes and a bulging forehead. Long, bending poles with banners fluttering on them stuck out to the sides. Vickery could see a goggled driver over the big aluminum-foil head, and two men swaying in the back, and he could just hear their shouted chanting over the noise of their engine.

The vehicle swerved among the cars and trailers, raising dust that blew across the plain and veiled the wide base of Giant Rock.

Vickery heard a thump and clatter close behind him, and turned—a sharp gust of wind had lifted the far side of the canvas, scattering rocks, and in the moment before he dove at it with his arms spread, the stark black lines on the upright white canvas were the brightest spot in the tan desert landscape.

Vickery banged his knee and his chin in falling on top of the canvas, and he rolled over painfully on it and sat up as the others swept the canvas flat and crouched between it and the jeep.

But the jeep had swerved toward them. Vickery pulled the .45 out of his pocket, holding it low, and saw Santiago glance away toward his motorcycle. Yoneda had drawn her little .380 semi-automatic; her teeth were bared in a tense smile.

Santiago was still looking back, but his hand remained in his jacket pocket.

The oncoming aluminum-foil alien face dipped its pointed chin to the dirt as the jeep slammed to a sliding halt thirty feet away. One of the men vaulted out of the back of it, and when he straightened up he was holding a revolver. He pointed it at Vickery and his companions and waved the barrel to the side twice, clearly ordering them to move away from the old pavement and the canvas. Vickery was aware that a car engine was approaching from behind him, and that it was probably what had caught Santiago's attention a moment earlier, but his eyes were fixed on the armed man standing beside the weird vehicle.

For several seconds nobody moved. Vickery knew he could get the .45 in line and shoot the gunman if the man were to swing the gun back toward them, and he was praying that the man would not do it.

But the man spread his arms and raised his shoulders in an exaggerated shrug; then, as if to emphasize his pantomimed order, pointed his revolver at the ground and fired.

And several deafeningly close simultaneous gunshots startled Vickery in the instant that his own gun jumped in his hand.

The man by the groteque jeep stepped back, startled—clearly he hadn't fired again—and Vickery quickly looked at the others crouched on either side of the canvas. Castine was flexing her empty right hand, Yoneda too had dropped her gun, and there was a smoking hole in the front of Santiago's hoodie. Plowman and Tacitus were sitting beside the canvas, looking around wide-eyed.

The man who had fired into the ground had climbed back into the jeep, and it was accelerating away in reverse, the aluminum-foil alien head nodding vigorously as the vehicle bounced over the uneven ground.

"Santiago!" shouted Vickery over the ringing in his and certainly everyone's ears, "are you hit?" He tapped his own side and pointed at the boy's abdomen.

Santiago shook his head and poked the muzzle of his pocketed gun against the hole in his hoodie.

Vickery looked closely at the others, but none of them had been hit.

He realized that he and Castine and Yoneda and Santiago had each fired a shot at the same moment—and it seemed clear that in each case it had been involuntary.

Vickery looked in the other direction. A black SUV was slowing to a stop a few yards away from the old pavement, and a white Chevy van behind it was doing the same; both vehicles halted and the doors swung open, and men with guns were jumping out onto the sand.

One man in a dark gray business suit and sunglasses stepped ahead of the others, his gun—a semi-automatic similar to Santiago's—held pointing up for now. He looked to be about forty, with gray streaks in his brown hair at the temples. Vickery noticed a ragged slit in the side of the man's well-tailored suit coat.

Four men had got out of the van; they all wore sunglasses and black nylon jackets, and, though one man was limping badly, each of them carried a handgun pointed toward Vickery's group. Sensitive Assignment

Specialists, Vickery guessed. And they've definitely got us covered.

"Let's see everybody's hands," the man in the suit called; and when all five of Vickery's party were holding up empty hands, the man went on, "Good, keep 'em up. I see Agents Yoneda and Castine, and Pierce Plowman, and one who must be Sebastian Vickery, and another who might be a GRU agent! Who are *you*, kid?" he asked Santiago.

"The caterer," said Santiago.

"And you," called Yoneda, "must be Agent Finehouse."

The four Sensitive Assignment Specialists looked tense and uneasy, and Vickery belatedly noticed bloody footprints and a hole punched in the tan boot of one of them. And there was a bullet-sized hole punched outward in the side of the van. Vickery looked more closely at the rip in Finehouse's coat.

"It happened to you guys too," Vickery said wonderingly, "didn't it? Your guns all fired spontaneously?"

Finehouse darted a quick, wrathful glance back at the SUV, then returned his attention to Vickery and his companions. "All of you on your feet," he said, "hands well clear, not kidding. Good. Now step away from the canvas." To the men beside him he said, "Pat, you and Mike frisk 'em and zip 'em, and Tommy, you roll up the canvas and stash it. Quick is good."

The back gate of the SUV swung up, and another man climbed down to stand unsteadily on the dirt. Vickery raised his eyebrows—the man's sandals and black turtleneck sweater were out of place among his companions, but the most jarring detail was his black goatee, which tapered to a theatrical point. He began lifting hatbox-sized cardboard boxes out of the back of the SUV and setting them on the sand.

Two of Finehouse's men shuffled forward, one crouching to toss aside the rocks holding the canvas down.

Beyond the SUV and the van, off to the right, Vickery now saw another vehicle plunging this way aross the packed sand—a gleaming white '70s-era Cadillac.

One of the two men by the van turned at the sound of its engine, and had just taken a step toward the back of the van when the driver of the Cadillac held a gun out the window and fired into the air and leaned on the horn.

And the area around the half-rolled-up canvas seemed to explode.

The agent whom Finehouse had called Mike had gathered the guns from Vickery's party and had been stepping back when all four of the guns he was carrying fired simultaneously; three of the guns sprang out of his hands and he spun and sagged at the knees. In the same instant the guns of the two agents by the van had jumped, and Vickery felt a bright, hot sting over his right ribs. He glimpsed fabric fragments flying up from the canvas, but any twang of ricochet was lost in the ringing concussion of the guns and the sudden blaring of horns from the SUV and the van and Vickery's Dodge.

Vickery was already diving forward, and he snatched Yoneda's little gun out of mid-air in the moment before his somersault slammed him into the knees of the two men by the van. As he rolled to his feet he grabbed one man's gun barrel and twisted it aside and struck the right wrist of the other with the butt of Yoneda's gun; and a moment later he had stepped back and was aiming her gun between the men's faces.

One of them had dropped his gun and was massaging his wrist, and the other slowly released the gun whose barrel Vickery's hand was still gripping and twisting. Both men seemed dazed, and Vickery realized that they had unintentionally fired their guns in that tumultuous instant three seconds earlier.

"Hands behind your necks!" Vickery shouted over the jarring clamor of the car horns, and both men hesitated and then complied.

Yoneda was backing away from the SUV, holding Finehouse's gun while Finehouse sat by the front wheel, apparently unwounded but visibly gasping for air. The man with the pointed beard was sitting on the sand in the midst of his cardboard boxes, weeping. The car horns stuttered to silence.

Vickery took a quick glance over his shoulder. One of the Sensitive Assignment Specialists was plodding back toward the van with his hands raised while Plowman kept Tacitus's revolver trained on him. The agent called Mike was sitting on the sand beside the old cement pavement now, clenching a gleamingly bloody fist; Tacitus had taken off his own belt and looped it around Mike's upper arm and was pulling it tight.

Castine had hurried to the SUV and pulled the bearded man to his feet. She carefully patted him down, and then pushed him to join his fellows. Santiago was unrolling the canvas and replacing the rocks around the edges, and the right pocket of his hoodie again sagged with its usual weight. Castine walked back and crouched to hold the canvas flat for him.

Vickery reached across to probe the rip in the side of his windbreaker. He could feel hot blood rolling down to his belt, and winced as he touched a gash over a rib. He wiped his bloody fingers on his jeans and made himself concentrate on his surroundings.

Twice, he thought, all the guns in this immediate area fired spontaneously! He raised the barrel of Yoneda's gun so that it was pointed a few inches above the heads of his two captives.

"Everybody!" he called. "Aim a bit to the side of whoever you're covering! Guns go off by themselves lately."

On the far side of the van, the Cadillac had rolled to a stop and the driver's-side door swung open. Anita Galvan stepped out, still holding the gun she had fired into the air while pulling up, and two men got out of the car after her. Vickery recognized Arturo and her nephew Carlos.

Galvan strode up to where Vickery stood and looked around with eyebrows raised. "Was that a grenade?" she asked. "Hey, that's the guy who offered me fifteen thousand bucks for you. Yo, mister! Do you have the money?"

Finehouse looked from her lowered gun to the raised guns of Vickery and Yoneda and Plowman, and shook his head in impatient dismissal of her.

Vickery turned to look out across the windy plain toward Giant Rock. People were staring in this direction or hurrying toward parked cars. He was relieved to see no one who appeared to have been wounded by either of the bursts of spontaneous gunfire, but several had their hands to the sides of their heads, clearly talking on cell phones.

"We gotta do this quick," he said. He turned back to the vehicles and walked carefully to the SUV and peered inside, then edged up to the open door of the van. He crouched and leaned in, scanning the interior over the barrel of the .380, but both vehicles were empty.

He straightened and stepped away from the van. He had noticed bundles of zip-ties at the belts of Finehouse's men, and he said, "Yoneda, kick all the stray guns over here, and Ingrid, get those zip-ties and bind all the ONI guys, and then bind them together. Pierce and Yoneda both cover her while she does that, but don't aim directly at anybody! Tacitus, finish up with that tourniquet and get over here. And everybody be aware of where guns are pointing!"

"I'm sorry!" wailed the oddly bearded man.

"Shut up, can't you?" said Finehouse.

Mike got to his feet, gripping the belt that was now cinched tightly around his upper arm. Castine unclipped the bundle of zip-ties from his belt, and Plowman waved the revolver toward where the man's companions leaned against the van.

Yoneda kicked a couple of government semi-automatics away from the vehicles as she held Finehouse's aimed at his shoes. "Get up and stand with your pals," she said.

When Finehouse had got up and joined the goateed eccentric and the four agents beside the van, Castine quickly looped a zip-tie around each man's wrists and drew them all tight—extra tight around Mike's wrists, slicked as one of them was with blood—then, standing to the side to give Yoneda and Plowman clear fields of fire if necessary, she ran a tie through all the loops, tugged it firm, and quickly stepped away.

Finehouse, crowded together now with the four battered Sensitive Assignment Specialists and the goateed man, looked up from his bound wrists.

"Sebastian Vickery," he called, "surrender to us now and Agent Castine will suffer no consequences for her actions during these three days. I'm authorized to promise that."

"He's got stuff to do," Castine told him as she stepped back beside Vickery.

"More important stuff, I'm afraid," Vickery agreed.

Finehouse looked away from them. "Agent Yoneda, turn the gun the other way or spend twenty years in Miramar."

"My money's on Vickery," she said, "God help me."

"Mine too," put in Galvan. "Literally."

Tacitus had joined Vickery and Castine beside the canvas. He looked down at the canvas and then up, nervously, at Vickery. "Now?" he asked.

Castine shivered, gripping her elbows.

Vickery took a deep breath and let it out, and nodded. "Now." He gingerly slid the .380 into his pocket and pointed across the plain. "Let's all three stare at the rock till we're seeing it in echo-vision," he said, "and then—" He paused.

— Then look down at the canvas, he thought. Samson pulling down the temple? *When they die they become mass*, Plowman had said at breakfast. *Unless we stop for lunch, this is probably our last meal.* Vickery looked at the bag full of sandwich wrappings and empty beer cans. Well, breakfast had not in fact been their last meal. Maybe this forced-march picnic hadn't been either.

He looked to his right at Castine, then past her at Tacitus.

Castine's lips twitched in an attempted smile. "The one in the riverbed on Sunday night didn't land on us." She took Tacitus's left hand, and Vickery clasped hers.

Finehouse took an awkward step away from the van, tugging the four men around with him, but slid to a halt when Yoneda stepped back and raised his own gun to point at his knees.

Finehouse flinched and retreated, but a moment later bared his teeth and shouted, "You *know* you're messing with enormous things which you don't remotely understand! Vickery, Castine, you used to be government agents—this is amateur, civilian!—acting in complete ignorance—"

"Go," said Tacitus quietly.

"Cendravenir!" Finehouse called. "Dammit, where are your balls?"

Vickery assumed he was shouting at one of his Sensitive Assignment Specialists, goading him to action; but Yoneda and Plowman were alert. Vickery stared across the plain at the towering boulder.

On Sunday he had shifted to echo-vision while sitting in his truck, but he had been staring at the slope of rocks to the left of Giant Rock. And he found it difficult now to impose a flat two-dimensional view on the imposing stone sentinel; the thing was too emphatically three-dimensional, too big and solid.

He didn't glance to the right, since he assumed that if either of his companions had achieved echo-vision it would have spilled him into it as well; and certainly Castine's hand would have tensed in his!

"You can still stop this!" cried Finehouse. "Abort, abort!"

With his left hand Vickery felt along the side of his denim jacket until he found the bullet-hole, and then poked his finger through it and scraped his fingernail along the gash a bullet had torn in his skin.

It hurt much more than he had anticipated, and his view lost its immediacy and scope—and it was easy in that moment to see in front of him simply a mottled brown blob bordered by expanses of blue and tan.

And he made himself look past the façade.

Instantly the sky was a remote bronze dome, and the great monolith stood far away across the glowing plain, displacing vast volumes of air, shining in the color that was out past red in the spectrum.

He looked down; and he exhaled when he saw the canvas, relieved that the echo-view was not showing him a time before they had unrolled it here. The lines of the negation symbol shone in that color now, against the dimmer background of the canvas. Unable to hear most sounds occuring in real time, he concentrated his attention on the jagged, tangled lines.

For perhaps thirty seconds they glowed steady in his sight—and then he winced as the symbol abruptly became black on white in glaring sunlight and he could hear the desert wind again. The retro-vision had ended.

He sagged and caught his balance, glancing around

quickly. Castine pulled both of her hands free and sat down, holding her head. Tacitus was alternately blinking at the figures around the three vehicles and up into the empty sky.

Castine lowered her hands and looked up at Vickery. "It didn't work," she said hoarsely.

Vickery exhaled, and realized that he had been holding his breath. He looked up into the vast blue vault of the sky, which was empty even of clouds. "Wait—there was a several-second delay on Sunday—"

"It *didn't work*," Castine repeated. "I sensed them *again*, just now—like last night on the boat, when I shared the mind of, of the *ghost* of one of them—I was open to it, the same *sensation*, like my little mind was shaking apart and falling out of everything as the *three* got closer, more real than me—but they—oh, English is no good for this!"

"Try," called Yoneda, not sarcastically.

Castine sighed and nodded. "They were responding to our—what was your phrase, Tacitus?—our *localized radiating discord*, and . . . came close? *Touched* the surface of the pond? But we didn't attract them close enough, didn't bring them into focus. A sort of field around this thing," she said with a wave at the canvas, "repelled them while they still had time to . . . step back, step out." She rubbed her eyes, then pushed herself up and got to her feet. "What's today? Tuesday? We gotta find a priest who'll hear our confessions."

CHAPTER TWENTY:
They Know Me

"Goddammit," Plowman burst out, "you didn't use the corncob pipe and the metronome! You move and I'll blow your head off," he added to one of the Sensitive Assignment Specialists.

"For God's sake," said Yoneda without taking her eyes off Finehouse. With her free hand she was fumbling in one of the pockets of her khaki jacket.

"I think you can release us now," called Finehouse. "I'm prepared to describe these three days in the best possible light in my report, if you'll all drop your weapons, cut us free, and get in the van. Several people here need medical attention. I see that you're bleeding, Mr. Vickery."

Castine inhaled through clenched teeth when she looked at the right leg of Vickery's jeans. He looked down and saw that the fabric around the right front pocket was blotted with blood.

"Get your shirt and jacket off," she said, and then helped him tug them off. She crouched to look at the

371

wound. "You're lucky," she said. She straightened and looked over at Finehouse. "You've got first aid kits?"

"In the van. Get him in there and we'll bandage him."

"I got it," said Galvan, trudging back to her Cadillac. She opened the door and groped under the seat, then closed the door and tossed a white plastic box to Castine.

Castine quickly tore open a package and smeared antibiotic ointment on a gauze pad, then stuck it on the gash in Vickery's side and wrapped an elastic bandage tightly around his torso to hold it firmly in place and put pressure on the wound.

Vickery put his shirt and jacket back on, carefully. "Better," he told Castine, "thanks." He pressed his palm hard against his bloody shirt over the wound, gritting his teeth but hoping to slow the bleeding.

Galvan leaned against her car. "No spacemen after all?" She seemed genuinely crestfallen. "Shit. Arturo can drive my Dodge back." She peered across the level sand at the car. "What the hell happened to my antenna?"

"We went under a low bridge." Vickery clenched his free hand in a fist and scowled at the empty sky. Maybe Notchett was all wrong, he thought. Maybe the aliens are just bubbles in the sky and grotesque animations of litter and sea water, and pose no threat. And maybe when they withdrew just now they withdrew for good. Hell, maybe the Earth *isn't* flat.

But he remembered the intense freeze and the column of not-snow over the bed of the L.A. River on Sunday night, and the undeniable fluctuations in gravity he and Castine had experienced on the bank; and the glowing thing that had descended into the sea last night, and the moments when the *Ouranos* had been weightless. And he remembered an image Castine had thought of when she comprehended the aliens' imminent kick-off from the scanty dimensions of the Earth—a burned-out flashbulb.

He glanced toward the zip-tie-bound captives and saw that Yoneda was pointing Finehouse's gun in their direction with one hand and pressing her old broken flip-phone to her ear with the other. She appeared to be listening, and after a few seconds began to speak into it, but was clearly interrupted. She listened again, and made a brief reply.

She snapped it shut and the cover fell off. As she stuffed it back into her pocket she met Vickery's eye and said, "Try everything."

Vickery nodded and took a cautious deep breath, then walked past the canvas to the Dodge and opened the door. Leaning in carefully, he set the emergency brake and snapped the pendulum off the dashboard metronome. "Boss," he called over his shoulder, "you got duct tape?"

Finehouse spoke up. "You want to *gag* me? Are you afraid of Agents Yoneda and Castine hearing what I have to say? You, Mister GRU—I can offer you immunity and a new identity."

Tacitus gave him a wan smile. "And thus does the warmth of feeling turn ice in the grasp of death!"

Vickery recognized the quotation from Bartholomew Dowling, and exhaled one syllable of a reluctant laugh; Yoneda knew it too, for she added the last two lines of the stanza, "A cup to the dead already, hurrah for the next that dies!"

"That's one way of looking at it," said Galvan. "Yeah, I got duct tape. Spacemen after all?"

"We need it," Vickery said. "Pierce, chock the Dodge's front tires and jack up the rear end."

"I got a floor jack too," said Galvan, "better'n what's in the Dodge." She tossed the keys to Arturo. "Both in the trunk. *Andele!*"

Vickery kept anxiously watching the road south, but the only vehicles raising dust along its visible length were cars leaving the area. Santiago wedged rocks against the Dodge's front wheels, and when Arturo came puffing back, Plowman slid Galvan's floor jack under the Dodge's back end and pumped the handle enough to lift the rear tires several inches above the sand.

Arturo handed Vickery the roll of duct tape, and Vickery crouched beside the Dodge's left back wheel, wincing as fabric dragged across the gash in his ribs. He took the old corncob pipe out of his shirt pocket and held it against the car's quarter-panel; then with his teeth he tore off a foot-long length of the silvery tape and laid it over the pipe, with several inches pressed to the panel on either side. He used another strip of tape to firmly attach the metronome to the sidewall of the tire.

He straightened, slowly, breathing deeply to stave off dizziness, and walked back to the canvas spread out on the old pavement. "Castine, Tacitus," he called, "once more into the breach."

Both of them hurried to their previous positions, and Vickery took Castine's left hand while she clasped Tacitus's with her right.

"Pierce," called Vickery, "lean in there and start the car."

"About time," came Plowman's reply, followed by the growl of the Dodge's engine. "Quick," Plowman added, speaking more loudly as he shifted it into gear, "your doohickey is likely to fly off the wheel."

Vickery looked from Tacitus to Castine. "Again," he said.

He stared across the plain at the towering stone, and his recent thoughts of the aliens and their perspective made it possible for him to see even this stark natural monument as just a feature on a small, limited world adrift in an infinite incomprehensible void.

In moments all he saw was a meaningless collage, shades of blue and tan—but this time he looked only partway past them, in what he thought of as *underpainting*. The sky became bronze and the sand glowed with the indescribable color of infrared radiation, but he could also see the shadowy form of Castine standing next to him in real time. The roar of the Dodge's engine was only half muted.

He looked down at the canvas, and it was a double-exposure: black lines on white, and glowing lines on a dimmer background. The canvas had been moved slightly since they'd first laid it out, and he had to shift to the side a few inches to get the two images exactly lined up.

Castine's hand tightened painfully in his. He kept his double-exposure gaze on the overlapped lines, and after a few seconds the glowing lines and the sepia world flickered away, leaving only the black lines on the white canvas in bright sunlight. The Dodge's engine was fully loud again.

Castine sagged, and he let go of her hand to slide his

arm around her waist and take some of her weight, ignoring the pain in his side. He could feel that she was shaking. With his free hand he cuffed sudden sweat from his eyes and squinted up at the deep blue sky—and it was still empty. The edges of the canvas fluttered in the wind.

"It didn't work—again," said Tacitus.

Castine straightened up, stepping away from Vickery, and she pushed her hair back from her face with both hands. Her voice was hoarse as she said, "Oh yes it did." She turned to Vickery. "You did your . . . *underpainting*. I could see it."

Vickery looked up again and again saw nothing, then glanced toward the Cadillac and the ONI vehicles. Finehouse and his men were staring in his direction; looking the other way, he saw Plowman standing next to the open door of the Dodge. Galvan, having apparently concluded that Vickery's second attempt had failed too, had walked across to the immobilized Dodge and was standing beside Plowman and peering in through the open driver's side door. Santiago had looked sharply at Castine when she had spoken, and was now staring warily into the sky; a medallion on a string dangled from his right fist.

Vickery followed the boy's gaze—and in that moment the sky erupted in darting silvery shapes far overhead; their eerie silence emphasized the hiss of the wind and the low roar of the car engine.

Someone in the group by the SUV screamed, and when Vickery spared them a sideways glance he saw that one side of the cluster of ONI personnel had sagged because the bearded man had fallen to his knees. A moment later the boxes on the sand by the van burst open and half a dozen chromed spheres flew up out of them.

Vickery watched them as they whirled away into the sky. The alien shapes far beyond them were darting at incalculable speeds from horizon to horizon, instantly changing course at acute angles, and the chrome balls were yanked back and forth on a smaller scale as if attempting to mimic them.

Castine was gripping his hand again. She whispered, "Almost . . ."

A change in the pitch of the Dodge's engine caught Vickery's attention—Santiago had kicked away the stones blocking the car's front tires and lowered the jack, and now he was in the driver's seat. Vickery saw him hang the medallion on the rear-view mirror.

The car began to roll forward, directly toward the old pavement on which the canvas was spread, and Vickery leaped out of its way, pulling Castine with him and knocking Tacitus off his feet.

Plowman sprinted after the car and pulled the driver's side door open. Running to keep up with the car, he reached in, grabbed Santiago's arm and hauled the boy right out from behind the wheel, and as Santiago tumbled to the sand, Plowman leaped over him and slid into the driver's seat. Vickery could now see the head of another man sitting beside Plowman, and he believed he recognized him.

The car rolled right up onto the cross-shape of cracked cement and stopped when the left rear wheel was resting on the canvas; and Plowman must have stood hard on the brake, for when he hit the gas pedal the car only lurched in place while the rear wheels spun furiously. In a moment the canvas was sucked up under the car and disappeared, no doubt wrapped around the axle and the shock absorbers, and acrid smoke billowed out around the wheels and flew away on the wind. Galvan was hurrying toward the car, waving angrily.

The roar of the engine must have been too loud for Plowman to hear even a shout, and certainly it was too late to save the canvas, but Vickery started forward, yelling, "What the hell are you—!"

But Castine caught his arm. "Wait," she said into his ear. "The pendulum and the pipe—and the symbol is always flat, in their view, even when—"

The ground under Vickery's feet jumped sideways and he fell to the sand on his left hip, with Castine tumbling down on top of him. Shadows were moving across the shifting ground, and when he looked up through a sudden cloud of dust he saw something like twisted scaffolding at least momentarily unsupported in the air; the bearded man's chrome spheres were rapidly circling it counterclockwise. Vickery rolled over to cover Castine, but the grotesque structure didn't fall.

The ground was still shaking, but Vickery rolled back off of Castine and sat up, grimacing and coughing. The tangled shape in the sky, the same color as the desert sand, hovered in the air at a height of perhaps a hundred feet, and only because he had spent hours last night tracing its lines in chalk and paint was he able to recognize Plowman's negation symbol—viewed from below.

Far above it, the quicksilver fliers were now circling in the same direction as the closer chrome balls—mimicking *them?* Being drawn down toward the symbol?

A moment later the sky was empty of everything except the hovering negation symbol, and after a few more seconds it dissolved in wind-blown dust. Vickery's ears popped, as if he were suddenly at a higher altitude, and Castine gripped her head and moaned, rocking on the still-gyrating ground.

The Dodge's engine was allowed to subside to a normal pitch and it began to move forward off the cement slab— but it roared again as the slab dropped out from under the back end; the car was gunning steeply uphill in the moments before the doors and Plowman's grimacing profile and the hood and the front wheels slid backward and disappeared into a newly opened sinkhole.

A geyser of dust erupted from the widening hole, and instead of dispersing on the wind it coalesced into a thrashing, angular shape, and with huge hands at the ends of skeletal arms it pulled itself out across the shaking sand. Its elongated head swung blindly back and forth, its shovel fingers dug trenches in the sand, and its mouth opened so wide that its lower jaw fell off and disintegrated; another jaw was extruded in its place, and also stretched so far open that it fell off and broke apart. A windy whistling issued from the open throat.

Vickery got to his feet and pulled Castine up, and they hopped and slid across the rocking ground away from the creature. But there were other patches of the desert floor sagging and breaking up to fall away into new holes, and other deformed creatures made of clumped sand flailing their huge hands in the wind. And the wind was very hot, and parchingly dry.

Through the flying clouds of sand Vickery saw several of the groping, misshapen forms, and to the extent that the things were able to move, they were crawling toward himself and Castine.

"Get," Castine gasped, "away—they *know me.*"

Vickery remembered the sea-water apparition on the deck of the *Ouranos* last night, and the ghosts at the cemetery and along the Fairfax Avenue sidewalk.

He didn't try to answer in the hot, whistling wind, but took her hand and pulled her along in the direction of the three remaining vehicles.

The alien ghost-figures were moaning now, the bell-like tones echoing one another. One long clotted-sand arm swung heavily toward them through the dust clouds, and Castine hooked a heel behind Vickery's ankle and punched him in the chest, and they both sprawled on the sand as the limb swept past over them.

Vickery's shoulder was pressed against the shifting ground, but a moment later it wasn't pressing against anything, and a *cold* wind from below him fluttered his hair; Castine was half on top of him, her chest against his face, and the two of them were tipping into a new hole that had broken open at his back.

Vickery convulsed forward and rolled over, and then he and Castine were digging frantically with toes and hands to push themselves back from the edge—and in the few seconds before they had got clear of the hole they were both able to see very far down.

Below them, at such a distance that clouds obscured

sections of their view, a vast white ring encircled a worldwide ocean, with distorted but recognizable continents clustered around a white central patch. In the light from some unseen sun, glassy needles could be seen standing up vertically from hundreds or thousands of points, most thickly along three straight lines—skirting the west coast of North America, crossing eastern North America through the north pole to east Asia, and stretching from southern England across Europe and the Caspian Sea to India. The lines were parallel.

Even as he and Castine had glimpsed them, the needles had broken apart and were gone.

When the two of them had scrambled on their hands and knees away from the crumbling edge of the hole, the earth was still rocking violently, and Vickery gripped Castine's arm to keep her from trying to stand. He couldn't see any of the grotesque creatures through the blowing dust, but a rough white block as big as a car impacted the sand a dozen yards away, and flying chips of it hit his face; he picked up a fragment and realized that it was ice.

Through his palms flat on the swaying ground, Vickery felt jarring impacts that must have been other ice-boulders crashing to the ground, for shards of ice were flying in all directions in the dust cloud that made it impossible to see more than a few yards.

He took a deep breath of the hot air, leaned toward Castine and yelled, "Can't sit still."

She nodded, and they got to their feet and began plodding forward. Vickery stumbled against a line of cracked cement, and he recognized the old pavement on which they had spread the canvas. He caught Castine's arm to keep her away from the hole Plowman had fallen into—but there was no hole now. The old cement slab lay there intact, and the ground around it showed no signs of having broken. Plowman and the Dodge had fallen through a hole that to all appearances had never been.

The impacts of more giant blocks of ice were jolting the ground, and Vickery and Castine hurried at a hopping lope away from the slab. Through the churning turbulence of wind-blown sand he soon saw the outlines of the SUV and, more dimly, the van, and he took Castine's arm and led her that way.

Finehouse and his men had at some point cut themselves free of the zip-tie restraints, and two of them were lifting a third man onto a stretcher. When Vickery and Castine blundered up and leaned against the SUV's hood, Finehouse stepped close to them to be heard.

"Get in now," he said harshly, "we're leaving."

Vickery saw that Yoneda was among them, leading the oddly bearded man, who was clutching a crumpled chrome sphere. The ground shook again, and Vickery could see the enormous chunk of ice that had just fallen and broken into tumbling, barrel-size pieces. It could have crushed either of these vehicles, and the hot wind carried the jarring crash of two more blocks hitting the earth somewhere nearby.

"Let's not," said Castine into Vickery's ear.

The shape of another car nosed into view beyond the van. A door opened and a figure stood up on the driver's side, and above the wind Galvan's voice shouted, "Vick! Come on!"

Vickery remembered the .380 in his pocket and pulled it out. It was sticky with blood from his side, but he held it steady, pointed at the ground.

"We're going with Galvan," he told Finehouse.

"Rayette," called Castine, "come with us. We can show you how." The wind tossed her hair across her eyes, and she held it back with one hand.

Vickery couldn't make out Yoneda's face, but he saw her shake her head. "What we did worked," she called back. "I'm willing to do the next scene." After a pause, she added, "You come with us. It's the real world, rough or smooth."

"Vick!" came Galvan's yell. "Last call!"

Vickery pushed away from the SUV's hood. He heard several booms of what must have been ice boulders striking the ground not far away, and his rib stung, and he was tense and breathless with the urge to run to Galvan's car before she drove it away.

But Castine had a decision to make.

After no more than two seconds she took his arm and told Yoneda, "The real world and I never did get along."

And then the two of them were hurrying toward Galvan's Cadillac. Galvan got back in, and Vickery saw that Tacitus was in the passenger seat and Arturo and Carlos occupied the back seat. He looked around for Santiago and couldn't see him in the murky turbulence; then he heard the yapping motorcycle engine start up and saw the boy riding away, standing up on the footpegs as the bike bounced over the still-shaking ground.

Castine had been looking that way too, and now turned to nod at Vickery, and at an impatient snarl from Galvan she hurriedly opened the passenger-side door and slid in beside Tacitus, while Vickery opened the back door and pushed Arturo far enough across the seat for him to crowd in. He was pulling the door closed as Galvan clicked the big Cadillac into reverse and backed around to face south, and then she was accelerating toward the road.

The dust cloud abated within a few hundred feet, and on the road ahead Vickery could see the piercing blue and red lights of police cars approaching. He didn't see Santiago. He looked back, but saw no other vehicles emerging from the maelstrom.

"This could be awkward," said Castine, her voice hoarse with exhaustion. "A gunshot wound, residue on our hands . . ."

"I think you two should have gone with Mr. Finehouse," was Tacitus's mournful observation.

Galvan barked a sharp phrase in Spanish to Arturo and Carlos, then slowed the big Cadillac to about ten miles per hour. She was squinting through the windshield at the approaching lights.

"I can stop 'em when they get within a few hundred feet," she said thoughtfully. She reached out and unsnapped a hinged plastic disk on the dashboard, exposing two recessed buttons. "And tracing the license plate on this thing will dead-end at the secretary of state's office in Wyoming. But I don't like dashcams and body cams."

Castine leaned back against the headrest. "I think I can get you a . . . a partly obscuring entourage," she said, "if you slow down to walking pace."

"Whatever you're talking about," said Galvan, "do it."

Castine rolled down her window. The sage-and-stone scented breeze was hot, but not as hot as the churning dust cloud behind them had been.

The police cars were close now, three of them, two in front driving abreast to block the dirt road. "About now, I think," Galvan said. She pushed one of the exposed dashboard buttons. "The resistor takes fifty seconds to charge."

"What have you got?" asked Tacitus.

"There's a big-ass EMP generator in the trunk," Galvan said, "looks like a giant spool of wire, and a resistor and a couple of capacitors like bazookas hooked up to it." She nodded—with, Vickery thought, wary confidence. "Electromagnetic pulse. It'll fry the microprocessors in their cars when we get a bit closer. This car's old enough so it's got no computer stuff, but if any of you have cell phones, they're toast."

Tacitus frowned and looked from Galvan at his left to Castine on his right, as if estimating his ability to clamber out of the car. "You've used it before?"

"Well I paid enough for it," Gavan said. She glanced at Castine. "Invite!" she said.

"Slow down." Castine leaned her head out into the breeze, and just because he was sitting directly behind her Vickery heard her whisper, "Will you come?"

Galvan said, "Fire!" and pushed the second button. Vickery heard a muted whine from behind his seat. Arturo caught his eye and shrugged.

The light bars on the roofs of the police cars went out, and the cars slowed to a stop fifty feet in front of the Cadillac; and then, out in the bright sunlight, there were people standing between the police cars and the Cadillac, and standing on the sand among the tumbleweeds on either side of the dirt track.

The figures in the conjured crowd, men, women and children, were dressed in every possible variety—T-shirts and shorts, business suits, worn denim, pajamas, while a few were simply naked—and the arrangement shifted, so that the appearance of a man might be in a business suit at one moment, and in swimming trunks in the next, and nudity was a state that flickered among them. They were all smiling and waving at Galvan's car—specifically, Vickery saw, at Castine. She shook her head, then sighed and waved back at them.

Beyond the ghosts, out among the sparse weeds, wavering images of trucks and cars appeared and moved across the landscape for a few seconds before disappearing. Vickery glimpsed Santiago riding his bike through them.

The Cadillac was idling forward at less than five miles an hour, and Galvan steered to the right, off the track and out onto the looser sand. The ghosts bowed and moved back to clear her way as tumbleweeds scraped under the front bumper.

Vickery looked back. The ghosts who had been on the other side of the road were crossing it now, spinning and floating like a drift of balloons, their insubstantial feet sometimes not touching the dirt at all though still going through the motions of walking. Half a dozen police officers were out of their cars, but they were shouting at one another; several were pointing at the phantom vehicles and the ectoplasmic figures moving past, while the others gestured toward Galvan's car. Beside Vickery, Carlos's face was turned to the left toward the police, but Arturo gaped around at the crowd of ghosts.

Galvan had passed the three police cars and rolled back onto the road. Several of the officers got back into their cars, but two others started running after the Cadillac.

Galvan accelerated to fifteen miles an hour, and the pursuing officers fell back. The ghosts had followed the Cadillac for a few yards, still waving and smiling, then one by one had vanished, whisking up brief whirls of sand.

The police cars remained motionless where they had stopped. Their light bars had not come back on. Santiago, still standing up on the bike's footpegs, was pacing the Cadillac now, a hundred feet away among the weeds.

Galvan peered at the rear-view mirror. "Hah! Worth every penny." She glanced at Castine and said, "Thanks. Their report is gonna be a crazy mess, and I think what they mainly got with their body cams is views of each other."

Vickery shifted around on the seat to look back, and in the sandstorm beyond the police cars he saw a last giant hand lift into the air and then burst into dust. The black SUV and the van had not appeared.

"Their report is going to get a whole lot crazier," he muttered.

"How did you do that?" Galvan asked Castine; and when Castine gave her a blank frown, she added, "Call all those ghosts? Ghosts aren't supposed to be able to even *see* this car."

"*Ella es la reina de los fantasmas,*" muttered Arturo.

"They can see *me,*" Castine said, watching the

passenger-side mirror. "I was *in* a ghost, I shared its identity, last night, out on the ocean. It wasn't human, but it was sentient and dead—and I was too, in it. So I guess ghosts are specially aware of me . . . and I find I'm aware of them." She gave a shaky sigh that was almost a laugh. "Like I'm an honorary ghost myself, now."

Ella es la reina de los fantasmas, thought Vickery. She is the queen of the ghosts.

"Oh." Galvan seemed momentarily disconcerted. "Well—yeah, thanks." For several seconds she drove on in silence. Then she said, "This is far enough." She was stepping on the brake now, and when the car slowed to a stop she shifted the engine into park. She climbed out, then leaned back in and waved toward the glove compartment. "Bag of jack rocks in there," she said to Castine. "Haul it out and give me half of 'em. Quick, the Navy guys are still back there!"

Vickery leaned forward to look over Castine's shoulder, and saw her pull from the glove compartment a big plastic bag full of angular twists of black steel. She tore the bag open and shook half the contents into Galvan's cupped hands, and Vickery saw that each of the things was four hollow spikes welded together to point in different directions.

"Scatter 'em thick across the road," Galvan told Castine, who nodded and opened her door to get out. Galvan looked at Vickery and grinned as she held out one of the objects. "Hollow, see? Even stop self-sealing tires." She straightened and yelled across the hood, *"Behind us, imbecil!"*

Out by the front bumper, Castine nodded and picked

up the few of the things she had already thrown; she hurried to the rear of the car and scattered them back there.

There was still no sign of the ONI vehicles. Vickery got out of the car and limped around to the back, nervously keeping well clear of the trunk and its EMP generator, and he helped kick sand over the spidery iron stars that Galvan and Castine had by now scattered liberally across the road, noting that the things always sat with one spike pointed upward.

In the Secret Service, he recalled, they had called them caltrops, and government limousines had been equipped with "run flat" tires that had support rings inside, so they could still function even if they ran over the things. He hoped Finehouse's vehicles didn't have that kind of tires.

He heard the 125-cc engine shift gears, and looked up. Santiago was riding this way now across the weeds and the humped sand, and when the boy got to the road he stopped his bike beside the Cadillac's back bumper, well away from the spikes.

His lean brown face behind sunglasses was expressionless, and when he spoke his voice was tight. "Mr. Plowman is dead, you saw." He looked from Castine to Vickery. "Did it work? Is the big winter stopped?"

"Yes," said Castine. She looked warily back toward the police cars, then went on quickly, "I felt it. The things in the sky saw the negation symbol—comprehended it, internalized it!—when Sebastian projected it in the past *and* the present, overlapped. The views were too widely separated in time for the things to miss, to step over."

Vickery too looked back along the road, but the police cars were still stationary and the officers were clustered around them. Finehouse's ONI vehicles still weren't visible beyond—disabled, destroyed? "We should get going."

But Castine went on, as if she had to get it out. "I felt them die today—I felt them fall right through the state of being ghosts this time, into—into fossilization." She shook her head and exhaled. "As inert as that corncob pipe."

"Mr. Plowman did it," Santiago insisted, "with that pipe and the piece from the clicker, and my medallion. Putting those right on top of the lines, spinning."

Castine nodded. "And he's the one who found the lines in the first place. He and his friend carried them right down into the aliens' view of our world."

"His friend?" asked Vickery.

"You didn't see the ghost in the car beside him? It was Frankie Notchett."

"He carried my Dodge away too," said Galvan, walking up. "Back in the car now, quick."

Vickery turned to speak to Santiago, but the boy had tapped the bike into gear and twisted the throttle, and all Vickery saw was his receding back and the bike's bobbing tail-light.

Galvan was already in the car, gunning the engine, and Vickery and Castine hurriedly climbed in. Galvan stepped on the gas, and the car surged forward, faster now.

In the front seat, Castine had bowed her head, and Vickery couldn't see her. He raised his arm to reach over the seat and touch her shoulder, but his arm, his whole body, was trembling with delayed reaction. He didn't look at Arturo or Carlos, but just clasped his hands tightly in his lap.

After another couple of miles Galvan was driving on a paved road, and soon they were passing the lonely white dome of the building known as the Integratron, which according to Plowman had been built without nails or screws by the same man who had started the UFO conventions around Giant Rock. The building was supposedly a focus for time-travel and anti-gravity, but Plowman had said he'd spent four days in the dome in the '70s, and it had been as bogus as the man's story of touring an alien space ship.

Vickery looked away from it to peer past Galvan's shoulder at the road ahead. Your negation symbol worked, though, old friend, he thought; that pattern of lines you completed by laboriously tracing it on the floor of the parking garage at the Cathedral of Our Lady of the Angels. And in spite of your age and reluctance, in the end you didn't just hand the job over to us—you braved the cultists at the Zeta Reticuli Chess Club to check their celestial seismograph, and you piloted Notchett's boat out to face the perils of a dying alien, and finally you took the negating symbol right into their—and your!—flat Earth. Rest in peace, in it. And I hope you're with Becky again, somehow, for the first time since her tenth birthday party.

"I think we're clear," said Galvan, glancing at the rearview mirror and then to the sides at the desert and the occasional distant house that they passed. "Those cops' radios are cooked, and any that see us now got no reason to stop us."

Upholstery creaked as her passengers relaxed, and

Castine inhaled and lifted her head. She shifted to look out the back window. "Will they get out?" she asked quietly. "Yoneda and those others?"

"Their vehicles were facing east," said Tacitus. "I'm sure they fled in that direction."

"I'll pray for them," said Castine, and Tacitus nodded soberly.

And somebody's tires are going to get wrecked for nothing, thought Vickery.

Galvan caught Vickery's eye in the rear-view mirror. "I saw those things with the big hands," she said, "and the ice blocks falling, and the holes in the ground that closed up again." Her tone was determinedly matter-of-fact, but Vickery caught a quaver of concealed awe in her voice. "Did you save the world again?"

Vickery sat back and emptied his lungs in a long sigh. He took a deep breath and said, "We all did. Yes."

Galvan nodded and lifted one hand from the steering wheel to wipe her face. "I'll—" she began; for a couple of moments she didn't speak, then went on, "I'll write off the Dodge, and the gas. Yeah. That guy drove it into a hole, and so the bamboo antenna and the fingerbones would have been lost anyway. But none of this gets you out of paying that hundred a month."

"Wouldn't have presumed," Vickery said.

"What a mess, eh?" Galvan stretched, straightening her short arms against the steering wheel. "I'm gonna find a storage place in Landers and hide this car till I can set up a new out-of-state limited liability company to register it—and now find a pay phone and call the yard for a ride back. We can drop you all somewhere."

"I might stay in Landers," said Tacitus. "It seems an appropriately remote place in which to . . . begin life anew."

"I'll hold that painting for you," Vickery told him, "in case we ever meet again."

Tacitus's mouth opened in a soundless, mirthless laugh.

Vickery's hand was steady enough now to tap Castine on the shoulder. "How seriously are they likely to come after us?"

Castine shifted in her seat to look back at him. "Oh— I don't know. We tied up some government agents and held guns on them . . . they might make an issue of that. Heh. Did we do anything else? Major?" When Vickery rocked one hand in the air, she went on, "It might be a good idea for us to retrieve your truck and then hide out at your studio for a while." She looked out the window at the endless desert. "And I've got to get in touch with Plowman's daughter."

Galvan turned south on Old Woman Springs Road, and Vickery recalled that it led south to the Twentynine Palms Highway, which after fifteen long miles would at last deliver them to the westbound onramp of Old Man 10.

EPILOGUE:
I Have No Idea

The close hangars and parked single-engine Cessnas and Beechcrafts swept past on the edge of the runway at the Yucca Valley Airport, and as the sleek C-37A jet lifted off and gained altitude, Joel Finehouse was able to look past the three-mile-wide cluster of small houses to the rugged hills of the Mojave Desert.

Agent Yoneda and Vilko Cendravenir were seated two rows behind him, both silent. Finehouse had talked with both of them, but had not decided which of the events he had seen out there today were ones he would accept as having been real.

He had had a phone conversation with Commander Lubitz this afternoon. Lubitz was being transferred immediately to the American Embassy in Helsinki, and Finehouse was being restored to his previous position at the Naval Research Laboratory in Washington D.C., back to developing alloys for vehicle armor. He was strongly looking forward to it.

The expenses of Operation Pleiades were being quietly stripped of itemization and specifics and shuffled into the accounts of the Materials Science and Technology Division.

The operation itself had been retroactively recast as a response to illegal GRU activity. It seemed clear that the deaths of six Sensitive Assignment Specialists on Sunday had in fact been the result of an actual rogue GRU operation, and two men who'd been killed in a grenade blast in Huntington Beach last night had—probably and fortuitously—been a part of it.

Agent Yoneda was already negotiating an agreement by which she would corroborate Finehouse's report that the injuries of three agents today were incurred during the ONI's fictitious counter-GRU operation. If anyone were to discover and correlate the Top Secret/Sensitive Compartmented record of the operation, they wouldn't find much, and there would be no mention of Anomalous Aerial Phenomena.

Vilko Cendravenir would be paid as a cvilian consultant on crowd management. A team from the Office of Naval Intelligence was already at work establishing falsifying details for today's events out by Giant Rock, and anything Cendravenir or anyone else might say about it all would be preemptively discredited.

Cendravenir had admitted that his chrome balls had got away from him and apparently accelerated whatever it was that had happened this morning—which seemed pretty clearly to have been the destruction of the UAPs, the end of Lubitz's hopes for establishing communication with an alien life-form.

Lubitz had mentioned reports of catastrophic "hail storms" in England and Germany. More reports, with more appalling details, would surely follow soon from other nations. An enduring mystery.

Finehouse turned away from the view of the desert through the airplane's window to look behind him. Agent Yoneda met his gaze and looked away. Cendravenir was asleep in a seat across the aisle, looking like some morbid commedia dell'arte marionette, and Finehouse considered getting up and leaning over the man and simultaneously shouting and yanking on his ridiculous goatee. But Cendravenir's reaction might be to propel Finehouse through the cockpit door, or even tear the plane in half.

Finehouse relaxed in his own seat. They had all certainly failed.

But maybe sometimes, he thought, it's a good thing, on the whole, to have closed a knife that someone else had opened.

A police car and a big plywood-sided truck were parked in the driveway of the derelict ranch-style house at the end of the cul-de-sac, and Santiago stopped his 125-cc Honda at the corner of Woodruff Avenue and flipped down the kickstand to watch. One of the few neighbors he'd been aware of was talking to a policeman next to a Century 21 real estate sign, and Santiago decided that this had nothing to do with the blown-up boat or the spacemen raising hell out by Giant Rock this morning. He had known that the day would come when he would lose access to his hideout.

For the first time, he pulled from his pocket the envelope Plowman had given him, and opened it. He counted twenty-five worn twenty dollar bills inside, and closed it and tucked it back into the inside pocket.

He glanced at the sky, which of course was empty now of anything but a few feathery clouds; but he shivered, wondering how the things he had seen today, particularly Mr. Plowman's slide into nowhere, might join the other memories that appeared in his dreams—his parents rebounding from a speeding car and tumbling to the shoulder of the 5 Freeway south of Oceanside, and old Isaac Laquedem, his eccentric surrogate father, lying in a puddle of blood on an L.A. sidewalk.

He nudged the kickstand back up and turned the bike around. He could have used the fake IDs in the house, and sold the handguns. The nearly empty bottle of peppermint schnapps was a memento of an evening he had spent with a young lady a few months ago, and he had been saving the last swallow in the bottle—he wished now that he had not sentimentally refrained from finishing it the next morning.

At least he had taken Laquedem's medallion, and given it to a man who, like Laquedem, had shown courage when it had proved to be necessary. And always on his wrists were the leather bands that contained the subsumed ghosts of his mother and father.

On Sunday night Galvan had asked Santiago to find Vickery for her. *I'll pay you a hundred dollars and a month's free food at any of my taco trucks,* she had said. He wondered now if anything he had done during these last two days had constituted finding Vickery for her.

Worth looking into, once she got over the loss of the Dodge and the floor jack.

He clicked the bike into gear. He could disappear into the freeway-side gypsy nests for a while, until he found another den. Los Angeles was a maze of hidden chain-blocked stairs and boarded-up theaters and forgotten rooftops.

He let out the clutch and sped away toward the 605 Freeway.

Ingrid Castine could feel sand inside her blouse and her shoes. She set her glass down on the roof planks beside her deck chair. "When does your . . . landlord go to bed?"

"Around seven, usually," Vickery said, leaning over to refill his own glass from the bourbon bottle. Castine noticed that he didn't wince as he lifted the glass and sat back.

After Galvan had sold him a null license plate for his truck, which fortunately hadn't been towed from the parking lot around the corner from her lot, Castine had insisted that they stop at a CVS drugstore and buy bandages and a lot of Terrasil Wound Care ointment, and when they had got here she had cleaned the gash over his rib and dressed and bandaged it. She was hopeful that no infection would develop—though he'd certainly be left with a big scar. They both agreed that it would be unwise to go to an emergency room with an obvious gunshot wound.

She judged that it must already be about five o'clock—the sun was silhouetting the hills to the west, and the early evening breeze was chilly enough to make the heater Vickery had carried up onto the roof useless.

"I'd pay a hundred dollars for a hot shower right now," she said, hugging herself in a borrowed overcoat.

"You haven't got a hundred dollars."

"I bet I could use my ATM card." She began to cast her mind back over the events of the last three days to identify instances when they had broken laws—but opening the memories let images crowd forcefully into her mind: the misshapen giant in the L.A. River bed on Sunday night, dead but groping blindly in the moments before it fell apart, and the great freeze and the failures of gravity that had followed; the tumult around Giant Rock six hours ago, gunshots and blood and ice-boulders crashing to the ground everywhere, huge crumbling hands clenching and flexing on the ends of spindly arms made of sand, Plowman and Frankie Notchett's ghost sliding away into a hole to an impossible world that she had for a moment seen clearly spread out below her; and, worst of all, the endless ego-negating moments in which she had physically occupied the sea-water form of the dead alien on the deck of the *Ouranos* last night.

Without having intended to move, she realized that her elbows were suddenly pressed hard on her knees and her fingers were knotted in her hair. She tried to take a breath, and remember what she had been saying, but she could breathe only in gasps, and she was shaking. She had no idea what she had been saying.

Her chair tilted on the planks as Vickery knelt beside her, and she felt his arm around her shoulders; and she restrained the reflex to spring away from him.

"Hey," came his voice. "You okay?"

"I—don't know," she whispered. "I have no idea."

She was grateful that he had the sense not to say anything.

After a few moments she straightened up, and her fingers found her glass and brought it to her mouth; and a swallow of the warm bourbon let her begin to breathe steadily again.

"I want to say," she began carefully, "that it's been a long time since lunch." She sighed deeply. "But I said that on Sunday night, and the next thing that happened was your bowl of scrambled eggs hit the ceiling."

"I remember."

"You still got any . . . what was it, beef stroganoff?"

"Yeah. Or lasagna. I can heat up a couple and bring them up here."

"No, I—it's getting dark. I don't want to be up here when the stars come out." She waved aside the obvious point. "I know the things weren't from our space at all, but I don't want to see lights in the sky." She laughed softly, then bit her lip.

He got to his feet and walked to the ladder.

She stood up, gripping the chair and frowning at the top of the ladder and wondering if she would ever again trust her balance.

"I'll go first," he said, "and catch you, if necessary."

She found herself thinking, *I'd rather hit the ground.* Than what? she asked herself a moment later. And she wasn't able to evade the answer: *Than overlap with anyone, in any way.*

"That's okay," she said. "But I can stay here, at your place? For a while?"

"As long as you like. As long as we can." He cocked his

head. "Under what circumstances do you think you might want to . . . return to the real world?"

The real world and I never did get along, she thought.

"I can't imagine," she said.

de Towaji Lutui and his fellow malcontents take to the far reaches of colonized space. The goal: to prove themselves a force to be reckoned with.

Lost in Transmission
TPB: 978-1-9821-2503-5 • $16.00 US / $22.00 CAN

Banished to the starship *Newhope*, now King Bascal and his fellow exiles face a bold future: to settle the worlds of Barnard's Star. The voyage will last a century, but with Queendom technology it's no problem to step into a fax machine and "print" a fresh, youthful version of yourself. But the paradise they seek is far from what they find, and death has returned with a vengeance.

To Crush the Moon
TPB: 978-1-9821-2524-0 • $16.00 US / $22.00 CAN
MM: 978-1-9821-9200-6 • $8.99 US / $11.99 CAN
– Coming Summer 2022!

Once the Queendom of Sol was a glowing monument to humankind's loftiest dreams. Ageless and immortal, its citizens lived in peaceful splendor. But as Sol buckled under the swell of an "immorbid" population, space itself literally ran out. Now a desperate mission has been launched: to literally crush the moon. Success will save billions, but failure will strand humanity between death and something unimaginably worse . . .

AND DON'T MISS

Antediluvian
HC: 978-1-4814-8431-2 • $25.00 US / $34.00 CAN
MM: 978-1-9821-2499-1 • $8.99 US / $11.99 CAN

What if all our Stone Age legends are true and older than we ever thought? It was a time when men and women struggled and innovated in a world of savage contrasts, preserved only in the oldest stories with no way to actually visit it. Until a daring inventor's discovery cracks the code embedded in the human genome.

THE FORGOTTEN WARRIOR SAGA

Son of the Black Sword
9781476781570 • $9.99 US/$12.99 CAN

House of Assassins
9781982124458 • $8.99 US/$11.99 CAN

Destroyer of Worlds
9781982125462 • $8.99 US/$11.99 CAN

THE GRIMNOIR CHRONICLES

Hard Magic
9781451638240 • $8.99 US/$11.99 CAN.

Spellbound
9781451638592 • $8.99 US/$11.99 CAN.

MILITARY ADVENTURE
with Mike Kupari

Dead Six
9781451637588 • $7.99 US/$9.99 CAN

Alliance of Shadows
9781481482912 • $7.99 US/$10.99 CAN

Invisible Wars
9781481484336 • $18.00 US/$25.00 CAN

KNIGHT WATCH

A new urban fantasy series from
TIM AKERS

KNIGHT WATCH

After an ordinary day at the Ren Faire is interrupted by a living, fire-breathing dragon, John Rast finds himself spirited away to Knight Watch, the organization that stands between humanity and the real nasties the rest of the world doesn't know about.

TPB: 978-1-9821-2485-4 • $16.00 US / $22.00 CAN
PB: 978-1-9821-2563-9 • $8.99 US / $11.99 CAN

VALHELLIONS
Coming in March 2022

When a necromancer hell-bent on kicking off the end of the world shows up wielding a weapon created by Nazi occultists, John and the Knight Watch team will go to great lengths—even Minnesota—to find out who's responsible and foil their plans.

TPB: 978-1-9821-2595-0 • $16.00 US / $22.00 CAN

Praise for Akers' previous novels:

"A must for all epic fantasy fans." —*Starburst*

"Delivers enough twists and surprises to keep readers fascinated . . . contains enough action, grittiness, magic, intrigue and well-created characters." —*Rising Shadow*

"Full of strong world building, cinematic and frequent battle scenes, high adventure, great characters, suspense, and dramatic plot shifts, this is an engaging, fast-paced entry in a popular subgenre." —*Booklist* starred review

Available in bookstores everywhere.
Orderr e-books online at www.baen.com.